A Serpent Cherished

A SERPENT CHERISHED

Ann Roscopf Allen

iUniverse, Inc.
New York Lincoln Shanghai

A Serpent Cherished

iUniverse, Inc.

For information address:
iUniverse, Inc.
2021 Pine Lake Road, Suite 100
Lincoln, NE 68512
www.iuniverse.com

ISBN: 0-595-32209-3 (pbk)
ISBN: 0-595-66493-8 (cloth)

Printed in the United States of America

for my parents

Charles and Mary Anne Roscopf

I fear me, you but warm the starved snake,
Who, cherish'd in your breasts, will sting your hearts.

—2 Henry VI, III, i, 343-44

Then a beautiful serpent glided into our home in the person of Mrs.
Mary Eliza Pillow. She whispered in our ears that she had been sent by
Heaven as an angel to fill the void in the heart of the husband, by a
companionship disinterested, pure, chaste, divine.

—Colonel H. Clay King
September 10, 1893

Acknowledgments

My introduction to the saga of Mrs. Mary Eliza Pillow and Colonel H. Clay King came in the form of an 1893 letter that Colonel King wrote from prison, "To My Friends throughout the United States of America," a fifteen page summary of his complicated personal, financial, and legal interactions with Mrs. Pillow. The late Gibson Turley of Helena, Arkansas, copied the curious letter for my father, Charles Roscopf, who later showed it to me. I am deeply grateful to both of them for keeping and sharing this story, thus giving me the opportunity to research the historical events and to embellish them through this novel.

An essential resource for me about the life of General Pillow, his first family, and Mary Eliza Pillow was *The Life & Wars of Gideon J. Pillow* by Nathaniel Cheairs Hughes, Jr., and Roy P. Stonesifer, Jr. (Chapel Hill: UNC Press, 1993). The *Memphis Commercial Appeal* has graciously allowed me to reprint their early articles, and the *Arkansas Democrat-Gazette* has allowed me to quote from theirs.

Michael Freeman assisted me with research into the Memphis newspapers and provided a great deal of detailed information about that city's history. Carolyn I. Macheak of the University of Arkansas at Little Rock Ottenheimer Library helped me locate the *Arkansas Gazette* articles. Also helpful to me were Kareen Turner of the University of Arkansas Mullins Library in Fayetteville and the Reference Staff at the Wicomico County Free Library in Salisbury, Maryland. John Carbonell sent me a copy of a matrimonial magazine from 1880 which provided a model of how personal ads from that time might have been written.

Friends and family generously shared their expertise, encouraged me, read all or parts of my manuscript, offered suggestions, and politely endured my monologues and e-mails about nineteenth century personal ads, the pink house, cemeteries, et cetera. These include Charles and Mary Anne Roscopf, Kathryn Adkins, Ann Casey, Elise Crockett, Pepper Crutcher, Peggy Genvert, Lisa Kurts, Lynn O'Reilly, and especially Brenda Ware Jones. The very patient Mike Altman at iUniverse provided excellent professional guidance. My children Gil and Kate encouraged me constantly, and my husband Gil took care of real life while I tapped away at my keyboard. Thank you all.

The Incident

March 10, 1891

"You damned bastard, I've got you." The crack of his pistol echoed off the brick buildings of Main Street, where the shooter swaggered out of the doorway right across from Court Square, squinting in the sunlight but not missing his target. Looked like he walked right up into that man, holding that pistol to his stomach. Looked almost like that man, angry arms waving, walked into that pistol on purpose.

"Oh, Lordy!" the wounded lawyer moaned, stumbling before falling over the tobacco boxes on the sidewalk. He staggered and started back around toward where he came from, holding his bleeding side, making his way down the street a piece, groaning, with the shooter following along right behind him, watching him calmly, less excited than if he'd just shot himself a deer and was watching it die. Just as the victim started to fall to the sidewalk, a big man with a beard ran up to catch him and dragged him inside Mooney's Cafe, and laid him out in there. The bright red puddle on the marble floor seemed ordinary, just another spill for the help to clean up and complain about. Sliding his pistol back into his overcoat pocket, that ivory handled pistol he'd got from a Yankee, the shooter stood just outside the door in a trance, silently staring down at the man.

By then I realized people were gathering. "What happened?"

"Who saw it?"

"Was it a shootin'?"

"I saw the shooter cross the street from over at the Memphis and Charleston ticket office right before it happened. Had his hand stuffed down into his overcoat pocket."

"Looked to me like he came out of that cigar shop over there. Lee's, right there where the shootin' happened."

"I saw him earlier with that gun hanging right by his side."

"Look at him. He looks drunk!"

"Hey. That's the guy that wandered into the barbershop a while ago. Just stood there and stared like a wild man. We all figured he was crazy."

"Drunk or crazy, that's for sure."

"All right, mister, you just settle down there." The policeman's trembling fingers reached carefully for the shooter's arm. "You give me that gun right now, you here?" When it became clear the quiet man wasn't going to put up a fight, the policeman thrust his hand into the overcoat pocket to get the pistol, announcing gruffly, "Consider yourself arrested."

"Don't take it out here on the street," the shooter whispered, pleading, as if people seeing him walking around with a gun was even worse than shooting a man. He always was more worried about his reputation than good sense ought to allow. "You can keep your hand in my pocket. I'll go with you." He looked down into the officer's eyes.

The policeman grabbed the gun but held on to it deep in that pocket, not removing it, his tensed arm the only chain tethering the shooter. He tugged at the shooter, who willingly walked away with him. I don't know why that policeman didn't just take the pistol. The man sure didn't seem to be of a mind to start shooting again. I reckon he'd done what he came to do, and wasn't liable to shoot anybody else. The funny looking pair—two men connected by an arm and a dull brain—waddled down the sunny street toward the jail, looking like the two headed beast in a sideshow. A crowd followed behind, men shouting and dogs barking and little boys skipping along behind eager to watch the circus that this parade would surely lead to.

The pale victim gasped for air. A few of the bystanders tried to help out—one man brought him a glass of water and another held his head gently—but most people were just staring and whispering. Mr. Mooney, wiping his hands on his apron, didn't look too happy to have a dying man on the floor of his café right at lunchtime.

"Kizzie!" The shout of my name broke the solemn mumbling. "Kizzie Biscoe!" I recognized the voice before I saw the little boy pushing his way through the crowd.

"You shush, Jeremiah," I scolded in a whisper, steering him hurriedly back out through the crowd he'd just run into. "You ought not to be hollering like that in there. He's practically dead."

"Did you see it? Did you see the shooting?"

A carriage stopped in front of the café. I strained to see who was getting out. "Is your lady here? Did she see him?"

"No. She's not here." Although I was annoyed that I had to be tending to the boy, I just didn't think it was fitting for an excited ten year old to be disturbing a dying man, even that one.

"Well, I thought I saw her in the crowd. I was sure she seen it. I just knowed this was going to happen, onct I heard all the yelling. This is the biggest news I ever heard about—a shooting right here in downtown Memphis. I betcha there's going to be a special on this one, don't you think?"

The victim was carefully lifted into the carriage.

"There's sure to be a special on this one. I better run on down to the *Avalanche*. Why, I might even make five dollars—people will surely want to buy papers about a shooting. See ya." Jeremiah scurried back up the street toward the newspaper building, his three legged dog limping along behind. There wasn't no good going to come from a tragedy like this, so it's just as well that an orphan boy should make some money off of it.

That was the first real shooting I'd ever seen. I'd seen that man too much, puffing his cigar, cussin' everybody, full of fire and spit, not at all like the pitiful bloody mess laid out there in front of everybody. I never did like him too much. I had been delivering legal papers to his office when Jeremiah came running in to find me, panting, reporting about the man shouting and growling threats down on the street. When that lawyer heard, he ran outside to confront the scoundrel. I followed along and saw the shooting with my own eyes.

Good thing Miss Marie wasn't with me. No telling what she might have said or done, watching one man kill another one, all on account of her. I wondered what she thought about all this, how she'd driven that man to such distraction that he'd shoot somebody. I wondered if she'd feel guilty. I don't imagine she ever did.

CHAPTER 1

Lest there be any misunderstanding, she came to me first. There was never anything untoward between us, never. Why, even in denial of this falsehood, there is the suggestion of an undeserved shame. Quite simply, she had many complicated legal and financial affairs, made more so by her spendthrift ways, and I assisted in whatever way I could. Simply that.

My first encounter with Mary Eliza Pillow came in a Memphis courtroom in 1872 when she was still Mrs. James Trigg. Leaning over two little girls, the dark haired woman whispered harshly, angrily. The child who looked most like the woman listened obediently. But the other, the one sandy haired and freckled, seemed frightened to tears by what the woman was threatening. Any woman who would scold a child to the point of terror … but then she turned. The soft loveliness of the woman's face seemed incongruous with her clearly volatile temperament and the intensity of her piercing brown eyes.

Ironically, my adversary in this case was General Gideon Pillow, my commanding officer during the War. I had never felt adversarial toward him in the least. In fact, we shared a bond that only warriors know, a bond of friendship, loyalty, and secrets never to be shared with others. Somehow General Pillow had been engaged by this beautiful young widow to represent her in a case against her own mother-in-law. He leaned near his client. This pair fascinated me—the older gentleman soldier coming to the aid of a wronged maiden, the ancient tale of courage aligned with beauty in conquering some demon. My reverie ended abruptly with the stench of garlic, onions, and worse—the sour breath of my client awakened me to her raspy whispering. This Cajun (she of Unionist sympathies, no less) was attractive only by way of having the means to pay my fee. The elder Mrs. Trigg had engaged my services and thus required my attention.

The facts of the case were straightforward enough. John Trigg of Louisiana owned 800 acres of land in Tipton County, Tennessee, which he deeded by will to his son, James. When James Trigg died, predeceasing his father, he left a sixteen year old widow Marie and a two year old daughter. When the father John Trigg subsequently died, leaving a sixty year old second wife as his widow, the younger Mrs. Trigg filed claim to the land. "Second wives should not be considered in determining an inheritance," the younger Mrs. Trigg protested in her letter accompanying the papers. After reading the filing, I expected to find some loathsome gold-digger on the other side of the courtroom. What I discovered was something altogether different.

Occasionally during the argument, I found myself staring at her, the elegant widow who could not have been more than 22 or 23—too young to be subjected to such familial contention. But the lawsuit was won—the elder Mrs. Trigg had her day, received fair rights to the land. I barely noticed the skeletal hand squeezing mine in gratitude, the rank asthmatic utterances, for watching her, angry, animated, blaming the little girls' misbehavior in court for her loss. The smaller child, sharing her mother's beauty, sat unaffected while her mother spewed her venom, but the other child, so unlike the mother, was weeping, trickles of tears evidence of her fear. The music of the woman's voice, all poison and anger, was surely a most blissful torment.

As is customary after a court proceeding, I crossed the aisle to greet the opposing counsel, and I was especially inclined to do so because of my kinship with him.

The General extended his hand. "Colonel King, always the worthy adversary. I'd like you to meet Mrs. James Trigg."

"How do you do?" I inquired to the back of her head.

She turned to face me, scowling, her choleric eyes boring through my own, into my innermost being. Blushing, I felt as if she were scrutinizing my most private musings, the reverie of the knight and the maiden, my distaste for my own client, my admiration for her determination and strength of character. Regaining herself, she smiled demurely. But rather than feeling relief, I shuddered, for momentarily, just for an instant, the smile seemed a hideous leer, a ghoulish expression lurking behind this mask of exquisite femininity. When I blinked, the horrible image disappeared.

"How do you do?" she replied in a businesslike manner, still staring through to my very essence.

I could say nothing but practiced courtesies. A perfectly normal woman, more charming than most, perhaps, hardly frightening. A lack of sleep, no doubt, caused fearful images of the night to appear in my mind in bright daylight. Yes, certainly that. But that moment never left me, the enigma of the litigating beauty, the horrible grimace, my intense attraction.

Although I had been married for several years, I took the opportunity of my wife's absence from Memphis to visit the young widow in her hotel, to extend my heartfelt apologies for her loss in the case which I was too shaken to express to her in the courtroom. But before I had even visited her a third time, she was engaged to be married to her own legal counsel, General Pillow himself. Although he certainly deserved much happiness after the tragedy of his own wife's death, General Pillow was only slightly older than I. She would have nothing to do with me, she declared after my first visit, she could not be seen with a married man.

And so it was that I watched her from afar. I watched as the General doted on her, traveled with her, glowed in the presence of his new young bride. I watched as they had three children of their own. I watched him champion her legal causes—her first husband's cotton, confiscated by the Union Army during the War, estimated to be worth $90,000, had yet to be paid for. I imagined them, in their home, discussing the legal strategies of those procedures, for this woman understood the law only slightly less than she understood her entitlements. But when the General encountered financial difficulties, I could watch no more. I could not leave them penniless. I could not be disloyal to General Pillow and his lovely young wife. They needed me, and as General Pillow had helped me in the War, I would help them. Perhaps it would please the young Mrs. Pillow. Surreptitiously, I purchased their properties out of the bankruptcy and deeded them to her.

But I could not let my name be associated with their scandal, or more scandal might have ensued, affecting my law practice or my family. I could not let anyone know of my connection to her, financial or otherwise, a connection made stronger by the indelible memory of a smile.

CHAPTER 2

First thing we heard was the laughter. The sparkling cut glass in the closing front door, the tinkling lamp crystals, the glittery beads of her gown, all reflected the soft light of the evening, a prettier, more fragile light than the harshness of daytime. I hadn't seen Miss Marie smile in weeks, but that night she beamed the glow of a bright full moon as she held the arm of our visitor and led him into the hallway. "Children, I want you to meet Colonel King. This is the man who has helped your father so much."

The four children and I stood on the steps of the tall, narrow stairway in the hall of our Adams Street home. Colonel King looked familiar.

"He's so handsome," Laura whispered to me and giggled, quick to make sure her mama didn't hear her.

"Laura, check with Cook and see how close we are to dinner. Kizzie, see that the others are all washed up." Laura slipped around the younger children and clattered down the stairs, cantering back down the hall to the kitchen, her dark curls bouncing. I always did think she was the prettiest one of all, being from Miss Marie's first marriage. But I was partial to Laura. I'd known her my whole life—she was just a year behind me and we were more like sisters than anything. When my mama died back during the War, Miss Marie took me to raise. That was down on the first plantation in Louisiana, in Feliciana Parish. Since Mama had worked for her on the old Trigg place, Miss Marie taught me to help her just like Mama used to. She'd rather have a white girl like me to help her with her personal things—she didn't want no colored girls close around her or Laura. And she'd rather make me sound fancier than I was, so she called me her "companion." She taught me to read and write and to take good care of all her pretty things. I wrote all her letters for her and helped in the kitchen and generally worked around the house for her. Sometimes Laura helped me with my chores. I nodded politely to Miss Marie and shepherded the little ones down the stairs and toward the back hall.

It was good to see Miss Marie happy again and to hear laughter at dinnertime. Her sadness always sat on me hard, so I was relieved it was gone. She chattered, sparkly words and laughter bubbling up from inside her, reminding me of when we were rich, back before General Pillow went broke. Miss Marie and the General used to go to parties at the Peabody Hotel. She wore her lavender silk from Paris, he drank brandy and laughed. One time he even took her to Washington to meet President Grant. The General bought her just about anything she wanted, including our pink brick house on Adams Street, what they used to call "Millionaires' Row." Miss Marie liked that name.

How a man goes broke being a lawyer, I'll never know. But sure enough, the General did, and they were going to sell everything he owned: our pink house, his plantation over in Arkansas, even all his books. Miss Marie was not happy. That was such a frightening time—I don't even like to remember it.

So it was a real relief to me to hear them laughing again. General Pillow smiled wisely and said very little, letting Miss Marie charm our dinner guest and entertain him. It was this man, this Colonel King, who had made it all happen, who helped us keep our home. Our meal was as big as Thanksgiving, but we were even more thankful.

At the end of the party, the Colonel kissed Miss Marie's hand. "Not even a cigar and brandy?" she offered, disappointed that he was leaving. General Pillow stood silently behind her.

"No, Mrs. King prefers that I not smoke, and that I be home by nine," he laughed. Something tense and lovely was in the air, the sweetness of her perfume, the bitter scent of whisky, the silent glances he gave her. We watched him walk down the front hill toward the street, 'til even his shadow from the moonlight had disappeared.

❖   ❖   ❖

It was good to have our happy life back, if only for a little while. I felt safe again. But after such a scandal as that, going broke and all, Miss Marie decided she didn't want to live in Memphis society any more. Instead, she decided we would move down to the country in Lee County, Arkansas, and she would play lady on their plantation.

That's how such a fine lady like Miss Marie ended up on a farm. And because she was such a fine lady, she spent money like a fine lady—on more pretty clothes and silver and whatnot. She was always spending money. We were there at Mound Plantation when the yellow fever epidemic hit Memphis. General Pillow still stayed in Memphis sometimes to practice law, so when word finally got out about the sickness, he escaped across the river in a row-boat—the ferry wouldn't run for fear of the fever—hoping he'd got out soon enough. But he didn't.

We had to bury the General right there on the farm because we didn't have enough money to do any different. And she had to start selling things again: the pink house in Memphis, the books. That man, he didn't leave us much of nothing. And because of all her spending, we owed a lot of money.

We scraped by for a few years, trying to farm. There were still some farm hands who hadn't moved on to work her fields. We were able to make a few cotton crops, but eventually the land went bad, and the field hands were get-ting older, and we didn't have any more money to pay them with. We went to Memphis to sell some of her things—her china, silverware, even some of her grandma's furniture. (Of course, she wouldn't sell her dresses.) Every trip up to Memphis, she'd fuss and fume. Every trip back, she'd cry. After a while, there wasn't nothing left to sell.

Colonel King helped out Miss Marie again with her business dealings and with the lawsuits about the money she owed. I could understand why he would, us being the General's family and all, and him being in the War with the General. And of course, it probably didn't hurt that Miss Marie was such a beautiful woman, and she was smart, too. That's why I never understood why she took a notion to get rich again by making eyes at him when he was another woman's husband. Making eyes ain't the half of it. Making trouble is more like it.

CHAPTER 3

The Mississippi River was hardly visible from the front porch of the mansion house at Sterling Hill through the thick foliage of the spring and summer, just a palpable presence of something larger, more powerful away in the distance. But by October, when the leaves began to fall, the presence slowly revealed itself in the broad gray stripe meandering across the land, no longer hidden and lurking but fully realized in its awesome winter presence.

At first I didn't understand the Pillows' desire to take up residence in what I thought then was merely a desolate cotton field. Clearly, Mrs. Pillow wanted nothing more to do with Memphis, perceiving the General's bankruptcy to have been too scandalous for her, and understandably so, considering the inevitable snobbery inherent to stupid people. But once I visited Lee County, I understood. The beauty of the isolated land led me to purchase my own country retreat, set in the hills along the river only a few miles from their Mound Plantation. Because the Helena and Iron Mountain Railroad ran very near, there was ample opportunity for escape to Memphis—or from it.

When word came that General Pillow had died, never had such sorrow and such joy filled my heart—to know that the human being to whom I owed the greatest debt of gratitude had departed this life and to know that in his death I could be of use, of some service, to his lovely young widow. At first I did nothing. I waited, kept abreast of her affairs, watched for whatever opportunity that might present itself to come to her aid. It was not long. She came to me, and she said she needed me. There were lawsuits, there was money owed, her financial situation was complicated and unpleasant enough to repel an ordinary man. Who would possibly desire to become entangled, even professionally, in such unsavory affairs? Yet who could resist? Despite her protestations that the debt had been incurred solely by General Pillow, I concluded that, in fact, she had come to him already heavily indebted, hid that fact from him, and continued to deceive him until his death. I found her childlike denials to be irresistible. Only after his death did the creditors decide to pursue, so that I then could become her champion. For several years I undertook the valiant fight on her behalf.

My plantation became a living entity during the fall harvest, bustling with urgent movement and noise. Heavy sacks filled with precious cotton bolls were loaded onto wagons, the earthy manifestation of the wealth which energized Memphis society. But I knew that at Mound Plantation just a few miles west, the cotton sacks were few and easier to load, that in fact it was unlikely that Mrs. Pillow and her family would break even on this crop. After years of legal and financial wrangling, her battle was over and she would have to surrender. She and her family were about to be forced off their only remaining property.

Stepping off my porch, I walked toward the edge of the steep hill to spy the river more clearly through the spaces in the almost bare trees. Taking a few steps into the tall grass, I heard that distinctive shivering *ch-ch-ch-ch-ch*. A yard ahead of me, coiled and ready, a rattlesnake had assumed its position of attack, warning me to move no closer. In my heavy boots I was in little danger, but I nevertheless slowly stepped backward, and again, and again, until I could more quickly move away.

"Malcolm. Malcolm. Get your shotgun. There's a rattler over in those weeds."

I could not shake the thought of her. The Arkansas countryside could be an inhospitable place for anyone, especially a woman of her sensibilities. How such beauty and intelligence could reside within the same woman was incomprehensible to me. She needed a home, so I would provide one. We would allow her to live here at Sterling Hill, to take up residence in the guest house, to supervise. Her shrewd business sense enabled me to leave the care of the entire plantation to her. Certainly, hiring a woman to supervise a farm would seem extraordinary. But, as was clear to me, this was no ordinary woman.

Malcolm ran up the hill from the quarters with his shotgun in hand and began hunting in the dead grass. The dark man stepped carefully, searching and listening.

My last conversation with her remained vividly in my memory. "He's still there," she wept, tears in abundance, those sparkling gemstones of grief embellishing her sorrow. "I can't leave. He's still there, in the land, left to be forgotten..."

The blast from the shotgun reverberated through the hills, ducks flapping and rising in fear in the distance. Malcolm turned to me in disgust.

"Dangit. Done slithered away."

CHAPTER 4

One of the men must have lost hold of the rope, because when they were hoisting General Pillow up out of his grave, rotten wooden box and all, the rope slipped, the bottom tilted, and the dead man himself started to roll out. Only thing I saw was his leg, dangling, still in its gray pants, before I covered up my eyes so I wouldn't have to see any other parts. I didn't specially enjoy looking at the General when he was alive, and I sure didn't want to see him now that he'd been dead for seven years. I took a step back, just in case that yellow fever was still catching. "Rest in peace" just didn't seem the fitting thing to pray, since there they were, digging him up all over again and there he was, falling out. Didn't ever seem to be much peaceful about the man.

Luckily the three men doing the digging must have gathered him up and scooped him right back in where he belonged, because when I peeked between my fingers, they were setting the box, or what was left of it, right there on the hard dirt. Shivering, I drew my shawl closer around my shoulders, not so much on account of the cold, and I was just glad Miss Marie wasn't around to watch the whole proceedings. She had sent me along with Mr. Worley and some of the Colonel's other men so I could show them just where the right spot was to do the digging—we never did have any more than an old wooden cross there to mark it. Mr. Nichols from the bank was there, too, just to make sure we didn't take nothing but the General. The wind was whipping up something fierce as they heaved him up onto the back of the wagon for the trip up to Memphis. Mr. Nichols cussed and started sucking on his finger—must have got a splinter when he pitched that half rotten cross into the back of his wagon. It just wasn't right to be taking the Lord's name in vain with a dead man lying right in front of you, but that banker didn't care. He was still muttering as his horse trotted off toward the east and into the evening.

It was only fitting for me to stand with the family during the reburying of General Pillow. Elmwood was the biggest graveyard I ever did see. Cedars and magnolias stood tall and silent, guarding the tombstones and the dead people underneath. Their late afternoon shadows scared me, stretching long and threatening over the brown grass and wilted bouquets. The General wouldn't be alone there—plenty of other Confederate generals and colonels and such were buried there—you could tell from their names carved on the tombstones.

Wearing her Confederate gray, Miss Marie moaned and sniffled while the preacher read from the Bible, and gray haired Colonel King stood right there by her side. "I just couldn't bear to have him buried in obscurity," she whimpered, not worrying that she might be interrupting the Scripture reading.

The Colonel stepped closer to her, holding her arm so she could lean into him.

Looking down at the fresh heap of dirt her daddy was lying under, I squeezed little Annie's hand, just to remind her she'd be all right. Giddy was getting fidgety, like little boys will, but he stayed put pretty well. Mary just looked bored, but she didn't say so. When their mama needed them to, they could all behave real good. A howling wind gusted and struggled to raise our skirts in that cold graveyard and made the cedar branches dance and sway, like they were celebrating getting another body among them.

The Colonel offered Miss Marie his handkerchief, and he patted her hand. When the preacher finished praying, I gave Annie a big hug, and the three children watched as their mama hugged the Colonel, too. Colonel King tended to Miss Marie like she was his own wife, and she played the part of the poor widow woman full out. And come to find out, that Colonel paid for the whole funeral, too, with his own money. He knew how to do the right thing, him being a gentleman and all.

"Colonel King has promised to give me the plantation where he and his wife now live," Miss Marie sniffed. "So it makes perfect sense that we should move there." The cold morning sunlight crept across her dusty bedroom floor, then cloud shadows, then light, 'til finally the sun just gave up and disappeared, leaving us with the dark. She clutched the only piece of jewelry she had left, holding the memory of the dead General in the safety of that gold locket, snapped shut and well out of sight. "The fact that he is married, Kizzie, should be no concern of yours."

We were packing up whatever it was we had left to take over to the new place. I reckon I mean *I* was packing it up. Miss Marie was better at directing. She walked over across the uneven wooden floor that creaked in the middle, so she could check all the dresser drawers and make sure I wasn't leaving nothing of hers behind.

"You want me to pack up all these beaded dresses, the ones you don't wear no more?" I asked her, peeking inside the dark wardrobe next to the window. That house was a wreck, but she was careful to keep her party dresses clean and safe.

She looked at me crossly. "'*Any* more,' and yes, I want you to pack everything. We're moving there permanently."

I carefully folded all those sparkly pieces, set them in her trunk, and smoothed them out just so, just wondering about it all. I couldn't rightly believe that such a fine lady like Miss Marie was fixing to move in with a colonel who was already married, and his wife wasn't supposed to mind, neither. The whole thing seemed mighty strange to me. But I didn't dare say so.

She'd married General Pillow for his money, I know, but his respectability too. She really wanted that, to be a general's wife. And being a general's widow was probably even better. But I reckon by the time we were moving over to Colonel King's plantation, with his wife still living there, she wasn't after respectability no more.

That was in the fall of 1885 when we had to leave the Pillow place on account of the bank foreclosed on us. We packed everything up that we had left, tied the mules together to the back of the wagon, and set out. It wasn't but a little ways down to the Kings' plantation over in the hills on the Mississippi River. But it was a bitter cold fall that year. I started that old wagon down the ruts and bumps in the lane that used to be smoothed out regular by the folks that worked for the General. That was such a long, trudging trip for it being only a short piece to go. The steady wind blew strands of my hair straight out in front of me, whipping my eyes if I dared look to the side. The mules didn't like that cold wind any better than the rest of us did—tugging, pulling, slowing us down. The three children were huddled up close in the back, sitting on Miss Marie's trunks and a grip or two. We'd pulled out all the blankets for them to wrap up in. Miss Marie sat up front next to me. She was bundled up, too, but she didn't huddle over. She sat up real straight and proud, like she always did.

"Kizzie, did you pack that old plantation bell like I asked you?"

"Yes, ma'am. Just like you told me. Just about ripped the skin off my fingers when I tried to pick it up, it was so cold. Heavy, too."

She didn't say nothing about that, and we were both quiet for a minute, listening to the creaking of the wagon wheels and the mules tromping along.

"Why are we taking that thing anyway? We don't have need of that bell."

"It's mine." That's all she said. I reckon that was enough.

CHAPTER 5

My eyes were level with her bosom when she tripped from the trolley steps and fell into me. Instinctively, my arms grabbed onto the strange woman, as much to catch my own balance as to rescue her. Realizing my left hand was clutching her derriere for a moment too long—yet even a moment is too long to fondle a stranger on the street—realizing my error, I knew I must rearrange—nay, release—my grasp of her once the woman recovered her balance. Yet fearful I might offend her further by giving unwanted assistance to some other part of her person, I held fast. Using my body to steady herself, she removed her face from my overcoat and looked up to see who had broken her fall. Such strange blue eyes. She smiled impishly at our newfound intimacy. She regained her composure, and I attempted to regain mine, helping to steady her briefly before assuming my usual dignified stance. She looked in my eyes wistfully as she backed away, kissing her brown fingers and blowing an imaginary thank you in my direction. Despite the serendipity of my encounter with the mulatto beauty, I hastily boarded the trolley lest anyone recognize me and mention the incident to Mrs. King at an inauspicious moment.

The spot of rouge on my collar would be signal enough to send Sallie into a fury. Jealousy did not become her, and I never gave her reason to grapple with the green eyed monster. Nevertheless, she would not understand the chance meeting between her husband and a harlot falling from a street car. I rubbed the spot with my handkerchief, determined to remove it before my arrival home, and decided to dispose of the cloth so as not to arouse further suspicion.

The trolley ride down Poplar to my home was always my best opportunity to reflect on the business of the day, which recently consisted almost entirely of the engrossing plight of Mrs. Pillow. Because my assistance to Mrs. Pillow would be a mutually beneficial circumstance for us all, Sallie would no doubt be fully supportive of my decision. After all, our Arkansas property needed a supervisor and Mrs. Pillow needed a home. There was nothing objectionable about my helping a client, especially the widow of a dear friend. My wife's penchant for jealousy would not be an issue in a mere business transaction.

The route took me by Orleans Street, and through the dark magnolias I tried to get a glimpse of the Pillows' former residence down the block at the intersection of Adams. Since the reinterment of General Pillow, I became more certain of my decision to give her a home. Mrs. Pillow advised me that her married daughter Laura in Virginia thought our arrangement not only proper, but deserving of the gratitude of their entire family. I had requested that she consult her about the suitability of our plan, as her presence on my land could so easily be misconstrued. Thus, with her family's blessing, she, her three younger children, and her companion would be given our guest house, just down the hill from the mansion house. She would manage my plantation and would be allowed to raise her children on our property. Her companion would make herself at home in the kitchen with our cook. It seemed to be an altogether beneficial situation for everyone concerned.

Conveniently, Mrs. King never appreciated our Arkansas plantation. She preferred to spend her time in the city, among her social peers, as she described them. Having Mrs. Pillow on my property would enable Mrs. King to be where she most wanted to be, behind the alluring façade of Memphis society, which, like their ubiquitous cut glass doors, sparkled with beauty from the outside but distorted and concealed the lives behind them. I wanted nothing more than to please my wife by allowing her to live where she was most comfortable, a proper goal for any devoted husband. Despite our unhappy union, we shared a mutual respect and desired each other's happiness and comfort above all. Mr. Haughton's willingness to release me from my unhappy mismatch with his daughter remained a bittersweet memory, embittered by her mother's unfortunate pronouncement that we must grin and endure it—they were a Catholic family and believed firmly in the sanctity of marriage—yet sweetened by her promise of an ample inheritance, making the endurance that much easier. So being a practical man, and one who respects the religious beliefs of those dear to me, I could not refuse.

The clanging of the trolley startled me. The contraption made sure to jostle its exiting passengers but good one final time before it screeched to its regular stop. I descended the steps carefully, determined not to repeat the mishap which began the ride. It was time to discuss my decision with my wife. Her reaction would undoubtedly be not only hospitable but charitable, for a finer Christian woman you could never meet in this lifetime.

Mary Eliza Pillow would come to live with me—with us—on my Arkansas plantation. I looked forward to a fruitful partnership of business relations with her, hoping that we might be of service to each other in whatever way possible. Charity, as they say, is its own reward.

CHAPTER 6

❀

1885

Nobody said anything for a minute, but I half expected hissing. Like an arched cat with hairs on end, Mrs. King stood beside her husband, stretching her small self into something bigger. She stared at the woman who was welcoming her into her own mansion house that evening, threatened but trying to look more threatening. Face to face, the women filled the silence with their anger.

"Colonel King! How wonderful to see you!" Miss Marie broke the awful tension, but Mrs. King's eyes still watched her suspiciously until she spotted something. Without warning, his wife swept right past them over to the front hall table and began to rearrange the flower vase, the book of poems, and the little painting sitting there, switching them back to the way they used to be.

"Can I get Ginny to make you some coffee?" Miss Marie offered, as she led the Colonel into the parlor, Mrs. King quickly returning to her husband's side.

"Well, I see you've made yourself right at home, haven't you? Calling on *my* servants. Oh, yes, you remember my wife Sallie?"

"Of course. Sallie. What a quaint name."

"How do you do, Mrs. Pillow."

Miss Marie looked all the way down Mrs. King's dress and back up to her face, without smiling. "Quite well, thank you." Their eyes met again, but this time Mrs. King looked away first, excusing herself to go out to the kitchen, without even giving me a chance to introduce myself.

"I want to thank you again for all you've done for us." Miss Marie found herself a comfortable spot on the sofa. She never had any problem at all just looking right into that man's eyes.

"It is my pleasure to help you in any way I can. I had planned to help with your move, send Haughton and some of the men to help with the trunks and the livestock, but I didn't realize you were planning to come so soon."

"Well, we are most grateful for your hospitality." The Colonel turned to stoke up the fire. Miss Marie watched him carefully. "I know how honored you must have been to be able to serve with General Pillow during the Tennessee campaign. So of course it meant so much to us all for you to accommodate our wishes to have him buried among his peers at Elmwood." She touched her handkerchief to the corner of her eye.

"General Pillow was a great patriot, and it was indeed an honor to serve with him." Colonel King was a tall man, a little thick around the middle, with a full head of gray hair. But I could see that once upon a time his hair was about the same sandy color as mine, even though I don't believe my face ever looked so red.

She sighed. "It just would have been so terrible for him not to have been given a proper burial." She sniffed. "Oh, Colonel King, how can we ever thank you?" I knew what was coming next.

"There is no need," he started, turning back toward her. "Mrs. Pillow? What…what's wrong?" Her eyes had welled up, and she started with the usual routine, going from the soft weep to the serious crying. I reckon that Colonel didn't know what to think, seeing as how she'd gone from being smiling and gracious one minute to being a poor pitiful widow woman the next. She was good at the quick switch.

"No, really, I'm all right. It's just that…" She held out her hand as if to stop him from worrying, but she didn't stop her sniffling.

Colonel King stood for a minute, his strong face puzzled with wrinkles, like he didn't have any idea what to do with a crying woman, at least not in his own house with his wife around. But he moved over to the sofa anyway and sat down beside her, putting his arm around her and comforting her. Miss Marie wiped her eyes and whimpered.

"Is something the matter? I thought I heard…" Mrs. King came out of the kitchen and spotted the Colonel cozied up to Miss Marie. She stood perfectly still, holding her hands in front of her like a schoolmarm, one hand squeezing the fingers of the other until her knuckles turned white.

The Colonel had the guilty look of a youngster caught spooning with the neighbor girl. He jumped up and out of the situation. "She's…she's still grieving, poor dear." He noticed me in the doorway, looking mighty relieved to have a distraction from those dangerous tears. "And you are…?"

"I'm Kizzie," I replied.

"And you are Mrs. Pillow's…" he hesitated and then asked, "sister?"

"Shoot, no. I'm her 'companion'. You remember me." I wasn't too worried about Miss Marie's tantrums. Seen too many before. Meanwhile, she was just weeping on the sofa and being glared at by Mrs. King, whose own body was heaving, too, with all those angry feelings she was trying to hold in.

"Of course. Kizzie. So nice to see you again. Do you know what we can do to relieve her, uh, distress? Anything she might need? Does she take tea? Coffee?"

"She likes sherry. Do you have some of that?"

Colonel King showed me to the cabinet in the dining room where he kept his whisky and such. He pulled out the sherry and his own bottle. He took a swig right out of his. I came to be very familiar with that particular cabinet.

I took Miss Marie the sherry, just as she was calming herself down some. She didn't say nothing to me, just took it and started to sip. By that time Mrs. King had sat down beside her, trying to be a lady and accommodate her guest, enjoying her company about as much as she'd enjoy a toothache.

The Colonel sat safely across from them, and Miss Marie told them both the whole sad story all over again—the General dying, farming the place, selling the Memphis house and all her pretty things, then finally losing the farm, gathering steam as she was showing off her pitifulness. I reckon he already knew all about it, seeing as how he was her lawyer and all, but she told it again anyway, thanking him kindly for each particular thing he did. It was all a terrible thing that happened to her—I know because I lived it, too. But Miss Marie was awfully good at spinning a tale. She made it all sound even worse than it was, if that's possible. Mrs. King sat with her hands clenched on her lap, nodding politely. Colonel King listened to everything she said, smiling. Yellow flames danced happily inside the fireplace, like they didn't have any idea how sad the widow's story was supposed to be.

Their cook Ginny waddled in and announced that supper was ready, for all of us. Miss Marie walked beside the Colonel as they strolled into the dining room, followed by Mrs. King, who was studying the floor. I went to round up the children so we could introduce them all. Mary was about 12 that fall. She was just as pretty and dark haired as her mama and just as spirited, too. Annie was ten, kind of quiet and sort of plain looking, if that don't sound too ugly of me. I don't rightly know who she took after. And then there was little Giddy. Least that's what I always called him. His mama always called him Gideon. He was eight when we got there, so he was the baby. And we met their teenage girls, too—Ruth, Ida, Mary, and Fannie—who reminded me of the four March sisters, except they all looked exactly the same: four different sizes of the exact same straw-haired girl. But none of them could have been Jo—they were all too shy.

"Your husband is quite an effective advocate," Miss Marie remarked at the dinner table. Since she always did the most talking, she was always the last to finish supper. They were still sitting around the Kings' big dining room table, enjoying their hospitality, getting acquainted, even though the Colonel and Miss Marie seemed pretty well acquainted already.

"He has enjoyed some success in his legal practice, that's certainly true," Miss Sallie replied without looking at her.

Miss Marie eyed her and practically sang, "Oh, but not just success. He cuts a most impressive figure in the courtroom."

That got Miss Sallie to notice that Miss Marie was smiling over at the Colonel who was gazing back. The lamplight behind Miss Sallie brightened their faces but kept her face in shadow, as if she was a stage actor whose footlights had gone out.

"What exactly did your most recent case involve, Mrs. Pillow?"

"Oh, it was a silly little thing, of no consequence," she replied, her silver knife carving easily through the fleshy pink meat.

"Colonel King?" Miss Sallie asked, her face still almost invisible in the shadow.

"Mrs. Pillow was being harassed by the Corbin Banking Company for back payments on her mortgage on Mound Plantation."

"Oh, this business talk is so dry. Sallie, darling, do you remember that lovely evening we all spent together at the Gayoso when General Pillow was alive? At the Mystic Memphi Mardi Gras Ball? What a wonderful memory!" Miss Marie took a bite of beef and chewed it slowly, smiling.

"Yes, Mrs. Pillow, I remember. So you owed them money. Tell me, Colonel King, how did her case turn out?" Miss Sallie already knew the answer.

"I'm afraid the banking company convinced the judge that they were right and we were wrong."

"You mean Mrs. Pillow was wrong," Miss Sallie corrected him.

Miss Marie stopped chewing. The Colonel responded quickly, "As her attorney, acting on her behalf, I was wrong as well, I'm afraid."

"And because you had no money, you lost your land," Miss Sallie concluded, not sounding real sympathetic.

Miss Marie acted wounded. "It has been a most unfortunate turn of events."

"Yes, it must have been," Miss Sallie sighed, placing her napkin, rumpled into a ball, beside her plate.

"And so we are quite lucky, aren't we, darling, to be able to bring Mrs. Pillow here with us to manage the household?"

"Oh, yes. Very lucky indeed." She studied her empty dinner plate a whole lot longer than it took to see that there was nothing there.

CHAPTER 7

❧

"Kizzie, what exactly is Mrs. Pillow's name?" My idiot husband had decided to disgrace me by bringing a money-grubbing social climber into our midst, so I was determined to uncover everything I could about the bitch.

"Oh, it's a long one," she replied, dishing up the eggs for breakfast. "Marie Eliza Dickson Trigg Pillow. On account of she's been married twice."

"Married twice. I see." Concentrating on a newspaper through his ridiculous looking spectacles, he didn't respond. "So, Clay, why does she now call herself 'Mary Eliza'? I thought her name was 'Marie.'"

"I don't really know—there's only a slight difference." He didn't even look at me, now distracted by the pile of eggs on his plate. It's not that I cared for the man—far from it. His whisky bloated body was reason enough for me to be relieved that he hadn't been a husband to me in years, and I certainly didn't need his money, or what was left of it after he rescued the damned woman.

"Well, you see," Kizzie offered, gesturing with the serving spoon, "General Pillow's first wife was named Mary. Mary E. Pillow. So when Miss Marie got married to the General, I reckon she decided it would just be easier if she went by the same name, seeing as how hers was so close anyway." Gliding about the table with the grace of a debutante, Kizzie expressed herself with all the eloquence of a Louisiana cotton picker.

"And why do you call her Marie?"

"Oh, I've always called her Miss Marie, since I was a little thing down in Feliciana Parish. That's her name."

I glanced over at him. "It just seems so strange for a woman to change her name to read exactly like the name of her husband's first wife, don't you think?"

"Not strange at all," he muttered gruffly, concentrating on his breakfast. "Mere personal preference, I'm sure."

"It's very odd, if you ask me." I looked at him skeptically, taking a slow sip of my coffee. "General Pillow was so fond of Mary. Perhaps that's why the new Mrs. Pillow began to sign her name that way, to please him. I understand trying to please one's husband, but going to such lengths…"

"She did it with Giddy's name, too," Kizzie interrupted. "General Pillow had a son named Gideon, after him of course, with his first wife, Mrs. Pillow, but he got killed in a steamboat explosion. So when little Giddy came along, they just gave him the same name. I think Miss Marie just wanted him to be happy with a new son, since he was so sad when the first one died."

"Hmm." I held my cup to my lips without drinking. "So she gives her son the same name. It's almost as if she was trying to recreate his first family."

"She's doing nothing of the sort," the Colonel grumbled, annoyed, finally glancing up at me.

"I don't know nothing about that. I just know Miss Marie knows how to please a man," Kizzie explained.

I set my cup down carefully in its saucer, unable to avoid the brittle clatter of fine china against its own.

After Kizzie was dismissed, he repeated the same tired story. "You know that I feel indebted to General Pillow because of our service together during the War. And that's the same reason I asked you to go care for him during his illness after Mary died—because I feel beholden. Very beholden."

"Yes, but General Pillow is dead and buried. Twice buried, in fact. There's nothing more you can possibly do for him."

"Well, I'm going to try. His widow and his children are destitute. It is our Christian duty to help them. And having her here as manager of the household will do us as much good as it does her." He was simply making excuses, arguing with himself. My silence dared him to continue. "And besides, with her here, you'll be able to stay in Memphis for as long as you like." Memphis. Holy Mother of God. If anyone in Memphis ever found out about Mary Eliza Pillow living with us, my reputation would be trampled. I'd be a laughingstock. I had had to endure a great deal in my marriage, but I would not tolerate the gossip that was bound to arise from our association with her.

"You know as well as I do that it's a lot more than that," I snapped. "She knows, doesn't she?"

Avoiding the issue like the coward that he was, he said nothing.

"I asked you a question."

The hall clock chimed. The morning sunlight revealed the floating dust of the now silent house. "There is a possibility that she knows."

"And you think she'd use that information against you?"

"I don't know. I just don't know. I can't imagine that a woman of her background and discretion…"

"And so she's blackmailed you into giving her this farm," I interrupted.

"She's done no such thing. Nothing of the sort. It's just that, well, we don't need it, and it would certainly be perceived as uncharitable if we didn't help…" His filmy eyes looked at me with a kind of pitiful sincerity, a prodigal begging for pennies, not yet knowing that he will squander even those.

I had tired of his excuses. "This is your farm and your business. I really want nothing to do with it."

"But it is important that you agree…"

"Leave the girls and me out of it. That's all I ask." Oh, dear God in heaven, if only he had.

CHAPTER 8

The chill of the winter evening made me long for the soothing burn of Kentucky whisky. Sallie's inquiries of the morning brought forth dangerous memories of disasters best forgotten. With my bottle I sat, long into the evening, guilt-ridden, indebted, taking my only comfort from that blessed dusky liquid, painfully recalling truths from the necessary haze of the past. Expecting those stories would stay locked away, perhaps even buried for eternity, I now knew I must act with renewed vigilance. Perhaps he had whispered my secret. Perhaps she knew.

Kentucky would not secede, would not follow the noble Southern cause as it rightfully should. I had argued strenuously with my neighbors, my clients, anyone who would listen, of the rightness of the Cause. No government has the right to impose its will on sovereign states. Kentucky and its people should determine the law of Kentucky, not a lily-livered native son, traitor to the South, son now of Illinois and leader of the mass of misguided Yankees. Lincoln was not my president and would never be.

The arguments were ever present, echoing in the halls of the courthouse, shouted in battle cries in the fields, cursed and sworn in shadowy taverns. Most agreed that Kentucky had been wrong in not joining the Cause, but not every native son proved to be a loyal Kentuckian. One prattling attorney had the audacity to challenge me to my face, shamelessly staring me straight in the eye as he spouted condemnation against the Confederacy. The imbecile had no reputation for violence, but his capacity for violence nevertheless became apparent to me, through his wild gesticulations, his threatening stance, his narrowed eyes. His adversary could bear no more. The noble soldier waited for an opportunity, which came late in the evening outside McCain's Tavern. From the blue midnight shadows the champion grabbed the dupe, wrapped his forearm about his sweaty neck, held the angry blade to his throat. Comrades of the soldier, following too closely throughout the evening, begged him to desist, not to draw blood within the boundaries of civilization but to take his wrath to the battlefield. They understood the zeal of the loyal soldier and knew that his actions were necessary to the Cause. The imbecile was released, stumbling, half choking into the night.

Rumblings, threats of retribution for his action, I ignored. I could not be encumbered with bloodless threats or with the law. I was compelled to fight for the honor of my beloved Kentucky. Thus, issuing a call to arms, inducing men to leave their homes under my leadership, I created a battalion of 2000 men, six companies in all—King's Tigers, Pillow's Guards, among others, we took the names of brave warriors, intimidating to others and inspiring to ourselves. We met with only skirmishes in the woods of Tennessee, but we were zealous warriors, eager to do our part for the Southern Cause.

In April of 1862, after spending the better part of a year fighting independent of any formal association with the Confederate army, I learned that several officers wished to consolidate my battalion with four other companies to become an official regiment of the Confederacy. I received word that the commander of this new regiment was to be Colonel Claiborne and that he would select his own subordinate officers. Chagrined, I concluded that with the destruction of my battalion my office as its chief was also destroyed. Who was this upstart Claiborne? Certainly, the leaders of the army would not choose a lesser man than I to lead my own troops. Certainly, they would recognize the importance of keeping leaders to whom the troops were loyal to maintain morale.

As leader of my fellow Kentuckians, I had been the unanimous choice of the entire battalion. I knew that under other leadership my men might indeed mutiny, so loyal to me had they had become. Having organized and led the battalion thus far, I felt slighted that my hard work and effort and contributions would not be recognized by my elevation to commander of the regiment. I raised the battalion unaided, armed it nearly entirely myself—became surety for all the horses purchased. I took from the state of Kentucky six brass pieces of artillery, caissons, and 800 stand of arms and ultimately gave these items to the Southern Confederacy. Certainly, these contributions and my own personal sacrifices should have been recognized.

He was easily distinguished among the fray of the new company's arrival, anxious horses tramping, almost tripping on each other in the throng, their riders swaying with confidence and exhaustion. He slouched upon his mount, unimpressive and unimpressed by the unit to which he had been assigned. Reluctantly swinging his leg over the horse and dismounting, he sauntered toward our collection of curious soldiers to mark his territory.

Stepping out beyond the shade of the elm to be recognized, I inquired respectfully, "Colonel Claiborne?"

"I'm Claiborne," he snorted. "And you must be the country cousins from Kentucky."

Distracted by his coarseness, his rudeness, his clipped manner of speaking, I nevertheless heard him inform me that he had been appointed colonel and that I was to be major of the newly formed regiment, if I so desired. If I so desired. He spoke these words, boldly, with a tone of condescension toward my men and myself that I had seldom before heard from any man, Union or Confederate. His impudent gray eyes glared into my own, daring me to defy him. *If I so desired.* He refused to let me look away, engaged me, forced me to attend to those steely, unforgiving eyes. I tried to resist, but he held control, assaulting me with that gray of gunpowder, spent shells, angry ashes.

He turned to leave. "You are to remain under my command," he ordered, taunting me without looking at me, speaking over his shoulder in an aside which would more rightly be delivered in bold soliloquy, face to face.

"I must refuse," I replied, my voice rising with indignation. "Sir, I have been turned out of office if only because of the destruction of my regiment, the consolidation of the troops. I will not accept the appointment. My men and officers do not want me to accept offices under you."

He stopped his progress and turned, once again directing his impudent gaze toward me.

"There would be no benefit," I continued, louder than I intended. "My presence would only add to the dissatisfaction existing among the men. They are virtually mutinous as it is, in the consequence of the change."

"Mutinous?" he snickered. Turning his back, he returned to his mount and galloped from the camp. He left the conversation hanging, the smoky haze remaining from a yet unresolved battle. He never intimated to me that he nevertheless recognized me as major of the regiment from that day.

In the evening he called me to his camp, just outside our own. Beside the firelight, he gulped liquid from his tin cup, sighing with the sound of whisky well swallowed. He offered me none.

"Captain, you've been commanded by the leaders of the Confederacy to join us officially, to defend our homeland."

Watching the dying blaze before me, I ventured to question him. "Whose homeland?"

"Why, mine. And yours. All of the South."

"And where exactly are you from, sir?"

"North Carolina." The embers glowed beneath the blackened logs.

Crickets whirred. In the distance, an owl warned its prey in careful hoots. I considered my response. "You don't sound like a Tarheel."

"Born and raised in Massachusetts. Moved down south about five years ago. Been farming tobacco, had a lot of success, too, until the Feds decided to take it upon themselves to tell us whatfor about how we farm."

I breathed deeply, inhaling the smoky night air. I gazed at the silent tree branches, reaching their fingers up toward the twinkling stars. Slowly, the stars darkened, then disappeared from the night sky completely. Clouds obstructed the spangled sky, confusing light and dark, muddling the heavenly image above.

He spat into the dirt. "Can I count on you?"

A lone star was uncovered by the slowly moving cloud blanket, sparkling restlessly. "Count on me?" Slight laughter escaped quietly, louder, rising up from deep within me, overwhelming me in the face of the absurdity that I, Henry Clay King, would fight under the command of a damned Unionist in defense of the Confederate States of America. I stood and stumbled away from the campsite, not answering the fool, my belly aching with torrents of laughter.

In the brilliant sunlight of that next day, I drew up my battalion on dress parade and formally handed it over to Colonel Claiborne in his presence taking a public leave of them, exhorting all to obedience to him. That same day I took up my quarters a mile and a half from camp visiting the colonel's head-quarters nearly every day and sometimes several times a day, setting up the business of the battalion—I was under the firm conviction that Colonel Claiborne would undoubtedly appoint another man as major—I did not know who that man might be. Thus I remained until the 17th day of April.

On that unusually warm spring night, when many in our companies left their tents open to encourage cooling breezes, a mutineer in our ranks, I shall not say who, one dissatisfied with Claiborne's leadership, intended to right the wrong. The moon presided boldly over the lesser lights, illuminating the entire camp, delineating each pebble, each blade of grass under the feet of the soldier as he stealthily departed on his mission. A quiet crackle in the brush—perhaps an animal—he paused, listening but hearing nothing more. The bright still-ness reassured the assassin that he was indeed alone. Grasping the cold steel at his belt, the soldier took the pistol and aimed at the open tent before he was within shooting distance of the despised colonel. A soft breeze brushed his uncovered head, anointing him, urging him onward. Three more steps, now two, now positioned, the soldier pulled tight on the trigger, the shot reverber-ating through the valley in which they were camped. The colonel flinched, waking, realizing he had been targeted, but not seeing the shadowy figure flee-ing into the Tennessee woods.

A shout, another, a growing urgent chorus of mumbling, talking, cries in the night. Awakened from my sleep by the stir, hearing of the dreadful event, I was encouraged to leave lest, as the former leader of the mutinous group, I be blamed. Most fortunately, of course, Colonel Claiborne survived the attempt. But, as my comrades argued, Colonel Claiborne might yet be killed and myself be blamed by his friends regardless that the colonel was so despised among all of my men. Even if the assassin were discovered, doubtless none of my men would arrest the mutineer. My only choice was to leave, that very night, never for once dreaming that I was violating any duty as an officer or gentleman. Through the warm spring night I hastened, the darkened roads of northern Tennessee leading me toward a greater destiny, to continue in fighting for the Cause. Grating voices in the distance halted my progress, angry accusations shattering the night, rushing toward me under gentle starlight. Wincing, cow-ering, I took the blows: Dereliction of duty, they shouted. Insubordination. And attempted murder.

I explained to my captors that I had resigned out of honor, expecting the colonel to appoint his own subordinates. I had not deserted, never, but was seeking other regiments with more amenable leaders. Binding and scratching my wrists with the coarse rope, they said there was no record of my formal res-ignation, that I had deserted the regiment and had acted as a spy against Colo-nel Claiborne. Forcing me along that road at gunpoint, they said that men within my battalion reported my frustration and anger with the colonel's lead-ership over them, that they were quite happy now to have a leader with moral courage. Throwing me into the dank cell, the iron gate locking with finality, they said that I had threatened the colonel before my men. Worst of all, accus-ing me of instability, stigmatizing their own commander, my men described to them a fractious mind unable to adjust to change, unable to lead them further. Lies, all of them.

Imprisoned, dejected, dishonored, I saw no hope. Only the darkness of a prison cell and a future of inevitable dishonor awaited me, as foul and squalid as the moldy walls surrounding me. Then nothing short of a miracle occurred. Silhouetted in the otherworldly light outside my cell door stood my deliverance, the "Hero of Chapultepec", General Gideon Johnson Pillow. Having never met the great man, I nevertheless nicknamed my part of my battalion "Pillow's Guards" in honor of him, being well familiar with his heroism and loyalty. It was an honor, I cried as I nearly bowed my head to the floor. He said he'd heard of my case, thought there might have been mitigating circumstances. Perhaps I'd been wrongly accused. He agreed that Colonel Claiborne was a difficult man and even more difficult it would be for a loyal son of the South to fight under a man of questionable birth. He himself had been familiar with the vagaries of reputation and misinterpretations of honorable actions. He knew of my reputation as a fierce warrior, and having lost several of his subordinates, he needed me to give personal assistance at his next assignment, Fort Donelson on the Cumberland River. Having the authority to wield influence, the great man altered my official record, in essence wiping the slate of any reference to the damned crime of which I had been accused.

The heavy iron gates were opened, and I was released, liberated by this great man to whom I was then held in thrall for the rest of my days. I was gladly beholden to him if my reputation could be restored and my wartime sins could be forgiven by the stroke of his pen.

Fort Donelson was a cold, bitter fight, with frostbite afflicting the ragged men who fought for us, many of the wounded freezing to death. We held on as the Union navy sent their gunboats, firing relentlessly. General Pillow vowed never, under any circumstances, to surrender to the Union army. But the battle was lost. There would be no victory: surrender was inevitable. General Pillow refused, and more men died as the battle wore on.

General Pillow arranged to leave his post as leader of the fort, to pass the position to General Buckner, who was reluctant but willing to surrender to Grant. With true conviction, Pillow pronounced, "As for myself, I will never surrender the command or myself; I will die first."

So in the bitter frozen night, too clear, with ice floes thickening around the muddy shores of the Tennessee River, in a tiny scow we fled. Not in fear, mind you, but in the cause of honor. General Pillow had given his word never to surrender–what harm was there in letting a lesser man take responsibility for the humiliation at Fort Donelson?

After we left our little boat on the shores, we began our slow trek through the woods. We traveled all night, crossing the bridge then boarding a steamer for Nashville. The General explained his actions to everyone he encountered—the intrepid Tennesseans, the overwhelming numbers of the Union troops—but within a few short weeks he was relieved of his command. Having accompanied him on the night of his purported dishonor, I knew a compassion and deep commiseration I had never before experienced—doing an honorable thing for himself and his beloved Tennessee, he was nevertheless treated dishonorably. That injustice toward him and his great effort on my behalf forged an unbreakable alliance between us.

I continued in the war effort by gathering conscripts and deserters, damnable men who fled from the battlefield. Ultimately, I was captured at Shelbyville by Union forces and remained imprisoned for the rest of the War. This time, imprisonment came without shame. General Pillow redeemed himself by leading the Volunteer and Conscript Bureau and never again saw battle.

After the War, I first saw him again in the clerk's office of the Shelby County Courthouse, as by coincidence we had both set out to practice law in Memphis. At first we merely exchanged pleasantries, but over time our conversations flowed from the practice of law, to the recounting of the fates of common friends, and finally to my great indebtedness to him.

I could not possibly express my lifelong gratitude for his great act of forgiveness and understanding. But he, who had been misunderstood by so many, especially regarding the incidents at Fort Donelson, understood the caprice of reputation. I did not run to the safety of my home, I ran to fight in other battles, which I did, most valiantly. I had not shirked my duty to my Kentucky brigade, only considered the privileges of appointment of my new commanding officer. I feared the subject of the attempted assassination of Colonel Claiborne, of my alleged insubordination. He smiled, his sympathetic eyes shining the approval of a watchful master, and he said nothing, understanding as I did that our most wrenching defeats need never be revealed. We were of one mind.

In honor, a lesser man will find dishonor. In courage, he will see cowardice. In all that is good, noble, beautiful, he will uncover evil. All this tangled paradox, this damnable knot, is best unremembered in the glow of this amber bottle, Kentucky born, full of anger and sleep.

If ever I can repay you, if ever…

"I will never surrender; I will die first." To you, General Pillow.

CHAPTER 9

"She was from somewheres over in Miss'ippi, but I b'lieve they met up in Memphis. She's such a kind Christian lady. But I guess the Good Lawd didn't see fit to give her no good looks." Ginny set her large self down at the table and rested for the first time that morning. Her coffee was the same color as the plump hand that stirred it. "Don't you tell nobody I said this," she whispered real loud, "but I think she's just plain homely, 'less she's smilin'. When she's smilin', that makes up for a lot."

Ginny was easy to listen to, and she seemed to know all the important details about everybody: whether they liked butter or jelly, scrambled eggs or fried, and all kinds of personal information, too. Even though I was trying to be polite, just getting to know her, I sure didn't mind her stories.

"Now, you see they decided they didn't like bein' married to each other. I don't know why not. No, the Colonel and Miss Sallie ain't married like reg'lar folks. I don't know why they don't just go ahead and git a dee-vorce, 'ceptin' that Miss Sallie and her mama, they's Cathlick. They don't believe in dee-vorces." She paused to take a sip from her cup.

"That Colonel King, he treats her real good, though, with this big old house and her carriage and all the pretty things she keeps, dresses, china, and knick-knacks. The Colonel lets her stay up in Memphis whenever she pleases, 'cause she's got lots of friends up there. And you should see the big old house they got up there, too. I've worked there some. Miss Sallie don't know too many folks over in Marianna. So I believe she's pretty lonely when she's here at Sterling Hill, unless she has somebody visiting her for a while. Must be an awful sad thing to have a husband who don't want nothing to do with you, even if you do live in a great big old house. Miss Sallie, she ain't no farm wife. No, ma'am, she's a real lady."

The kitchen still smelled of bacon almost burned. It would be another good day for staying inside, but when I was working in the yard I never missed the chance to stop and take in the view. The Kings' mansion house was perched up at the top of a steep hill surrounded by gray cottonwood trees that had lost all of their leaves by the time we got there that November. Sometimes among the crowd of trunks and bony limbs, an open space allowed a peek at the river in the distance, like a secret that couldn't be kept, and even farther away, the bare fields of Mississippi. At the bottom of the hill sat the guest house and over toward the picked over cotton fields and the river were the rest of the buildings—the barn, the quarters, the workshops. Puffs of smoke from each little shack marked the presence of life, dark families gathered around their tiny hearths, secure in their homes and happy that the crop was in. The gray of smoke, of trees, of empty fields seemed as full of promise to me as the yellow buds of spring.

"But when it comes right down to it, they're just like the rest of the menfolks in the world. They ain't gentlemen at all. And, see, that was how Colonel King got his end of the bargain. He had this nice little wife—that he didn't have nothin' to do with—sittin' in her big old house, and she allowed him to spend time with whoever he wanted. Least that's what I heard tell.

"I don't rightly know how much wanderin' the Colonel does any more, now that he's older." She looked at me hard like I was supposed to know. "But I know this—I ain't never heard the Colonel say nothin' bad about Miss Sallie. Not one bad thing. I heard her daddy was rich. He was a Miss'ippi planter after all. That ought to keep a man int'rested in a lady, even if she ain't pretty."

I swanny, that woman could talk a blue streak, and she said all kinds of things I reckon she shouldn't. I don't rightly know if Miss Marie already knew all that about the Colonel and Miss Sallie, but looking back, I reckon that's what she liked about the situation. She wasn't the type to go messing up a real good marriage or nothing. No, Miss Marie had good breeding. She wasn't fixing to mess up something that was just fine. But seeing as how the Colonel and Miss Sallie were messed up to start with, and seeing as how this was her time of need, I reckon there wasn't no harm in taking advantage of the situation.

The creak of the kitchen door startled me, and an oil smeared man walked in the kitchen door, stamping the dirt off his feet. I stood up, fearful of who he might be.

"Oh, sit yourself on down, Miss Kizzie. That ain't nobody but Tom."

He studied me a minute before speaking. "I believe I met you before. Over when we were digging up…"

"Oh, yeah. Howdy do." I was glad he didn't say nothing about the General falling out of his casket. That was just too awful to remember.

"It's Kizzie, is it? Tom Worley."

"He's the farm manager," Ginny explained. "Now, Tom here, he's knowed the Kings for some time, ain't that right, Tom?"

"Well, I know the Colonel. Ain't never seen too much of Miz King, though. She ain't here all that much." He walked over to the stove and poured himself a cup of coffee before joining us at the table.

"That's right," Ginny agreed. "She don't have much truck with farm life. But she do like to say that she's the one gave him the idea to buy this place. She done told me that onct when General Pillow was sickly—that was before he was married to this Miz Pillow—Colonel King sent her down from Memphis to Mound Plantation to take care of him. I don't know what all she did, but she says that's when she saw how beautiful these hills along the river are. And the Colonel thought so, too—if it was good enough for General Pillow, then it was good enough for them, I always heard him say. Especially since they named the county after General Robert E. Lee and all."

I watched Tom Worley peering at Ginny over the top of his coffee cup, hiding his grin.

"Of course, this place was named after a little town called Sterling, not very far from here. One year when the river flooded, the whole town just plum washed away. At least that's what I always heard. I never did think it was too lucky for them to be living on a farm named after such a place."

"Washed away?"

"Oh, you don't need to worry none, Miss Kizzie," Tom Worley assured me. "That's just going to happen now and then on a river as powerful as this one. She's a changeable woman, she is, and sometimes she gets mad enough to do some damage. You'll be just fine as long as you stay right up here on this hill, especially during high water."

Ginny and Tom laughed at me worrying about the flood, so I laughed uncomfortably, too. Tom Worley and I had a real enjoyable time together listening to Ginny. He didn't say too much more, but he had friendly eyes. When her rest time was over, Ginny made her way over to the sink and started washing, her soft, broad back toward me. Tom Worley stood up slowly and said goodbye, leaving me sitting at the table, glad to make his acquaintance.

Realizing I needed to get back to work, too, I stood up quickly and moved towards the door.

"Kizzie?" Ginny called after me. When I looked back at her, she winked.

❦   ❦   ❦

We were hard up for money, and Miss Marie was bound to get some. So that Saturday evening, while Miss Sallie was bathing her girls out in the kitchen, Miss Marie did what she came for—or what I thought she came for. She wanted me to be there as her witness while she talked business with the Colonel in the parlor, but I stayed back in the shadows near the door. I knew my place.

"As you know, our cotton crop this year didn't cover the debt on the farm," she began, standing behind him. "This is so embarrassing. Because I also have some responsibilities to some creditors in Memphis that need attention."

"More creditors?" He didn't look up from the papers he was reading at his desk.

"Well, the truth is, I owe a dressmaker $150. And there are our debts to the feed store in Marianna."

"Is that all?"

She looked down at her hands, and dabbed her eye with her handkerchief. "And I owe some money to the milliner in Helena. Just a little." He didn't look up. "Ever since you lost that case for me, and I had to pay off those creditors so as not to declare *bankruptcy*, I have had almost nothing to meet my obligations with." He frowned at the papers in front of him. "You know, General Pillow was a wonderful man, but he left our finances in such a shambles. It's just been so hard, trying make ends meet and feeding these children and paying my employees…" She started crying, just a little. Just enough to seem pitiful. He still didn't say anything, so she tried again. "And my widow's pension from the War Department—it hasn't even come through yet." A tear ran down her cheek.

"You haven't started to receive the pension?" He turned around and looked at her over his spectacles.

Miss Marie seemed surprised that he had finally taken the bait. "No, not a penny."

"How ever in the world do those imbeciles up in Washington expect a widow—a general's widow of all things—to survive on nothing? And after all that General Pillow did in Mexico."

"Colonel King, I hate to have to do this, but because of my situation, I must. Would you be willing to lend me $600, at least until my widow's pension comes through? Oh, I feel just horrible with even the imposition of the request." She covered up her eyes with her hands and her handkerchief and wept softly.

He paused a minute, I reckon still trying to understand why the government wasn't taking better care of her. "Six hundred dollars? No, that shouldn't be any problem. Can you believe that? No widow's pension." He shook his head, not believing it at all.

She smiled through her tears and shook his hand with both of hers. "Thank you. Thank you so much. I will always be grateful to you for your generosity. And this must be a loan, not a gift. I still have my cotton claims pending."

He smirked. "Your cotton claims? You mean you haven't given up yet?"

"Of course not. There's a great deal of money at stake, you know. I have had such a time of it, since I was just a minor when that cotton was stolen and then when Mr. Trigg died. But when I get what I am owed, I shall have more than enough to live comfortably." Then she remembered to add, "And to repay all my debts, of course. And you of all people know about my land in Tennessee…"

He frowned playfully at her silly talk. He knew and I knew there wasn't no land in Tennessee that belonged to her. The judge had already told her that, years ago, when I was just a little girl sitting there in that courtroom.

"I don't have much as security," she continued, "but I do have some mules and the wagon and the bell. That bell came from my parents' home in Feliciana Parish. It belonged to my great-grandfather. It's bronze, you know, cast in France, a valuable antique. If you would draw up an agreement, I would be happy to offer what I have as security."

"However you would like this to be arranged, I can arrange it," he finally offered, turning around to his desk to find paper. Just like one of those old timey knights in armor, Colonel King seemed happy to oblige his damsel in distress.

So he wrote up an agreement. He said he'd keep the mules and our wagon, and even that old bell just in case she couldn't pay him back. I don't think they were worth all that much, but that's what they agreed on. They made me sign my name as a witness.

The next morning Miss Marie directed Malcolm to install that old plantation bell on a post out in the yard. The white sun appeared and disappeared among the clouds, too busy hiding to warm up the day.

"Who lifted this thing for you, Miss Kizzie, when y'all were coming over?" he asked me, shaking off the cold from his hands like invisible dust. He was a strong shouldered man, with an easy smile showing off the space where a tooth used to be.

"I did it myself."

"You a strong young lady," he commented, finishing his work. "I'm surprised you can do such a thing, this bell's so heavy."

"I imagine a body can do just about anything it has a mind to." And I believed that, too.

A darker gray cloud spread over us quickly, like a sooty quilt, bringing the smell of winter rain. Even the strong gusts of wind couldn't make that bell clang. It wouldn't budge. Between the weight of that heavy brown metal and Malcolm bolting it on so tight, that bell wasn't going nowhere.

*   *   *

After supper that night, Miss Marie decided to read to us all. The Colonel stoked up the fire real good in Miss Sallie's pretty parlor, and the children lounged together on the Persian rug. Miss Sallie said she wanted to go on up to bed, but her girls and Miss Marie persuaded her to stay. Now, Miss Marie wasn't particular about where she'd pick up reading a book, finding a little bit here, a little bit there that she wanted to recite, not usually taking a book from start to finish when she read to the children and me. I always preferred to start at the beginning and work my way all the way through a book in order, but I wasn't one to tell Miss Marie anything. She decided to read from *Jane Eyre*, one of my very favorites. I always enjoyed her reading. Why, she could make the catechism sound like a swashbuckler if she was of a mind to. She put so much feeling into it, you'd think you were in a theater and she was acting all the parts.

"'*Jane, you look blooming and smiling, and pretty,' said he: 'truly pretty this morning.*'" Miss Marie deepened her voice just like she was Mr. Rochester in love. Made him sound like he was from England, too, which I reckon he was.

"'*It is Jane Eyre, sir.*'" She changed her voice to be real sweet and clear when she read that. And she looked down, acting shy. Miss Sallie frowned at her.

"'*Soon to be Jane Rochester,' he added: 'in four weeks, Janet; not a day more. Do you hear that?*'"

*"I **did**, and I could not quite comprehend it: it made me giddy. The feeling the announcement sent through me was something stronger than was consistent with joy—something that smote and stunned: it was, I think, almost fear."*

The girls giggled when they heard their brother's name in a book, but I just wondered why on earth anybody who was in love would be afraid. It would seem like love would only make you happy. Jane Eyre must have been one of those people who never thought she was as good as everybody else.

"'Yes, Mrs. Rochester,' said he; 'young Mrs. Rochester—Fairfax Rochester's girl-bride.'" That part reminded me of Miss Marie. She sure was a girl-bride, getting married at 13, getting widowed at 16. But other than that, I don't think she was much like Jane Eyre at all.

The parlor was the most inviting room in the house and one of the prettiest places I'd ever seen, even in the evening. Sitting on the floor in front of the fire that Malcolm had kept burning in there all day, I leaned my face against one of the carved wooden roses on the arm of Miss Sallie's sofa. Such finery seemed almost magical in the firelight. Pictures of her ancestors hung on the wall in big gold frames. I tried to look into their painted eyes without being scared, their faces half hidden by the shadows, and couldn't figure why anybody would want such frightening folks staring down at them all the time. But that's what fancy folks like. I sure am glad I won't never be fancy.

The children yawned and blinked sleepily as Miss Marie read on and on. Giddy put his head in Mary's lap and fell asleep there. Miss Sallie was plaiting one of her girls' hair. The Colonel's eyes never left Miss Marie.

"'And then you won't know me, sir; and I shall not be your Jane Eyre any longer...'" Miss Marie glanced an eye over to Miss Sallie to see what she was doing, and then she looked straight at the Colonel and said the rest, without even looking at the book: *"'and I don't call you handsome, sir, though I love you most dearly...'"*

That's when I looked up and noticed that Miss Sallie was looking at the both of them, too.

CHAPTER 10

The dry branches of the fir tree drooped under the weight of the ornaments and melted candle wax. Christmas in Memphis was a bigger chore in the cleaning up than in the preparations, especially without Ginny's help. Pine, oranges, gingerbread—the fragrances of the season made me sick to my stomach.

My German glass ornaments had been a sparkling distraction to me during the holidays, a new addition which kept me from thinking of uglier matters. But the time had come to put them away. Removing them from the tree and carefully wrapping each one in paper, I tried to seem preoccupied with my task while he talked. I was not surprised that he had come to Memphis after Christmas to announce what he had done.

"I have thought a great deal about this, and I wanted you to know that it is now official." I could not help but turn to face him, but he was pacing anxiously, avoiding my eyes. "I have written a will in which Mrs. Pillow will inherit Sterling Hill at the time of my death. As much as I have wanted to retire to the plantation and live out the rest of my life there, it is quite obvious that you have different feelings about the matter. So the only condition to my bequeathing her the property is that she agree to give me a home there for life."

"A home there for life." Those words echoed a warning in my mind, the faint wail of an unwelcome train in the distance.

"You and I have been very fortunate in financial matters, with my law practice and the inheritance from your father," he continued, "and we have the wherewithal to arrange this, since you and the girls have already been amply provided for. And I always had tremendous respect for General Pillow, who helped me so much during the War, so it is only fitting that I should show my appreciation by assisting his widow and their children during this time of need. And this appears to be the appropriate way for me to act on my kind feelings toward him, even after his death."

"Toward him or toward her?" A shining glass angel dangled by a ribbon from my quivering fingers.

"Well, toward both of them, I suppose. She is a charming woman." He examined the half undecorated tree for the first time.

I had left Sterling Hill because I could not bear to stay in that house another minute. I was sickened by his embarrassing behavior, following her around like a lovesick puppy, placing his money and our reputations in peril. That woman was certainly out for money—probably more—and he was more than willing to accommodate her. As my excuse, I explained that I didn't want my girls to miss any of the Christmas parties in Memphis and that our home there was a more suitable setting for our Christmas festivities. Of course, there was nothing festive about it.

"Clay, your behavior with Mrs. Pillow is embarrassing, especially in front of the girls," I snapped. "The way you smile at her, the way you both flirt with each other. What is a 60 year old man like you doing flirting with a 39 year old anyway?"

"She's 37."

The ornament shattered onto the floor, startling us both. Blue and silver shards lay rocking, glittering before me. Kneeling to pick up the broken glass, I fingered the cracked piece that had been the angel's face. "I should never have agreed to this damned situation. It was wrong, and I knew it was wrong."

"Sallie, you obviously have some great bias against her that has impaired your judgment."

"Impaired my judgment? Who's the one who created this situation and brought her into our home?" Disregarding my broken treasure, I stood and glared at him, pinching my fingers to stanch the bleeding.

"And what would you have me do, put her out on the highway, wave farethewell, and hope she'll find a means to feed her children? Come on now, Sallie. Somebody's got to take care of her and of her children, and we can certainly afford to do so."

"And then you fall under her spell, giving her money and land and God knows what else?" Despite my bleeding finger, I continued my task, reaching into the tree too roughly, the ornaments tinkling and swinging precariously.

"I have not fallen under anyone's spell," he laughed. "I have all my faculties in good working order." He had made his way to the liquor cabinet, bending down in search of some particular bottle.

"Clay, you're 60 years old. Of course you're flattered when a lovely young woman pays attention to you. But can't you see she's playing you for a fool? You know you can't trust a woman like that. Especially if…"

"If what?" he asked, obliviously. He continued his search, rattling bottles.

"Clay, she's disgusting. Just look at her. Her attitude, her tone of voice. She's just so condescending toward me and always fawning over you…"

He stood upright, bottle in hand, his cheeks flushed. "Mrs. Pillow is a kind, honest woman who has helped us immensely over the past few weeks."

"My God, Clay, can't you see through that 'poor, pitiful widow' drama?"

"Mrs. Pillow is a woman who needs our help, and she *is* a widow," he replied, turning his back toward me and pouring himself a glass.

"I just can't believe you don't see it. It's as if she's bewitched you. You don't seem to see how manipulative she is."

"Bewitched? That's ridiculous."

"You've left her the farm in your will. Is that the kind of Christian charity you'd show to just any poor downtrodden soul?"

"Of course not. But she's General Pillow's widow and…"

"I've heard so much about the great and mighty Gideon Pillow that I could just scream." He stared at me, motionless, not believing my outburst. "I just have a feeling about this woman. Someone as poor as she is, well, she might resort to desperate measures…"

Shrugging his shoulders, he returned to life, noticing the empty glass in his hand and chuckling. "Do you think she's going to steal the silver?"

I eyed him skeptically. He knew what the consequences could be to our situation in society. "I just don't trust her. I think you should determine some other arrangements for her welfare. Or let her determine them for herself."

"Are you suggesting that we turn her out? Leave her to the elements? Sallie, I'm surprised at you." He sloshed more whisky into his glass.

Each time I touched the tree, brittle needles scattered down through the branches to the floor. The facade of the holidays was over; the sooner this dead tree could be removed from my home, the better. "All I know is that I am not happy with your entangling our lives in hers. She means nothing but trouble for all of us. And I think it would be best for all concerned if you would do something about it."

But he left Memphis and returned to his wilderness, as if he expected to find there something other than empty gray fields of bare cotton plants and a hopeless, destructive passion.

CHAPTER 11

1886

"There's a smudge down the middle of this one," Miss Marie observed, holding up one of Miss Sallie's silver bowls just like a mirror. The sunlight found a spot on the rim and brightened it with a glare as she turned it. While the Colonel was in Memphis, she had taken to bossing everybody around, just like she was hired to do. So when she decided that Miss Sallie's silver needed polishing, we gathered it all up and took it into the kitchen, as much as would fit. She held up each bowl and tray, studying the bottom, and then turning it over and looking at the shiny front, admiring her reflection. "Now, you and Ginny get this finished up before suppertime," she ordered and left us in the kitchen to do the work.

"Miss Sallie has so much silver." All the shining pieces spread out across the kitchen already seemed pretty well polished to me.

"Honey, you ain't seen the half of it. She's got most of her silver up in their Memphis house," Ginny remarked, pulling out the rags and piling them on the table.

"You'd think one house would be enough for one family."

"You'd think. But I done already told you, they ain't a reg'lar family."

"I just don't understand why two married folks don't love each other any more than that," I commented, grabbing a couple of rags for myself.

Ginny eyed me carefully, sizing me up, and then didn't say anything for a little while. She looked angry, but I knew she wasn't. "Kizzie, tell me about her."

"Who, Miss Marie?"

"Tell me about her." I believe Ginny knew full well what kind of person she was, since we'd been living there for over a month. What she wanted was gossip.

"Well," I thought about what it was I should say about her. "I've lived with her my whole life, so I guess I ought to know her pretty well. She's one determined lady, that's for sure. Like our cotton. The way I've always heard it, the Yankees came down to her Louisiana plantation back during the War and took away all our cotton, so we weren't left with nothing. And after that husband died and the War was over, she started trying to get her cotton claims paid for by the government. I don't ever remember a time when she wasn't fighting about it. She said they were worth $90,000. Can you imagine that much money?"

"Hmm."

"Well, I can't hardly imagine it. I'm not even sure it's all true. Of course, I'd never say that to her. But she hadn't never, ever stopped fighting for those claims. And for just about anything else she thought was rightfully hers."

Ginny was listening, so I kept on. "Just like the way she fought for that land in Tennessee. When I was about nine years old we traveled up from Feliciana Parish to Memphis for her lawsuit over some land in Tennessee she thought she should have got when her husband died. She got in a big lawsuit with her voodoo mother-in-law."

Ginny chuckled at that. "Her voodoo mother-in-law? Musta been a frightening thing."

I laughed, too. "Maybe so. Maybe that's why Miss Marie lost the lawsuit." I put down the sugar bowl I'd just finished and tried to decide which piece I should start rubbing next. "That's how we met General Pillow. He was our lawyer." I picked up a little tray.

"Colonel King was in a lawsuit onct." She was frowning and rubbing that silver, like she was more worried about that shiny pitcher than what she was telling me.

"Colonel King was always in lawsuits, Ginny. That's what he does for a living."

"He was in a lawsuit up in Memphis over some land. He won it, all right. But he done lost his heart to the woman on the other side." She looked off in the distance out the window, eyebrows raised. "Things ain't never been the same between Miss Sallie and the Colonel ever since."

I listened without hearing what she had said. "Miss Marie thought it was important for us two little girls, Laura and me—that's her married daughter, you see—she thought it was important for us to be in the courtroom with her during the hearing so that we'd all look even more pitiful—a young widow with two little girls in tow. She thought that would help us win our lawsuit. She's real good at tugging at people's hearts when she needs to. She'd warned us over and over about keeping quiet, and I did. I was always scared of her and her angry eyes, and I didn't want to get in trouble.

"After the hearing Miss Marie was furious and blamed us that she didn't get that land in Tennessee, because we weren't quiet enough. I was truly scared of her, always. I was so ashamed and so sorry. I didn't ever want to make Miss Marie mad, especially about something that important. I was always so sorry about that, even when I was old enough to know it wasn't me and Laura that was the reason. It was the Colonel that got the best of her in that case. She never did get that land in Tennessee, but she landed herself a general. I'm not rightly sure which one would have made her happier."

Through the window, I studied the hills that spread westward for a short ways, before the gray Delta land began. The old place was just a few miles over to the west. The leaves had withered and fallen, baring the bony skeletons of the trees underneath, the ugly part better left dressed and hidden with their green cover. I pondered the memory of that courtroom, now understanding that Miss Marie was the reason…

Ginny was quieter than I'd ever known her, busily rubbing and polishing, her strong hands working each piece as if by memory. Her eyes were intense, scared and anxious.

"But surely Miss Sallie wouldn't allow…" I began to ask.

"Honey, they both allow," she replied slowly. "Just as soon as Colonel King started looking around at that other woman, I do believe Miss Sallie started looking around some herself."

My brain rattled with this new information. "Who?"

She polished, wanting to tell what she knew, but probably wondering whether she could trust me. "They's a lot of things that happen out here on this farm. Lot of funny things. Lot of things you can't even explain," she observed, mysteriously. "The folks that work in the fields, they see things they ain't supposed to see, and sometimes they say things they ain't supposed to be saying."

"About Miss Sallie?"

She kept polishing the compote dish, working it around in her hands without looking at it, but she didn't say no.

"What do they say?"

"They talk. They whisper about things that they see, things they hear."

Our quick hands worked the silver anxiously, silently. I wanted to ask what she meant, but I was afraid to hear the words that even Ginny would not speak.

CHAPTER 12

❁

"Colonel King, tell me about Malcolm," Mary Eliza asked, studying her elaborate embroidery. While Sallie was away, it had become our evening ritual after dinner to retire to the parlor, she to her stitching, I to my paperwork and spirits.

"Malcolm? Why do you want to know about him?" Reviewing documents at my desk, I was amused to find myself with her rehearsing such a mundane but altogether pleasurable domesticity.

"He seems like such an intelligent man for a Negro."

"I think he is. He's always been most helpful to me."

She sat composed, engrossed in her handwork. The firelight illuminated her face, warmed and rosy, half hidden with her head bowed in attention to her art. The glinting needle led the long thread up through the fabric to its farthest extent, holding it taut, suspending the motion momentarily, before gracefully dipping down to jab the cloth again. "Helpful to you?"

"Yes. Why do you ask?"

"Has he been with you long?" Her midnight eyes caught a glimpse of mine before returning their focus to her work.

"Ever since we bought the place. He was born here."

"Ever since you bought the place? Hmm." She pulled the needle up again.

"Really, why are you so interested in Malcolm?"

Her eyebrows raised as if in surprise, she continued her concentration. "Me? Oh, I'm not interested in Malcolm," she responded, and hesitated before saying, "and I wouldn't worry at all that Sallie might be, either." Once again, she poked the sharp point at the fabric until she found just the right spot to push it through.

I stood up from my desk and walked over to where she was sitting. This time her eyes followed my every step.

"'Wouldn't worry'? Why would you say such a thing? And why would Sallie be interested in Malcolm more than any of the other hands around here?" I sat down in the chair beside her.

She drew the needle back up in a smooth rhythm. "Oh, I don't mean *interested* interested. I would *never* say such a thing. It's just that I've heard some talk among the servants, and I noticed that when she was here she sometimes came walking with him up from the quarters early in the morning. After working with him, no doubt. I suppose she must find him a very useful companion."

"'Companion'?"

"Well, not in the usual sense of the word. 'Companion' as in, oh, helper. Yes, he's her helper. A very intelligent helper. And fairly attractive, too, for a Negro, of course."

We sat in silence for a moment as she continued her careful stitching, rhythmically pushing the needle through and pulling it back up tightly, creating some as yet undetermined design. Finishing her work, she quickly turned over her handiwork and knotted the thread, before snipping the end with her tiny scissors. "I must check on the children," she concluded, gathering her sewing and leaving me wondering.

Malcolm. A good man, a gentle man. An able and willing worker. He followed instructions well and served Sallie's household needs well, building the fires, splitting logs, doing all the necessities required of a proper home. He was a good man to have around.

I must admit, he was inclined to sleep late. There had been many a morning I had to wake him by walking down to the quarters and shouting, because he would be the only one not already up and working. And on occasions when I had to be away, Sallie naturally would have to direct the workers in whatever needed to be done. On the mornings when Malcolm might be slow in rising, being a lady, she probably wouldn't shout to awaken him, but would simply walk down to the quarters and knock on the door of his shack. Yes, very likely. If anyone ever saw her returning from the direction of the quarters in the early morning, it was undoubtedly because she had had to make a special effort to awaken him. Undoubtedly. Without question. Anyone who would suggest otherwise—

CHAPTER 13

He lay on the bed, naked, unconscious, drooling. Completely uncovered, the vulnerable white mountain of flesh heaved slovenly. Liquor had left him in this state often, reason enough for me to avoid him and to seek respite elsewhere, though I was surprised to find him so shamefully uncovered well after the sun was up, especially with children running about the house.

I had returned from Memphis for personal reasons. There were things I needed, errands that had to be attended to. In the abstract, I knew that this weak man had fallen prey to this horrible woman. Seeing his drunken, prostrate body before me brought cold reality to those thoughts I preferred to avoid.

"What are you doing here?" she asked impudently, poking her finger between my shoulders, startling me. I turned to see her in the hall, fully clothed and hair neatly arranged, with a distinct manly smell about her, difficult to ignore at such a close distance.

"This is my home." I tried to muster some indignation, but was too shocked when she pushed by me and walked over to the naked man on the bed. "What are you doing? You can't go in there. Colonel King is…"

"Resting. I know. I left him this way a little while ago." She smiled with satisfaction as she admired her handiwork.

"Why, Mrs. Pillow, you have no business being in here when my husband is so, so indisposed." I jerked the covers up over him, the oblivious object of my concern, and she just stood there, as if nothing shameful or embarrassing were occurring before us.

"Oh, really, Sallie, there's no point in hiding the fact that you refuse to be a wife to him. So I have taken it upon myself. Truly, you have no standing…"

"Have you no shame?" I hissed. "Get out of this house right now."

"I will do no such thing," she laughed. "He wants me here, and he wants you in Memphis. So I expect you should be the one to leave. You have another home. For a while, at least."

"I don't give a damn about how you've manipulated my husband into giving you this god-forsaken piece of property. Take it, for all I care."

"I will. I will enjoy all of the properties that Clay has left me in his will." I shuddered at the familiarity with which she referred to him. "You don't know, do you?"

"Know what?"

"He is going to leave me all of his properties, here and in Memphis. All of them. Including your other home."

"Don't be ridiculous. He would never…" But there she stood beside my naked, drunken husband. My knees collapsed beneath me, as I dropped to the bed, sitting, stunned. The mountain of flesh groaned weakly.

"Unfortunately, you'll have to have access to both houses as long as he's alive. There are many advantages to your returning to Memphis, of course. Your friends, the parties, fine social circles. And if you stayed here, your poor girls would have to remain as they always have, running about barefoot with the pickaninnies, like a bunch of savages."

"My girls would never run barefoot. I buy their shoes at Lowensteins." All I could think, all I could say in the face of her smothering insults.

"Well, of course, you do," Mrs. Pillow responded, strutting over to the corner rocker and placing herself in it with affected daintiness. "And wouldn't your friends in Memphis be impressed to know how well you yourself get along with all the colored field hands here."

I stared at her, smirking at me. "What do you want from me?"

"From you? Oh, Sallie, I want nothing from you," she responded, blithely.

"Why have you intruded upon our lives so?" I could no longer restrain the tears. "We have the law…we can use the law to keep you away from us."

"Oh, the law can be a very useful tool indeed." She stood slowly, and began to move toward me. "I have seen it used effectively by my husband and by yours. It can hone an argument. It can screw. And it can unscrew. It can trap a man like a vise. It can chop a life in two. Why, the law can practically chisel a name into stone once that name is added to a will. But when the law and wagging tongues work together, almost anything can be accomplished." She looked down at me, smiling derisively.

I stared at her blankly.

"You know what I mean by wagging tongues, don't you? Gossip, reputation. And you know about the power of reputation, presumably, from your time in Memphis. Once destroyed, a good reputation is impossible to regain."

"Of course, but even you would never...why, Colonel King...and General Pillow..."

"Oh, no. I don't mean them. I mean you." Her dark eyes were riveted on me. She paused before she asked, "Are you familiar with the miscegenation laws in Arkansas? There is little more shameful, wouldn't you agree, than sexual intercourse between a Negro man and a white woman? And what would happen to that woman if such charges were brought?"

"Mrs. Pillow, I have no idea what you mean, but falsehoods would surely be found out in a court of law."

"Perhaps. But in the court of Memphis society? If it were ever revealed that you, Sallie King, had taken a Negro lover..."

Standing, in my fury finding energy I did not have, I slapped her, more easily than I might have imagined, a hard spank. My hand tingled with pain. But she grabbed my shoulders and attempted to wrest me to the floor, surprising me with such force as was hardly imaginable in a woman. I attempted to resist, my knees crooking, but I fell. The sound of footsteps in the hall stopped her. Kizzie appeared in the doorway.

"Miss Marie? Oh, Miss Sallie, are you all right?" She ran over to me and knelt down.

On seeing her, Mrs. Pillow stood up and stepped back. "Oh, Kizzie, I'm afraid Sallie has tripped and fallen." She extended her hand to me in mock helpfulness.

I stood up under my own power, rejecting the hand that had just knocked me to the floor. Straightening my dress, I left the room, the triumphant eyes of Mary Eliza Pillow on my back as I retreated.

※   ※   ※

"I thought I'd already told you," his whisky voice croaked. Leaning against the door frame of my bedroom, he looked barely awake, but was at least fully dressed.

"You gave her our home in Memphis, too?" Blinded by my tears, I could not see and did not care what I had thrown in my trunk, but I intended to leave this godforsaken place as soon as I could.

"It's just a bequest in my will."

I slammed the top of the trunk. "Oh, is that all. First you take her in, then you give her our farm, now you've given her our home? What in the world are you thinking?"

"Sallie, we have so much, and she has nothing. We can afford to do this. I've helped her before."

"Are you out of your mind? That woman just assaulted me. In my own home. You should be calling the law, not defending that damned tramp." I heard nothing but the faint sound of dishes clattering in the kitchen below. I remained on my knees in front of the trunk as if in prayer to some indifferent god. He leaned awkwardly against the door frame, one leg crossing the other, a stupid satyr casually explaining away the morning orgy.

"Have you no shame?" I challenged him through my tears.

"There is no shame in representing her legal interests, as I have done for several years," he argued, wiping his mouth with the back of his hand and finally balancing himself on both feet. "And there's no shame in offering to help a family friend who's in need."

"And there's no shame in having a mistress as long as no one knows about it." I wondered if he was sober enough to detect my sarcasm.

"How can you say such a thing?"

"Oh, God, don't even try..."

"Sallie, I tell you, I have no more taken up with Mrs. Pillow than you have...have...taken up with..."

"With who? Who do you think I've taken up with?"

He bowed his head, the disheveled gray locks making him look more comic than pitiable.

"Has that woman been feeding you lies? Has she been saying things about me?"

He would not look up.

"How could you?" I implored through my tears. "How could you?"

"Sallie, I am truly sorry. I did not mean to imply... I was just trying to show you how ridiculous...I didn't mean..."

"Look at you," I finally said, sniffling. "Look at what you've become. You've insulted your own wife. You've taken a mistress. And not just any mistress. One in the *same social circles as our friends.* Don't you see what this could do to you? Just look at how she's poisoned your mind with these...these...base allegations... Do you think she would hesitate to do the same about you? In Memphis? Around all your professional friends?"

"I did not mean to suggest anything untoward about you. I apologize once again. Please, accept my apology, and let's be done with this subject."

I opened the trunk and impatiently tossed the rest of my things into it. "You've clearly made your choice. And I refuse to be a part of this disgusting situation any longer. You've never wanted to stay married to me, especially since you met that serpent. Well, now you're going to get your wish. I won't give you a divorce. I will not debase myself and my reputation in that way. But I will give you the freedom to make a fool of yourself. I certainly hope no one in Memphis finds out what you're doing. I just can't imagine!" I slammed the trunk angrily and fumbled fastening the locks.

"Sallie?" He looked at me half pleadingly.

"Go to Hell."

CHAPTER 14

❀

1886–1887

"Kizzie, you and the children go back to the guest house and go to sleep." Miss Marie had been unusually helpful in clearing the dinner dishes that night.

"But Mama, aren't you coming too?" Giddy whined.

"I will be there shortly. Kizzie, take them," she ordered.

"But Mama, I want *you* to put me to bed." He hugged her skirts, wrinkling the fabric with his anxious clasp. If I'd pulled him off, he would have ripped her dress. But she pushed him away gently, indifferent to his pouting lip and sleepy whines, and he let her loose. She spread her arms wide, trying to herd those children and me out the kitchen door. "Shoo! Now you go back and go to sleep! I'll be there shortly."

But she wasn't.

It was a pleasant evening, for February, but still too cold to sit out on the front porch of our guest house. So I read by lamplight in the tiny parlor, waiting for Miss Marie. I figured she would be back at any time, seeing as how she had stayed over there so long after supper. Giddy was all tucked in. No more giggles or whispers in the dark from the girls. Colonel King had let me borrow *The Adventures of Huckleberry Finn*, and Huck made good company that evening.

After a short while, I shuffled into the back hall and put on my bedclothes. Crawling onto my cot, I thought I heard a scratching sound. I sat still and listened to be sure it wasn't Miss Marie before I put my feet back on that cold floor. I listened, but there was no wind, no tree branch, no scratching. Wasn't nobody there.

A quiet moan came from the room where the children slept. Reluctantly, I tiptoed out into the cold house to check on Giddy, only to find him lying in bed with his mouth wide open. I tucked in the covers real tight around him and kissed his shadowy forehead.

"G'night, Kizzie," Annie whispered, a ghost child in white sheets, her eyes already closed and her soft voice fading.

"G'night. You go on to sleep." I went back to bed. I figured I'd let Miss Marie tend to herself this time.

That next morning waking up early in the cold darkness, I started the coffee and slipped back to the bedrooms to check on everybody. The children were in their beds, still as death. I tiptoed back to where Miss Marie slept. She wasn't there. Her bed was still made up. She hadn't even come in from Miss Sallie's house that night. Lawdy, mercy, she'd gone and done it. She'd laid with a married man.

Now, I'd been suspicious that something was going on that shouldn't have been, but I didn't want to think that. But night after night of her staying over there a long time after supper had been over, I knew she wasn't reading no book, neither. I just didn't want to believe that Miss Marie had sunk so low as to be having relations with the Colonel.

After I got the children up and helped them dress, we went up to the mansion house for breakfast, and there she was wearing that same dress she wore the night before, puttering around the kitchen. Ginny shook her head slowly from side to side, not believing it, and then she giggled silently behind her hand, rolling her eyes, but only because Miss Marie wasn't looking.

There wasn't no hiding what was going on. Wasn't no point. But I wasn't fixing to say anything about it. I didn't ever want to get slapped across the face again like I did when I was 13. I hadn't been slapped since, and I didn't plan to.

It wasn't too long before she moved us all over into the mansion house, too, with her and the Colonel. She told me I was to sleep in the servant's quarters right off the kitchen. The two girls slept upstairs in their own room. Giddy had his own space up in the attic. Seemed like she got us all exactly where she wanted us to be.

❖   ❖   ❖

The bushes of golden bells all over Sterling Hill began to blossom, like bright yellow fountains set here and there among the hills, and then directly we started to see the daffodils peeking out their little heads. Those chattering catbirds were busy just a-mewing and fussing, building their nests in the brush along the lane. Mary spotted the first robin that year, and we saw it building a nest up in the old magnolia tree right outside Miss Sallie's bedroom window. We decided we'd watch out that window for the little blue eggs. I knew Miss Marie wouldn't mind, since she didn't sleep in there anyway.

When springtime came, I got to help plant the flower seeds out in the garden. Planting flower seeds wasn't that much different than planting vegetable seeds, but knowing that they were going to turn out different made all the difference to me. It was a warm spring, and the area for the flower garden was right next to the house. Over near the front were the rose bushes we had already pruned in the wintertime. I hadn't ever grown roses before, and I didn't know you were supposed to cut them back. Like you had to have less before you could have more. There was a lesson in that. The red shoots on those bushes were already starting to sprout. Seemed like we were going to have a bumper crop of roses. They were Miss Sallie's pride. It was too bad she wasn't there to enjoy them.

Even Miss Marie seemed to feel spring in the air, because she was wearing her pretty colors again. She had taken to wearing gray after the General died, even on dress up occasions. She always said black was "too severe" for her fair complexion, "too dramatic." She thought gray would be more fitting and would remind folks that she wasn't just any widow woman, but the widow of a Confederate general. But when she decided to dress up in her pinks and blues and greens, she was a mighty beautiful woman.

Giddy took to climbing the trees in the yard in the springtime. He liked to hide up there when it was time for him to do his chores. I'd call and call for him, and finally find him sitting way at the top, grinning like a monkey. One time before I'd even started looking for him real good, I heard a scream, and then I saw him fall plum out of that tree where the robin had built its nest. He was lying on the ground, crying and carrying on, more mad than hurt. The smudges on his face showed that this hadn't been his only adventure that day.

"What caused you to be falling out of that tree? You could have broke your arm," I scolded him, pulling him up from the dirt.

"That ol' catbird flew at me." He rubbed his elbow. The sound of birds fussing right above us told me he'd riled them up somehow.

"I never heard of no catbird flying at anybody."

"Well, he did. Those catbirds in the brush done moved over here in this tree. Right near the robin's nest."

I didn't believe his story. He just lost his balance is all. Didn't much matter, but he had gotten closer to the nest than any of the rest of us. "Did you see any blue eggs?"

"No. I didn't get that close. That bird flew right at my head. Dern bird."

"Now you just shush with that kind a language and help me find your sisters. You've got chores to do. And don't let your mama see you out here all covered with dust. Brush yourself off. Go on. Git." It scared me to see Giddy fall out of that tree like that. He was usually a lot more careful. But little boys are going to do what they want, no matter how many people tell them not to.

❦   ❦   ❦

The Colonel would still go up to Memphis for a couple of days here and there on business like he always had—he had a law office right on Main Street. I imagine he stayed with Miss Sallie and the girls when he was there, but I don't rightly know. They were his family, after all. But then he'd come on back down to Sterling Hill and take up with Miss Marie like nothing ever happened. Strangest thing I ever did see.

When he was gone, that left us with that whole big mansion house just to ourselves. Miss Marie had Ginny cooking her Louisiana recipes again, and she enjoyed worrying with all Miss Sallie's fine things. We sat out on the front porch in the evenings, watching the lightning bugs blink while she sipped her sherry. Couldn't see the river through all the darkness, but I knew it was over there in the distance. Couldn't hear it, neither. It was frightening to imagine that something that quiet and beautiful could be that dangerous, and that it ran so close.

The Colonel and Miss Marie worked hard getting the cotton crop in that fall. And he even came back down to Sterling Hill the day after Thanksgiving, after he'd been up to Memphis. He always seemed relieved when he got back to Miss Marie. And seemed like she was good-natured almost that whole time. Wasn't unusual for me to see them sitting on the sofa in the parlor, spooning. Seemed to me they were like the perfect husband and wife.

The winter was a lot milder that year than it had been before, and we had an early spring, just perfect for taking walks in the sunshine. The children and I would follow them sometimes as they strolled, arm in arm, down beside the cotton fields, even before we'd got the cotton planted, and even further down toward the river.

"Will you take me shooting next week?" Giddy asked, tugging on the Colonel's sleeve.

"I'm afraid I have to be in Memphis next week for a trial," he replied, rubbing the back of the boy's head. The weeds down near the river were almost tall enough to hide Giddy when he was standing up.

"Aw, please?"

"Gideon, you mustn't hang on Colonel King that way," Mary scolded her brother. "It's not manly."

"I ain't a man yet."

"You 'aren't' a man yet," Miss Marie corrected him. "Clay, can't you see this child needs a man's influence? He spends so much time around the help that he's beginning to speak as they do. It would be much better for us all if you could stay here all the time. Won't you consider retiring from your law practice and becoming a full time gentleman farmer?"

The Colonel laughed. "So you want me to be part of the landed gentry, hmm?"

"Well, I guess you already are. And some day I will be as well."

"Oh, so you're anxious for your inheritance, are you?" the Colonel teased her.

"Oh, no! I didn't mean that. I just meant that when you retire, we'll be here together. I have a home for life here. You have a home for life here. It will be almost perfect."

"Just almost?"

"Yes," she sighed. "If only we could be married."

We continued our walk without talking. Colonel King walked the shoreline to survey how much of his lower fields had been flooded. Giddy threw sticks in the river, watching them twirl in the eddies and sometimes be pulled under. Annie broke off a willow branch as a switch, and began carefully picking off the buds.

"Why can't you make it happen?" she asked, once the children were just out of earshot. "You can divorce Sallie. She hasn't been a wife to you in years. That must be grounds."

"Now, Mary Eliza, you know it's much more complicated than that. You are very dear to me. But I made a solemn commitment to her parents that we would remain married. And don't you think it would reflect badly upon her in Memphis society if she became known as the 'spurned woman'? I have to think about what's best for her, too, you know."

"Her father has been dead for years, and her mother is a vindictive old shrew," she argued sourly. "And if you no longer spent any time in Memphis, you really wouldn't have to worry about her status in society, now would you?"

"Colonel King! Colonel King! Look what I found." Giddy ran up from behind holding a piece of driftwood, hardened smooth by its adventures in the current.

"Let's talk about it later, dear. Well, Gideon, I don't believe I've ever seen a piece quite that large."

When the trees start to sprout their little yellow-green buds and the flowers start to put on their show, it just seems like the perfect time for two people to be in love. But as that spring wore on and the summer started to heat up, she wanted to talk about being married more and more, and she wasn't near as patient about it any more.

"Is it her money? Is that it?" Her shrill voice from his bedroom could be heard at the bottom of the stairs.

"We've discussed this over and over. I simply cannot justify divorcing her."

"But you can justify living with me? Giving me your homes?" I climbed one step at a time, careful not to make any noise. I needed to put away the girls' frocks I had finished pressing, not wanting to disturb their conversation, but listening just the same.

"I can justify living with you because you are the woman I love. I want to be with you. Always. But I have no cause to divorce her, at least not honorably."

"Then why not dishonorably?"

I stopped at the top of the stairs, hoping the floorboards wouldn't creak. "What in the world are you talking about?"

"You are not the only one with a lover, you know. For all you know, Sallie has had a whole string of lovers."

"Mary Eliza!"

"What do you think she was doing with General Pillow—my husband!—all those months when you sent her down to care for him? Hmm?"

"You hadn't even met the General yet, so he wasn't your husband at that time. What am I saying? Of course, there was nothing untoward between Sallie and General Pillow. What a ridiculous allegation!"

"How do you know? Were you there?" I slipped quietly toward the wall and took a step toward the girls' room.

"Mary Eliza, Sallie is as chaste as a snow-flake, as honorable a woman as you are ever likely to meet."

"Is that so? More chaste, more honorable than me?"

"No, that's not what I meant. You get me so confused sometimes…"

"And then there's Malcolm."

He was quiet. "You don't actually think…?"

"Let the evidence speak for itself. She certainly spent plenty of time out with him early in the mornings, and I saw them more than once walking back from the quarters together."

"She was just waking him up, getting him to his chores, doing perfectly normal things that the wife of a plantation owner would have to do in her husband's absence."

"Well, if you actually believe that, I can't stop you. I just know what I saw. And Kizzie saw it too. There, that makes two witnesses. If having intercourse with a Negro isn't grounds for divorce, then…"

I had quickly made my way to the girls' room by the time the Colonel walked out and slammed the door.

CHAPTER 15

1887

"If I am to inherit this property some day," she finally asked, "then doesn't it make sense for me to have a deed?"

I leaned back from the table and considered her inquiry quite seriously. She had picked at her dinner and said very little, clearly preoccupied by some issue in that busy mind of hers. It had been over a year since I had written the will and we had spoken little of it since. "No, I don't think that's necessary. When I die, the property will be yours. The lawyers will worry with the deed so you won't have to."

Mary Eliza shook her head slowly. "I suppose I just don't understand all these legal matters. I thought when a person owned a piece of property, she had to have a deed."

I laughed at her childish misapprehension. "Yes, you're right. People who own property do have deeds. But generally they are recorded at the courthouse, not kept with the property owner."

"Well, it certainly makes sense to me that I should have the deed." She tossed a sulking looked toward me, then affected an interest in the lace on her napkin.

Even when she was being unreasonable, I could not resist her charm, and she knew that. I nevertheless had my doubts about her request. "Well, it's not really necessary." She fixed her brown eyes on me. "I could possibly draw up a deed of sale in support of the will. But I'll have to think about it." Her eyes softened, pleading with me, as if I held the world before her—I could not resist offering it. "But if it would please you, then yes, I think I can write up a deed."

She exhibited the very response I had hoped for, wrapping her delightful arms about me, kissing me repeatedly, unabashedly showing her gratitude without regard for the presence of her children or her companion or any servants who might be about.

Within days I had arranged it and set out to explain my gift to her. Uncertain of the possible consequences of my actions, I requested Kizzie's presence as it was my habit always to have witnesses at any potentially significant legal proceeding. As brilliant a woman as Mary Eliza was and as unfortunately experienced in the ways of law as she had become, I nevertheless attempted to make my explanation as simple and as clear as I could to eliminate any possible misunderstanding.

"Now, the usual way of conveying a piece of property involves not only the deed, which is basically a description of the property and a statement of who owns it, but also a contract of sale. There must be some consideration given."

She looked at me quizzically.

"An amount of money given by the buyer to the seller. The amount for which the land is bought."

"But this is to be an inheritance, a gift. You don't expect me to pay for it, do you?"

"No, no, no, not at all. I know you don't have any money. No, what I meant was that I think it would be best to indicate that some sort of payment was made, the consideration, in order for the transfer of the land not to look, well, untoward."

"It can't just be a straightforward gift?" Her keen eyes once again took me in their sights, not releasing me, until I would give the answer she wished.

"It can be, but I think it would be best for us to arrange it this way. Yes, I think so. This is all so unconventional, you understand. It would probably be best for anyone in the future looking at this transaction to consider this an outright sale—for your benefit and for mine. And, of course, for Sallie. We have to consider how this would be perceived, and I certainly wouldn't want any of this to reflect dishonorably upon any of us."

"Oh, no, we wouldn't possibly want that." Her lack of concern for appearances surprised me, but I hoped to be hearing truth in what sounded like sarcasm.

"I just want to make you happy, Mary Eliza. I want you to know how important you are to me. That's why I've agreed to write up this deed, to prove it to you. But this deed is not to be recorded, you understand. It is just a token between us, a token of my feelings for you." I tried to look into her eyes, but she was distracted by the papers.

"Yes, a token of our affection," she responded seriously.

I read through the papers and explained them all, signing both documents and then asking her companion to sign them as a witness.

"Ten thousand dollars!" the young woman exclaimed. "We've got to pay you $10,000?"

"No, Kizzie. This isn't real money changing hands. Mrs. Pillow isn't actually buying this land. This is just a legal technicality, to make it appear that this is a sale. It's actually a gift. A bequest, to be precise."

"Oh," she replied, clearly not understanding. She spoke as she signed, as a child would—"Kesiah...Mae...Biscoe. How's that?"

Amused, we exchanged a smile, waiting for the ink to dry before I sorted and filed the papers. I gave Mary Eliza her copy of the will, explaining its importance and suggesting she take special care with it.

"But shouldn't I keep the deed and the contract? Aren't they also an important part of the transaction?"

I was concerned by her apparent dissatisfaction. "No, I don't think so. I think I'd better keep those in my files."

She frowned. "Why?"

"Honey, you just let me handle it," I replied, closing the papers in my desk drawer. She studied my hand holding the drawer shut. "But any time you would like to look at them, I will be happy to oblige. Now, would anyone like to join me to enjoy the lovely sunset outside on the back porch?" She took my arm loosely, sighing as we moved toward the door.

As the three of us were making our way outside, I excused myself, explaining that I wished to pour some spirits for us all in honor of the occasion. Returning to the parlor, I felt in my pocket the reassuring presence of cold metal—my desk key—and knew I would not regret one small act of prudence.

CHAPTER 16

❁

"Kizzie, have you been rummaging around in my papers?" The Colonel didn't usually come around to the kitchen, so that summer morning we knew he was concerned about something. Ginny and me stopped peeling the peaches and held our sticky hands dripping over the bowls.

"No, sir. I always stay away from your desk, just like you told me."

"Ginny, have you?"

"Oh, no, sir. I wouldn't dare," she replied.

"That's good." He glanced around the room, not at us, as if he was looking for something. "I seem to be missing some important documents. I'm missing the deed and the contract that I was talking to Mrs. Pillow about a couple of months ago. If you find any of my documents elsewhere in the house, make sure you lay them back on my desk. Do you understand? This is very important."

"Yes, sir, I understand. If I see 'em, I'll do just that," I answered.

Of course, I didn't tell the Colonel I'd come in upon Miss Marie reading over that very deed the night before up in her room. Seemed like she was determined to get a good look at all those legal papers that he wrote up. Some time, I don't know exactly when, she must have broken open that drawer and stole whatever papers she didn't have already, so she could read them.

"Miss Marie, you need anything?" I asked her when I saw her that evening, curious to see what she might say.

"No, Kizzie, don't bother me now." She didn't look up from her reading.

I sat down on the edge of the bed, watching her. I could see she was just a-thinking, but I didn't know about exactly what. I don't rightly know why she wanted that deed so bad. But she wanted it in her own hands. "If I record this deed," she pondered out loud, "then I'll own the land. I won't have to wait to inherit it. And then he'll have to marry me, won't he, Kizzie? If he wants to keep his land."

"Ma'am?"

She was quiet for a minute. "Kizzie?"

"Yes, ma'am?"

"Go get me some sherry, quickly."

"Yes, ma'am."

When I got back, she wasn't reading the papers no more. I didn't know where she put them at the time, but I figured she hid them, seeing as how she wasn't supposed to have them in the first place. I couldn't rightly tell the Colonel that I knew what she had, just not where it was. What would have happened to me if she thought I'd betrayed her? I was in a fix.

All he meant for her to have was her copy of the will. I heard him say so. I knew he wasn't real sure about the deed part, on account of the way he sounded when he talked about it. He didn't mean for her to have all those important papers, least not yet. I reckon she saw owning this land as her chance to get out of debt and get rich again. But the way she went about it, sleeping with a married man and then getting him to write up a deed and then stealing the deed he didn't mean for her to have, why, I wasn't sure I liked all this. Once she said she couldn't even spend any time with the Colonel on account of he was a married man. I wasn't sure what she was up to, but I knew it wasn't good. But I couldn't very well tell the Colonel that.

When we were children, Laura and I used to go down to the banks of the Mississippi River that ran by our place in Louisiana. We'd wade along the shore, up to our ankles, but only if there was an adult with us—that river is mighty strong, and you don't even know it. Why, I heard of a fellow from our place down there who went swimming out into the middle and just disappeared—got pulled down by the undertow, never saw him again. So we were properly fearful of that big old river.

So it was a memory to me when we moved to Sterling Hill and there we were, right on that same river again. I knew that river could fool me, that it was a lot more deadly than it looked. That we needed to be careful even though it didn't look like we did. This time I was the adult. I walked down to the river barefoot with the three children, through the canebrake, until we got to the willow trees that lined the banks. Annie was too afraid to even touch her toes in that cold brown water. Mary looked curious, but still stayed close. But little Giddy marched right out into it up to his knees, trying to show the girls how brave he was. I had to go running in after him, with my skirts all pulled up, too high, shouting, "Boy, you git on back here, now! What is your mama gonna say when she sees you all wet!" And he just laughed and went out just a little further. But when the girls started whining at him to come on back, he was going to get them all in trouble, that's when he minded me.

I saw the whole Mississippi River on a map one time, saw how it starts way up in the north and comes on down past closer places: Memphis, Helena, Baton Rouge. I reckon the land along side it looks a lot different depending on where you are. In Arkansas, we had tall hills all along it, at least for a while. The hills down in Feliciana Parish were smaller, softer ones. Across the river in Mississippi there was nothing but flat land for miles and miles. You could see all the way over to the sunrise when you were looking at Mississippi. But the river itself looks pretty much the same no matter where you see it. If you see that muddy river from far away, it looks mighty calm. You almost can't tell that it's moving at all. But that ain't the way it is. What's true about the river is how it moves on and on, how it can pull a man down, and how it can kill him. That's why I was always watchful.

❧   ❧   ❧

"Colonel King, there's something I think I want to talk to you about."

"Yes, Kizzie?"

I found him in the downstairs hall, sunlit and a mite too public. "Can we go sit in the parlor? Would that be all right?"

"Of course, but you're being mighty mysterious." We stepped into the parlor, and he pulled the door to.

I stood in the middle of the Persian rug, trembling, following the intricate swirls and designs with my lowered eyes, hoping I could say what needed to be said.

"Well?" he asked, leaning against his desk casually.

"It's about that deed. You know that deed you wrote for Miss Marie?"

"Yes. What about it?"

"Well, I saw her with it last night."

He stood up straight. "You saw her with it? Where?"

"She was reading it up in her bedroom." I knew it wasn't really her bedroom on account of the bed was never messed up, but that's what she called it, so I did too.

He walked over toward me and sat in the gentleman's chair, releasing his breath in a loud sigh. He stared at the floor silently.

"And I heard her say something about it, something I knew you wouldn't like."

He looked up at me. "What did she say?"

I bit my lip so hard it hurt. "She said she was going to record that deed." I was too afraid to tell him about the marrying part, so I didn't.

His eyes turned angry, looking over at the desk and beyond it, as if he could see through the very walls. He didn't say anything, and I was just as glad. I was thinking of what Miss Marie would do if she knew I was down here talking to him.

"I think I better get on back upstairs..." I said, stepping over toward the closed door.

"No, Kizzie. Please. Come sit down." He sounded serious, but kind. I sat down over on the sofa. He was still just staring through that desk, not saying anything, so I was quiet, too.

I don't believe I'd ever sat for so long alone with a man, a gentleman at that, without not saying a word. I watched the specks of dust floating in the sunlight that was shining through the window. That sun seemed too cheerful to be shining down on such a serious talk.

"Kizzie, do you understand what recording a deed means?"

"No, sir, but I know you didn't want Miss Marie to do it."

"Yes, you're exactly right. Recording a deed means to take it down to the courthouse and make it official—the transfer of land from one person to another. Do you understand?"

"I think so."

"The deed I wrote was only to appease her. Only to make her understand how much she means to me, and that I was serious about leaving her Sterling Hill when I die. If she recorded that deed now, there would be some very negative consequences. I wouldn't be able to make any decisions regarding the land. If we ever had any differences, she might not even allow me to live here, because it would then be *her* land. That's not what I meant to happen. This is my land. I want her to have a place to live now and financial security when I'm gone, but I want to be able to use this land, make decisions about it, farm it, as long as I'm alive. Do you understand?"

"Yes, sir. Miss Marie is a mighty changeable woman. You'd have to stay on her good side to make sure you got to run your own place."

"If she recorded the deed," he added.

"Yes sir. If she recorded the deed."

"So I must make sure that she does not record that deed."

"How are you going to do that? She's not liable to be talked out of anything she sets her mind to."

"Yes, I know that. That's where you can help me, Kizzie. I need to get that deed back. As soon as possible."

I looked at him in disbelief. "You mean you want me to do it? To get it back?"

"Where does she keep her most precious things? Does she have a cupboard or a box where she keeps her jewelry or her sentimental items?"

"She doesn't have any more jewelry, to speak of. We had to sell it all." I thought for a minute. "She's got a tintype of General Pillow she keeps in a leather case. She keeps that in the wardrobe. I believe she's got a couple of his letters to her in there, too."

"Look in there and see if she's got that deed and the contract in there and then bring them to me."

"I can't. She keeps that leather case locked. Always has."

"Do you know where she keeps the key?"

I thought real hard for a minute. "No, sir, I don't." I really didn't want to disappoint him. "But I bet I could look for it and maybe find it, if you give me some time to think about it."

"Kizzie, there's not a lot of time. If that deed gets recorded, I could lose all legal rights to my own farm. There would have to be a lawsuit, at least if I fell from her good graces. I think you of all people would understand that I wouldn't want to be beholden to her in that way."

"Oh, yes, sir. I understand that. She's not an easy one to have to live with."

"Look for whatever opportunity you can, as soon as possible."

"Yes, sir. I'll do just that."

❦   ❦   ❦

Miss Marie wore her gold locket almost all the time, the one that General Pillow gave her as a wedding present. She hadn't ever showed me what was inside, and I wasn't really all that interested. I figured it was just another picture of General Pillow, and that sure didn't interest me. That was the only place

I could think of where she might hide a key—I'd been all over the rest of her things. Me and her, we didn't have any secrets, usually.

As it happened, that evening Miss Marie decided she wanted a bath. The Kings had left one bedroom without any furniture in it for Miss Sallie, and now for Miss Marie to wash in. It would have been a whole lot easier for her just to wash in the kitchen, like the rest of us, when that day came, but instead Ginny and me were all the time toting hot water off the stove, up the stairs, and around into that empty bedroom, pouring it into that big old tin tub just so she could take a bath "like a lady." Miss Marie probably took more baths than she needed to in Miss Sallie's special bathtub room, she liked it so much. It occurred to me that while she was in the bathtub might be a good time to look in that locket. So when I forgot her special mint smelling soap on purpose, I told her I had to run back to her room (the one she never slept in) to get it. And while I was in there, I looked at that locket she left lying on that dresser.

I wanted to do the right thing and not disappoint the Colonel, him being a man and the bossman of the plantation. But I sure didn't want to make Miss Marie mad. I hadn't ever been in such a place before. But I decided that I'd rather have Colonel King in charge of the farm and not Miss Marie, seeing as how she hadn't done too well when it came to farming, judging by how we lost the old Pillow place and all. So I got up all my gumption and opened up the front of that gold locket, and when I did, a little brass key fell *clink* on to the floor.

That sounded to me like I'd dropped an iron skillet, and I prayed to the Good Lord that nobody heard it. Good thing, though, that Annie was in talking to her mama about one thing or another, I wasn't listening. I picked up that key off the floor and went over to the wardrobe where she kept that leather case. And of course, the door on that thing *creaked* just as loud as you please. The voices down the hall stopped talking for a second, and I held my breath. Then they started back up again. So I pulled out that case out from under some of her underthings and unlocked it, and lo and behold, there it was. That deed.

I stuffed it into my apron pocket just as fast as I could, slapped that little case closed again, creaked that wardrobe door shut, and hurried back over to the dresser to put the key back in the locket.

"Kizzie!" she yelled from down the hall. That startled me so much I dropped that darned key, and sure enough, it fell under the dresser.

"Yes, ma'am. I'm coming."

"What's taking you so long?"

I didn't answer. I got down on my knees and reached under for that key (good thing it didn't fall under too far, I would have really been in a mess then), and I carefully put it back in its little bed inside the locket. I saw General Pillow's face just staring straight at me from that little picture inside.

"Well, don't look at me. You're the one that got us into this mess in the first place," I whispered to him, as I set the locket back where I found it.

❧   ❧   ❧

That next night I was having a hard time sleeping. Seemed like the hoot owls were hooing at each other more than usual. I couldn't get comfortable in my bed. I thought I heard some talking, so I got up and tiptoed out into the kitchen. There was somebody talking all right, but it wasn't Miss Marie and the Colonel. It was Mr. Tom Worley and the Colonel. I could see them through the dining room and past the hall. They were in the parlor.

They were burning something in the fireplace.

I heard the Colonel saying to Mr. Worley, "You're my witness," which didn't make any sense to me. I couldn't figure out why anybody would have to be a witness to burning a piece of paper. But I knew I was watching something I shouldn't have been, so I decided to go back to my bed.

When I moved, a board in the floor creaked, and the men stopped whispering. I don't think they saw me, it being so dark, and I was hiding behind the door frame all the way back in the kitchen. But I was scared. And I'd never been scared of the Colonel before.

Suddenly, something screeched out in the yard, some little animal swooped up to be killed by one of the owls. The Colonel must have heard it, too, because I heard the longest, most frightening space of silence I'd ever known, and my heart was pounding. Finally they started whispering again, so I tiptoed back to bed.

Shooo! I was never so glad to be back where I belonged, under the covers.

CHAPTER 17

Every clink of silverware against china seemed a torturous water drop upon me, punctuating the increasingly unbearable silence of the dinner table. Mary Eliza ate little, infuriated that the deed was missing from her room, most likely stolen. I didn't want to embarrass her by accusing her of stealing it to begin with, nor did I wish to embarrass myself by admitting that I had stolen it back. And I did not want to implicate her very helpful companion Kizzie. Anything, anything to break the silence.

"Tell me some more stories about you and Daddy in the War," Gideon asked me. Relief! The dear boy. I believe the young boy was simply trying to fill the damnable quiet at the dinner table, for I had many times recounted our exploits, only slightly exaggerated, and I knew that Gideon already had heard all of them. But I happily acceded to his request.

"Well, let's see," I began, clearing my throat. "Have I ever told you about the time that he and I fought together alone in the wilderness?"

"I think so," Giddy responded, honestly. "But I want to hear it again."

Mary Eliza stopped eating and eyed me.

"As you know, I gathered a brigade of men right at the beginning of the war up in Kentucky, before we came down to Tennessee—we called ourselves 'King's Tigers.'"

"I want to hear about how you shot the Yankees." The impatient child wanted to get to the meat of the matter.

"Girls, help Kizzie clear the dishes," Mary Eliza said suddenly.

Annoyed by the interruption with household matters, I nevertheless began my story. "Well, that's certainly what we were in the war to do." I proceeded to tell him my story about being out in the wilderness and shooting three Union soldiers all by himself.

During all of this, Mary Eliza said nothing. After a while, she interrupted again. "Gideon, that's enough war stories for one evening. Now you go get yourself ready for bed."

"Yes, ma'am," he said reluctantly, and headed into the hall and up the stairs. The girls had already excused themselves, and we found ourselves uncomfortably alone.

"Do you actually expect him to believe these tales you tell?" she asked me, leaning back in her chair, as if drawing some sort of conclusion.

"Well, of course," I responded. "They're all true. Or maybe General Pillow didn't tell you about all of our exploits. It was really quite an amazing time." I gazed into the candle flame, proudly remembering my service. I felt it was safer to maintain the ruse than to admit to wrongdoing she might not be aware of.

"'Amazing.' Yes, that's a good word for it. Or maybe even 'incredible.' After all, aren't most war stories pure fabrications?"

"Of course not. Those are not fabrications. How could you think such a thing? That is a true story. I did shoot three Unionists."

"Oh, I don't know. I guess I've learned a little in my years. Especially about men and their attempts to protect their honor. And to cover up whatever there is in their pasts that they might consider dishonorable."

I studied her face, trying to determine what and how much she knew. "You don't actually think these war stories I've told Gideon are attempts to cover something dishonorable, do you?"

"Perhaps."

"Why, I'm surprised at you. I thought you had more respect for me than to question my integrity."

"Oh, I have tremendous respect for you. Of course, I do. It's just that, well, sometimes we never really know the truth of a situation, do we? Sometimes there's no way to tell what did or did not happen."

I listened, trying to hide my trepidation.

"For example, suppose there was a general who swears on his honor never to surrender to the enemy. Then when it becomes clear in the course of battle that his forces cannot prevail, he retreats and leaves his men to fight under a new commander, just so that the general can retain his 'honor.'"

"Yes, and...?"

"Wouldn't retreating under those circumstances, leaving one's men to die and another commander to take the blame just to preserve one's honor, wouldn't that actually be *dis*honorable?"

"Surely you are not doubting the honor of your late husband's actions?" I was incredulous that a woman so loyal to her late husband would in any way suggest something disreputable about him.

She stood up and walked behind me as she continued. "Well, perhaps I should give you another example, just for argument's sake." She leaned over the back of my chair. "Suppose there is a colonel, a *very honorable man*, who deserts his troops…"

I sipped my coffee, almost missing my mouth.

"…and who attempts to assassinate his commanding officer?"

Stunned, I rattled my coffee cup onto its saucer and began to sputter a response.

"But," she continued, "when he tells his superiors what happened, he explains that there was a misunderstanding, that someone else was to blame, and further fabricates explanations for his dishonorable behavior. Wouldn't that colonel be, well, a traitor to the Cause?"

"Traitor?" Intelligible words finally came to my tongue, despite my fury and fear. "That's preposterous. I don't know what you mean. Wherever did you…"

"Oh, of course, I'm just speaking hypothetically. I don't mean to suggest anything. It would be very difficult to tell, would it not, the truth of that entire situation. It could be interpreted as an honorable action, resigning to allow the Confederate officers the chance to appoint one of their own. Or it could just as easily be interpreted, well, differently." She stepped to my side and watched me, the predator toying with her wounded prey.

"How do you know about all this? There is nothing in my official record…It was just a misunderstanding. It wasn't right for me to stay in charge…"

She seemed satisfied. "There is just so much in war that can never be known for sure. So much in love and war, as a matter of fact." She leaned over the table smiling and snuffed the candle with her fingertips.

CHAPTER 18

❀

"I've drafted that deed that we discussed." The Colonel had been in Memphis for two weeks and called Miss Marie into the parlor as soon as he got back. When I heard him mention the deed, I stood outside the parlor door and kept still.

"Oh?" As if she didn't have any interest in deeds.

"A deed of sale is not appropriate, since there will be no actual sale. This new deed of gift is only intended to support the will. It is *not* to be recorded and will have no power at all until my death. Do you understand all this?"

I didn't hear anything.

"As you requested, I have included my other Memphis properties," he sighed. "This amounts to all my personal property and my real property—Sterling Hill, the home on Mosby Street, the adjoining lots, the one on Alabama and Exchange…" On he went, reading off a whole list of properties, including a law library.

"And the conditions?"

"As with the first deed I am giving you a life estate. You will have a home here, if you need it, for the rest of your life. As with the first deed, you must provide a home for me here throughout my life. You must provide a comfortable living for me from the rents of the farm and a decent burial, as indicated here."

"Anything else?"

He paused. "If you should move from the property, or marry, then all the rights to the property will revert to me. And if any of your creditors try to attach your interest in this property, all your rights to the land will be forfeited." She never liked him talking about all the money she owed, but since what he was doing seemed so generous, I reckon she would have to like it all just fine. "Now, do you understand all this?"

The silence was as full as that tiny second right before a spark bursts into a flame. "I understand perfectly."

"Mary Eliza, that contract. The one I signed with the first deed? I would like to have that back, since it no longer applies." He knew she stole it when she stole the first deed, and he was as much as calling her on it.

"I *burned* it," she sneered. She must have snatched that deed right out of the Colonel's hands, because she came tearing out of the parlor, carrying that paper. She would have knocked me over, if I hadn't heard her coming and got out of the way.

"Mary Eliza, wait," the Colonel called after her, following out into the hall. I'd made my way back down the hall a piece, so he wouldn't run over me, neither. He turned and saw me, sighed, and went back into the parlor, shutting the door behind him.

I headed upstairs just in time to hear her bedroom door slam. I was scared to knock on her door and scared not to.

"Kizzie! Is that you? Come in here."

I slipped around inside the door, just barely in the room.

"The nerve of that man. The nerve of him. My creditors. He thinks my *creditors* are going to take his precious farm." The new deed was lying over on the floor where she'd thrown it.

"You want some sherry?" I whispered, my voice trembling.

"How dare he?" she snarled. "How dare he? My *creditors*. There is no provision for marriage, nothing for my protection. Nothing. I only get the property if I take care of him for life. He'll always have a home in my home. *My* home." She picked up the deed from the floor and shook it at me. "Look at this, Kizzie. If I marry another man, I have no claim to this property." Her fists were clenched, rumpling the paper. I decided to go back downstairs and get her some sherry. This time I figured I'd best get the whole bottle.

When I came back up with the tray, she was sitting on the bed, studying the new deed. She didn't say anything to me, just took the glass I poured for her and downed it. She held it out to me, and I filled it up again. This one she sipped.

"He plays this all up as if he's making a gift to me, as if he's being generous and kind and doing his Christian duty, when all he's really doing is setting me up to be his mistress, so I can take care of him. I'd rather die than record this deed and look like I'm a kept woman."

"But Miss Marie, ain't it awful nice of him to provide for us at all by leaving all this land to us?" I asked quietly.

"Shut up, you stupid fool. He's left it to me, not to you. And no, it's not awfully nice. I've earned an interest in the property by all the work I've done here, deferring to his little blithering wife, polishing her silver, caring for her things. Leaving this property to me is the least he could do. It's just the way he's written this deed. It's absolutely insulting."

I didn't say nothing else. I didn't want to disturb her, but I was just curious enough to stay, so I stood there watching her for a while, and then sat down in the rocking chair and looked out the window. I never, ever understood why she thought Sterling Hill should have been hers, just because she worked on it some. If that's true, then I ought to own the old Pillow place and that big pink house in Memphis, too, as much work as I did there. Sterling Hill, too. I watched that old catbird out in the tree, fluttering in the robin's nest.

I don't rightly know where she slept that night, or the nights after that, but I know things weren't ever right between them again. I reckon he didn't trust her any more, after she'd been scrounging around amongst his important papers and stole that first deed. I reckon she didn't trust him neither—can't say that I blame her after what he did to her by burning that first deed without her knowing. I felt bad that I'd been a part of all that. But I didn't know what else to do. I wanted to do the right thing, and from my experience, I knew that what Miss Marie wanted wasn't always right.

Next morning, after she settled herself down a mite, she went downstairs, deed in hand, and went up to the Colonel at his desk. "I apologize for my outburst last night. Will you forgive me?"

The Colonel looked at her skeptically. "Of course, I will." I couldn't tell if I should believe him or not.

"I would like to go ahead and execute this new deed you have drafted, if you don't mind. But there is one other thing." I wasn't sure how she could ask for anything else.

"What is that?"

"I want you to include in here the promise that you will provide for my children and their education in the event of my death."

He looked down at the floor and took a deep breath. "I can include that. We can write that in the margin. But you understand your promise. Your promise not to reveal…?"

"Why, Colonel King, what ever do you mean?"

He must have been satisfied, because he sat down and wrote some more on that deed. "Now, I'll need to sign this, and we'll need some witnesses. Kizzie, why don't you run get Tom, and you and he can witness the signing of this deed."

"Yessir." I was always happy to get the chance to see Mr. Worley.

So that's how it all happened. The Colonel signed the second deed, and Mr. Worley and I signed it, too, to show that it was actually Colonel King who wrote it and that that's what he meant to do. Miss Marie said she thought she ought to sign it, too, just to be sure, even though the Colonel said she didn't need to. So she did. She thanked him politely, but this time there wasn't any hugging. I reckon this time it was strictly business.

CHAPTER 19

"Why did you bring that woman here?" A brisk November breeze, whistling around the front porch, accompanied my husband into the front hall of our home.

"The girl is too sick, she has no chance down in the country. She needs a real doctor," he explained sheepishly. His mistress's entourage had already arrived, her trunks sitting on my front porch for the entire neighborhood to see. One of his colored men tramped through the brown stubble of my chrysanthemums, the only thing left of my garden at this time of year.

"Dr. Cooper was good enough for me when I was at Sterling Hill. Why can't he take care of her?"

"Mary Eliza is just distraught over Mary's sickness, Sallie. I couldn't in good conscience refuse her." The crunching of the fallen leaves signaled the arrival of the patient, carried by his men across the yard, up the steps, right past me into my front hall. "Can't you see it in your heart to help with this poor child?"

"What if she infects the rest of us?" I didn't care if anyone else, particularly that woman, heard us. Like Queen Victoria herself, she stepped from my carriage, assisted by Kizzie, and cast a skeptical eye at the outside of my home.

"We will keep her quarantined, in the room off the kitchen. No one but Mary Eliza and Kizzie and the doctors have to be around her. Here, let me show you where to put her," he spoke to the man with the pale, wasted girl in his arms. His decision already made, he walked away from me, pleading, "Please, Sallie, it's her only chance."

She entered my home, our eyes meeting. She played her new role as a concerned mother rather convincingly. "Thank you for allowing us to stay here while we attend to Mary."

"Miss Marie, I've got your shawl right here." Rushing through the doorway, Kizzie interrupted before I could respond. "Oh, Miss Sallie, it's awfully nice of you to let us stay here for a while. I just don't know what we would have done without you." Mrs. Pillow had already started back toward the kitchen, and Kizzie followed. Swirling sycamore leaves dashed themselves in confusion against the steps and the porch as I pushed the door closed against the wind.

I could not believe he had the gall to bring his mistress into my home, which had up to that time been my refuge from her. Her daughter had typhoid, undoubtedly, and there was no hope. There was no chance that the doctors in Memphis could save her, and everyone knew that before she was even presented to me, without my foreknowledge of their arrival. I saw no point in risking my life or the lives of my own children because of her. But before I could object, that woman was ensconced in my home. She stayed there for twenty-two miserable days.

Naturally, I sent the girls down to Mother in Aberdeen, to avoid the contagion, not only of the disease but also of that hideous woman. Although I spent as much time as possible with friends to avoid the misery and the wailing, I could not abandon my home entirely—good God, the woman would become a squatter, laying claim to everything in it. I had to protect my home, so I had to endure her presence. That woman epitomized selfishness, but she seemed uncharacteristically genuine in her concern for her daughter's plight, the child who looked and acted the most like her with her dark hair and slippery temperament.

The girl finally died. Only Kizzie's sorrow moved me, such a sensitive young woman. I could not help but feel compassion for her, not only that she had lost an acquaintance, but that she was condemned to spend her life with that godawful woman.

Mrs. Pillow's mournful widow act paled in comparison to her legitimate grief. She locked herself in Mary's bedroom, from whence the noisy melodrama swelled. Kizzie dutifully tended to her there. The curtains stayed drawn, sheltering her from the sunlight of the otherwise beautiful autumn days. She seemed to thrive on the darkness and refused to emerge. Not seeing her for several days would seem to be a blessing, but the way Kizzie fretted over her made her presence continually felt. When she finally did appear, her eyes swollen with grief, she was even haughtier than before, with her new entitlement to attention and pity.

Of course, my husband took it upon himself to give the poor child a proper burial, because the woman remained indigent, despite the money he had lent her. And of course, he insisted on the most expensive burial at Elmwood, beside her father. I did not attend. I was afraid I might make suggestions proposing the next object of mourning at that gravesite, words which would not be suitable for a woman of my standing to say.

CHAPTER 20

I finally understood how awful Jo March must have felt when her sweet little Beth died. I cried and cried when Mary left us. Miss Marie just couldn't bring herself to write Laura and tell her the terrible news, she was so heavy-hearted, so I had to do it myself. That was the saddest letter I believe I ever had to write. I'd already told her all about the Colonel and Miss Sallie, but I never got around to telling her about how her mama had taken up with the Colonel and that Miss Sallie had moved back to Memphis. I reckon I must have said too much in that letter, I don't remember exactly what it was I did say, because before I knew it, she was writing me telling me that she was coming to fetch us right out of there.

It was Christmas time when they got to Sterling Hill, she and her husband John. They had just moved to Birmingham and were starting a new dairy business. But she wanted to come see her mama, on account of her little sister Mary dying and on account of the living situation.

"Mama! Mama, are you here?" she bellowed as she marched through the front hall of the mansion house. An angry bull would have sounded sweeter than Laura in a fury. She was truly the prettiest of Miss Marie's girls, with all of her best features, and some of her worst.

"Kizzie, darling!" She squeezed me hard when she saw me and held me firmly at arms length. "Oh, it's wonderful to see you. But what dreadful circumstances. Tell me it isn't true." By that time her husband John had caught up with her, breathing heavy, and he set the grips down in the dining room where we were standing.

"Tell you what's not true?"

"Oh, Kizzie, has Mama really taken up with a married man?"

"Well, I don't rightly know if they've taken up, but we're all living here in his mansion house. Isn't it pretty?"

"And this Colonel, he must be a horrible man, to have mesmerized her so that she would be behaving in such a way."

"In what way?" Miss Marie had walked up behind her.

"Oh, Mama!" She turned around and hugged her mother's neck. "What has this man done to you? Has he bribed you? How has he manipulated you into this horrid mess?"

"Now, Laura, on you go, and we've hardly greeted one another. Hello, John, it's lovely to see you again. Why don't we all go sit in the parlor? Kizzie, bring us some coffee, please."

So Miss Marie guided them into the parlor, with Laura still fretting, just not as loud, and John wandering behind them. I didn't want to get in the middle of that conversation. Miss Marie and her girls were fine ladies, full of spirit and smarts, but when they got their dander up, you wanted to make sure you were in the next county.

"But Mama, he's a married man. And a colonel at that. Think about General Pillow. Think about his honor. And about your reputation. We'll all be ruined if word gets out." I could hear her all the way back in the dining room as I was coming through with the refreshments. "You must remove yourself from this wretched situation and come live with us." Laura always had been kind of loud and ornery.

"You just don't understand this at all. The Colonel and I have a mutually agreeable situation." Miss Marie poured the coffee daintily into Miss Sallie's china cups.

"How can you say that?"

"He has left me this plantation in his will."

"He what?"

"He has left me this plantation in his will."

Laura narrowed her eyes. "Why?"

"Oh, Laura, really. You mustn't worry so," she responded, handing her daughter a cup with four lumps of sugar on the saucer. "Just be glad of my good fortune and let's all enjoy Christmas together again, as a family. We certainly deserve some happiness after all our grief."

"What do you have to do in order to inherit this land?" Laura asked suspiciously, not worrying too much about her mama's grief.

"Oh, it's what I've already done."

Laura listened, waiting for her mother to explain.

"I have been the manager of the household."

"Yes, Mama, I'm sure you have. But I'm just afraid—oh, do I have to say this?—I'm just afraid he's doing this if you'll remain his *mistress*."

"I am the manager of his home and his farm," Miss Marie continued, speaking each word carefully and ignoring Laura's comment. "His wife didn't have the sense God gave a flea. She would leave the silver to tarnish. She never waxed the wood. She certainly couldn't have handled the accounts. She is much better suited to the frivolous world of Memphis society."

"I understand that you are a very capable woman, Mama. But you have to consider how all this looks. When you told me you were moving here, you told me it was for financial reasons. You never said anything about his wife moving away. You just told me…"

"Sterling Hill is a most comfortable home for all of us, including your brother and sister." Miss Marie took a final sip of her coffee and set her cup on the tray.

"This just can't be happening."

"And when you meet Colonel King tonight at dinner, I expect you to have straightened yourself up and to act as graciously as I know you can. He has been a magnificent host to us, and he deserves no less."

That was a frosty night at the supper table. Everybody was being so nice and polite, asking about this relative and that time that something lovely happened and how wonderful everything was. It was mighty tense.

Christmas came and went. We tried to decorate a pine tree like we used to, sing carols and such, but it was all just make believe, like those shiny ornaments on the tree—they made the tree look magical, but underneath it was still just a dead pine tree, shedding its needles. There were presents for us all—the Colonel was always a generous man—but there wasn't any excitement. We were all smiling and polite and saying "Please" and "Thank you", but didn't nobody mean none of it.

After a couple of days of all that terrible politeness, Laura just couldn't stand it any more. "Mama, you simply must persuade him to divorce his wife and marry you. What if anyone hears about this? Think of what people will say."

"Oh, don't be ridiculous. There is a perfectly innocent explanation for all of it. He *and* his wife have approved of my living here. Even she agreed to his bequest of the land. I have a deed to the land. Marriage is not necessary." I stared at her, then realized I'd best not.

"But what if your friends in Memphis find out? Think of the scandal! You simply must marry him."

Miss Marie sighed, tired of arguing with her, I reckon. "Laura, he simply will not divorce his wife. I've done everything I know to persuade him. But at least my powers of persuasion have gotten something out of him."

"Oh, Mama," Laura sighed disgustedly. "I know the money is important to you, but it can't possibly be worth all this…this…*shame.*"

Well, they talked and they squabbled and they raised their voices and they lowered their voices. Usually Mr. John would leave and go some place else for a while—outside or wherever the Colonel had taken off to. And the women just kept up the talk. They never did ask me what I thought. I would have told them that I liked Arkansas just fine and that I didn't want to go some place else. I liked the Colonel and Sterling Hill. I liked my Mr. Worley, too. But seemed like I didn't have a choice. Miss Marie and her family were all the family I had. But I don't think they must have cared what I thought.

Finally, Laura made the pronouncement: "John, you must confront the scoundrel and demand that he divorce his wife and marry Mama immediately and make all this right. Otherwise, she must move to Birmingham and live with us. With the children. Kizzie, too, of course. You must confront him, and, well, threaten him with bodily harm if he doesn't."

"Bodily harm?"

"Yes. No doubt you can persuade him to act on his honor instead of his, oh, never mind." With her decision made and her orders given, Laura marched out of the parlor, leaving Mr. John standing in the middle of the floor, scratching his head.

CHAPTER 21

John Shields sheepishly opened the door to the parlor and stood awkwardly behind the sofa, waiting to get my attention. He quietly cleared his throat.

"Well, Mr. Shields, can I interest you in a libation?"

"Oh, yes, sir. And please call me John."

"John. Yes, a noble name indeed. Here, here, have a seat. It's important that we men have our opportunities for more intellectual engagement after the grueling niceties of a dinner with the ladies, right?"

"Oh, yes, sir."

"Lovely they are, quite charming even, but a tad tedious for too much attention."

He laughed. "Yes, I agree." That evening's dinner with the Shields had been more tense than usual. Laura, a dignified young woman, seemed too sophisticated for a rube like John Shields, despite his family heritage. She spoke at the edge of politeness, not from the depth and warmth of her heart, if such a place existed, but from a place where only propriety reigned, and not necessarily for long. She inquired about my wife, producing an awkward silence at our table, and seemed little concerned about the grief her dear mother had only recently experienced. She pressed the issue about Mrs. King, wanting to know why we were estranged, why we were still married, and finally, whether I indeed loved her mother. I successfully evaded each inquiry with generalities or by allowing the natural flow of dinner to present its own inevitable interruptions. Kizzie, who had proved so helpful to me at previous occasions, once again showed her worth, engaging the Shields in conversation long enough for me to find my bottle in the cabinet and make a polite departure from the dining room.

The voices in the other room became louder, sharper. We sat in nervous silence, sipping our whisky, listening to the crack of the fire.

"Colonel King," he finally began.

"Did you say your family had fought at Manassas? I knew several soldiers there."

"You did, sir?" he responded with relief.

"Why, yes, Lieutenant Stokes and I had been friends from childhood up in Kentucky. He later moved down toward Petersburg and joined the 7th Cavalry. He was wounded at Chancellorsville."

John had been a child during the war, he told me, but since his family was from Virginia, he had many relatives who had fought for the Confederacy—at Richmond, Manassas, even Antietam. He went on to describe boastfully how various of his family members fought in different battles, where they had been schooled, where they were from. Mere child, rightfully bragging about his family, but not at all the type who would himself fight valiantly. I laughed to myself and tolerated his arrogance, knowing that he, unlike myself, knew nothing of the honor of battle. The whisky dulled the edges of the evening. I heard the thick mumbling of voices from the dining room, waves of sound, sometimes louder, sometimes mercifully soft, and I heard words here and there from him.

"Charlottesville...artillery...lost his leg riding...survived the battle and went home to father three young boys...my third cousin was a Lee...the instincts of a coward...Fort Donelson was always misinterpreted, misunderstood..." Raucous laughter. Another dose of *elixir vitae*. "Antietam?...No, but he held fast at Richmond...Stonewall..." A new friend, just a child during the War, but an ally in the family war, at last.

He must see my pistol, I remember thinking, and I went upstairs to retrieve it, unsteady but pleased with my newfound friendship. Stumbling going up, I searched and found my prize in the hard shadows of my dresser. Losing my balance briefly, I turned toward the stairway, feeling for the banister, and began my descent, pistol in hand, John's eager face below. A missed step, I tripped, fell, rolling, rolling, banging my shoulder, knocking my forehead on an unyielding stair. The pistol fired, the sharp explosion of sound piercing the air. My face pressed hard upon the cold floor.

Screaming. "Colonel King, are you all right?" Hearing the gathering, facing the pain, my eyes closed. But we have guests, I must, trying to sit up, pain pounding my shoulder.

"What in God's name do you think you're doing? You could have killed us with that thing!" she screeched.

"Whisky and guns don't mix, Colonel King."

"Oh, he just tripped. Happens to the best of us." A hand extended, helping me stand. Opening my eyes, there was John Shields, wobbling. I had not realized he was drunk. "And do tell. Look at that gun. I believe that's a Federal pistol. Where'd you come upon such a thing?"

Rubbing my head with one hand, and holding my pistol out with the other. "I traded mine in for this one. Got it from a Union man. Colt .44. Nice square ivory grip. Blued barrel."

"I should have known you got it from a Yankee." Angry voice fading. Yes, I should have known.

CHAPTER 22

1888

Sitting next to Mr. Worley on the wagon, bundled up from the cold, I shivered and watched the dead, frozen weeds as we passed, crowds of them lining each side of the lane, bowing their heads from the weight of the ice. We didn't speak the whole way into Marianna, where we were catching the train to Memphis on our way to Birmingham. The few townspeople along the streets moved slowly that early morning, wrapped up and unrecognizable in their dark coats and hats. He drove us right up in front of the station, helping us each down from the wagon, his warm grasp of my hand as our only goodbye. I couldn't watch him leave.

We had already sent all of Miss Marie's belongings to be delivered to Mr. John's house down in Birmingham. But this time we didn't take that old bell.

Without explanation she crossed the street toward the courthouse, and out of habit, I followed her, our boots leaving footprints in the morning frost. She shoved the door open into the warmth of the office.

"May I help you?" the clerk there asked, closing the grate on the stove.

"I would like to record this deed."

The clerk went to his desk and looked at the papers she pulled out of the envelope. "Let's see, this all looks in order—deed, contract of sale, but there's only one acknowledgment page."

"It applies to both documents."

He tapped his chin, thinking. "Usually, there's one acknowledgment page for the contract and one for the deed," he explained. She said nothing. "This is a little unusual." He turned his head toward the back of the room to see if there was somebody there who could help him. There wasn't. It was just the two of them, a determined woman and hesitating man. "Well, I reckon just one acknowledgment will be all right."

She had told the Colonel that she'd burned that contract, but, lawd, if she hadn't saved it. With that contract and that second deed together, it looked like she bought Sterling Hill for $10,000. But she never had $10,000. I'd by lying if I said she had $10. The Colonel even had to give us the money to buy our train tickets for Birmingham. And there she was recording that deed, the deed that wasn't supposed to be recorded, the deed that wasn't even supposed to count if she left Sterling Hill. But the clerk didn't know all that.

They went through the procedures for doing the recording, and she paid him some money before we returned to the train station where the others were waiting for us.

Arriving in Memphis, we carefully made our way down the frozen street to the Shelby County Courthouse there on the bluff overlooking the ice-lined river, where she recorded the deed to the Memphis properties, too, before we boarded the train and left for Birmingham.

CHAPTER 23

The smell of cow manure in summertime is sweeter than the factory smoke that spewed out of the smokestacks down in Birmingham. Except for that nastiness, it seemed like as good a place as any to get a fresh start. Mr. John's dairy was at the foot of Red Mountain, just down from the railroad station and not too far from the post office. Birmingham was a growing city, not as big as Memphis, but still too big for me. I liked living on a farm better, just as long as I didn't have to work it. I liked the smell of a farm better, too.

We all worked in the dairy, every one of us, even Miss Marie. She didn't milk the cows, mind you, not that she couldn't have (it ain't that hard to do). She decided to work with the money, counting it and taking it to the bank and making sure nobody cheated her. But Mr. John wasn't much of a businessman, bless his heart, and no matter how hard we worked, there never seemed to be much money around. Things were pretty dismal, right from the start. Miss Marie was always in a sour mood, having to work in his dusty office and be polite to customers. I believe she missed the Colonel, too. But seemed to me she'd pretty much give up on him.

"Kizzie, what words would you use to describe the way I look?" Miss Marie asked me one Sunday right after breakfast. She had out her writing paper and was getting organized with all her things around the tiny kitchen table.

"Everybody's always said you were the prettiest lady in Memphis. So you're sure the prettiest lady in Birmingham. Why are you asking me that?"

"Would you say 'pretty' or 'beautiful' or what?" She looked down at her paper, with her pen in her hand. "I don't want to sound too conceited."

"'Pretty' is good. 'Beautiful' sounds kind of, I don't know, kind of…"

"Narcissistic?"

"Ma'am?"

"Oh, never mind. How about 'attractive'?"

"Miss Marie, what on earth are you writing?"

"What I am writing, darling Kizzie, is a matrimonial ad. An ad for a husband. For *The Matrimonial News and Special Advertiser*. And I want to word it just so."

I picked up the newspaper she had lying in front of her. "'A Monthly Journal of Love, Courtship, and Marriage'. Hmm. 'The Only Paper of its kind in America. Chicago, Illinois.' I never heard of such a thing."

"Hmmph." Miss Marie kept writing.

I flapped the paper open to the inside. "'A widow, fat, fair and forty…'"

She looked up with a scowl.

"Wishes to correspond with an intelligent gentleman about 50."

"Please, Kizzie. Can't you see I'm concentrating?"

I laid the paper back down on the table. "Why are you doing that?"

She sat back in her chair and sighed dramatically, rolling her eyes. "Look at me. I am a widow. I have to work for a living at a God-forsaken dairy, of all places. You don't actually expect that I want to remain in these circumstances? So I need a husband, someone who will provide for me and lend me some—respectability. Yes, that's it exactly." She looked down at her words and decided. "'Attractive.'"

"What about the Colonel?" I asked, then I thought better of it.

"I have to consider all my possibilities." She fiddled with the paper and the pen and the inkwell a minute, and then just got frustrated and told me to do it. So I took her place at the table and began to write down everything she said. It wasn't because I wrote any prettier than she did. She made real pretty strokes. I think it was just because she liked the idea of having a "secretary." She changed it and reworded it and fretted about it, but what she came up with was this:

> *A wealthy Southern widow of 30, owner of a large plantation in Arkansas, with brown hair and brown eyes, height 5 feet, 5 inches, graceful appearance and affectionate disposition, attractive, intelligent, and of good social standing, desires correspondence with a temperate gentleman of means and refinement with a view to matrimony; best of references given and required. Editor has address.*

"But Miss Marie, you're not 30. You're 38." I didn't want to get into the "wealthy" part. That seemed like an even bigger stretch.

"Oh, you just hush," she scolded me as she folded up the letter neatly and slid it inside the envelope. She handed it to me without a word, intending for me to take it to the post office. I just took it and went.

So that's how she thought about herself, attractive and a landowner. She was a beautiful woman, that wasn't a lie. I didn't think too much of her telling folks about it, though. I don't know about the landowner business. Maybe she was and maybe she wasn't. She'd moved away, so that deed wasn't supposed to be any good any more. And if she got married, then it sure wasn't supposed to be any good. Wonder what kind of man would be taken in by that kind of advertisement?

I don't know if she ever heard anything from that ad, whether any man answered it and wanted to marry her. I doubt it.

❦   ❦   ❦

"Miss Marie," I called to her walking as fast as I could without looking like I was running. "Miss Marie." The street was muddy from the rain earlier in the week, but I was able to sidestep the puddles.

"Really, Kizzie, must you shout at me from the street?" she fussed as I hurried through the office door.

"It's from Colonel King," I panted, handing her the envelope.

She studied the outside as if she didn't believe I could decipher the Arkansas postmark. With her letter opener she ripped it open with one quick stroke and read eagerly, hungry for his words.

> *My dearest Mary Eliza,*
>
> *Honey, I miss you greatly and wish that we could come to some agreement. You are such a delight to me, and my life seems so much darker without you in it. I cannot divorce Sallie, for reasons we have discussed many times, but you have been more of a wife to me than any woman, and I do not want to be without you.*
>
> *With loving thoughts,*
>
> *Clay*

Her eyes welled with tears as she stood silently absorbing the message.

"Excuse me, is Mr. Shields in?" A slight man with red whiskers had entered the office.

"Come with me." She grabbed my wrist and pulled me toward the office door.

"But Miss Marie…"

"Ma'am, excuse me, Mr. Shields?"

"He doesn't matter, you fool," she barked, bumping into the puzzled man on our way out.

She marched me back over to the house, and sat me down with her pen and paper. Pacing anxiously, she composed her thoughts, and after several small changes, she wrote him back, telling me just what to say.

> *My dearest Clay,*
>
> *It is with great dismay that I write to you from such a great distance. The days seem interminable being away from you and all that I love. I desire to hear from you with greatest expectation. I will be forever grateful to you for your many gifts, including your gift of Sterling Hill. I assume that the planting has gone well and that we can expect an abundant and profitable cotton crop in the fall.*
>
> *However, I urge upon you an appreciation and discharge of your duty towards me and my family. With my spotless reputation in mind, I beg of you, my darling, please consider a poor widow's plight. I love you dearly, and wish above all to become your wife. Divorce the woman to whom you are attached but for whom you bear no affection. Allow me to return to that home which I love so much and be everything to you that a woman can be. For without the divorce, I cannot return to you with my honor intact.*
>
> *With fondness and affection,*
>
> *Mary Eliza*

❧   ❧   ❧

"We've just got to give the dairy a chance. There's bound to be plenty of business, if we can just wait it out," Mr. John said.

"If we wait it out, we may starve," Miss Marie remarked crossly. She prodded the beans on her plate with her fork as if she expected them to respond.

"What choice do we have?" Miss Elizabeth asked. She was Miss Marie's sister from Louisiana who'd moved to Birmingham, too, since all their people were gone. She hadn't taken a bite of her supper, probably because she wasn't used to having the same meal three nights in a row, but she was pretty bony to begin with. She probably just plain didn't like to eat.

"You couldn't make a living in Virginia. Now you can't make a living in Birmingham. We've got no property and no money." Laura was always so dramatic. Miss Marie had taught her well.

"But darling, *I* own some property." Miss Marie gestured towards herself grandly.

"Where do you own property? Not in Louisiana. Not in Tennessee. And it sure don't look like your beloved cotton claims are ever coming through." I believe Mr. John was getting irritated with his mother-in-law's talk of being rich. "No, don't tell me. You think you own that property in Arkansas? You don't actually believe that, do you?"

"I not only believe it, I have the deed recorded to prove it." She turned her attention back to her supper.

"Does that really make you entitled to the farm?" Laura asked.

"Certainly it does, if Clay King ever dies. He's left it to me in his will." There was an uneasy silence, as they all looked at her. She took a small bite of beans.

"Mama, you couldn't possibly be thinking…" Laura gasped.

"I will use whatever means I have at my disposal."

Laura glanced at Mr. John, who took a sudden interest in his shoelaces. Miss Elizabeth stood up and carried her plate to the sink. Miss Marie didn't say anything else, but broke open her cornbread and buttered it, dropping crumbs.

By April, Miss Marie had started writing letters back to the Colonel pretty regular. I imagine she figured he was the best chance she had at getting rich again.

Dearest Clay,

I so desire to see you and be held in your loving arms once again. But my reputation is at stake, and I think you must understand that. Without a proper marriage between us, I can only be considered a kept woman, and the widow of a great general cannot possibly be perceived in that way. Divorce Sallie and marry me as soon as possible. I'm afraid my children feel just as strongly, and my son-in-law John has unfortunately mentioned coming back to Arkansas for a confrontation if you do not divorce your wife and make an honest woman of me.

With love,

Mary Eliza

She read it over when I was done writing it, and when she put it in the envelope, she kissed the back of it. I shook my head as I walked out the door with it. I didn't know why she'd say such a thing about Mr. John. I hadn't ever heard Mr. John say anything about going back to Arkansas, and he sure didn't seem of a mind to confront anybody, especially his old drinking buddy.

Every day I'd run down to the post office to see if he'd written, and every day I'd trudge back to the dairy with empty hands. Miss Marie was getting more and more frustrated. She wrote to him a couple more times, asking would he divorce Miss Sallie and marry her, but he still didn't write her back.

One evening, Miss Marie stayed in the kitchen after supper to help me with the dishes. I knew then something was up. "How long has Mr. Worley been at Sterling Hill?" she asked.

"Since the Colonel bought it, long about '76. Why do you want to know?"

"He's such a handsome man. I certainly understand why you like him so," she remarked, stacking the dishes she'd dried in the open cupboard.

I wasn't sure whether or not I liked her calling him handsome.

"Would you ask him to do a favor for me?"

"What kind of favor?" I asked, suspiciously.

"I would like to communicate with the Colonel, but he obviously is too busy to communicate with me. I was hoping that your Mr. Worley might act as a sort of 'go between' for us. Do you think he might be willing?"

I studied her face. "I reckon. Do you want me to write him and ask?"

"That would be most helpful. Thank you, Kizzie." I handed her another clean dish to dry off, but she had already left.

So I wrote to Mr. Worley. I asked how things were on the farm, how the crop was going, if they were getting any rain. And then I asked him would he mind talking to the Colonel for Miss Marie. About two weeks later, I got a nice letter back. In it, he answered all my questions about the farm, but he didn't say nothing about Miss Marie. He did sign it "Kindest regards", which I liked a lot.

After a while, she decided that she should write to him. She thought that since she was more important than me, that he would listen to her. Important according to who? I wanted to ask, but I held my tongue. Even though she came up with the words, she still read them out to me. I wondered what Mr.

Worley would think when he got a letter from her in my handwriting. But I didn't even try to understand her any more.

> *Dear Mr. Worley,*
>
> *I am writing to inquire as to how the planting is going this spring at Sterling Hill. As you may know, I have a vested interest in the property and would like to see to it that it remains a profitable operation, even in my absence.*
>
> *I am planning to return to the property, or send my proxy, to look out for my interests there. I shall contact you with further information at a later date, but I want you to be prepared to act on my behalf, lest there be some unfortunate breach with Colonel King. Do not mention to the Colonel that I wrote this letter, or I will have your job.*
>
> *Yours truly,*
>
> *Mrs. Mary Eliza Pillow*

I took that letter down to the post office, like I did with the others, and we waited and waited to hear from him, but we never did. I don't think Miss Marie ever did understand why he'd write to me and not to her. Seemed to me she was trying to catch that fly with vinegar, and I knew that wasn't going to do much good.

So after all the other ideas she'd tried didn't work, I reckon she decided that she just didn't have no other choice.

CHAPTER 24

Something about her seemed familiar, her dark eyes and haughty demeanor. I had never met this woman until Kizzie introduced me to her just minutes before when they arrived at Sterling Hill, but something about her eyes suggested that she was clearly who she said she was.

"You must pay my sister $10,000 in cash," this Dickson woman said to me, positioning herself stiffly on the sofa.

"For what?"

"For you being in a predicament."

"What predicament?"

"Mary Eliza has recorded the deed of gift and wants ten thousand dollars for a quit claim."

I swallowed the rest of the bourbon in my glass and painstakingly set it on my desk. I heard but I did not comprehend her words. Mary Eliza. The room began to blur. Mary Eliza's deed of gift. My heart pumped. Ten thousand dollars. Closing my eyes, I tried to grasp the words. "She's recorded the deed?"

"Yes, and she wants her money for this property."

The blurriness transformed into a terrible cleanness of line. The chair on which Kizzie sat was exaggerated in its outline and color. The furnishings were still, bright, strange. My eyes followed the unearthly clearness over to the sofa where Mary Eliza's eyes pierced right through to my soul. But it wasn't she who glared. "A quit claim?"

"You destroyed the deed that showed she paid $10,000 for this property. To release her interest, you must pay her $10,000." She enunciated the words too precisely, needles pricking my brain, words I didn't want to hear again and that I could not conceive.

Out the window, the clear blue of the day had begun to dissolve into a humid haze. On the post in the yard perched that old plantation bell, an ancient reminder of her presence. "She never paid me $10,000. That's ludicrous. I don't believe she sent you here to ask for that."

"She asked me, and she was quite serious. You deeded her this land, and she intends to have whatever its value might be."

I could see the air, outside around the trees, inside around my face, my arms. The smothering heat pressed down on everything near me, pressuring, discomforting, infuriating. "Why, this is nothing but…but…blackmail." The anger rose within me until it erupted into expletives. Why would she blackmail me? After I sent her…Blackmail?

The eyes that responded no longer exhibited the same intensity I had known for those many months, but shielded themselves in fear. "And how will you answer this demand, Colonel King?" she asked less boldly than before.

I closed my eyes tightly, seeing too much, breathing too hard. "This is blackmail pure and simple, and I will not submit to it. Kizzie, you haven't said anything. What do you know about this?"

"I don't know nothing," she responded quietly. "I know y'all wrote up some kind of deed and all, but I sure don't know none of the particulars. She just said we were supposed to be her 'proxy', but I didn't rightly know what she meant." Her frightened eyes watched the floor. This simpleton who had helped me retrieve the damned deed earlier was clearly not bright enough to help me now.

The words bellowed from me almost without will. "Mary Eliza has no claim to this property. She moved from here, voluntarily, and according to the terms of that deed, she's forfeited all her interest in my land. *My* land." She recorded the deed? I wanted to kill that woman. Then I heard those very words echo from within. "I'm going to kill that woman."

I glared at the woman messenger. "And I'm going to kill anybody that helps her, giving me trouble about my property." I charged out of the room, sloshing and spilling the whisky from the decanter, whose cool glass in my hand was the only relief from the stifling thickness of the air. The women's sibilant voices. Quit claim. The piercing, demanding eyes. Ten thousand dollars. Mary Eliza. *Mary Eliza.* Crystal shattering against wood, the sweet smell of bourbon from the slowly dripping wall. Silence, and then, footsteps. A sharp, sparkling puddle at my feet. *I'm going to kill that woman.*

CHAPTER 25

"Now, ladies, let me make this offer," the Colonel said, with his hand on his forehead shading his closed eyes from the morning sun. We had stayed the night in the guest house and were fixing to head back to Birmingham when he joined us out in the yard. "Tell Mrs. Pillow she should come on back here for a visit so we can discuss this face to face."

"If that's how you would like it," Miss Elizabeth responded in her most businesslike voice, as if she hadn't been terrified of the Colonel just last night.

"Colonel King," I asked quietly, "would you mind too much if I stayed here while Miss Elizabeth goes back to fetch Miss Marie?" I glanced over at Mr. Worley who was already looking at me.

The Colonel peered out from under his hand in confusion, standing still but swaying.

"There just doesn't seem to be much point in me going off to Birmingham and then turning around and coming back again," I explained, fearful of what he might say but hoping for the best. I didn't want to go back to all those cows down in Alabama.

"Why, Kizzie," he said, walking over to me and then putting his arm around my shoulders, "that would be just fine." He squeezed me uncomfortably hard, and I smelled the whisky on his breath. "You're right, that's an awful lot of coming and going for you to do. Besides, I think there might be someone else here who'd like for you to stay a bit." He grinned at Mr. Worley. I didn't realize that the Colonel knew about our interest in each other. Or that the Colonel was liable to drink whisky in the daytime.

❧   ❧   ❧

May was a pretty time of year in the hills. Miss Sallie's purple irises seemed a friendly welcome back to this place where so much kindness had been shown to me. The sun shined and the cotton plants were growing and the air itself felt warm and inviting.

I didn't have any particular chores to do, and since the Colonel went to Memphis shortly after Miss Elizabeth left, there wasn't nobody there to boss me. I tried to make myself useful, helping Ginny in the kitchen, but mostly I just enjoyed the Colonel's books and wandered. Miss Marie never had let me go down to the quarters, so since she wasn't there, I decided I would do just that.

That was when I first met Mr. Alfred, a kindly old colored man. I heard tell he'd lived on that farm since he was a young man, back when he was still a slave, and that he hadn't ever left even after the War. I reckon a body gets used to one place and doesn't want to change, no matter how awful it is, or how good some place else might be. Mr. Alfred was sickly and wasn't strong enough to be much help. His job was to gather up kindling from out in the woods and pile it up near the mansion house. Sometimes he would pull weeds. But being an old man, he tired easily. So he mostly just sat and smoked his pipe on the porch of his little house.

At first, Mr. Alfred kept quiet when I came around. Seemed like most everybody down in the quarters knew I was Miss Marie's companion, and that nobody liked her much. So most folks were pretty careful about me. But after a couple of days of me coming around and visiting with some of the colored girls in the evening, I reckon he figured I was all right.

"Kizzie? Come on over here, lemme talk to you," he hollered over to me one evening, when I was headed back to the mansion house.

"Yessir?" I walked closer.

He cackled. "What d'you mean, callin' me 'sir'? I ain't yo' boss. Didn't yo' mama teach you no better?"

"I didn't have a mama. She died when I was a baby."

"Poor little thing. Didn't even have a mama. Come on, come sit down next to ol' Alfred. I wanna talk to you."

So I sat down on the step next to him, and we didn't say nothing at first. Children giggled and shrieked over at the next house, until their mama came outside swinging a spoon and fussing. Someone was humming a familiar tune.

All the folks were slowing down into the purplish evening at the end of a long day. I watched Alfred blow smoke rings into the air. "You ever seen anybody do that before?"

"Yessir. General Pillow used to do that, from time to time."

"Oh, the General did, did he? Well, then, I must be in good comp'ny, havin' the same habits as a general." He chuckled.

He showed me how he used his tongue to make a smoke ring. He even offered to let me try, but I said I couldn't ever do such a thing, smoking a pipe. What would Miss Marie have said? Finally, he persuaded me to try one time. I sucked in on the smoke from that pipe, and it burned so in my throat, I liked to never stop coughing. Mr. Alfred just laughed and laughed at me.

"Girl, I don't b'lieve you'll ever be a smoker. You too much of a lady to smoke no pipe."

"Oh, I ain't no lady," I choked out.

"Oh, yes, you is. You come down here, call me 'yessir', try my pipe when I'm tryin' to be friendly. You a fine white lady. And I be proud to call you my friend." He sucked in on the pipe, and puffed out three blue rings. "But tell ol' Alfred somethin'. What causes you to be workin' for the likes of Miz Pillow? She cain't be nothin' but trouble."

"She raised me. She's always taken good care of me. I try to take good care of her, too."

He shook his head slowly, spitting out a thin stream of smoke. "That woman ain't nothin' but trouble, and she's liable to git you in some, too, if you ain't careful. You ain't got no business stayin' with the likes of her. Neither does the Colonel. Why, she's just an ol' *Delilah*—gonna give him the kind of cuttin' he don't want. He oughta git shed of that woman and quick."

"Mr. Alfred, she's like my family. You don't leave your family, unless you've got a good reason. She's not as bad as you think."

"Young lady, you ain't got no idea what kind of evil thing that is you livin' with. You git away from her and quick. There ain't no tellin' what kind of misery a woman like that can make." He looked at me seriously.

I didn't try to argue with him any more. But I sat and listened as he told me stories from when he was younger, when he lived in the cabin that used to be near the front entrance of Sterling Hill. He called himself "the gatekeeper," because he used to look out for trouble back during the War. He weaved back and forth between now and then, so that I wasn't real sure he could tell the difference. He was some kind of storyteller, Mr. Alfred was.

The evening had turned to darkness. As I was standing up to go, he grabbed my hand and shook it. He looked me straight in the eye, and he said, "You come on back and visit with me some more another time. You a real fine lady, Miss Kizzie. Don't let nobody ever tell you no diff'rent."

❧   ❧   ❧

On that Sunday, Mr. Worley asked me did I want to go on a walk with him through the hills, and I said yes. So we set out toward the north, walking right at the top of the ridge. Crowley's Ridge is what he called it. The woods were a tangle of greenery, the tall cottonwoods and pines, the ferns nestled in the shade beneath them, fat grapevines snaking around tree trunks, thick masses of cane down at the bottom of the hill. "That land where the cane grows, that's the best land," he told me. He pointed at the river, hiding behind the trees off in the distance. We must have walked a good piece because the hills weren't so close to the river any more, but we were still close enough to spot a steamboat out in the main channel, way off.

"Here." He led me through the undergrowth out onto a hogback, he called it, a little arm of the hill sticking out into the valley and made just perfect for sitting. Spreading out a blanket, we had ourselves a picnic, surrounded by the shelter of green leaves and branches.

The afternoon was quiet, with an occasional twitter from the birds. Just down the hill, a giant woodpecker circled a tree pecking his way farther and farther up. His hammering echoed through the valley.

Mr. Worley wiped the crumbs from his mouth when he finished his biscuit. "My mother had freckles, too."

My cheeks grew warm. "She did?"

He nodded, still watching me. He lay back on the blanket with his arms behind his head, watching the leaves above. I fingered a patch of moss beside me, so soft. A tiny black ant scurried over giant twigs and leaves and clods of dirt back to his home, a small anthill just a few feet from us. A squirrel chattered from a branch above, and a pine cone fell down on our blanket.

He covered his face with his arm and laughed. "He must think we're trespassing."

I held up the pine cone. "I'm not scared if you're not." I giggled.

He looked at me for a long second. "Hers weren't as dark as yours when I knew her." Embarrassed, I studied the pine cone in my hand. I'd never had a man look at me so hard.

"I believe we'd best be going now, Miss Kizzie."

"Yes, I believe so." As I packed our things in my basket to leave, I carefully set the pine cone among them.

CHAPTER 26

Miss Marie was careful not to prick her finger as she broke a rosebud from the bush in the garden. "How does it look?" she asked, poking it into her hair and patting it in place.

"Just fine," I answered, trying to keep hold of her grip while balancing her hat boxes on my hip.

"Oh, Kizzie, don't be clumsy and drop them." Waltzing up the steps and through the front door, she seemed unusually cheerful. I followed her in, setting the boxes carefully on a chest in the hall. She had made her way back to the kitchen.

"Yoo hoo, Ginny." I heard her excitedly telling Ginny that she would be there for supper and what to cook. Then she hurried up the stairs, like she'd never left the place. Ginny came out into the dining room, wiping her hands on her apron and shaking her head in disbelief.

"Looks like the cyclone's back," she said.

Colonel King hadn't returned from wherever he was, so the two of us had dinner together, alone in the dining room, eating off Miss Sallie's good china, using Miss Sallie's pretty silverware, and drinking out of Miss Sallie's crystal goblets.

"Is Annie still afraid of old Ginger? I don't believe she'll ever get over that cow stepping on her foot." I set her plate in front of her and took my seat. "How's Giddy's ankle?" Naturally, Giddy had found the best climbing trees in Birmingham, too, and had fallen out of a few.

"Oh, never mind all that, I have the most wonderful news." She beamed. "Guess what Colonel King sent me?"

"What's that?"

She opened up her hand satchel and pulled out an important looking paper to show me.

"Petition for Divorce," I read out loud. And on it I saw the Colonel's and Miss Sallie's names scrawled in a messy hand.

"Can you believe it? He's agreed to divorce her! We can be married soon and then I can finally be Mrs. H. Clay King!" she practically shouted. "And he wrote me this letter, this dear, dear letter, and told me that he had sent a copy of this to the judge in Memphis, too. I just can't believe it!" she laughed, as she pulled out the other sheet of paper from the satchel.

I congratulated her and listened as she chattered happily throughout dinner. I reckon it was good news. Maybe that would put an end to all the differences they had over the deed. And maybe her recording it wouldn't make any difference, if she was married to him. Looked like Sterling Hill would belong to both of them after all.

❧   ❧   ❧

"Lawd, have mercy, I do b'lieve he's been drunk almost every day since she left," Ginny whispered as we were cleaning up after supper. "Sometimes he's just a little tipsy, but sometimes he flies into an awful rage. I shore hope Miss Sallie's done got him straightened out. She never cottoned to him doin' all this drinkin.'"

"He's been with Miss Sallie? But Miss Marie just told me they were getting a divorce."

Ginny had her back turned toward me, working a dishtowel around a teacup.

"Oh, I reckon he just went up there to tell Miss Sallie all about it, seeing as how she's part of the divorce, too," I concluded, thinking out loud.

Ginny concentrated harder on that same teacup.

"What is it? What aren't you telling me?"

She turned around toward me, her eyes watering. "Oh, Lawdy. Don't you know he must have been drunk when he wrote that dee-vorce paper. Why, he was raisin' all kinda Cain through the house—I couldn't help but hear him. He even started axin' me about it all one night at supper. Why, he was good 'n' drunk that night. And he axed, 'You like Mary Eliza, Ginny, don't you?' That's what he called her, 'Mary Eliza'. He said, 'You're a good judge of character?' And I just said, 'Yes sir, I like her just fine,' even tho' I don't. And he started just a-jabberin', 'bout how a man like him deserves a beautiful wife, even if she ain't rich, and on and on, until he ended up in tears, just messy drunk. And then he was talkin' 'bout wanting to get her back, 'I just gotta git her back' and then he mumbled somethin' 'bout a dee-vorce. Why, he just about knocked the chair over when he got up from the supper table, stumbled on into the parlor. He was sittin' at that desk for a long, long time, 'til he fell asleep, with his face flat down on it. I found him that way in the morning and went to jostle him, to git him on up, and that's when I saw it."

Ginny hands trembled. "I don't know for sure what it was he was doin'. But if Miss Marie got a dee-vorce paper down in Birmingham, I 'magine that's what he done wrote up that night when he was drunk. That was right before y'all got here, you and Miss Elizabeth." She shook her head sadly. "I'm just afeared that dee-vorce ain't from his heart but from that ol' whisky."

I kept quiet, trying to absorb all that she had told me. I knew that asking for that quick claim made him awfully mad. I reckon that's because he didn't know she'd recorded the deed. Lawdy, mercy. That's when I figured it out. He was going to divorce Miss Sallie until he found out that Miss Marie had gone against him and recorded that deed.

Pondering it all and worried, I poured some sherry for her. The front door swung open suddenly, and the Colonel walked in. Rather than the stiff soldierly stance he usually took, his shoulders sagged and his arms and legs hung loosely, as if a slight breeze might set them drifting.

"Good evening, Colonel."

"Good evening, Kizzie." He saw the sherry glass in my hand. "Is she here?"

"Oh, yes, sir—she's right there in the parlor."

I followed him into the parlor, almost hiding behind him. She stood waiting, holding her book to her chest and still wearing that wilting rose.

"Oh, Clay, it is wonderful to see you again!" She opened her arms to him and hugged him tight.

His arms stayed by his side. "I didn't realize you'd be here so soon."

"Well, of course, I wanted to get here as soon as I could when I heard you wanted to see me. Kizzie, do you have my sherry?"

"Yes, ma'am."

The Colonel stood with his hands in his pockets listening to her and looking down. She positioned herself daintily on the sofa and sipped her sherry, bubbling excitedly about everything and nothing. Nothing that mattered much, anyway.

"Kizzie," the Colonel interrupted, "I would like to talk to Mrs. Pillow privately, if you don't mind." He looked frighteningly serious.

"Oh, yes, sir. I'll go out and take a walk. See who I can see."

"And Kizzie, on your way out, tell Ginny I won't be having supper tonight."

❦   ❦   ❦

It wasn't quite dark yet when I went outside, that eerie time of the evening when you're not sure if you see shadows of things or the things themselves. Feeling uncomfortable alone in the twilight, I went looking for some company. I walked down the hill to the barn to see if I could find Mr. Worley.

He was in there, finishing up from the day's work, but he seemed happy to see me. He asked if I would give him time to wash up a little, that he wanted to visit with me. So I wandered on over to the porch of the guest house, where he told me to meet him, and sat and enjoyed, since the darkness had come on.

It had been a warm day, but the evening was pleasant, with just enough of a breeze. The orange moon sat low, just off the ground, glowing as big as I'd ever seen it. Its shadows stretched across the ground like patterns in a dream. The house, the barn, the tree all seemed longer and larger and darker and not even real. I heard the hooing of an owl, and the bullfrogs began croaking their evening song.

I wondered about Miss Marie and the Colonel. She was smiling when she saw him, and he sure wanted me out of there, but I just didn't understand. She was so happy about the divorce, and he was so angry about the deed, I just hoped they could settle things between them. I never did like a fuss.

Mr. Worley came walking up through the darkness, taller than I realized, with his hair freshly combed. "Do you mind if I sit with you?"

I made room for him on the swing, but he still sat close, the unmistakable scent of witch hazel drawing me near him. His leg touched mine as we sat, the closest I'd ever been to him. He rocked the swing with his foot, causing the thick chain to squeak in an easy rhythm. After a minute he stopped rocking altogether, and the squeaking stopped, too. Then he rocked and squeaked only once. Then he started all over again. He grinned at me, and I laughed at his silliness. And shortly, without saying a word, he put his strong arm around me and clasped my shoulder. I was afraid to look at him.

"Miss Kizzie." His soft blue eyes looked at me intently, before he closed them and leaned toward me to kiss me on the lips. And when we opened our eyes, he didn't talk, and neither did I. We only looked. And we enjoyed it all—the moon, the shadows, the breeze, the closeness.

CHAPTER 27

The only recourse was whisky.

I excused myself to find libation and when I returned, still she prattled. I continued my silence, soothed by my Kentucky bourbon. She began questioning me, smiling, worrying, her words swarming about me. My reticence shielded me, and I did not listen. Like Fort Donelson, the chill became deadly. Like Fort Donelson, I intended a fight.

I would not surrender to her. There is no honor in surrender.

Here she was, this alluring woman, who had wanted me, who was more a wife to me than either of my others. Who knew my deepest secrets. But poverty was her scourge, and having attempted to save her, I had almost destroyed myself.

Sallie would turn her head to my mistress, but if I divorced her, I would lose all. If only Mary Eliza had been satisfied with our lives as they were. If only meddling Laura had abandoned her self-righteousness and ridiculous concerns about her mother's honor and left us to our happiness. But a thing begun must be completed. Had she never come, had they never threatened, we might have returned to our previous idyll. But a thing begun...

There is no honor in surrender. There is no balm in Gilead. There is nothing I could do but force her. God, how I wish she had not betrayed me. And how I wish this beautiful serpent had dripped her venom dry rather than turn her poison on me. Yet she did betray me. I trusted her, stupidly I trusted her. Why would a sensual woman prefer the cold, crusty earth beneath her to the flesh and blood of a man willing to satisfy her every want? Can money be as great a temptation?

The seething anger beneath the veneer of gentility slowly seeped forth with the revelations of the liquor. The soldier took her to bed. Tenderness was not all that he had encountered with her—a strong woman, eager and lusty, a battle waiting to be fought. He held her siege, her cries the moans of a captive. Like an ambush of an enemy, his force, his roughness were unexpected, enhanced by the pleasing power of liquor. Shrieks like battle cries, this adversary was no frightened victim, no weak prisoner, but a fervent warrior, zealous and bold. Her pleas for surrender did not deter this soldier. There is no honor in surrender.

Curled, crying, naked, she seemed much weaker than the powerful Nemesis he had previously encountered. He groped along the tabletop for the documents—difficult to see through the haze—she need only sign them. A mere stroke of the pen to save him. Beside the documents, the glinting pistol. He confronted her with them both. If she would not be persuaded by the power of his physical person, she would be persuaded by his fury.

She seemed to gather resolve from his threats. She rose from the bed, her shadowed face streaked with tears, not of mourning but of fear, standing naked in front of him. She dared him to use the gun. Grabbing the flimsy gown from the foot of the bed, she struggled to dress. She refused to sign. Each refusal became louder, matching his threats and warnings, matching his obstinacy. She dared him to use his gun. She refused to have the recordation revoked. She refused to accede to his wishes, turning her back to him she refused, the rumpled papers in his sweaty hand now less a weapon than a flapping white flag during a war of wills. His pistol did not intimidate her. His faltering hands defied his swelling anger. She slipped his grasp and rushed from the room, an angry specter in white, she did not fear his weapon, fleeing, crying, descending into the darkness.

Momentarily I stood watching the movement below, hearing the sobbing, the darkness surrounding me whether or not I opened my eyes. Where had she fled? The cold steel smeared with sweat had been useless, cowardly. Opening the chamber, returning to my room, emptying the bullets into my hand, onto the floor, stepping on slippery papers, finding my bed. Where was she? Oh, God. With eyes closed, spinning. My churning stomach emptied itself. Head pounding. Please. Comfort. Sleep. Anything...

CHAPTER 28

❀

The moon had risen higher and smaller by the time Mr. Worley walked me back up to the mansion house, holding my hand. I knew I'd never forget that night, and I hoped he wouldn't, neither. Since I didn't like being in the guest house all by myself, I'd taken to sleeping back in my own room off the kitchen, but I didn't want to disturb anybody when I went back inside. Before I could step onto the back porch, he took both of my hands in his. He kissed me gently on my lips again. My heart was fluttering too fast for my mind to think what to say, but I didn't have to. He touched his fingertip to my lips and smiled, guiding me up to the back door with his hand barely touching me.

"Good night, Miss Kizzie Biscoe."

Good night, Mr. Tom Worley.

By the time I'd closed the door I had my wits about me enough to hear the shouting. Puzzled, I tiptoed into the dining room and could tell that the ruckus was coming from upstairs.

"I told you not to record that deed, you goddamn traitor." The voice was too loud and too slurred to be the Colonel's. "And you went behind my back and did it anyway."

"How dare you speak to me that way."

"Sign it."

"I will not."

She gasped. "You...you wouldn't use that thing...you wouldn't dare...I don't believe you..."

"Sign it!"

I heard the sounds of a struggle and footsteps coming down the stairs. Then a figure in white ran to the front door. Miss Marie—all she had on was her nightclothes, running out into the night. I stepped into the hall far enough to see the Colonel at the top of the stairs with a gun in his hand, but he didn't see me in the shadows. I slipped back into the kitchen and went running back out the kitchen door.

The brightness of the moon didn't help me find her. I ran down the hill a piece to get away, and then I heard a door slam and saw a lantern light inside the guest house. Too frightened of the Colonel to return to my room, I ran down to find her.

"Miss Marie! Miss Marie! Let me in! Please!" I banged on the door of the guest house, but I didn't hear her coming. I didn't hear nothing. Sobbing, I banged harder and yelled for her. But she didn't come. The bushes on the path rustled, and I was sure it was the Colonel come down to shoot us both. I was too scared to scream.

"Miss Kizzie?" It wasn't the Colonel's voice. "Miss Kizzie, what the devil is wrong with you? Are you all right?"

I ran to him and threw my arms around him. "Oh, Mr. Worley, Mr. Worley. The Colonel drew a gun on Miss Marie…"

He calmed me down, and we sat down on the swing. I told him what I knew. He knocked on the guest house door, again and again, and called for her, but she wasn't budging. I don't rightly know why she wouldn't let me in that night. I reckon she was as afraid of the Colonel as I was.

I didn't want to go back into the mansion house, but he said I'd be just fine there, that he'd check in on the Colonel. For the second time that evening he walked me to the back door, but this time he walked me all the way inside, right up to the door of my room.

"Does this door lock?"

I nodded, trembling.

"Well, you lock it. You'll be all right." As I closed it gently, I knew he was waiting on the other side of the door for the sound of the bolt. And then I listened for his heavy footsteps as he walked away and into the house.

❀   ❀   ❀

The next morning I could hear her before I was halfway down the hill, making a racket in the guest house kitchen, banging pans. She dropped the fireplace poker with a loud clang. I stood at the door for a minute, trying to get up my nerve, but she opened it before I even knocked. She held up a skillet with both of her hands, ready to swing.

"Oh, Kizzie. Thank God it's you." Her eyes were swollen from the tears, and she was still in her nightgown. "That man tried to kill me last night. He tried to kill me."

"Yes, ma'am, I know about that."

"You know?"

"I was in the kitchen. I heard it."

"Did you see him? Did you see the gun in his hand?"

"Yes, ma'am. I peeked out into the hall just as you were running away. I saw him up at the top of the stairs."

"So you're a witness, aren't you? You know what he tried to do to me." She fell back into the rocker and wept. "He tried to kill me."

I knelt down beside her and squeezed her hand.

"It was that damned deed. He's furious that I recorded the deed. He wanted me to sign my name, but I refused. I couldn't do it. But he threatened me. With a gun."

"Miss Marie, you know the Colonel loves you and he wouldn't never…"

"I know no such thing. He drew a gun on me. The look in his eyes was just so *vicious*."

"But he sent you that Petition for Divorce, so y'all can get married…"

"Oh, Kizzie, that was just a ruse—a trap to get me back here so he could force me to sign that document. All he wants is his property."

I didn't believe the Colonel would do a thing like that, trying to trick her that way. But I reckon a man who'd point a gun at a lady is liable to do most anything. "Was he drinking whisky last night? Maybe it was just the whisky made him act like that."

"No, it's not just that. He was certainly drunk, but he was being so, so cold and so violent." She sobbed for the longest time. She told me how she had wanted to make things right between the two of them since he was willing to divorce Miss Sallie. Now what she meant by "right", I don't know. Said she was trying to use her "womanly charms" to keep him from being so angry with her, to make everything all right, like it was, now that they were back together again. But that didn't change his mind. All he wanted was for her to sign those papers. He even told her it was a mistake for him to try to help her in the first place. I know that must have hurt the worst.

I made us some coffee, and Miss Marie kept talking, her sorrow turning into fury, explaining to me why she was justified in being so angry. With everything she said I could see she was building up her courage for a fight.

"I've got the law on my side, you know, since I've recorded those deeds. Right there in those courthouses, they've got in black and white that I bought Sterling Hill, fair and square. The will shows his intention, and the recorded deed shows that it's a *fait accompli*. There's nothing he can do about it. Sterling Hill is mine." She wiped away her tears, and I fetched her some water so she could wash her face. I didn't want to say nothing about how I knew she didn't really buy the land. I didn't want her to get any more upset. We sipped our coffee in the morning quiet, calming ourselves from all the excitement, but knowing that was just the beginning of other troubles ahead.

We stayed at Sterling Hill because Miss Marie wasn't fixing to leave. We didn't go into Miss Sallie's mansion house, and the Colonel didn't come down to the guest house. Miss Marie wasn't happy living in a little clapboard house when there was a fine house full of fine things just a little piece away, where she used to live.

I reckon rich folks don't know how to be poor. I reckon they want things always to stay the same, even if they don't have any more money. Miss Marie grew up with fancy things down in Louisiana. Why, she might have even had ancestors hanging on the wall, although why anybody would ever want them, I'll *never* know. She probably got used to furniture with roses carved into it. I know she liked using shiny silverware, after she had to sell off her own when the General died. I don't see much difference, myself. It's shiny, or it's not. Shoot, I'd eat with my hands and be glad the Good Lord gave me something to keep me from being hungry. Not rich folks. I reckon you don't ever want to get rich, because then you have to stay that way to be happy.

But I think the Colonel finally must have had enough of us being on his property, eating his food, using his people for whatever we needed. Miss Marie was just lording it over everybody there, like she used to, except she was doing it from the guest house and not the mansion house. I think the Colonel tried to ignore us for a long time, pretending we weren't there, but after a while, he was finally ready for us to leave.

"Mrs. Pillow, I need to speak to you." The husky voice outside surprised me. I set down my chopping knife and walked around to the door. The Colonel stood on the porch looking down at her while she was sewing. It was the first time he'd talked to us in probably a month. She didn't look up.

"I have to leave to go to Chicago, and I will be gone for several weeks. I think it's time for the two of you to go back to Birmingham."

Miss Marie continued her stitching, ignoring him.

"I believe it would be more fitting for the two of you to return to Laura and John in Birmingham and make your home there."

"I believe we can make our own decisions about what is best for us." She glared at him coldly.

He noticed me in the doorway. "Kizzie, would you excuse us for a moment? Mrs. Pillow and I need…"

"Kizzie, you stay right where you are. Anything Colonel King has to say to me can certainly be said in front of you. Now, Colonel, is there anything else?"

Things seemed to be mighty chilly for June, with all the "Colonel" this and "Mrs." that. I reckon they were a far cry from first names now, after all that had happened.

He shut his eyes for a minute, mustering up his words, trying not to explode. "I want you both gone before I return." He turned and hiked back up to the mansion house. Miss Marie turned her attention back to her sewing and didn't say nothing else.

I really didn't want to go back to Birmingham, and I know for sure that Miss Marie didn't. But he told us we had to leave and be gone before he came back. I reckon I'm used to doing what I'm told, so I figured we were fixing to leave.

The next morning I went up to the edge of the yard and watched as Mr. Worlcy and the Colonel left for the train station. When I got back to the guest house, I found her sitting in her bedroom with her grip open, ready for me to pack up her things.

"Kizzie, today I want you to take my things back over to the mansion house."

"But we're supposed to be going back to…"

"We are not going back to anywhere except where we belong—in *my* mansion house."

"But Miss Marie…"

"That house is rightfully mine, and I have no intention of leaving."

Nobody was there to tell us not to. So we packed our things and started to set up like we had before. Miss Marie marched into that house and up those stairs, followed by Malcolm carrying the grips, followed by me. Ginny heard the commotion and came out of the kitchen to watch what was happening, staring at us with a peculiar expression. I shrugged my shoulders and just kept going, knowing I'd need to unpack her things.

Well, I reckon it didn't sit too well with Mr. Worley when he came back from Marianna that evening and heard from the others what we'd done. He and Malcolm and some of the other men gathered themselves up and knocked on the front door. I knew what it was going to be about. I let them all into the hall.

Miss Marie came out of her room upstairs holding her hands behind her back.

"Good evenin', Miz Pillow," Malcolm spoke first.

"Good evening, gentlemen."

"We come to find out if there's anything you need us to do for you."

"No, I am just fine, thank you. I believe you all better get back to your quarters now. We'll have a full day of work tomorrow."

Mr. Worley spoke up. "Oh, just put a sock in it. What makes you think you can just move your stuff into the Colonel's house when he done told you to leave? We come over here to git you and your things on outta here…"

I had seen General Pillow's pistol from the War at Mound Plantation, but not since we lived at Sterling Hill, at least not until that moment. She pointed it right at them.

At first, they didn't say nothing. Neither did she. "We sorry to bother you, Miz Pillow," Malcolm said. "We'll be goin' now. Come on, Tom."

"Look, lady," Mr. Worley growled. "You ain't s'posed to be here, and you know it. The Colonel told me to help you git your things together and git you on down to the train station."

"My things are staying right here in my house. You are the ones who have to leave."

"And are you gonna shoot me if I stay?"

She pulled the trigger and shot a hole in the downstairs wall—right above where the men were standing, the blast echoing through the hall. The men turned tail and ran out through the front door, all except Mr. Worley, who had his arm up over his face.

"Somebody's gonna git hurt with you shootin' off that thing indoors!"

"I'll kill you or Clay King or anybody else who tries to keep me out of this house." And she pointed the gun right at him.

"Miss Marie, please, don't." I was trying to keep my sobbing quiet.

"Kizzie, you git on outta here." Mr. Worley ordered. "Go on back in the kitchen. This is between her and me…"

"Mr. Worley, don't…"

"Are you gonna shoot Kizzie, too?"

"Get out of my house right now. I don't care who gets hurt. This is my house, and you will not drive me from it." She pulled the trigger again, and this time it shot right above his head so that he had to duck, making another hole in the wall. I couldn't help but scream.

"All right, all right. I'll leave. This is between you and the Colonel. He made this mess, and he'll have to clean it up. You just make sure you don't hurt Kizzie, or else I'll come back in here with my shotgun. Kizzie, you git on back to your room," he ordered me.

Watching her and stepping backwards carefully, he made his way to the front door. Once he was all the way out, she dropped her arm so the gun wasn't pointed down at him no more.

"Kizzie, you get on to bed now," she directed. I had already begun running back to my room quick as I could, and I bolted the door. I was too terrified to be in the house, just in case she was going to take out after me, but I was too terrified to leave, too. I don't know what made her want to live there so bad that she'd shoot a man. I reckon she was just bound and determined not to lose what she thought was hers. Or to get revenge on the Colonel.

In a couple of weeks, Miss Elizabeth came back from Birmingham again, and this time she brought Annie and Giddy with her. We were going to set up like we had before. Giddy got his attic bedroom back, and Annie got her room, and Miss Elizabeth slept in the room that was supposed to have been Miss Marie's but never was. Ginny did the cooking, and Malcolm did anything we needed outside. Miss Marie didn't have too much to do with the farming, though. She let Mr. Worley take care of that. She must have figured he knew more about it than her, and I imagine she was a little anxious about having another quarrel with him. Next time she might not win. Besides, letting him handle the farming made it a whole lot easier on her.

"Well, Kizzie, this is a surprise. Do you and Tom have some news you want to announce?" The Colonel had been gone for almost three weeks when we picked him up at the Marianna train station.

I blushed. "No, sir. I'm just along for the ride."

"Then why are you still here? Tom? What's going on?"

"I'm sorry, Colonel. She had a gun and she drew it on us. We were going to try to talk her out of staying, after you told her to leave, but she wouldn't listen. Just pointed the gun at me and Malcolm and the others. Even shot a couple of holes right in your walls. I figgered, well, I figgered you better handle it. I didn't want to git into no shootin' match with her."

"You mean she's still here? At Sterling Hill?"

"Yeah, and she moved back into the mansion house."

"She said it was only fitting for her to be living in her own house," I added. I realized then that I shouldn't have said that.

His face turned red and then the hollering started. And then the cussin'. It was mighty embarrassing, with all the people on the street turning to look at us, but that didn't stop him. He said some awfully unkind things about Miss Marie. I wouldn't dare repeat them, to nobody.

The Colonel didn't even go out to Sterling Hill. I reckon he knew what was waiting for him out there, so he grabbed his grip out of the back of the carriage and hustled back into the station. Said he was going to Memphis to see a lawyer.

❦   ❦   ❦

Storm clouds were gathering up in the west when the stranger on the black horse came riding up the hill that Friday afternoon. The horse pranced into the yard, and he tugged tightly on the reins.

"Mrs. Mary Eliza Pillow?"

"No, sir. But I work for her."

"Then make sure you give this to her," he said, leaning down and handing me a letter. Before I could ask him what it was all about, he had turned around and galloped off. What he handed me was an official looking envelope addressed to *Mrs. Mary Eliza Pillow, Sterling Hill, Lee County, Arkansas.* Just the look of it made me nervous.

"I don't know, Kizzie," Mr. Worley said, looking at it over my shoulder. "I bet you the Colonel sent her this. You sure you don't want some company when you take this in?" He didn't think too much of her, ever since the gun incident.

"No, I don't want you to get in a fight with her. I know you're a mighty charming man, but you might have a hard time charming her," I flirted with him. "Besides, she's my family. She won't ever do nothing bad to me."

So I took the letter inside where she was sitting, reading over some papers.

"A man just brought you a letter," I said, quietly.

"Oh?"

"Looks like it's just from somebody in Marianna," I offered, as I handed it to her.

She looked through her spectacles set on the end of her nose. She pulled out her silver letter opener from the drawer and ripped open the envelope. She began to read it out loud.

Col. H. C. King vs. Mrs. Mary Eliza Pillow

The more she read, the slower and quieter her voice became until she stopped reading altogether.

"Miss Marie, is there something wrong?"

She moved over to sit on the sofa, studying that letter. We were quiet for an uncomfortably long time. "Do you realize what this is?"

"No, ma'am. Is it from the Colonel?"

"Of course, it's from him, you fool."

"What's it say?"

"It says, Kizzie, that he has filed a lawsuit to remove me from Sterling Hill and to make it official that he owns it." Her cheeks were flushed. "And furthermore, it says something here that you apparently forgot to tell me."

"What…what's that?" I asked, trembling at how angry she had become.

"It seems that Colonel King had some assistance in stealing that deed from me. Or that's what he says here in this lawsuit." She stood up and walked over to me.

"Assistance?"

"It says here that he persuaded you to take that deed from me. Is that true?"

I was too scared to answer.

"I said, is that true?" she asked again, raising her voice.

"Yes, ma'am," I replied, carefully.

"And why did you do that?"

"I didn't think he wanted you to have that deed."

"And why would you be listening to him over me? Why would you betray me? Hmm? Did you have a relationship with Colonel King that I am unaware of?" She stepped closer to me, her brown eyes sharp and furious.

"I…I didn't mean to betray you, Miss Marie. It was just that…"

She slapped me hard across the face. I held my hand to my sore cheek and started to cry.

"It's clear you don't know a thing about loyalty," she barked. "I've raised you since you were an ugly, mewling little baby. I've given you food and shelter, even when I almost didn't have the means to provide them for my own children. And this is how you repay me. You stole from me the one chance I had to be wealthy again. That just shows me how stupid you really are."

I stood, frozen, too afraid to move, but at least she turned her back and walked away. She stood still for a minute, breathing hard, and then turned back to face me. "I will not tolerate disloyalty," she growled, pointing her finger at me fiercely. "I'm going to get what's mine, one way or the other, and if you won't help me, you'll be out on the streets. Do you understand?"

I cried, holding my face, not believing that she'd hit me again. Miss Marie had hit me again.

"Stop your sniveling and go get me some sherry." And I did.

We found out that the Colonel had filed his lawsuit both in Marianna and in Memphis to get her out of his house and off his property, because a couple of days later, she got another one of those letters, this time from the court in Memphis. When Mr. Worley brought it back from the post office, he just left it on the table in the hall. I stayed as far away from her as I could.

Miss Marie had always been good to me, considering. She always gave me something to eat and a place to live. I had to put up with her moods every now and then, but that didn't seem like too much. But other than that time she slapped me when I was 13, she hadn't ever hit me. Not once. At least not until she got that letter. I don't like to speak bad about somebody who's been good to me but it seemed like there were starting to be as many bad times as there were good. I couldn't leave, because I didn't have any family to go to. And my Mr. Worley lived at Sterling Hill to manage the farm. I wanted to run away, but I couldn't. The two people who'd been nicer to me than anybody in the world were right there, so I couldn't go no place, no place at all.

CHAPTER 29

February 1889

I had no choice. Her betrayal pained me deeply. I had no choice but to protect my own interests. I had moved back to Memphis where Sallie took me in, not happily, but because of appearances—she did not wish to be viewed as a shrew if our acquaintances understood that I was in Memphis but living elsewhere. Very few people had known about our arrangement with Mary Eliza, but once I filed the lawsuit, everyone knew. I thought that receiving justice would be a greater reward than any harm publicity might do. Little did I know. The Memphis media were like green flies, seeking refuse everywhere, buzzing noisily for no purpose but annoyance.

For a number of years I had edited *King's Tennessee Digest*, my own legal periodical, which proved to be a blessed distraction from my personal legal entanglements and enabled me to visit Chicago several times a year, to get away from everybody and everything. That February was no exception—I left Memphis gladly to spend several weeks in scholarly pursuits.

Mary Eliza had written me regularly at my office and even at my home, an act of audacity which surprised me and infuriated Sallie. I did not read all of the letters, but I read enough to know that she still wanted me to divorce Sallie and marry her. On occasion, I responded.

Dear Mary Eliza,

Once again I am writing to you in the hope that we might come to some understanding. I would prefer to work this out between the two of us, rather than in the courts. I would like very much to sit down and discuss the farm and its operations with you before spring planting begins. I will be in Chicago during

the month of February overseeing the publication of the new edition of my
digest and thereafter I shall be in Memphis. Let us consider meeting, without
conditions or preconceptions, so that we may do what is best for all concerned.

Fondly,

Clay

❧   ❧   ❧

Several inches of snow on the ground in Chicago made travel almost
impossible, but fortunately the library where I wrote and researched was not
far from my usual residence, the Hotel St. Benedict. I would not be deterred
from my work by mere weather, so I donned my boots and traipsed through
the snow daily to meet my publishing deadline. Arriving back in the lobby that
Friday afternoon, I discerned a familiar silhouette, the curve, the bearing, the
distinctive profile. As I moved closer to the two women, who were apparently
seeking a room there, I realized she was wearing gray. "Mary Eliza?"

"Clay, what a lovely coincidence, that we should meet so far from home."
She took my hand in both of hers. I did not for one minute believe that our
meeting was coincidental, but I was too surprised to feign anger.

"What on earth are you doing in Chicago?" Glancing around the room, I
was concerned that somehow someone I knew would see us together.

"Good afternoon, Colonel King," Kizzie greeted me, smiling. "It sure is
good to see you."

"It's good to see you, too, Kizzie." Mary Eliza's gloved hands had not yet
released mine. "I didn't expect to see you both here."

"It was your letter. I knew you were serious about having a meeting of the
minds when I got your letter."

"But I didn't mean for you to travel all the way to Chicago."

"Well, regardless, we're all here together. Let's have dinner, the three of us,
shall we?"

"Yes, that would be fine." She squeezed my hand. "But I'm afraid I'm off to a
meeting in just a little while." She continued to gaze into my eyes. The awk-
wardness of my standing in a public place, not simply speaking to her, but
touching her—I did not want to offend her, anger her, but I pulled my hand
away. I did not know what to say to her. "Perhaps you'd like to rest up in my
apartment? I shouldn't be more than a couple of hours."

"How gracious of you. We could freshen up before dinner. Thank you, Clay."

❧   ❧   ❧

"Don't you think we can work this out somehow?" she asked at dinner, free from the presence of her companion, a mere shadow to her. Attired in her favorite lavender silk (she never failed to mention that the gown had been designed in Paris), she seemed perfectly at ease with bare shoulders in winter, veiled alluringly with a stole of diaphanous tulle. "It's really just a misunderstanding. Surely we can work it out."

"And what is it you want, Mary Eliza? You have taken over my property, endangered my employees, and you think that I still want to be with you?"

"Oh, Clay, let's not let a little property dispute come between us—and all that we've had," she entreated me, leaning over the table towards me, revealing more of her fair sanctum of decolletage than was becoming. Once again she tried to take my hand.

"It's not just a little property dispute." I pulled away as she touched me.

My retreat deflected her. For a moment, I worried how she would respond. Regaining her gracious demeanor, she adjusted her stole more modestly. "We won't talk business now. We'll have plenty of time for that later."

I believe she thought she could charm her way back into my life. Although she said nothing about marriage that evening, or the others afterward, I was sure that was her goal. I was no longer deceived into thinking that she loved me. It was my money. It had always been the money.

As the days passed, we did talk business, about the year's cotton crop and whatnot. I wanted to make sure that she was going to get it planted properly. How grateful I was that Tom Worley was willing to endure her presence to insure that Sterling Hill was taken care of. I tried very hard to discuss only the specifics of farming without provoking her by discussing the recorded deed. I did inform her of my decision to remove our Mosby Street home from my bequest and to retitle it in Sallie's name. She was my wife and that's where she and the girls were living. Mary Eliza said nothing about it, didn't respond negatively, even though that was one of the larger properties listed in the deed. As much as I wanted to resolve the conflict over the property, I knew I had to leave those negotiations to the lawyers who could be objective. Finally believing that no one from Memphis would be a witness to our meeting in Chicago, I decided to enjoy as much subjectivity with her as I could—she owed me that, at least.

CHAPTER 30

�֍

When we stepped onto the hotel elevator one morning after we'd been in Chicago a few days, the fresh scrubbed attendant greeted us. "Good morning, Mrs. King, Miss Biscoe."

"I am Mrs. Pillow," Miss Marie corrected him, irritated that he didn't already know that. I just smiled at him.

His eyebrows arched up so high they got lost underneath his little monkey hat. He stared a minute longer, before remembering his job and closing the clanking gate in front of us.

Since I was born in Louisiana and lived most of my life in Memphis and Arkansas, I didn't really understand what cold meant. But I got a good idea of it while we were walking around Chicago. I'd seen snow before—every three or four years we'd get a little—but I never saw so much snow in one place. Why, there was snow everywhere. I had to wear my work boots all over town, which just wasn't fitting, because my dress up shoes sure wasn't the way to get around in Chicago in February.

Miss Marie and I went shopping in the daytime, while the Colonel was working. But at nighttime, we were right back in the apartment, with him. We never did have to get our own room. The Colonel's apartment had a couple of bedrooms, and I was happy to have one all to myself. He took us out to dinner and even took us to the theater once. She'd brought some of her prettiest dresses to catch his eye, and she was always flattering him and touching him. He looked a good deal older than he had over three years ago, when we first came to Sterling Hill. His hair was completely gray, and his face was more wrinkled. Miss Marie called him "distinguished looking," but he just looked awfully tired to me. She was as beautiful as ever, even though she was going to

- 127 -

turn 40 later that year. I don't believe she ever looked any older, the whole time I knew her.

Several days later, when we entered the elevator that same attendant greeted us with a big smile. "Good morning, Mrs. Pillow, Miss Biscoe."

"Good morning," she replied politely. He didn't stop grinning at us, even when we got to the bottom floor, and he opened the doors.

Walking into the lobby, I saw a group of ladies sitting and talking. One lady noticed us, and with the purple feather in her hat bobbing, she leaned over to whisper something to the lady in blue, who stopped talking and stared at us as we walked past. Then three or four hat feathers began bobbing, and those ladies began cackling like excited chickens in a henhouse.

Whispers, stares, and grins seemed to follow us everywhere around the Hotel St. Benedict, and within a week of our being there, the man at the news-stand, the grocer, even the milliner were ogling us. I felt uncomfortable about it, but Miss Marie didn't seem to notice. She wasn't inclined to look at what other people were doing unless she decided she was interested. But on the way back into the hotel one evening, she couldn't help but notice.

As we approached the front door of the hotel, a scruffy looking man came stumbling up behind us, and he slurred, "Hey, Mrs. Pillow, when you're fin-ished with him, why don't you come on over to my place? 325 Oxford St. I can treat a lady real nice." He grinned.

The Colonel was too surprised to say anything right at first, just glared at the man, who wiped his lips with his sleeve.

"Have you no decency?" she hissed angrily, looking at both of them.

"Let's get inside. He doesn't deserve the dignity of a reply." The Colonel grabbed her arm and pulled her through the doorway. The heavy bags under the stranger's eyes and his scraggly whiskers couldn't completely disguise the face of a gentleman, a grimy, drunken old gentleman. I saw it in his bloodshot eyes, his refined features. "Good evenin', Miss." He doffed his hat and winked at me before staggering back across the dark street.

"How can I ever show my face in Memphis? Everyone will think I'm his mistress." She tried to talk her way through to an answer as we made our way carefully down the slushy sidewalk. The sun peeked out every now and then and melted just enough snow to make it slippery. "And that's probably what he wanted all along—to embarrass me, to *blackmail* me so I'd have no choice but to go along with his schemes."

After a month in Chicago, Miss Marie still hadn't got the Colonel to promise to divorce Miss Sallie. I reckon he was liable to be as stubborn as she was. Or maybe he just finally understood what kind of woman he was dealing with in Miss Marie. He seemed to enjoy her company, but he didn't want to live with her any more. And she could no longer ignore the stares and whispers.

"If he won't make good on his obligation to me, then I will give him exactly what he deserves," she promised with a frosty breath, as if her words demanded the visibility of that icy cloud.

❦   ❦   ❦

"I'm not sure I can help you with this, Mrs. Pillow. I really don't see how we have anything to do with this issue at all."

We had found the office of the *Matrimonial News and Special Advertiser* where we were talking to the editor and his wife. They were nice enough folks, but they looked busy. He had ink on his fingers, and she was wearing a dirty apron, not fitting for receiving company, but I reckon we hadn't given them any warning, neither.

"But you just don't understand," Miss Marie pleaded, her eyes welling up. "I have been singled out for persecution by a very powerful man, a colonel. He is trying to destroy my reputation. I am simply a poor widow who has been duped by this conniving lawyer. He has caused me to lose all my money. He has taken my farm. And now this. Because I refuse to marry such a horrible man, he has set out to ruin my reputation in polite society!" She sobbed into her handkerchief.

"Now, now, Mrs. Pillow, why don't I fix you a nice cup of tea? I can see you are very upset," Mrs. Scott frowned at her husband as she walked out of his office.

"Oh, I know," Miss Marie sighed. "You don't know who I am, and you probably don't care. But can't I impose on your sense of human decency to help a poor widow in distress?"

I hadn't ever been in a publisher's office before. I imagined this is what the inside of a newspaper office would look like, or the place they printed *Godey's Lady's Book*. I just never thought that the folks that did all the publishing would be quite so dirty. Miss Marie looked as out of place as a peacock in a pig sty—especially compared to Mrs. Scott. Now, don't misunderstand. Mrs. Scott was a right nice looking woman. But with her straggling pieces of hair and her smudged cheeks, she looked like she was a good deal older, or like she didn't know how to take care of herself. She sure didn't have on clothes as fine as Miss Marie's, neither. Hers were a whole lot more like mine, except that she wore an apron, and I knew better. I saw the way she looked at Miss Marie when she greeted us at the front door, like she wasn't accustomed to having such a fine lady around, and I could tell she wanted to treat her right.

"Here you go. Some nice hot tea. I'm afraid I don't have any lemon," she added apologetically.

"This is just fine, thank you." Miss Marie sniffled again.

"Mr. Scott, isn't there anything we can do to help this poor lady? She has obviously been hurt very badly," she reasoned with her husband.

"Oh, all right, all right. It'll be quicker to help you than to sit around and argue about it. What is it you want me to write?" He made a space on the desk in front of him and pulled out a writing pad.

"Oh, thank you, thank you ever so much. Now, if I could just have from you a written statement, declaring that Colonel King himself delivered that matrimonial ad you published, why, that would be quite enough."

"But that's a lie," the editor objected. "I've never met this Colonel King in my life. I'm not going to swear to a lie."

"Oh, just a tiny white lie. That's really all I need. And you don't have to take an oath of any kind. And in writing that statement, and signing it, of course, you will have done a poor widow and her fatherless children a great service."

Mr. Scott looked at Miss Marie and then looked over to his wife, who was scowling at him. "Oh, all right. Tell me what you want it to say."

Mrs. Scott smiled broadly, like she'd just done an act of Christian charity that was sure to open the pearly gates of Heaven just for her.

CHAPTER 31

July 1889

"Ma'am, it is a most unfortunate situation you find yourself in, but if you excuse my saying so, it sounds to me like you're blackmailing the poor man," Mr. Gantt remarked, leaning back in his chair behind his desk. Out his window, you could get a good view of the brick buildings on Main Street, and all the other lawyers' offices we'd already been to.

Almost every one of those lawyers said the same thing, that Miss Marie was blackmailing the Colonel. I couldn't figure how they would know such a thing since all they know is what she told them. Miss Marie went calling all over downtown Memphis to find her a good set of lawyers, but the problem was that Colonel King already knew all of them, since he'd been practicing law in Memphis for so long. Even though General Pillow was a lawyer, that didn't seem to matter to them, I reckon since he was dead. It ain't easy suing a lawyer. Or maybe they thought she didn't have the money to pay them with. Seemed like everything always came back to money.

Finally she was able to find somebody who thought the widow of a general was somebody important, at the law firm of Poston and Poston. It sure wasn't her first choice, but the fact that they would take her case was good enough for her.

Cigar smoke wafted from the lawyer's office, marking our path to Mr. Poston who sat behind a big oak desk, puffing blue gray clouds of stench, the likes of which I hadn't smelled since the rancidness of Birmingham's smokestacks. He stood up and leaned over the desk to stick out his hand to Miss Marie, without ever taking that cigar out of his mouth.

"How do you do. I'm David Poston."

"Yes, how do you do. I am Mrs. General Gideon Pillow."

"Ah, the General's widow. Do sit down."

"You've heard of my late husband?"

"Oh, yes, I know of General Pillow. Fought in Mexico, right? Spent some time in Tennessee during the War. Didn't he run for Vice-president at one time?"

"Yes, he did, in '52." She smiled proudly.

"Yes, yes. Well, it's a pleasure to meet his lovely widow. And this young woman must be your daughter?" I wasn't sure I liked him mistaking me for her daughter.

She laughed. "Of course not. This is my companion Kesiah."

"Howdy do," I said politely, extending my hand. He ignored me, left me standing there with my arm stretched out to nothing. I didn't much care for that.

"Now, how may I be of service to you today?" he asked, gesturing for us to sit.

Miss Marie took her seat on the edge of that hard wooden chair. "Yes, well, down to business. I am currently engaged in a most unpleasant property dispute with Colonel H. Clay King, and I need an advocate."

"Colonel King?" His eyes gleamed with recognition.

"Are you familiar with him?"

"Familiar with him? Why, yes, in a manner of speaking." He leaned back in his swivel chair with a loud squeak. "Colonel King and I have been engaged on opposites sides of many lawsuits for a number of years. I guess you could call ours a 'friendly rivalry.' He's a good man, Colonel King."

"Colonel King has treated me with dishonor and disrespect, and I intend to have representation in this case which will see to my interests first and foremost. If your previous relationship with Colonel King was of a friendly nature…" She started to stand up.

"Now, now, Mrs. Pillow, I didn't mean to suggest that I couldn't be an aggressive advocate on your behalf. The legal community in Memphis is quite a complicated entanglement of personalities and interests. But that never gets in the way of my loyalty to my clients," he explained with a grin. "Now tell me some of the particulars of your lawsuit. Girl, go get us some coffee. Katie will show you where it is."

Now, I didn't cotton to being called "girl." It was bad enough that he wouldn't even shake my hand. But I didn't like being treated like a nobody. I've been with Miss Marie a long, long time and had to put up with more bad than good from her, but I didn't like her hiring a rude man like this.

"Yes, Kizzie, that would be lovely, if you don't mind," she said as she pulled the letters she'd got from the Colonel's lawyers out of her hand satchel. I knew she was putting on airs, so I just put on a few of my own. "Yes, ma'am, Mrs. Pillow."

When I came back in with the tray, Mr. Poston was studying those papers. "Now, Mrs. Pillow, I don't mean to get too personal with you, but if I'm going to represent you, I have to know the facts behind all these allegations."

"There are no facts in those letters—just lies."

"So tell me why he would say these things, 'She exercised undue influence over me.' What does he mean?"

Miss Marie smirked. "He has been desperately in love with me for years. He's tried to blackmail me into marrying him. Perhaps what he's referring to are these improper feelings he has developed. I have no earthly idea why he would say that, unless that's what he means."

Mr. Poston observed her skeptically. "Now, he says here that you persuaded him to deed his properties to you—that's a number of properties here in Memphis and then the plantation," he peered over his spectacles, "'Sterling Hill.' Is that the name of it?"

"Yes. That's the plantation I bought from him."

"Says here it was a bequest. When you received the deed you agreed not to record it. And then that you 'took forcible possession' of his land. How do you respond to that?"

"That man is a thief and a liar. I lent him $10,000, and when he failed to repay me, I asked for a quit claim to Sterling Hill in repayment. That would have fully satisfied the debt." I know she didn't lend him $10,000. She wasn't telling Mr. Poston the truth at all. But I wouldn't dare try to correct her.

"So what is this business about 'forcible possession'?"

"That's just another lie. He gave me that plantation and everything on it and then left it for good, never to return. And the only force ever used in my dealings with him was the time—no, the two times—he tried to kill me."

Mr. Poston craned his neck toward her. "He tried to kill you?" he asked, I reckon not believing the Colonel would do such a thing. I was just wondering what the second time was.

"Yes, once he called me to his bedroom when he was drunk and drew his pistol on me, ordering me to sign some documents that would have somehow revoked the deed I recorded. The other time was when he violently drove me and my poor little children away from Sterling Hill for a time, when we moved to Birmingham. Kizzie here was a witness to both."

"Well? Did you witness these events?" Mr. Poston turned his wolflike eyes toward me.

I hesitated. "I did see the Colonel holding a gun and some papers when he was drunk one night, and I saw Miss Marie running from him. She wouldn't even open up the door to the guest house to let me in, she was so scared."

"And were you also present for the second assault?"

"Sir?"

"When you all were driven by force from the property?"

I felt like a treed squirrel, not sure where to jump next. "Well, um, well, the night before we left Sterling Hill, I did see the Colonel with his gun." He didn't ask nothing else, so I didn't say nothing else.

"Now, Mrs. Pillow, I have to ask you this, and I mean no disrespect, but as your attorney I must know the facts behind this whole situation."

She sat composed, daring him to ask.

"Did you have a relationship with Colonel King that was of a personal nature?"

"Of course not," she snapped. "Ours was strictly a business relationship. Not that he didn't want it to be more. But I always rejected his advances. He was just a deluded old man, trying to cheat me out of what was rightfully mine."

"I'm sorry to have to ask that, but I hope you understand that as your attorney…"

"I understand that there are some unsavory aspects to this case, because of Colonel King's involvement. But even he has attested to the purity of my character—here in Memphis, to his friends. But the innuendo in this lawsuit is positively defamatory."

"Back to the deed." Mr. Poston retrieved his cigar from the ashtray where it had been smoldering. "He says he never actually delivered the deed to you. Is that true?"

"I had witnesses. They saw him give me that deed."

"It says here there were two deeds," he said, looking down at the papers. "A deed of sale and a deed of gift. Did he deliver both to you? What is that all about?"

She sighed, as if she was tired of having to explain it all. "The first deed he gave me had a contract attached which showed that I paid the $10,000 for the property. Kizzie witnessed that deed and contract, didn't you Kizzie?"

"Yes, ma'am." I was glad I could tell the truth without fudging.

"But he manipulated poor Kizzie into stealing that deed from me, didn't he?" I nodded. But I didn't want her to start thinking about that again.

"Now let me get this straight. After he signed that first deed, he gave it to you?"

"Of course. In front of several witnesses, including Kizzie." He didn't ask me about that, and I was just as glad. I might have told him how I saw him lock that deed in his desk instead of giving it to her. Or maybe telling the truth would have been too dangerous. She was telling just enough of the truth to sound honest, but then she twisted it to make it work in her favor.

"But he says here that you stole it from him."

"*He* stole it from *me*, after having given it to me. And then, THEN, of all things, he burned it. Burned it right there in the parlor fireplace. It was after he destroyed the first deed that he gave me the second one. But it is the first one, the one that showed that I bought the land, which I believe to be more important. I never agreed to the conditions set forth in the second deed."

Mr. Poston took off his spectacles. "Then why did you record the second deed, if you thought it wasn't as important?"

"I wanted to file it as notice to the world that I had rights, and to prevent Colonel King from selling the property, and to give me time to establish the deed which he had burned."

Mr. Poston puffed his cigar and thought for a while in silence. I didn't understand what lawyers could do, listening to so much that might be true and might not and asking all the right questions to figure out what was and wasn't so. But I didn't understand Miss Marie, neither, lying just as easy as you please so she seemed honest and the Colonel seemed like a villain. The truth was probably somewhere in the middle. I reckon that's why they have judges.

"Mrs. Pillow, it seems to me that you would probably have a stronger case for your ownership through the second deed. After all, that deed is still in existence—it hasn't been burned—and it has already been recorded." He sank down in his chair, with his fingers intertwined in front of him, pondering.

"That second deed was merely a gift he attempted to give me, to persuade me to marry him," she explained. "It was absolutely insulting—if I left the property, if I married someone else, I'd lose all interest in the property. And I would have to provide a home for him for life without benefit of marriage—which, of course, I would never have agreed to. I couldn't agree to those conditions. The first deed had no such conditions. The first deed, which he destroyed, showed that I bought that property fair and square. I want *that* deed restored," she tried to persuade him.

"Yes, I can see your point. I'll have to think about this." He frowned at the papers on his desk. "What's this about a conspiracy? This says that you and J. S. Shields engaged in a conspiracy to murder Colonel King?"

"That's nonsense. Just the ravings of a lunatic. My son-in-law, John Shields, is too innocuous a person—I hesitate to call him a man—to be a threat to anyone. He's never said the first threatening thing about Colonel King."

Now Miss Marie did tell me to write that letter about Mr. John threatening to confront the Colonel if he didn't marry her. But I couldn't imagine the Colonel would actually believe such a thing, knowing Mr. John like he did. Everybody knew he was too much under Laura's thumb to hurt anybody.

"Of course, you'll need to engage an Arkansas attorney for the issues regarding the Arkansas land. Tom Chambers is a good man. I could contact him for you. The properties being in two states makes this whole thing a bit out of the ordinary." Then he took a long draw on his cigar and blew the smoke up above us. "But this home on Mosby Street may cause a problem."

"Why is that?"

"The deed which you recorded describes all the properties in both states, and yet, he's already transferred the Mosby Street property out of your name. Did you receive any proceeds from that sale?"

Miss Marie looked worried. "Of course not. There was no sale. He just gave that house to Sallie. She was living in it, after all."

Mr. Poston sat silent for a minute. "The judge might question why you're fighting for only one of the properties listed in that deed."

"Well, they're all technically mine."

"No, not any longer. Mrs. King owns the Mosby Street house free and clear. The odds are against us trying to retrieve that property, Mrs. Pillow, since Mrs. King lives there with her children. I'm not sure we'd get much sympathy from a judge if we were trying to…"

"Oh, then don't make an issue of that house," she interrupted, impatiently. "It's not nearly as valuable as the plantation. And he hasn't transferred THAT to anyone else. All I want is Sterling Hill, or its value in cash."

"This is a very complicated case," he concluded. "It will be important for you to produce all your witnesses so that you can strengthen your position. It seems to me that you can sue for defamation of character and certainly assault…" On he went, laying out the different ways they could sue the Colonel. They talked about money and land and her good name. He took notes, and she sermonized about how cold-blooded and cruel and selfish the Colonel was to her, and how she was just a poor pitiful widow woman who'd been taken advantage of. She said she wanted to end the cross-bill by saying that the Colonel had destroyed her reputation and that he wasn't a gentleman at all, but that he was a "thing masquerading before the world in the form of a man." But seemed to me that her filing this whole thing wouldn't do much for her reputation, and pretty well showed that she wasn't much of a lady, neither. When she said that the Colonel's lawsuit had put her in a "compromising position," I knew that just wasn't so. She'd done that to herself.

CHAPTER 32

The wailing from the darkies down by the misty river rose eerily, solemnly, as they led a young man down to be held under the creek water, women in white, singing mournfully, their unsteady voices holding a note that wandered up and down without melody. At first a pleasant, comforting image, the singing became more and more ominous. I realized I was dreaming, but the wailing continued, reverberating through the hallway, up the stairs, to the doorway. The horrid sound turned to intermittent sobs and a lower discordant moaning began.

"Oh, Daddy!" a higher pitched voice exclaimed. Not darkies in a dream, but I knew with certainty these were the voices of my children.

"What's that?" Clay appeared sleepily at the doorway of my bedroom.

"Oh, God," a quieter voice from below began, reaching a crescendo of sobs.

"It's the girls." I quickly climbed out of the bed, and grabbing my housecoat, I pushed by him and headed for the stairs. By the time I reached the bottom, I heard a chorus of four female voices whining and crying. Hunched in a crowd at the dining room table, my daughters were reading the *Appeal-Avalanche*, spread out in front of them. As much as young girls enjoy their penchant for melodrama, I knew that this was more than romantic sadness, especially when the girls looked at me and were afraid to speak.

IN ARKANSAS

The Pillow-King Case Over the River

---

*Mrs. Pillow Uses a Little of the
Colonel's Plain Language*

---

*Indignant Denials and Applications
of Falsehood*

---

*His Said to Be a Crafty Spirit of
Vindictive Malevolence*

---

*"A Battle to the Death of the Integrity
and Moral Life of One, and May
God Defend the Right," Says
the Respondent*

"What is it? It can't possibly be as bad as all that."
Their continued silence was an unwelcome response.
Clay had entered the room by that time. "Oh, Daddy, how could you!" Fannie cried, running from the room, her sisters hurrying behind her in a parade of sorrow.
"How could I what?"

❈   ❈   ❈

"One hundred thousand dollars for defaming her character? That's absurd. I have somehow defamed her simply by filing a lawsuit to clear the title to my land? It's hogwash. There's no jury in the United States that would award such a gargantuan amount, even if the case had merit."
"It covers the entire front page, Clay. The entire front page. Can you imagine what our neighbors will say when they read it?" Agitated, I paced the room, not believing that his involvement with this woman had become so ugly and so public.
"She says here I owe her $10,000."

"Did you borrow that money from her?" Panicking, I did not know what to believe.

"Of course not. She's never had a dime to her name. She's been in debt up to her ears ever since I've known her. Look, what happened is that I wrote a contract giving $10,000 as the amount of consideration, when I gave her the deed to the land."

I eyed him skeptically.

"I wanted it to look as though she had bought it…I was afraid a gift of that nature would reflect badly upon us all."

"How prophetic of you." In the cabinet I searched for his bottle as he continued his silent reading. "You made the mistake of putting that damned woman in your will, of leaving her your properties. I just had no idea it could go beyond the will, that everybody would hear about it."

"A 'legal devil fish' who stole money from her. She calls me a 'devil fish.'" He chuckled.

"What in God's name is that?" I asked, pouring each of us a glass.

He shrugged his shoulders and smiled. "She's as creative in her descriptions as she is in her charges. I thought Dave Poston was a better lawyer than this. Maybe he's trying to take it easy on me by letting her take charge of the case."

He read as I sipped the bourbon. How he could drink that vile stuff in such vast amounts, I had no idea, but I craved relief from the humiliation he had heaped upon me. He remained silent for too long.

"What is it?"

"She's accused me of attempted murder."

"What?" I felt the dizziness hit me, and grabbing the back of a chair, I steadied myself. "Attempted murder?"

He read more intently than before, no more smiling or making light of her charges. I watched him uneasily.

"Clay, did you?"

"These are lies, all of them. When she returned to Sterling Hill from Birmingham, I tried to convince her to revoke the recordation of the deed, and she refused. Perhaps she didn't like my methods of persuasion. But I never drove her off the property violently. Hell, you know the truth—she's the one that was firing a pistol inside the mansion house."

"Attempted murder. If only you had succeeded, then we wouldn't be in this mess." I swallowed the last gulp of the bourbon. Reading over his shoulder, I saw it.

"A Petition for Divorce? Clay, you didn't. You wouldn't."

He didn't respond.

"Clay?"

"I thought I could use it to get her back in the state. You were in Memphis, I was alone at Sterling Hill. I couldn't exactly get her to revoke the recordation of the deed when she was in Alabama. I had to use something as bait."

"So you drew up papers to divorce me?"

"I didn't know it would all become public."

"Oh, God, Clay." I squeezed his shoulder, digging my nails into his flesh, and shoved him in frustration. "Right on the front page of the Sunday newspaper." I then became aware that I had been weeping.

"I thought it might work. I was drunk, and it was a drunkard's logic."

"That's your excuse for all of this."

"She says here she was offended by the offer. Sallie, you know as well as I do that she wrote me regularly asking me to divorce you, and I never agreed to do that. I never would. It was just a ruse. These charges are all lies. Can't you see that?"

Morning sunlight illuminated the silent room, bringing with it the heat of another summer day. I could hear the girls' muffled voices upstairs as they were getting dressed. Clay said nothing. He stared at the paper in front of him.

"What is it? There couldn't possibly be anything more." He didn't respond to me. "Clay, what is it?" I stood behind him and read. "Oh, God, no. You didn't. You wouldn't. Oh, God, no." The pain pierced me deep in my stomach when I saw those black words on the page.

"Sallie, truly, I never said this thing. Never. This is all from her."

I couldn't breathe, wouldn't remove my hands from my tear-stained face.

"Sallie, please, believe me."

Braying like a wounded animal, I had no control, no guiding principle of movement or feeling, only indiscriminate retching and sobbing. "What have I ever done to that damned woman to make her want to do this to me? Why is she taking it out on me? She says that *you* said it about me. You. In the newspaper."

"I am so sorry." Tentatively, he got up from his chair and walked towards me, cowering in the corner of the room.

"Don't." I pushed his outstretched hands away. "Don't." I could escape his embrace only by falling to my knees, the only posture appropriate for one so sickened with humiliation.

CHAPTER 33

May 1890

"Your Honor, the charge against Colonel King, as it has been filed, is 'assault with a deadly weapon,'" Mr. Weatherford explained, "which in Arkansas is a misdemeanor. And the indictment reads that the alleged assault occurred in May of 1889. It is now May of 1890. One full year later. The statute of limitations for a misdemeanor in Arkansas is only six months. The facts notwithstanding, this case should be debarred."

The distinguished W. G. Weatherford had fallen beneath himself, standing in front of this country judge and a jury of hayseeds in this godforsaken corner of a cotton patch called Marianna, Arkansas. Fortunately, Clay still had his wits about him enough to hire a reputable attorney, but I was certain the odds were against them both in this setting. Unlike the impressive courtrooms of Memphis and even Nashville with their marble and polished wood, this storefront hardly inspired confidence in the judicial process.

The judge was mystified. "Mr. Brundridge, what do you have to say to that?"

The prosecutor shuffled through the papers on the table before him with the assistance of his deputy, holding documents close to his bespectacled eyes and squinting so he could read them. "Your Honor, I believe there has been a mistake. The date of the assault was May of *1888*, not 1889. And the charge against Colonel King was supposed to be 'assault with intent to kill and murder,' which is the felony charge. The statute of limitations has not yet run for that. The other charge, 'assault with a deadly weapon,' that's a mistake."

The judge leaned back in his chair and stared at the lawyers in disbelief. "Mr. Brundridge, do you mean to tell me that the indictment includes not only the wrong date but also the wrong charge?"

"Yes, sir. It seems a clerical error has been made," Mr. Brundridge admitted, his cheeks aglow with embarrassment.

"Your Honor, we move that the charges be dismissed, because of the statute of limitations issue," Mr. Weatherford announced.

"But your Honor, the courtroom is full, we are ready for a trial, the original charges were simply miswritten..."

The judge frowned at them both. "I could rule on the statute of limitations issue, as a matter of law," he explained, "but because there is a discrepancy regarding the date of the alleged assault, which would be considered a matter of fact, well, we'll have to send the matter to the jury."

The lawyers argued at length over the proprieties of the law. The jury was dismissed so that they did not have to endure the proceedings, but the rest of us had no choice. After at least an hour had passed, Mrs. Pillow had had her fill, and in the middle of the argument, with a great distracting hubbub, she and Kizzie exited the courtroom.

There are no books of etiquette regarding how one behaves in court when one's husband has been charged with the assault of his mistress. The stupid fool—if only he had done it right and killed her, then there would be no ambiguity about this situation and I wouldn't be sitting here, behind his sweaty head in a courtroom full of Arkansas dolts. The humiliation was more oppressive than the heat. There I sat, Mrs. H. Clay King, with my dear son Haughton by my side, having to perform the masquerade that was my marriage in that public arena. Even the Memphis and Little Rock press were there.

Tired from the sitting and bored by all the legal wrangling, I was ready to ask Haughton to accompany me elsewhere, anywhere. I had to be there for our reputation's sake, but God knows, I didn't want to be. I was forced to sit there all during the whole terrible mess. I certainly hoped he appreciated my show of loyalty. I told him repeatedly that that woman could not be trusted, and now here was living proof that I was right. But even being right did not make up for the embarrassment of being entangled in this web.

On that Sunday morning when her damned cross-bill was published, the weeping and wailing of my daughters indelibly carved this whole tragedy into my memory, the pain he had caused us all. I shuddered. If only we had known it would be in print, on the front page in banner headlines, we might have had the chance to hide the newspaper, giving us time to explain, to warn them of the oncoming calumny. But how does one explain such dissolute behavior on the part of their own father? Shortly thereafter the Lee County prosecutor, this moron Brundridge, brought the matter of the assault before a grand jury. But I didn't hear about the indictment. Clay never even told me. We continued to live out our farce in Memphis. I did not know that Clay was being sought for trial in Arkansas, at least not yet. Not until I read in the paper that Mrs. Pillow and her daughter Laura had taken matters into their own hands.

Laura Shields made a trip over to Little Rock to see Governor Eagle, trying to persuade him to arrest Clay and extradite him to Arkansas for the trial. Her arrival there was treated as if the Queen herself were deigning to visit the backwoods. The *Arkansas Gazette* reported that "Mrs. Shields is no ordinary looking woman by any means; finely dressed, having the appearance of a refined, well-bred Southern lady, and exceptionally intelligent withal." "Refined" and "well-bred" my ass. Not reared by that she-devil. And it continued, "the little lady is making a brave fight for what she believes to be right." Utterly nauseated, I could stand it no longer. I did not want to read these sympathetic portrayals of this horrible clan. Before a formal extradition proceeding could occur, I persuaded him, nagged him, goaded him to face his accusers and return to Lee County.

Just as they were lighting the lamps in the courtroom in preparation for an evening of argument, Mrs. Pillow reappeared in the doorway of the courtroom. She had evidently been called back to testify. I was amused that she had been taken by surprise and looked so unkempt from the long day and the beginning of a trip back to Sterling Hill. For a woman so much in command of herself and those around her, she seemed confused and uncertain, touching her hair with her hand, straightening her skirt. Mr. Brundridge instructed her to get up on the witness stand.

"I have to do what?"

"You must give your testimony. Please come on up here so we can swear you in."

"But…but…I'm not ready."

"But it's time to begin."

"I need to talk to my lawyer first, Mr. Poston. He's right over there."

"Mrs. Pillow, you don't need a lawyer. This is the state's case."

"But don't I have a right to a lawyer? Don't I need to be prepared to answer? Mr. Poston?" She was on the verge of tears.

"Mrs. Pillow, I don't know enough of the facts of this case to act as your attorney," Mr. Poston replied, trying to whisper and still be heard. "You know I'm just here as an observer. I'm sorry."

The weeping began. Oh, God, that woman would flood the world with her tears to get what she wanted, not worrying that she was drowning the rest of us in the process. Mr. Poston's face softened when he saw her tears—he was obviously unfamiliar with her tricks. "Oh, oh, all right. Your Honor, may I have a moment to consult with my client?"

"We will not recess for it, but I will give you a couple of minutes. But don't belabor it," the judge warned.

Mr. Poston and Mrs. Pillow huddled over at the prosecutor's table for a minute. She was wiping away her tears and nodding her head. Mr. Poston helped her compose herself.

Mr. Poston nodded to Mr. Brundridge, who announced, "Your Honor, the witness is ready." I marveled that she could look so sincere placing her hand upon a Bible while intending to lie. She was calmer than she was when she was crying, but she still looked a little flustered.

Mr. Brundridge began the questioning. "Mrs. Pillow, please explain the events of the evening of May 12, 1888."

She took a deep breath and spoke deliberately. "Well, I was living in my home at Sterling Hill which I had bought from Colonel King…"

"Objection!" Mr. Weatherford shouted. "She is assuming facts not in evidence—her ownership of that property, which is in dispute in the courts."

"Sustained," the judge said. "Mrs. Pillow, we are only interested in the assault charges. Any references to the dispute over the ownership of the property are not to be included in your testimony." I'm glad they muzzled her with that lie.

"Yes, Your Honor."

"Now, Mrs. Pillow, tell me what happened that night," Mr. Brundridge asked again.

"I was living in the mansion house at Sterling Hill. Clay King was visiting me, and we got into an argument."

"And what was the subject of that argument?"

"Colonel King had sent me and my son-in-law a copy of a Petition for Divorce, showing that he intended to divorce Mrs. King. He wrote me a letter saying he had also sent the divorce petition to Judge Morgan in Memphis. He said his intention in doing so was to marry me. He was very much in love with me." My cheeks flushed with embarrassment.

The prosecutor looked down at his notes. "Did you and Colonel King have a romantic relationship prior to the time of his sending you the copy of the Petition for Divorce?"

She feigned astonishment. "Why, of course not! He's a married man. He was just a fool, a deluded old fool. He thought he had the strength of youth to per-suade me, but all he had was the *decrepitude* of age. I was not persuaded," she sneered. The gall of that woman, to insult my husband, her lover.

"Let's move on then. Tell us about the events of that night."

"He called me up to his room about nine o'clock." I heard a gasp in the courtroom. I took a deep breath.

"Are you in the habit of going to the rooms of male visitors in your home in the evening?"

"*No.*" She deserved that.

"Please continue."

"He called me to his room because he said he had some business he needed to discuss with me. And I wanted to express my outrage at the suggestion that I would marry him. So I went to his room, only to find him in a drunken rage, ranting, I could barely understand him. He was shaking a handful of papers at me. I did make out of his drunken babbling that he wanted me to sign some-thing. He wanted me to sign something, or he'd shoot me. And that's when I saw the gun, pointed right at me."

"Did he pull the trigger? Fire the gun?"

"No, but he threatened to."

"Were there any witnesses to this assault?"

"I believe my companion Kesiah also saw him with the gun."

"Now, Mrs. Pillow, had Colonel King ever said or done anything threaten-ing to you prior to these events?"

"Yes. I moved away from Sterling Hill after he threatened me with a pistol and said that if I ever gave him any trouble about who owned Sterling Hill, he would kill me."

Someone whispered, "I just can't believe it." And, of course, I doubted her, too. But I knew deep in my soul that it was possible.

"Objection, Your Honor. The witness is lying," Mr. Weatherford responded angrily.

"Who is lying and what is a lie are to be determined by the jury and the jury only, not by you or me. Overruled," the judge growled.

"Mrs. Pillow," Mr. Brundridge continued, "had you ever done anything regarding the ownership of the plantation which might constitute 'giving him trouble about who owned Sterling Hill'?"

"Of course not. I bought that land from him fair and square, and he knows it."

"Your Honor," Mr. Weatherford complained. The judge frowned but before he could say anything, the prosecutor concluded, "Thank you. Your witness."

Mr. Weatherford stood up thoughtfully and walked toward her. "Mrs. Pillow," he said genially, like the gentleman that he was, "Do you know the contents of the papers that the Colonel was 'shaking in your face', as you put it?"

"No, I do not. He was drunk and incomprehensible."

"Is it possible that these papers were somehow related to the deed to his property, a deed which was not meant to be recorded?"

"Objection!" Mr. Brundridge shouted with irritation.

"Sustained. Mr. Weatherford, once again we are not here to decide the dispute over the property," the judge said, impatiently.

"But Your Honor, this may help explain the extenuating circumstances…"

"The objection is sustained."

"All right, then." Mr. Weatherford walked over to the table where he'd been sitting and picked up a stack of envelopes. He held them out in front of him as he walked back over to her. "Mrs. Pillow, did you have a romantic relationship with Colonel King prior to this alleged incident?"

"I already answered that. I would never have had such a relationship and certainly not with this man." Her arrogance was offensive to me, and I hoped to the jury as well.

Mr. Weatherford held up the stack. "Do you recognize these?"

"I don't know what that is you're holding."

"Mrs. Pillow, these are letters from you to Colonel King, are they not?" Mr. Weatherford asked, holding them out to her.

She took them from his hand and inspected them. "Yes." She handed them back.

"And did you write these letters yourself?"

"I composed them and dictated them to my secretary, yes."

"Your Honor, the defense would like to submit these letters as evidence, defense exhibit number one," Mr. Weatherford said, showing the letters to the judge.

"The prosecution objects to this evidence on the basis of its relevance," Mr. Brundridge sighed.

"Mr. Weatherford, what bearing do these letters have on the case at hand?"

"The defense contends that Mrs. Pillow and Colonel King did in fact have a romantic relationship, and that these letters are proof of it. I intend to show that this witness is lying and that her testimony regarding the assault is therefore suspect. She was, in essence, spurned by Colonel King and is seeking revenge by bringing these false assault charges."

"Your Honor, these letters are presented only to embarrass Mrs. Pillow, and they have no relevance to the assault."

The judge studied the faces of both men. "The objection is overruled. Please continue."

"Now, Mrs. Pillow, would you please read this letter." Mr. Weatherford handed her the letter from the top of the stack.

"What?" Mrs. Pillow looked puzzled, but she took it.

"Read the letter out loud to the court."

"Your Honor, is this really necessary?" Mr. Brundridge whined.

"Mr. Weatherford?" the judge asked.

"If Mrs. Pillow does not wish to read her actual words to the court, then perhaps the prosecution would stipulate to the existence of a romantic relationship…"

Mr. Brundridge stood up. He looked at Mr. Weatherford and then at Mrs. Pillow and then at the judge and then back at Mr. Weatherford, thoroughly confused. He approached Mrs. Pillow and whispered something. She closed her eyes and nodded her head.

"So stipulated," Mr. Brundridge muttered as he shuffled back to his seat.

Mr. Weatherford took a deep breath. "Mrs. Pillow, is it true that in your letters to Colonel King you regularly asked him to divorce his wife and marry you?"

"Objection," Mr. Brundridge snapped.

"Your Honor, these letters have been admitted as evidence. The stipulation that there was a romantic relationship between them should not preclude my asking questions about their general content."

The judge shook his head. "Go ahead. But tread lightly."

"Did you write to him asking him to divorce his wife?" Mr. Weatherford held the stack of letters in front of her, as if he was threatening to read all the personal details in them if she didn't tell the truth.

"Yes," she spit out angrily.

"And did you write to him asking him to marry you?"

"Yes."

Mr. Weatherford started to walk away, when he seemed to think of something and turned back to face her. "What is the postmark on the letter you're holding?"

"October 25, 1888."

"And the alleged assault occurred in May of 1888? Is that correct?"

"Yes."

"Is it possible that this is one of the letters in which you asked him to marry you?"

"Hmmph." She looked to each side of her as if expecting someone to stop his barrage of questions, but found no one. "I suppose."

"So it is possible that you wrote asking him to marry you *after* he allegedly assaulted you with a pistol?"

She glared at him angrily. "I was not behaving rationally, that's why I wrote those letters. His threats and that ridiculous divorce petition and the lawsuit that he filed, they caused me to become mentally unbalanced, at least temporarily."

Mr. Weatherford paused for a minute to look at his notes. "Now, Mrs. Pillow, where were you during the month of February 1889?"

"I'm afraid I don't remember. I'd have to think about it."

"Mrs. Pillow, were you staying in the Hotel St. Benedict in Chicago at that time?"

"Why, yes. That's it. I was in Chicago on business," she replied nervously.

"Well, that's a question ripe for the asking..." Mr. Weatherford said under his breath, even though everybody could still hear it. I heard a little snickering. Mrs. Pillow blushed.

The judge frowned. "Mr. Weatherford...?"

"But I won't venture down that path. Now, Mrs. Pillow, did you happen to see Colonel King while you were in Chicago 'on business'?"

She held up her head proudly and tried to sound innocent. "Why, no, I don't recall that I did."

With the beginning of a smile, Mr. Weatherford asked, "Isn't it true, Mrs. Pillow, that Colonel King was also staying in the Hotel St. Benedict in Chicago during the month of February 1889?"

She spoke calmly, but her eyes were livid. "Yes, now that I think about it, he was. I do remember seeing him."

"And isn't it true that you followed him to Chicago and stayed in the same apartment with him for a month, in the hopes that you could persuade him to marry you?"

She was already standing up, ready to explode even before he finished asking the question. "He invited me to Chicago. He said he wanted to straighten out the dispute over the property. I told you I was not behaving rationally…"

Mr. Weatherford chuckled loud enough for me to hear. Then everybody heard the rest.

"I am the widow of General Gideon Pillow! You have no right to treat me with such disrespect!" She was red-faced and howling, a hellhound in lace and ribbons.

"Mrs. Pillow, sit down," the judge ordered her. She looked like she was about ready to strike the judge, but she didn't. She sat back down with thump. Then she started to sniffle, and pulled out her handkerchief and dabbed at her eyes. And then she started to bawl.

Mr. Weatherford was perturbed. I suppose he didn't want to look as if he were being harsh to a widow. He stood in the front of the courtroom for a minute, eyeing Mrs. Pillow skeptically. Then through her crying, I heard him say to the judge, "No further questions."

I was relieved but surprised. I had assumed Mrs. Pillow was going to be on the witness stand into the evening. When the judge announced that the court would adjourn for the evening, she remained in that same chair, finishing her sobbing, like the last remnants of distant thunder after the biggest part of the storm has already passed.

CHAPTER 34

❀

"The state calls Miss Kesiah Mae Biscoe."

I had only just got situated in the courtroom on that second day of the assault trial, and right away they were calling my name. I didn't know what for. I was afraid I might be in trouble. I looked up not knowing what to do, when Mr. Brundridge smiled and signaled to me that I should come on down to the front. So I stood up and walked by all those people, the lawyers, and the judge, and all those people just looking at me.

"Do you swear to tell the truth, the whole truth and nothing but the truth, so help you God?" They made me put my hand on the Good Book and make a swear. I was so scared, I just whispered, "Uh huh."

The prosecutor showed me the seat, and I sat down in that same wooden chair that Miss Marie had sat in the night before. The dark courtroom was brightened by the pale morning sun, casting shadows my direction and shining in my eyes.

"Now, Miss Biscoe, were you on the plantation known as Sterling Hill the night of May 12, 1888?"

Even though I'd been called "Miss Biscoe" from time to time in my life, I hadn't ever heard it sound so important. "Yes sir."

"And were you ever in the mansion house on that property during that evening?"

"Yes sir."

The prosecutor stared at me, and I looked at the floor. I didn't like the place I was at, not at all, having to tell the truth up here because I made a swear on the Good Book and being right up there so Miss Marie and everybody else could hear me.

"Well?"

"Sir?" I felt like I was going to cry.

"*When* were you in the mansion house that night?"

I took a deep breath. "Miss Marie and I had supper there together, before the Colonel got back from Memphis."

"Was that the only time?"

"And then when I came on back in, later on."

"Came on back in from where?"

I blushed. I didn't want to tell my private business to all those folks, but I reckon I didn't have a choice. "Outside."

The prosecutor looked frustrated with me. "Why were you outside? Were you with someone? Elaborate, *please*."

I looked down at my lap and answered, "Mr. Worley and I had been sitting together on the porch of the guest house, and before it got too late, he walked me back over to the mansion house where I was staying." Maybe that's what he wanted me to say.

"And what happened once you got back inside the mansion house?" He had turned around to face the crowd, and I decided I liked him a whole lot better that way.

"I heard an argument upstairs. I went into the dining room to see if I could hear what was going on."

He turned around again and looked at me seriously. "Did you see or hear anything?"

"Yessir. I heard them arguing, and then I heard footsteps running down the stairs and saw Miss Marie running out the front door."

"Is that all?"

"No sir."

He wrinkled up his forehead. I knew he was getting put out with me. "Miss Biscoe, did you hear them say anything? Anything of any importance?"

"Yessir. I heard the Colonel say 'Sign it' a couple of times and I heard some cussin'." I didn't want to tell him that, because I didn't want to get the Colonel in trouble, what with him being so nice to me for so long. But I'd swore on the Good Book. I didn't have any choice but to tell the truth.

"And did you ever actually see Colonel King upstairs that night?"

"Yessir. I saw the Colonel walk out into the upstairs hall with a gun in his hand."

I heard a gasp out in the courtroom somewhere. The whole crowd was mumbling. Mr. Brundridge looked satisfied, and the judge banged his hammer. "Mr. Weatherford, your witness."

Mr. Weatherford stood up and smiled at me. "Miss Biscoe, how long have you worked for Mrs. Pillow?"

"Well, I've been with her my whole life. I reckon I started doing work when I was, oh, I don't know, five or six."

"And how do you consider Mrs. Pillow? A friend? An employer?"

"Yes sir. Both of those. And family too, I reckon."

"So would it be fair to say that you feel a fair amount of loyalty towards her?"

I wasn't sure what he was getting at, but I said, "Yes," anyway. He turned and smiled at the jury.

"Miss Biscoe, do you remember writing the letters that I showed to Mrs. Pillow last night?"

I liked Mr. Weatherford better than Mr. Brundridge. He seemed a lot more gentlemanly. "I don't know if I remember any of them in particular. They were all an awful lot alike."

"All?" he asked. "How many were there in all, approximately?"

"I don't know for sure, but I reckon I wrote about eleven or twelve for her." I was just guessing, trying to be honest.

"And do you remember what she said in these letters that she dictated to you?"

"Objection!" Mr. Brundridge hollered.

"Sustained. Mr. Weatherford, we went over this last night," the judge reminded him.

"Did you accompany Mrs. Pillow to Chicago in February of 1889?"

"Yes sir. I went with her."

"And what hotel did the two of you stay in?"

"Just like you said, the Hotel St. Benedict." This was getting a whole lot easier.

"And is it true that you and Mrs. Pillow stayed in the apartment that belonged to Colonel King with the colonel himself during that month?"

I looked at my lap. I knew she wasn't going to like this. "Yessir."

"So in February of 1889, nine months after the alleged assault, Mrs. Pillow spent a month in Chicago in the same apartment with Colonel King?"

"Yessir," I said quietly. I was so sorry I had to say that, but I didn't have any other choice. And I didn't dare look at Miss Marie.

"Thank you. I have no further questions for this witness," Mr. Weatherford announced.

"Then the witness may step down," the judge ordered.

I was mighty glad that was over. I was so afraid of what Miss Marie would say or do to me. But when I walked back to where I had been sitting, right next to her, she didn't look at me at all. I was glad of it, too.

"The prosecution rests, Your Honor," Mr. Brundridge said.

The judge pulled out his watch and studied it. "Is the defense ready to proceed?"

Mr. Weatherford replied, "Yes, Your Honor. And we won't take long." I think he realized that the judge didn't want to take too long with the whole thing. I didn't blame him one bit. "The defense calls Colonel Henry Clay King."

The Colonel walked up to the stand, looking important and dignified, not at all like he looked that night he was drunk and pointing that gun at Miss Marie. They swore him in.

"Now, Colonel King," Mr. Weatherford started. "Why don't you tell us about the events of the evening of May 12, 1888."

The Colonel cleared his throat and started. "Mrs. Pillow had been living on my plantation in the role of housekeeper. My wife and I agreed that would be a useful thing to do, as Mrs. Pillow was destitute at the time we hired her."

"Objection. What is the relevance of this background information?" Mr. Brundridge wanted to know.

"Overruled. I will allow some latitude."

The prosecutor sat back down, and the Colonel continued. "At some point, Mrs. Pillow fell passionately in love with me and begged me to marry her. It was some delusion on her part. I believe all she wanted was my money, as was indicated by many of her actions."

"Your Honor…" Mr. Brundridge started to stand up.

"Sit down, Mr. Brundridge," the judge told him.

Mr. Weatherford asked, "And under what circumstances did Mrs. Pillow and her family leave Sterling Hill?"

"Her daughter insisted that they leave my land, and move to Birmingham to live with her."

"Did you threaten her with violence to cause her to move away?"

"No. The night before she and her family left, voluntarily, I did take out my pistol to show to her son-in-law, and I remember tripping on the stairs with the gun in my hand. But I did not threaten anyone."

"And what happened once she and her family moved to Birmingham?"

"That's when she began writing to me, pleading that I divorce my dear wife and marry her."

"Are these the letters she wrote to you?" Mr. Weatherford wanted to know, waving the stack of letters in the air.

"Yes, they are."

Miss Marie closed her eyes tight and shuddered. Those letters would have been awfully embarrassing if they had been read out loud in front of everybody. I wondered what all those jury folks thought of this mess, these two fine looking people, who didn't act real fine at all, least not to each other.

"Colonel King, did you invite Mrs. Pillow to Chicago to discuss a resolution to the property dispute?"

"I did not invite her."

"So when she loudly proclaimed to the courtroom last night that you had invited her, she was lying?"

"Yes."

Mr. Weatherford asked about the Petition for Divorce, but the Colonel lied about that. He said he never did send such a thing. And then the Colonel told about that night with the gun, and he lied again. He said him and Miss Marie never had so much as a quarrel. Now, I knew that wasn't the truth, because I heard all the yelling. And I heard him say he would kill her. And I saw him with the gun. I reckon everybody doesn't realize how important it is to tell the truth once you make a swear on the Good Book. At least, didn't seem like the Colonel and Miss Marie did.

When Mr. Weatherford said he was finished, the prosecutor said he had just a few more questions. He walked over to the Colonel and leaned over him. "Now, Colonel King, these letters that you presented to the judge. Are these all the letters you received?"

"I don't know. Probably."

"Are all the pages to all the letters contained in that stack?"

"I don't know. I don't remember separating them."

"Are all the pages to all the letters in the same pristine condition in which you received them?"

The Colonel looked confused. "'Pristine'?"

"Yes, 'pristine.' Are they in the same condition in which you received them?"

"Well, no. I broke the seals on the envelopes. I unfolded the papers. Is that what you mean?"

"Is it possible that any of these letters has been smudged or slightly torn?"

"Of course, but only slightly, if at all."

"So it is possible, then, that the letters you presented to the court may have been missing pages, may have words smudged, and may have been damaged in some way?"

"You are misstating my testimony," the Colonel warned.

"Is it possible that the letters you presented to the court are not in the same condition in which you received them?"

The Colonel sighed. "Yes, I suppose that's possible. But for all practical purposes…"

"So your answer is yes," Mr. Brundridge interrupted, looking down at an important looking paper he was holding. "Now, Colonel King, about this divorce mentioned earlier. Are you familiar with this document?" And Mr. Brundridge dangled the paper in front of the Colonel's face.

Colonel King took it from him and read over it, and placed it face down on his lap. "Yes."

"And what is this document?"

"It is a petition for divorce."

"Did you write this?"

"Yes."

"And whose names are included—which persons are named as the ones being divorced?"

"My wife and I."

"Colonel King, did you send this Petition for Divorce to Mrs. Pillow in Birmingham and to Judge R. J. Morgan in Memphis?'

"Yes."

"And so you were lying when you said there had been no petition for divorce sent to Mrs. Pillow in Birmingham, the paper she wanted to confront you about in your bedroom that night?"

"I was drunk when I wrote up that petition. I didn't want anyone to misconstrue my business relationship with Mrs. Pillow, and I did not want to marry her except that she insisted it was essential for her to maintain her reputation. I was drunk when I wrote that document." The Colonel tripped over his words, trying to explain, but not making a whole lot of sense.

"And were you drunk when you drew the pistol on Mrs. Pillow?"

"Yes. I mean, no! I never drew a pistol on Mrs. Pillow!"

"Objection, Your Honor, the prosecutor is badgering the witness!" Mr. Weatherford hollered.

"Sustained." The judge grumbled.

"No further questions," Mr. Brundridge said, smiling.

❦   ❦   ❦

Fifteen minutes after the judge sent the jury out to make its decision, the jury had made up their mind. We'd barely got outside under the shade tree before somebody came running outside telling us we needed to go back in. I didn't have any idea a trial could be over that quick.

"Have you reached a verdict?" the judge asked the jury when everybody got back into their seats. He looked a little surprised, too, that the whole thing was about to be over.

"Yeah, your honor, we did." A cock-eyed farmer stood up.

"Well, go ahead and say it."

"We, the jury, find the case debarred by the statute of limitations and the defendant, not guilty."

Seemed like the whole audience sighed. I understood the part about him being not guilty, but not the other. I looked at Mr. Poston to see if he was smiling, but he wasn't. Neither was Miss Marie. But lots of folks in the courtroom seemed real relieved, especially the Colonel and Miss Sallie.

❦   ❦   ❦

I had to be careful reading the newspapers to Miss Marie. She was pretty upset about how those reporters described her, and how they said the Colonel had been acquitted. And the jury didn't like it, neither, because they wrote a letter to the newspaper:

> *In justice to Mrs. Pillow, and our attention having been drawn to the article in the Evening Democrat, which says that the verdict of not guilty was antici-pated, we wish to state that the case was decided by us on the bar of limitations alone. If it had been tried on facts we, as members of that jury, would have given to H. C. King the uttermost penalty of the law.*
>
> *R. P. Crittenden,*
> *W. H. Hickers,*
> *J. H. Story,*
> *J. M. F. Branch,*
> *H. Bickerstaff,*
> *Wm. Walton,*
> *Ben Williams*

I knew Miss Marie would feel better about it all, having the jury on her side, even if they didn't find the Colonel guilty. That jury did the right thing according to the law, but not according to what really happened. That's something I reckon I'll never understand. The law's a funny thing, especially when it gets in the way of the truth.

CHAPTER 35

"But there have to be witnesses. That way the judges can see for themselves what kind of liars they are." My relief over the disposition of the assault trial did not last, for on its heels came the hearing to clear the title to Sterling Hill. Once again I sat in Weatherford's office preparing my case, only blocks from my former office where I had practiced law, back when clients still entrusted me with their legal matters. All that had ended, of course, with Mary Eliza's public assaults against me.

"Clay, you know that in a hearing of this nature, there are only depositions, no witnesses, at most an oral argument from the two sides."

"But those depositions leave wide open the possibility for her to manipulate the deponents. She's already persuaded her attorneys to conduct them at Sterling Hill. *At my home.* She's got authority over everyone they could possibly call—her sister, her children, Kizzie. And all of *my* servants and field hands. She will tell them precisely what to say, regardless of whether it's true, whatever works to her best advantage, and they will have no choice but to follow her instructions."

"I know, you're right, but I'll be there. I may be able to prevent some of the abuses you anticipate. And whatever lies make their way into the depositions will be seen for what they are by the judges. You have to believe that." Weatherford did his best to reassure me, but sitting comfortably behind his desk, lighting his pipe, he had no idea of the frustration I was facing.

"Well, once the depositions start, I'll do my best not to speak up. I'll let you take care of it all."

"You can't be at the depositions. I thought you understood that."

"Of course I'll attend the depositions. They'll be held at my own farm, for God's sake. I want to do what I can to insure they are conducted properly."

"Clay, you can't do that. For your own safety, you can't ignore the death threat. The assassins may be expecting you to be in Arkansas for the depositions."

"You mean John Shields."

"There is no reason to believe that John Shields has anything to do with this. That threat could have come from almost anybody."

"I suppose you're right." I slouched further in my chair. "The press has so demonized me, the evil, lecherous older man taking advantage of the poor widow of a popular general. I'm a veritable lurking menace, based on what the newspapers say."

"She certainly seems to thrive on that depiction."

"If it weren't for the allegations against Sallie, no one would be interested in the damned newspaper articles. This could go along silently and with dignity, like most civil cases." I searched in my pocket for a cigar.

"I'm afraid it's much more than that. You have sued a woman. That doesn't happen every day in our courts. And she happens to be a widow. The widow of a local hero. And she has counter-sued. This whole situation is a novelty, Clay, you've got to understand that."

"And so you would have me sit back and let her steal my property from me?"

"Of course not. But you must have known what you were up against from the beginning. I know part of the strategy was to pressure Mrs. Pillow through a public airing of her actions. I had no idea she would take the whole thing so much further."

"Aren't you going to ask for a retraction from the newspapers?" Remembering the lies those rags published infuriated me. Unsettled, annoyed, I paced the perimeter of his office. "They've ignored my letters, won't even print them, but they won't ignore you. Your reputation hasn't been ruined," I reminded him, pointing my unlit cigar for emphasis. "It's Poston that's behind it all, I'm convinced of it. He's feeding them these stories, leading those editors by the nose to the foulest lies he can concoct. Hell, all he has to do is take the elevator down to the ground floor of his own building and present to the editors whatever it is he wants them to say."

"I think the best course of action is to do nothing. Don't make an issue of the negative publicity. You'll only incite them to write with more enthusiasm.

Let the trials play themselves out. Vindication in the court of law will go a long way toward vindicating you in the eyes of the public."

Out the open window, the sing-song cries of a newsboy filled the air. "Get your afternoon edition right here, mister. The King-Pillow suit is set to be tried in July. A colonel sues a poor widow woman for her land. All the personal details you want to read. Get your afternoon edition…"

Flakes of tobacco from my broken cigar fell onto the wooden floor. Unclenching my fist, I let the rest fall as well.

CHAPTER 36

June 1890

"Do you swear to tell the truth, the whole truth, and nothing but the truth, so help you God?"

"I do."

"Please state your name for the record."

"Elizabeth Dickson."

The lawyers had turned the dining room from the main party room of the plantation into a law office, with Mr. Poston and Colonel Taliaferro on one side of the table and Mr. Weatherford and Judge Brown, the Colonel's lawyers, on the other side. After all the eating and drinking they'd done together at Sterling Hill during those two weeks, it seemed kind of silly to have them dividing up, taking sides in the lawsuit, since the Colonel's whisky had made them all so friendly with each other. Mr. Poston had a taste for drinking, so he just helped himself, and he kept helping himself, the whole time they were taking depositions. Miss Marie's other lawyer was Colonel Taliaferro from Birmingham, who knew General Pillow and Colonel King from fighting in the War. He started out quiet and gentlemanly, but after he got into the Colonel's whisky, why, he got louder and funnier, telling some of the most awful stories, ones I'd laugh at but never repeat. Even the Colonel's lawyers, Mr. Weatherford and Judge Brown, enjoyed the Colonel's whisky. Ginny had done it up big with her cooking—sugar baked ham, crusty fried chicken, field peas, cornbread dripping with fresh butter—and that was fine with me. I do believe those depositions were the biggest party I'd ever been to.

Mr. Pickle was a court reporter who'd come down from Memphis to join in the festivities, and he knew how to write everything down in little squiggles he called "shorthand." He sat right down there on the far end of the table next to whoever was going to be answering the questions. With the lawyers on each side of the table, Miss Marie and I sat together at the other end, situated just so Miss Marie could have a straight shot of looking at whoever was answering. She wanted me sitting right there with her, just in case she needed anything, and told me to not to say nothing.

Now, Miss Marie had another lawyer, Mr. Chambers, who handled the Arkansas part of the case. He hadn't come down for the two weeks of partying, and he didn't sit at the table with the other lawyers, neither, but in a corner all by himself, smoking his pipe. He was a courtly little fat man who was always hidden in a haze of that sweet smelling pipe smoke, almost sickly sweet. Sometimes he'd get up to whisper in Mr. Poston's ear, that white smoke following along with him, but he didn't ask any of the questions.

"And what is your relationship to Mrs. Mary Eliza Pillow?" Mr. Weatherford asked Miss Elizabeth, the first witness to be deposed.

"She's my sister."

"Would you please recount for the record the events of May 5, 1888?"

"Yes, sir. Let's see," she responded nervously. "I traveled from Birmingham with Kizzie, Mary Eliza's companion, and we were picked up at the Marianna train station by Mr. Worley. It was a drizzly day, as I recall, and I hadn't brought my wrap, so I was getting a bit chilly…"

"Miss Dickson," Judge Brown interrupted grumpily, "we don't have all day, and we've got lots of witnesses to depose. Please just get to the part about your interaction with Colonel King."

Miss Elizabeth scowled at him. She wasn't accustomed to rude treatment from lawyers, or from anybody, for that matter. "The Colonel and I sat right over there in the parlor, and Kizzie was there, too. I asked him for $10,000 for a quit claim to the property." If she could've stuck her tongue out at that man, I believe she would have.

"Now, Miss Dickson, do you know what a quit claim is?" Mr. Weatherford asked.

"Mary Eliza explained it to me. She said that it was a good way for the Colonel to pay her what he owed her."

"What he owed her?"

"Yes. He owed her $10,000. That's what she told me."

"So as you understood it, the quit claim releasing her alleged interest in the property was in repayment of a $10,000 debt?" Judge Brown asked.

"I think so."

Miss Elizabeth glanced over uncertainly at Miss Marie, who chimed in, "Yes, I lent him $10,000. Back in '84 or '85."

"Mrs. Pillow, you are not yet being deposed. Let us find out what your sister knows," Mr. Weatherford said in a most kindly way. "And what did the Colonel say when you requested the money?"

"Oh, what did he say?" She looked at Miss Marie and shrugged. Miss Marie silently mouthed some words, and Miss Elizabeth brightened up. "He, uh, he pulled a gun on me, and threatened to shoot me and Mary Eliza and anybody else if we, uh, gave him a hard time about who owned the property." She smiled.

Miss Marie crossed her arms and leaned back in her chair, satisfied.

"You mean when you asked him for the quit claim, he threatened you with a gun?" Judge Brown repeated her words as if to make sure she meant what she said.

"Uh, yes, he threatened me with a gun. Yes, that's what he did. And Mary Eliza too, right before she left for Birmingham. And you know about the attempted murder when she came back. Why, Colonel King is a violent man."

They asked her a few more questions, but I was just shaking my head. Colonel King didn't have a gun that day, least not one that I could see. And I knew he never pointed one at us. Or that night before we left, neither. All he did that time was to fall down the stairs. The only time I believe he tried to shoot anybody was that night up in their bedroom, but the court had already decided about that.

Next it was Giddy's turn. Giddy was just about 13 by then, so they took it pretty easy on him.

"Now, Gideon, how long have you known Colonel King?"

"We moved here when I was eight, so I guess about five years."

"And how did you and Colonel King get along?"

"I don't know, fine, I reckon. But if I saw him right now, I'd kill him."

All the lawyers stopped what they were doing when they heard those words from the little boy's mouth. She'd poisoned that child's mind. Colonel King had always been good to Giddy, always. He gave him toys at Christmas, taught him how to ride a horse proper, even gave him a hunting rifle one time. Colonel King treated little Giddy like his own son. And there was Giddy, saying he wanted to kill him.

"All right, then. Gideon, are you aware that Colonel King gave your mother a deed to this property?"

"Yessir, he did. I saw it."

"And are you aware that your mother paid anything for this property?"

"Yessir, she bought and paid for Sterling Hill." He looked at his mother, and she smiled at him.

"And do you know how much she paid for the property?"

"Yessir. She lent him $10,000, and when he didn't pay her back, she said she'd take the land instead."

Mr. Weatherford stared at the boy. Then he looked down at Miss Marie. Then he looked back at Giddy. "Mr. Poston, I would respectfully request that Mrs. Pillow leave the room during her son's deposition."

"Why?" Mr. Poston asked suspiciously.

"Because, if you pardon my saying so, the young man seems to have been coached."

"That's ridiculous," Miss Marie responded.

"Mr. Poston, I'm not aware of many thirteen year old boys who are knowledgeable about the details of their mothers' financial dealings."

"Well, you're looking at one now," Mr. Poston replied.

Mr. Weatherford and Judge Brown whispered to each other. Shaking his head in frustration, Mr. Weatherford finally continued, "Gideon, did you see Colonel King give your mother a deed to this property?"

"Yessir. I did." He seemed glad to be answering all their questions without having any trouble remembering what he was supposed to say.

"Was that the first deed he gave her or the second?" Judge Brown asked.

"I saw him give her both deeds. I saw him give her the one he burned up, and then I saw him give her another one."

They asked him question after question, and Giddy never hesitated. He said exactly what he was supposed to. His mama had prepared him well.

Then it was Annie's turn. She sat right down there at the end of the table, the same place that Miss Elizabeth and Giddy had sat. Yes, her mama lent the Colonel $10,000. Yes, she saw the Colonel give her the deed. Yes, he was a violent man. Knowing her like I did, I figured she didn't want to be lying. She never looked up at the lawyers, and never looked at her mama, neither.

❦   ❦   ❦

"Gentleman, let's get right down to business. I think the first witness to be deposed today should be Malcolm Davis."

We had only just cleared the breakfast dishes from the table, and the lawyers hadn't even sat down to start another day of deposing before Miss Marie made her announcement. They shuffled through their papers in a flurry. Finally, Mr. Weatherford asked, "Who is Malcolm Davis?"

"Why, he's the Negro man that Sallie King had relations with—the one described in the cross-bill."

"Mrs. Pillow." Colonel Taliaferro hesitated. "Mrs. Pillow, does he know anything pertinent to the ownership of this land?"

"Of course not. He's just a house servant. Occasionally he works out in the yard, if he can get himself out of bed in the morning."

Mr. Poston adjusted himself in his chair. "Mrs. Pillow, if he knows nothing about the ownership of Sterling Hill, then there is no point in deposing him. Did he see you with a deed? Was he a confidante of Colonel King?"

"Certainly not. But he was included in the cross-bill, and that makes him 'pertinent.'" Her cheeks were turning red. She didn't like folks telling her she couldn't have things her way.

"But if we submit this deposition to the court, and it contains nothing pertinent to the ownership issue, or to the deed, or the will, then it will be inadmissible."

"Then why could we mention that whole issue in the cross-bill if we can't use it in court?" Her shrill voice didn't do much to hide her anger.

"Now, Mrs. Pillow, calm yourself down. You're right, of course, that the 'criminal intercourse' charged by Colonel King was part of the cross-filing, but as you may recall at the time Colonel Taliaferro and I did not think it was relevant to the property dispute, it being such an ancillary issue—the purported grounds for divorce," Mr. Poston explained.

"That was completely Judge Chambers' doing, in representing the Arkansas aspect of this case," Colonel Taliaferro continued. "I just don't think…"

"That's all just lawyerly double talk. He must be deposed. Now," she demanded angrily. "We must get all the necessary information for all the aspects of the case. Whether or not the judge will accept the deposition shouldn't determine whether or not you will take the deposition."

"Gentlemen," Mr. Chambers said quietly, in his husky voice, the white smoke around him unsettled by his movements. "Why don't you let me handle this? If the 'criminal intercourse' charge was the reason given for the divorce, and the divorce petition is central to Mrs. Pillow's explanation of the events, then it would seem that a deposition of Mr. Davis would be in order."

Everyone was silent. I didn't know that lawyers on the same side of a case could disagree about something so important. And I didn't know that it was Mr. Chambers, and not Mr. Poston, who was behind that story about Miss Sallie and Malcolm. Of course, that didn't keep Mr. Poston from talking about it as much as he could.

"Kizzie, run get Malcolm, right away."

Kicking the dust in front of me as I reluctantly walked down toward the quarters, I wondered why she was being so hateful toward Malcolm. The grass around the bell post had grown too tall, and a vine had wrapped itself around it snakelike, stretching its shoots upward like tiny hissing tongues. The deep, mournful clang of that old bell had stopped the singing from down at the quarters just days before the lawyers had arrived, the dark silent people gathering to hear her words. Looking from face to face, smiling her terrible smile, she threatened them. "The lawyers are coming to ask questions," she said, "and you must oblige them. You must say only what I tell you to say." Coming from her, the words carried a heavy burden. "This is a good place to live, and there will always be plenty here for you and your families." But the promises of a good life were tainted with an unspoken threat. "Colonel King has given me Sterling Hill. He hasn't been back in months, has he?" No one listening knew the truth of it all, but must have felt it in their bones. Must have known that wasn't right. "My husband General Pillow was a hero to people here, people in Memphis. Everyone knows who I am." Disobedience would surely bring trouble to the people who spoke for themselves and not for her. "I will make you leave." And run away, through the lands belonging to all the people that she knew. "I will put out the word that any no account niggers who say they are from Sterling Hill are thieves and drunkards and not to be trusted. You won't find any work anywhere in Arkansas or anywhere in Tennessee. You might even find a lot worse." Even other colored folks wouldn't take in a wandering stranger, once the word got out. There was no choice. "You can stay if you obey me, or you can find yourselves wandering in the woods alone." Someone in the circle cleared his throat but did not speak. My toe swiveled in the dust, the same dust I kicked in a cloud before me, on my way to find Malcolm, recalling that he had to be obedient, too.

By the time Malcolm and I walked into the dining room together, Mr. Chambers had moved out of his corner and was sitting at the table beside Mr. Poston. He was puffing on that pipe, the thick cloud of white smoke hovering over the table, mingling with the blue gray clouds from Mr. Poston's cigar. The lawyers made Malcolm sit down at the end of the table to be questioned. They made him swear on the Good Book, and then Mr. Chambers began.

"Do you know Mrs. Sallie King?" he asked softly, as he wrote notes on a pad.

"Yessir. That's Miss Sallie. She used to live here."

"And what was your relationship to Mrs. King?"

"She's the lady of Sterling Hill. Well, she used to be."

Miss Marie shifted her chair noisily.

"And what does that mean regarding your job: is she your employer?" The words in the question seemed plain enough, but there was something ugly, something awful in those questions.

"Yessir, she was—is—Colonel King's wife, and he's my employer."

Miss Marie cleared her throat.

"Do you now or have you ever known Mrs. King in a more personal capacity?" Mr. Chambers asked, following the smoke with his eyes, looking less interested in Malcolm than in the wafting haze between them.

Malcolm lowered his head. "No, sir. I ain't never knowed her personally."

"Malcolm," Miss Marie barked. He must have seen the fire in her eyes, remembering what she said to all the folks in the yard.

"Mrs. Pillow," Colonel Taliaferro said politely, "you must not interrupt the deposition."

She frowned at him. The other lawyers were busy looking at their papers, and the court reporter was scribbling. Nobody in that room wanted nothing to do with this. Nobody except Miss Marie and Mr. Chambers.

"Did you ever have relations with Mrs. King?"

"Naw, sir! Naw, indeed! I wouldn't never do sech a thing!" Malcolm stood up and spoke angrily. "Why do you say sech a thing? That ain't true, no sir."

Mr. Chambers glanced up from his papers and said calmly, "Now, boy, you better just settle yourself down. You're not going to make it any easier on yourself."

By this time, Miss Marie's narrowed eyes were fixed on poor Malcolm, and he must have felt it, because he sat back down and stared at the table. He didn't want to look her in the eyes, I could just tell. Nobody wants to look at her eyes when they're fiery like that. I knew how he must have felt, scared and angry. And stuck. Because I felt that way. I didn't want to make no swear on the Good Book and then be made to lie. I knew him well enough to know he wanted to tell the truth. Least that's what I would have done. He sighed sadly.

"Now, Malcolm, did you ever have relations with Mrs. King?"

He didn't say nothing.

"Was that a 'yes' or a 'no'?" the court reporter asked, even though he was sitting right next to Malcolm.

"That was a yes," Miss Marie replied firmly. "How many times, Malcolm?"

Malcolm shook his head slowly, from side to side.

"How many times?"

Their eyes met, and he did not look away.

"Mrs. Pillow, is this really necessary?" Colonel Taliaferro asked.

She answered her own question, their eyes still locked. "He and Mrs. King were together at least a dozen times since I came on the property."

"Is that true, Malcolm?" Mr. Poston asked.

He looked around at the lawyers and at Miss Marie and at me, and just kept on shaking his head. Then he stood up slowly, simmering with anger, and walked out the door into the kitchen. We heard the outside door slam.

"We are not yet finished!" Miss Marie cried out, getting up from her chair.

"We've got all we need from him," Mr. Poston said, sullenly. "Let us move on."

Malcolm hadn't said a thing, not one thing. It was Miss Marie answering the questions. I wondered if the lawyers would know the difference when they read their notes.

That was the last we ever saw of Malcolm. Seemed like right after that deposition, he just up and went. Nobody knew where to. I like to imagine that maybe he made his way up to Chicago or St. Louis or some place exciting where a colored man stood a chance of getting a good job and meeting a pretty colored lady. Dear Malcolm. Could be some of what they said about him was true. Could be.

CHAPTER 37

"Girl, bring in some of that whisky," Mr. Poston yelled toward the kitchen after Malcolm stormed out. "It's going to be a long day."

Ginny brought the whisky from the cabinet, and every one of those lawyers poured themselves some, even though it hadn't been very long since breakfast. Since Ginny was already in there, they made her swear and then sat her down so they could see what she knew.

"And did you witness Colonel King giving Mrs. Pillow the deed to Sterling Hill?"

"No, sir, but I heard 'em talkin' 'bout it."

"And do you remember what they said?" That was a stupid question, I thought. Ginny never missed anything that was said or done in that house.

"Course I 'member. He said he was savin' Miss Marie from bein' poor. He said when he died, her and her young'uns would git the farm. That's what he said. I heard him."

"'Being poor'? Were you under the impression that Mrs. Pillow was poor at the time that she came to Sterling Hill?" Mr. Weatherford asked.

Ginny wrapped her big arms across her bosom, as if by hugging herself tight enough, she could keep the wrong answers from coming out. Her frightened eyes seemed to be asking me for help, but I was too scared to do anything but listen.

"Naw, sir. She wasn't poor. No, I don't believe she ever was. She was a real fine lady."

"But you said he gave her the deed to Sterling Hill to keep her from being poor."

"I don't know rightly what he said. I just know he wanted to take care of her."

The lawyers whispered together. "And did you ever see him hand the deed over to Mrs. Pillow?"

"Naw sir, I don't 'member him handin' it to her."

"So you heard him say he was giving her a deed, although you never saw it delivered it to her?"

"I only saw her holdin' it one time, and that's the time I caught her scramblin' around in Colonel King's…"

"That's enough, Ginny," said Miss Marie.

"…desk."

"You saw Mrs. Pillow doing what?"

"I said, that's enough. This woman doesn't know anything unless she imagines it. You may leave, Ginny. And make me some coffee. With some cake. Now." I reckon Miss Marie didn't take to drinking whisky in the morning with the gentlemen.

"But Mrs. Pillow, this may prove to be a useful witness," Judge Brown argued.

"She's just a busy-body, making things up half the time. Ginny, you run on." I've never seen Ginny move so fast, getting up from the chair and scurrying into the kitchen. "Oh Lord, thank you, Jesus," we all heard her say in a relieved sigh behind the closed door. Mr. Pickle started giggling.

"Is there anything wrong, sir?" Mr. Poston asked, annoyed.

"No, sir," replied Mr. Pickle, very seriously, as he looked back down at his scribbles with a grin.

"Mrs. Pillow, in order for you to see justice done, we must conduct this process fairly, but you are making it very difficult when you cut off these depositions." Mr. Weatherford complained politely.

"This is my lawsuit. It will be conducted in the way that I see fit." And that was that. Mr. Weatherford looked over to Mr. Poston for support, but Mr. Poston was keeping himself busy with his papers. I believe Mr. Poston already knew who was in charge. Mr. Weatherford was just finding that out.

❈   ❈   ❈

I didn't want to do it, but they made me. "Do you swear to tell the truth, the whole truth, and nothing but the truth, so help you God?" My left hand was on the Good Book, and my right hand was up in the air.

"Yessir." I hated to have to make a swear. Sometimes it's better not to say anything at all than to say the whole truth. Anyway, that's the way it seemed to me. But this time I reckon I didn't have any choice.

"What is your full name?"

"Kesiah Mae Biscoe."

"And what is your relationship to Mrs. Pillow?"

"She raised me. So she's kind of like my mama. She calls me her 'companion', though."

"And in what capacity do you serve her?"

"I'm her housemaid. I help her with her clothes. Help her some with the children. I just kind of take care of things for her."

"And in that capacity as housemaid, were you a witness to Colonel King making any promises to her?"

That was an easy one. "Yes, sir. He promised her he would let her live at Sterling Hill for the rest of her life."

"Did he say why?"

"Yes, sir. He said it was on account of all that General Pillow did for him during the War." At least that was one of the reasons.

"Are you aware of any special feelings Colonel King might have had for Mrs. Pillow?"

"I believe he was in love with her, but I don't know for sure." Now, that's what I really thought. But they didn't ask me how she felt about him, and I didn't tell them anything about that.

"Did you ever witness Colonel King giving her a deed to Sterling Hill?"

"Yessir." That was true. I just didn't tell him which deed.

"Was that the first deed, the one that was burned, or the second?"

I fidgeted. Here I was, with Miss Marie looking at me, expecting me to say what she wanted me to say, and I knew the Good Lord was looking down on me, too, expecting me to tell the truth. I swanny, I didn't know what to do.

"At one time or another, I saw her with both deeds." Now that was true. I did see her with the first one, after she stole it.

"Did you see him give her the first deed?"

Now, I was in a real fix. "I was there when he showed her what he wrote that first time."

"Did he give it to her afterwards?"

"I'm not real sure." Well, I'd done it. I'd gone and told a lie.

"I see here from Mrs. Pillow's statement that you were a witness to the signing of that first deed."

"Yes, sir. I was."

"And did you see that $10,000 was the consideration given for the purchase of Sterling Hill?"

"Yes, sir. I saw that." Because I did. I remember being so shocked by that amount of money. But the Colonel said it wasn't really money changing hands.

"Did he at any time ask you to steal that deed from Mrs. Pillow?"

"Yes, sir. And I did that for him." I was nervous talking about that, but Miss Marie didn't seem to be bothered.

"Are you aware that deed was destroyed?"

"Yes, sir. I watched 'em do it."

"You watched who do it?"

"The Colonel and Mr. Worley. I heard some noise one night and got up out of bed and saw them in the parlor, burning something."

"How do you know it was that first deed?"

"I don't know, for sure. I just figured when she was all frantic about finding it the next day, that that's what it was they were burning."

Mr. Weatherford sighed and leaned back in his chair. Then he looked down at his notes again. "Are you aware that Colonel King owed Mrs. Pillow any money?"

"No, sir." And that was the truth.

Just then Ginny came into the room with a tray full of cups and the coffee pot and another bottle of whisky. Judge Brown was down at the end of the table, nodding off. I believe he probably drank too much at supper. It had been another long day.

"Why don't we take our coffee in the parlor?" Miss Marie suggested. "You can get back to Kizzie tomorrow."

But they never did get back to deposing me. I reckon Miss Marie thought I'd said enough, and if they asked me much more, I might say too much. The lawyers didn't much seem to like Miss Marie calling an end to the proceedings, but seemed like they were starting to figure out that she was the boss, and she could direct them however she wanted. She would have done it anyway.

❧   ❧   ❧

For the next few days, they went through witness after witness, and they all said the same thing. All the field hands from down in the quarters said they saw the Colonel give Miss Marie that first deed. I don't believe most of those folks had ever even been in the mansion house before, let alone be invited to sit in the parlor during an important business conversation. But with every question those lawyers asked, those poor folks just looked at Miss Marie, hoping she'd see that they were saying what she wanted them to say. Of course, they wanted to stay at Sterling Hill, so they said what they thought they were supposed to, and they made up some pretty good stories about other things, too. At the end of the day, the last field hand escaped out the back door and down to the safety of the quarters, like a captured hen let loose from a crate, but still not free enough to fly the coop for good.

✤   ✤   ✤

The last deposition was going to be Mr. Worley's. He was too busy with farming, he told them, and couldn't take the time to be deposed. The truth was he didn't want to be answering any questions, and he'd just put it off as long as he could. But they finally got him in there on a rainy morning and sat him down at the dining room table, just like the rest of us had.

"What is your full name?"

"Thomas Lee Worley."

"And in what capacity do you work at Sterling Hill?"

"I'm the manager of the farm."

"And are you aware of any of Colonel King's business dealings?"

"I take care of the farm business for him, but I don't know nothin' 'bout his law dealin's."

"Are you aware that he gave a deed to this property to Mrs. Pillow?"

"I only heard about it."

"And from whom did you hear about it?"

Mr. Worley paused. "I reckon I first heard about it from Ginny. And then Kizzie. And then when all this lawsuit mess started, I reckon the Colonel hisself told me about some of it. I figgered it wasn't none of my business."

"Did you ever see the first deed?"

"Not until it was burnin'."

"Did you help burn it?"

"Yessir. And I was glad to do it," he said, glancing over at Miss Marie. She just said, "Hmmph," loud enough for all of us to hear.

"Did you ever see the deed in the possession of Mrs. Pillow?"

"No."

"Are you aware that the Colonel owes Mrs. Pillow $10,000?"

At that, Mr. Worley paused, with a curious look on his face. Then he started grinning. Then he started laughing.

"Why that woman ain't worth $10,000, even if he'd had relations with her 10,000 times!"

Miss Marie's face went white. I do believe that if she'd had a gun with her, she would have shot him.

"Mr. Worley, you are no gentleman. Why, to speak in such a way about this lady and your employer…" Mr. Poston roared.

Miss Marie was wailing. Mr. Worley was laughing.

"She ain't my employer, and she ain't no lady, neither." With that, he got up and left. I was proud of him for being so brave as to say that, even though it wasn't a very nice thing to say. I would never have said it, even though I might have thought it.

CHAPTER 38

July 1890

"Colonel H. Clay King, in his attempt to come to the aid of a poor widow woman, the widow of a Confederate general, Brigadier General Gideon J. Pillow, in his attempt to obey the Biblical principle of caring for those less fortunate, has himself been besmirched and besmeared in the process of maintaining his own farmland." Mr. Weatherford wore the stern face of a preacher as he spoke to the two judges, Judge Sanders from Marianna and Judge Estes from Memphis. They'd already told everybody in that crowded courtroom to keep still, but the buzzing and whispering didn't stop; it had just got softer.

"That Colonel and Mrs. King welcomed Mrs. Pillow onto their Arkansas plantation is without dispute," Mr. Weatherford continued. "That they assisted her financially is evident, although the defense questions the facts. Colonel and Mrs. King fed, clothed, and housed Mrs. Pillow and her family for two years. And the result? Slander and infamy. On the charge that he assaulted her with a deadly weapon, the Arkansas court has already found him not guilty. On the charges of his being dishonest, I think the court will find Colonel King to be the most upright and honest of gentlemen. As to the unfortunate and unwarranted personal accusations against Mrs. King, the complainant contends that this is all part and parcel of Mrs. Pillow's slanderous onslaught on his character. We have not dealt with the details of those charges in this case. In fact, the only dispute which concerns us today is the ownership of the land.

"We have deponents who have sworn that Mrs. Pillow took forcible possession of this property, armed with a pistol, and that she refuses to leave Colonel King's property unless she is compelled to by this court. It is the desire of the complainant, Colonel King, to have a decree issued, vesting the title to this property in Colonel King alone and setting aside the deed of gift to Mrs. Pillow. It is this final issue, the property dispute, that is the sole concern of this court. Thank you, Your Honors."

Mr. Weatherford sat down at his table beside the Colonel and Judge Brown. The buzzing and mumbling started up again until Judge Estes banged his hammer.

Mr. Poston stood up suddenly, startling those judges, and began to speak, just a little too loud. "Your Honors," he bowed slightly. "Ladies and gentlemen in the courtroom," he opened his arms dramatically. "Colonel King," he barely turned his head toward him and smirked. "This is certainly a most unusual occasion, having two distinguished jurists from two different states in one courtroom to hear a property dispute. But this is not simply a property dispute." He raised his forefinger and paced in front of the judges. "What we have here is an alleged gentleman, who made certain promises, gifts, and sales to a widow, and then reneged on the same. We come before you to show you that this person, Henry Clay King, is both a scoundrel and a thief!" He used that forefinger like a spear, jabbing it at the Colonel accusingly. "That he had as his client one Mrs. General Gideon Pillow, the widow of the heroic Confederate brigadier general, and as her lawyer, he preyed upon her, gaining her confidence and then robbing her of property that was rightfully hers. Mrs. Pillow was not left destitute after the death of her husband, but was in fact in a position to come to the aid of Colonel King and his family by lending them $10,000 of her own money, a bequest left to her by her late husband. Mrs. Pillow further understood that the security for this loan would be the Sterling Hill plantation in Lee County, Arkansas. Colonel Henry Clay King, and his wife, Sallie Haughton King, were living at their home in Memphis and encouraged Mrs. Pillow to make a home for herself and for her three young children (one of whom, God rest her soul, has since departed this life) at that same plantation." He placed his hand over his heart, looked down at the floor, and shook his head sorrowfully. "This encouragement, coupled with the fact that Colonel King not only bequeathed her that property but also delivered the deed to her safekeeping, is ample evidence that Mrs. Pillow is the rightful owner of that land.

"As Colonel King did not repay her the money he owed, Mrs. Pillow bought the plantation known as Sterling Hill for the sum of $10,000 as repayment, and thereafter he delivered to her a deed to that property." He gestured as if handing somebody a paper. "Colonel King, through fraudulent means, stole that same deed from her possession and burned it in the fireplace." He grabbed that imaginary paper back and squatted down to pretend to be sticking it in a fireplace, even though if he'd really stayed in that leaned over position as long as he did in front of a real fire, he would have burned his nose. "Clearly, he meant to cheat this poor widow woman of that which he had promised. This dastardly deed was performed by this thing masquerading as a gentleman, who himself, in his own words and with his own voice, accused his wife of criminal intercourse with a Negro…"

"Objection!"

"Sustained. Mr. Poston, limit your remarks to the issue at hand. You may continue."

"Thank you, Your Honor." Good thing Miss Sallie wasn't in the courtroom. She would have hated to hear that out loud in front of everybody. Mr. Poston just bowed his head and smiled.

"As I was saying, he not only took advantage of her in his position of being her trusted counselor, by promising a thing he had no intention to deliver and taking her money, but he attempted to force her to marry him by impugning her character with conditions set forth in the second deed which she found repugnant." Judge Estes scratched his head, looking confused.

"This man is not entitled to credit on an oath in a court of justice, because he not only abandoned his wife, but he took up with Mrs. Pillow *as his mistress*! Truly, this scoundrel should pay for his misdeeds and the havoc he has wreaked on this poor widow woman. We respectfully ask this court to divest Colonel King's ownership of this property and restore to Mrs. Pillow original deed of sale to the property which she rightfully owns."

I imagine Mr. Poston could have made good money as a stage actor, since he was so good at pantomime and face making. After he said his piece and sat back down, it occurred to me how silly that whole speech was. After all, Miss Marie had sued the Colonel for $100,000 for slandering her. Calling her his mistress sounded pretty slanderous to me. I don't know why old man Poston said such a thing. I thought the walls were going to start shaking on account of that remark. But Miss Marie just sat there with her head held high, looking proud of being called his mistress. She didn't even seem to be embarrassed that he was saying such a thing with Annie and Giddy right there in the courtroom.

"Now, counselors, are these all the depositions you are submitting in this case?" Judge Sanders asked after both lawyers had finished.

"No, Your Honor. We have one more," Colonel Taliaferro answered, finding the document on the table in front of him then presenting it to the judge.

"Objection. We have not seen this new deposition." Mr. Weatherford glanced at Judge Brown, who looked worried.

"We have made a copy of it for your convenience."

The Judge Sanders looked down through the spectacles on the end of his nose and read, "*Deposition of Mr. Hugh Scott, Chicago, Illinois.* Mr. Weatherford, what is the basis for your objection?"

"Your Honor, we are not familiar with this witness. We were not present when his statement was given and have not had the opportunity to question him. We don't even know which aspect of the case his testimony pertains to."

"Mr. Poston?" the judge asked.

"Your Honor, this statement was taken in Chicago. Neither Colonel Taliaferro nor I were present at the time Mr. Scott gave us his statement, but it has been submitted to us, and we have confirmed with this Mr. Scott that what he sent us was his actual sworn statement."

The Judge Sanders frowned at the document, and then whispered to Judge Estes, who nodded his head. "We'll read this statement and give it the weight it deserves: not as great as the sworn statements for which you all were present, but not insignificant. Mr. Weatherford, will you agree to that?"

"Your Honor, I'd like my objection to be noted for the record, but for the sake of efficiency, I will agree."

I thought and thought and couldn't remember anybody named Hugh Scott, but then it came to me. He was the man we'd visited in the publishing office with the ink on his hands. He was the one who put out the *Matrimonial News*. I didn't understand how a statement from him had anything to do with who owned Sterling Hill.

"Ordinarily, a trial in the Chancery Court consists only of depositions which the Court will read and consider in making its judgment," Judge Estes explained. "However, because of the unusually personal nature of this case and because of the obvious dissension between the parties and disagreement about so many of the facts, I think it might be helpful to request that Colonel King and Mrs. Pillow be available to take the witness stand if we need clarification of anything. Does counsel have any objection to that procedure?"

Mr. Poston jumped to his feet. "No, indeed, Your Honor. Mrs. Pillow is ready at any time to take the witness stand."

Mr. Weatherford agreed. "Colonel King is more than willing to testify before this court."

"Well, then. We'll take it up again on Monday. That'll give Judge Sanders and myself the chance to read over all these depositions and prepare some questions. Court is adjourned." And he banged his hammer.

✤   ✤   ✤

"Colonel King, when did you first meet Mrs. Mary Eliza Pillow?" When Monday came around, I was not looking forward to hearing all the details of my life for the past few years repeated and twisted for all the world to hear. Miss Marie had told her story so many times, it seemed more like the sad part of a fairy tale—Cinderella being mistreated by her wicked stepmother or Oliver Twist begging for food—than anything that really happened to us. But I was curious as to how the Colonel would tell it. Besides, it was cooler indoors with a fan than out in the sweltering July sun, and Miss Marie didn't give me a choice, neither.

"I met her during a lawsuit in 1872. She was represented in the action by General Pillow, and I represented her former mother-in-law, Mrs. Martha Trigg, of Louisiana."

"And when did you come to know her in a personal capacity?"

"After the lawsuit, I had the occasion to meet her socially."

"Were you married at that time?"

"Yes, I was. And I still am."

"Around 1876, I believe, General Pillow declared bankruptcy." Judge Estes was rustling his papers. "Were you involved in that proceeding at all?"

"Yes," he hesitated, "but I have tried to keep my financial dealings in this area private."

"Why is that?"

"I did not want to embarrass Mrs. Pillow."

"How were you involved in General Pillow's bankruptcy?"

"When his homes and library were sold, I bought them."

"To give back to General Pillow and his wife?"

"Yes."

"And what accounts for this amazing act of generosity on your part? These properties must have been worth multiple thousands of dollars."

The Colonel sat with his hands squeezed together and his elbows on the arms of his chair, leaning forward, ready for anything. "General Pillow was good to me in the war. I wanted to return the favor."

"Is this the reason that you took in Mrs. Pillow when she encountered hard times again?"

"Yes, because of General Pillow and also because of my Christian duty."

"Christian duty?"

"To help the poor, the widowed, the fatherless children."

Miss Marie rolled her eyes and sighed, "My God," loud enough so I'm sure even the Colonel up on the witness stand could have heard her. Judge Sanders gave her a look of warning, but he didn't say nothing.

"Colonel King, would you please describe the financial help you gave her from the time that she moved onto your property?"

He cleared his throat. "Well, almost immediately after she arrived on my plantation she asked to borrow $600, which I gave her. I allowed her to keep the income from the farm during 1886 and 1887, without argument. She took that income without my first giving her permission, by the way, but I did not stop her. I paid for the burial of her daughter at Elmwood Cemetery and also paid the costs of having General Pillow reinterred there. And when she left Sterling Hill, I loaned her the money for her trip."

"Colonel King, has Mrs. Pillow repaid you any of this money?"

"Not a dime."

"Now, Colonel, let us get to the matter of the deed. Please explain to the Court why it is that a married man would bequeath his farm and all his other property to a woman other than his wife."

He paused and looked over at Mr. Weatherford, who nodded at him. "I had already provided for my wife and daughters. They had income from other properties. In addition, my wife was well provided for by her parents."

"But why would you once again perform this amazing act of generosity for Mrs. Pillow? Did you have a relationship with her other than..."

"Yes. We did," he replied quietly. "And it was because of that relationship that Mrs. Pillow was able to persuade me to include her in my will and deed her the properties"

There was a long silence. Here he was admitting to the judges and everybody else what I knew had been going on the whole time. "Why did you give her a deed to your property if you had already included her in your will?" Judge Estes asked.

"To appease her. She begged me for it, so I gave her a deed. At first, when I was trying to decide how to arrange the bequest, I drafted a deed of sale with a contract. But I decided that would not be wise. I wasn't sure I could trust her. I never delivered that deed to her—I kept it locked in my desk."

"Why did you originally write a deed of sale? That would certainly suggest that she bought the properties from you."

"No. She did not pay for them. But I thought it would look less…less…suspicious, if it appeared to be a legitimate sale rather than simply a gift."

"Do you mean that giving her the land might look as if there were some special relationship between the two of you, whereas selling it would not?"

The Colonel looked down at his clasped hands. "Yes."

"Why did you destroy that original deed?"

"Mrs. Pillow had threatened to record it. That had never been my intention in giving it to her. I meant only to appease her." He glanced at Miss Marie with tear-filled eyes.

"Let's move on to the issue of the recordation," Judge Sanders suggested gruffly. "Mrs. Pillow claims you advised her not to record her deed because her creditors might try to claim the property."

"No, that's not true at all." The Colonel wiped his eyes and sniffed. "I asked her not to record the deed of sale because I wasn't certain it was the proper way to make the transfer. It was merely an appeasement—a way to make her happy—that's why I made out that deed in the first place, to assure her that I intended for her to have the property after my death."

"It seems she recorded a contract for sale when she recorded the deed of gift, and that the Recorder of Deeds accepted that. Did you write a second contract when you wrote the second deed, the deed of gift?"

"No. I wrote only one contract, and that was for the first deed. She apparently stole it from me when she stole that first deed. When I asked for it back, she assured me she had burned it. I believe what she did was save that contract that showed the $10,000 consideration, and attach it to the second deed. And then she must have used the acknowledgment page for the deed to apply to both documents. Her recordation of that deed was clearly fraudulent." Biting his lip, he nodded, as if he'd finally figured out how she did it.

"Now, Colonel King, we have this deposition in front of us from a Mr. Hugh Scott of Chicago, in which he claims that you delivered a matrimonial advertisement on behalf of Mrs. Pillow. Is that true?"

This new evidence woke him from his pondering, and he spoke with more energy. "I've never met Mr. Scott in my life. I don't know anything about a matrimonial advertisement."

"Mrs. Pillow suggests that you wrote and delivered it to make her appear as an 'adventuress.'"

"Your Honors, Mrs. Pillow lured me into doing things for her benefit that I would not otherwise have done. My association with her has been painful enough for me and for my entire family. Why would I want to make her look any worse and thereby make myself look worse, for taking up with such a woman?" He must have realized how pitiful he sounded. "No, I didn't write any advertisement, and I didn't deliver one."

"The advertisement in question states that she was the owner of a large plantation in Arkansas. If you delivered it to Mr. Scott for publication, aren't you as much as admitting that the property belongs to her?"

"I admit no such thing. I've brought this entire suit to clear the cloud upon the title. I wouldn't do anything to confuse the matter further. This must just be some fabrication of hers, to advance her case."

On it went, the Colonel giving his version of what happened. He seemed mighty sad. I knew a lot of what he was saying was true, but since I didn't know it all, I can't rightly tell if he told the whole truth, like he swore to. But most likely, what he said was right. Him being such a gentleman and all, I knew he didn't like making Miss Marie look bad. But I reckon he didn't have any other choice.

❧   ❧   ❧

That afternoon it was time for Miss Marie to answer questions. She had armored herself with her Confederate gray suit to protect the widow of a general from questions she didn't want to answer. Matching her little black cap was her main weapon, her dark eyes with their razor like glances. But until she needed them, until she wanted to show her anger or disapproval, she smiled demurely.

She went through the whole business of the General dying of the yellow fever, and us farming the property, even though they didn't ask her about all that. She was sniffling in all the right places. But again, she twisted her answers to make it sound like we weren't near as bad off as we really were.

"So why was it that you decided to move to Sterling Hill?" Judge Sanders asked.

"He owed me money. $10,000. I accepted the property as repayment. It was my property, so I moved there."

"What did you understand to be the reason that he bequeathed these properties to you in the first place?"

"First, because he owed me money. The properties were the security for the loan. But then," she sighed, "Colonel King had fallen passionately in love with me. He wanted to divorce his wife and force me to marry him. I filed a copy of the Petition for Divorce he sent me as evidence. I even have his letters to me, where he calls me 'honey' and says I was like a wife to him…"

"Yes, Mrs. Pillow, we are familiar with all the evidence in this case. And so he bequeathed you his plantation and the house in Memphis as security for a loan *and* because he was in love with you?"

"Yes, exactly. He concocted this elaborate entanglement to force me to marry him and to steal my money. The deed he wanted to give me had such insulting conditions—he was blackmailing me."

"Excuse me?" Judge Estes asked.

"If I didn't marry him, he was going to make me appear to be his mistress and ruin my reputation, which is exactly what he's done. He wrote that matrimonial advertisement, which he now denies doing. He said I had to give him a home for the rest of his life, that I couldn't move or marry without losing my interest in the plantation. I couldn't possibly accept those conditions on land that was rightfully mine. That's why I want my original deed restored."

"Didn't you voluntarily record that deed, the one with all the 'insulting conditions', as you describe them?"

"Yes, but what choice did I have? If I hadn't recorded it, he might have tried to sell the plantation. Recording that deed, even with all those conditions, was the only choice I had, except to marry him, which I would *never* do."

"Let's back up a minute." Judge Sanders looked confused. "You say you lent him $10,000 at some point. Do you know what that was intended for?"

"I believe it had something to do with completing their new home in Memphis."

"Mrs. Pillow, do you have any bank records to indicate that you did indeed have $10,000 to lend to Colonel King?"

"Oh, no. I was leery of banks. I was afraid to put any of my money in them, because I was afraid that the creditors—General Pillow's creditors from the bankruptcy, of course—that those creditors would try to take it."

"So if you had $10,000 to lend, where did you keep it?"

"My sister Elizabeth kept it for me."

The two judges put their heads together and mumbled for a minute, flipping pages and studying documents, when Judge Estes said, "Mrs. Pillow, what do you make of this statement in your sister's deposition, dated June 9, 1890:

Mr. Weatherford: Where did Mrs. Pillow keep her money?
Miss Dickson: She kept it in the bank
Mr. Weatherford: Do you know the name of the bank she used?
Miss Dickson: I believe it was the Corbin Banking Company

Now, Mrs. Pillow, how do you explain this apparent inconsistency with your statement that you were 'leery of banks'?"

Miss Marie cleared her throat and glared at the judge. "My sister must be mistaken."

Judge Estes peered at her over his spectacles at her.

But I knew what the judges didn't. She was lying. She was flat out lying. I don't know if she had any money, but if she did, I don't know why we had moved to Sterling Hill. That kind of money could have paid off her mortgage on the Pillow place. And if she'd had that kind of money, then she wouldn't have had to borrow the $600 that I know she borrowed, because I signed on as her witness. But I don't know how those judges were going to know all that.

I didn't say nothing, of course. I was sitting right there, right in the court-room, and I could have stood up and said, "Wait! I know what really happened!" I could have. But I didn't. Because I was supposed to be on her side of this whole mess. I reckon I could have stood up and give them all what for and told them what I knew. But I was too scared. And nobody asked me to. And I didn't have any reason to rock the boat, even though I felt uncomfortable about all of her lying when she had promised to tell the truth.

They continued with the questions into the afternoon. Sometimes Miss Marie would tell the truth, sometimes she'd lie. She looked mighty pretty up there on the stand in her Confederate gray. And she'd let herself get all teary eyed when it suited her. But when the day was over, they hadn't shaken her up too much. She stuck to her story. The judges said they'd know by that next day what their decision would be.

The Tennessee judge, Judge Estes, started off. "There are only two reasons that this case requires the representation of the Tennessee justice system. One is that Colonel King is a resident of Memphis, so it would be appropriate for me to hear a case involving him. The more important reason is the matter of the Mosby Street property and the other Tennessee properties contained in the deed. It is my understanding that in all these disagreements concerning the deed, both the Arkansas plantation Sterling Hill and the Mosby Street home were involved. They were included in the burned deed of sale and in the recorded deed of gift. The troublesome part of this whole case is the disposition of the Mosby Street property. It appears that Colonel King transferred this home to his wife, after he'd delivered the deed of gift including it to Mrs. Pillow, and that Mrs. Pillow did not object to this disposition. And, as I read the depositions, she did not receive any proceeds from that transfer, if there were any. That being the case, if she did not object to one piece of property she allegedly 'owned' being sold, then I don't understand why she would then lay claim to the other property in that same deed she says he delivered to her. And as the other property is Arkansas land, clearly I have no jurisdiction over the matter. Therefore, I defer to the decision of Judge Sanders regarding the Sterling Hill property."

That made sense to me. I was starting to understand more and more about law and how sensible it all was, once it was explained to me.

Judge Sanders cleared his throat. "We have read all the sworn statements submitted and considered carefully your own answers to our questions. There are so many inconsistencies, especially among Mrs. Pillow's witnesses, that it is difficult, if not impossible, to determine the truth of these matters. One puzzling aspect is Mr. Scott's deposition. If, as he said, Colonel King delivered the matrimonial advertisement to Mr. Scott's establishment, there would be in that action the implication that he acknowledged the statements therein were true—that she was in fact the owner of a 'large Arkansas plantation.' But the means by which this affidavit was obtained remains mysterious. No one is quite sure who contacted Mr. Scott, or how this statement ended up in the hands of the respondent's attorneys."

I wanted to look over at Miss Marie, but I didn't dare.

"Thus, the complainant has not had the opportunity to question Mr. Scott. In addition, the Arkansas plantation mentioned in the advertisement is not identified. It is possible that the writer of this advertisement was not even referring to Sterling Hill, or that the writer was simply lying. Added to that is the fact that we are making suppositions about Colonel King's thinking just by virtue of the fact that he was said to have delivered the advertisement. With these problems in mind, I think we must totally disregard Mr. Scott's statement.

"Furthermore, based on all that I have heard, the party who seems to have the least number of inconsistencies in his testimony is Colonel King. It seems to me that a good number of Mrs. Pillow's witnesses are mistaken, or lying. Whether or not that first deed was ever delivered to her can't be determined with any certainty. There is also the fact that nobody else—no neighbors, no acquaintances from Memphis, nobody except Mrs. Pillow's family members and employees subject to her control—no objective person had ever heard about Colonel King giving her the property. Therefore, in the matter of King v. Pillow, the property dispute, I rule in favor of the complainant and further make a judgment in the amount of $11,000 against Mrs. Pillow." He banged his hammer and all those folks in the courtroom buzzed even louder than before and swarmed toward the doors.

Now, seemed to me that those judges got it just about right, considering all the lies they had to wade through to get to the truth. Or what seemed like the truth. I knew Miss Marie wasn't going to be happy, so I figured that with all the bad feelings between them, this lawsuit business wasn't fixing to be over.

❧   ❧   ❧

Stepping out onto the marble steps of the courthouse overlooking the Mississippi River, I was stung by the heat. Miss Marie was already perspiring from her anger and didn't want to stand out in the bright sunshine any longer than she had to, so she sent me out to find the carriage driver. A steamboat was unloading its passengers down the hill at the riverbank, a colorful crowd of people who must have been happy to finally be in Memphis after floating down from somewheres else. Memphis didn't seem like such a happy spot to me, especially since I knew that Miss Marie had only just got started with her ranting about that hearing. I continued to watch the people pour out of the steamboat as I made my way slowly down the steps when I felt a shove into my stomach. The little boy fell backwards onto the hard marble, his face grimacing with pain. Newspapers were flapping about on the steps around him.

"Hey, are you all right? I didn't even see you coming." I gathered up some of the newspapers as I approached him.

"I'm sorry, ma'am, you don't have to do that. It was my fault—wasn't looking where I was running," he whimpered.

"Well, you just can't be running and not looking," I said, patting the back of his head as I handed him a stack of his newspapers.

"I heared that Mr. King and Miz Pillow was in there. You know—the ones in the lawsuits. They've been in all the newspapers for a long time, and I just wanted to see 'em."

"Well, I reckon I don't blame you for that."

"Who are you?" he asked, his eyes still glazed with tears he wouldn't admit.

"Kizzie Biscoe. And I work for Mrs. Pillow."

"You do?"

"Yep. I'm her companion. And I know more than I want to about all those lawsuits. So what's your name?"

"Jeremiah." At that point I noticed the little dog barking at him from the bottom of the steps. He only had three legs.

I gave him a hand up. "Well, Jeremiah, pleased to make your acquaintance."

"Nice to meet you, too." He brushed off the seat of his pants. "Who won?"

"The Colonel did. And Mrs. Pillow ain't at all happy about it."

"Kizzie!" Miss Marie shouted from the door of the courthouse.

"Is that her?" he whispered.

"Yep. And now I've got to run get her carriage before she gets any madder. You watch where you're going, you hear?"

"I sure will, Kizzie Biscoe. Looks like I'm going to have a whole bunch of new papers to sell." He waved to me as I walked down the rest of the marble steps. When I looked back at him, he was standing off to the side waiting for her to make her appearance.

❧   ❧   ❧

The train ride back to Sterling Hill was a sleepy one. I dozed off and on for most of the time. I woke up at the Forrest City station, but just for a minute, and as I drifted off to sleep again, the train lurched forward. It never got up to full speed. We rode slowly for about a mile, or for what seemed like only a mile, the train chugging and coughing and spitting, when we stopped dead still. We were in front of a clearing in the woods in the flat land. Deep in the darkness, in the trees that seemed more like monsters than trees, I saw a figure, hanging. The darkness made it almost impossible to see. Loose arms, limp heavy legs, large shoulders. The dark man hung motionless and alone by what seemed almost a tiny thread, until another man appeared on the ground with a ladder, climbing up to the limb with a glinting knife. The train let out a sorrowful wail and began to move again, away from the nightmare, away from the thing that was much too scary to be real.

CHAPTER 39

March 1891

"'Nope—they're white. No nigger blood in them.' To *my children* they say these things. Complete strangers walk up to my darling girls, look them over, and utter these obscenities." The intolerable indignity of my own offspring being treated like children of the gutter.

"Clay, there is no need to slam the door."

Weatherford sat behind his desk as if the world were not coming to an end. "Sallie cannot go out onto the streets without these insults. And they come even from friends. From *friends*. Comments, stares, whispers, it is unbearable." I felt the sting of tears.

"Please, Clay, lower your voice. There are other clients…"

"No suitors call on them any more. None of Sallie's friends look in on her. There is no respite from the pain. The stigma is simply unbearable."

"Sit down. Let me get you a drink. Here, take my handkerchief." His warm hand on my shoulder, the white cloth dangling before me. "We need to go over a few items related to the appeal."

"The appeal? You want to talk business while my life is being destroyed?" This brilliant man, too dull to understand the pain.

"Calm down. You look like a wild man. Get a hold of yourself." He moved toward a table, pouring the liquid, bringing me burning respite. "Now, it looks like Poston has filed the appeal to the Supreme Court of Tennessee as well, so we've got to write two separate briefs. I'm coming to believe that this has more to do with spite than ownership of the property."

"The stigma. The stigma." Certainly spite. Their pleasure derived from the intentional infliction of pain. My hands trembled. Head ached. The clouds of uncertainty began to part. The path became clear.

"Clay? Are you listening to me? I said Dave Poston…"

"Have you seen him any more? Have you seen him armed?" Remembering the fear when he was seen. Next time I would be ready.

"I have seen him on the street, yes. I can't help but see him with his office just down the block."

"Did he have the shotgun?"

"Only the one time. You have to get beyond this. He is no threat to you."

No threat to me except in honor and reputation and money and my life. "I saw John Shields on Front Street yesterday. He had said he was going back to Birmingham. But he lied. It's obvious, isn't it? He plans to confront me. They both do."

"If John Shields is in Memphis still, he will not necessarily confront you, Clay."

"But I will be ready. If Poston and John are armed, I shall be armed as well." I felt into my pocket. The cool steel in my hand reassured me, gave me power.

"Put that thing away! Don't swing it around in my office. Good God, man, get a hold of yourself!"

"I have no choice but to protect myself and my family." Honor, honor is all. There is no honor in surrender.

"You have the courts. Now, don't lose your perspective about this." His silhouette against the sunlit window, his ignorance, not understanding.

"There must be a duel. There must be. Call Poston. Let's get this over with, so no innocent party will be hurt in the gunfire."

"Clay, we must settle our differences in the courtroom and there alone."

The courtroom. A battlefield most unsuited for an affront so reprehensible.

❦   ❦   ❦

The same dark courtroom, filled with insinuation and insult, my pain and my prison. The Nemesis spoke: "Your Honor, I would respectfully request a continuance in this case. My associate, Colonel Taliaferro of Birmingham, Alabama, had to return to his home for family reasons. I would prefer to take up this case upon his return."

Late February and these damnable men. The eternal property lawsuit appealed; the slander lawsuit alive by spite and delay. Restless, quavering, I wanted it to be finished.

"Your Honor, Colonel Taliaferro is not even on the pleadings for this lawsuit. I don't see why we need to wait for him. We are ready to get this over with at once," Weatherford argued. Spite and delay.

Judge Estes asked, "Mr. Poston, you've already asked for one continuance of this suit on the basis that Mrs. Pillow was too ill to appear. And now you're asking for another one?"

"Your Honor," Weatherford began, "it would seem to me that if Mrs. Pillow was defamed to the extent that only $100,000 would appease her, that she and her lawyers would be eager to see this suit begin immediately. Perhaps this is only a delaying tactic?" Yes, but this was no time for smiling, my own advocate.

Poston roared, "We are entitled to be adequately prepared for any case we may bring, including having all the lawyers we want and including having the complainant present for the proceedings. If you are so much as suggesting that I am trying to manipulate the court for improper purposes, why..."

"Calm down, Mr. Poston," the judge said. "You're going to get your continuance. But only briefly. Only as long as it takes to get word to Colonel Taliaferro."

"We will agree to a postponement until such time as Colonel Taliaferro can be notified and have a reasonable time to come to Memphis," Weatherford sighed. Tugging at his coat, I whispered. "We request that the Court send Colonel Taliaferro a telegram notifying him of this change, at Colonel King's expense, since a telegram would reach him much more quickly than a letter, and we would like to proceed with this suit as expeditiously as possible."

Poston exploded. "Colonel King, that is an insinuation that you have more money than I have—that I am a pauper, and I won't submit to it!"

I stood, checking my emotions, one hand restraining the other. "Your Honor, in your great wisdom, the Postal Service is the usual method for the Court to make notifications, but I believe it is only appropriate for me to bear the expense of the more costly telegraph." Calm thoughts made very clear.

"I'll agree to that. Colonel King shall pay the expense of the telegraph, and this case is continued until such time as Colonel Taliaferro is able to appear. We are adjourned."

My anger contained, I attempted to leave the courtroom, the heat of fury warming my face, my eyes fixed on the floor lest I catch the eye of the Nemesis.

I shall not provoke him, and I have promised that I shall not speak to him, though it took the strength of Sampson.

Ranting, shouting. "That goddamned deserter had better be prepared to answer for that kind of insult." Sputtering loudly. "This kind of character assassination is beneath even a scoundrel like King."

He stared straight into my eyes, sneering, daring me. Fury rising. Desertion. Assassination. She had told him. The goddamned woman had told him.

❀   ❀   ❀

"Mary Eliza Pillow and David Poston are simply scheming to take away my property, that's all there is to it." The crowds at the Vienna Café this lunch hour were mumbling, great groups of people seated, animated, looking at me.

"It certainly seems that way," Stratton concurred. "The judges did find that all their witnesses were lying."

"Those people are nothing but liars, and all they want is to ruin my good name. They will lie, cheat, and steal to get their hands on my property. And I cannot tell you the damage they have done to Mrs. King and the girls with their scandalous lies." More customers turned to look. I raised my glass to them in spite, and swallowed it all.

A familiar face, Mr. Strickland appeared at my side, from some other part of the noisy room. "Colonel, I couldn't help but overhear what you were saying, and…"

I stood and faced him, nose to nose. "Tom Chambers, Mrs. Gideon Pillow, and Dave Poston concocted a damnable conspiracy to beat me out of my estate, and you can tell them that I said so." More faces turned.

"I am a friend of Dave Poston's and…"

"Well, he's a goddamned scoundrel and conspirator, and you can tell him I said so." I returned to my seat, Strickland looking down at me, mouth agape, flushed, faces all around staring. I lit another cigar, sucked in the bitter smoke, poured another glass of whisky, and relished an afternoon of diversion with a comrade not taken in by the demon.

❀   ❀   ❀

The soldier waited calmly on the warm March day, reconnoitering the battlefield, brick streets crowded with civilians, horses, carts. The sun, almost directly above his head, beat with an unseasonal intensity, causing a glare as he gazed at the passersby. He felt his pocket to insure it was there–the hard cylinder deep within his overcoat pocket gave him assurance that he was ready for whatever assaults he might encounter.

He wandered, slowly, glancing to both sides of the street, walking, zigzagging unsteadily toward the park, where the shade was less relief than too cool. He felt his pocket. Watching, looking, hunting, he moved purposefully across the street yet again, into the barbershop, where he searched. "Have you seen him? Is it over yet?"

The man with the blade in his hand moved toward him, threateningly, blade pointed directly toward him, ordering his retreat. The soldier cried out—you misunderstand, I'm only seeking my position, my enemy—overwhelmed by war whoops from the men in flapping white uniforms, foamed faces, angry expressions. He retreated into the street, the bloody red stripes, cylindrical, like the steel in his pocket after the victory.

The sun shone bright enough that he could easily see the stones under his feet, could easily be seen, would hide in the obvious daylight crowds, meandering, cheerfully chattering, admiring their reflections in shop windows. No one would notice. No one would see. He stopped, leaning on a barrel, he—I shall not say who—stopped only momentarily, long enough to look up into the admiring sun, shining approval, promising vindication like a forgiving commanding officer.

Hearing the noise of the streetcar, knowing someone in the crowd would hear, he shouted through the din, "Have you seen him?" People stopped, stared, heard him despite his attempts at staying unheard. He spied them, not provoking or speaking, but continued to walk.

The buildings seemed to meld into the blue sky, reaching, lifting the encompassing blanket, covering all, protecting all, in its endless blueness, too beautiful, too godly a penumbra for his deed. He knew it was wrong, knew it was violent, against all law of God and man, except that he must save his honor, even if it meant having his honor lost. The blue of the sky rankled him with its bright honesty. Few white clouds hung over the scene, causing all below to squint, to close one's eyes to the brightness.

Face blended into face, the woman's smile, the man's snarling visage, the child's empty eyes, each separate and one, part of the vast society which judges and judged the honor of better men. Why that pursed lip, that wrinkled mouth, those vacant uncomprehending cavities, why are they in judgment of the intentions of a man? And why not? Had he not similarly sat in judgment of others, men in his ranks, men above his ranks, colonels of ill-repute whose audacity and coarseness he could hardly explain? Why was there not snow, ice, bitter freezing wind? The biting sunlight was all that was offered this day, enough to make one perspire in the middle of the street, and shiver in the shade.

Honor is good, a decent thing, a thing worth killing for, a golden shield protecting the weak and wielded by the strong on the battlefield. Honor is what he was killing for. Honor is all.

This man, this damnable enemy, on the same side of the politics, of the same learning, allies with the same leader, this man was no man. Accusing those less guilty, perhaps not guilty, of that which they did not do, supposing so. This loathsome, foul mouthed toad dragged the honorable soldier into his own sordid depths.

There in front of him, a grotto, his place to be obscured. A cigar shop, fragrant and manly. Inhaling, he made his purchase, stowing his reward for later pleasure.

The sound of shouting in the street, the voice of the Nemesis, loud, threatening, the thunderous blows of the naval cannons, he heard. Slowly, stealthily, his back to the wall, he slid, three steps away from the door, now two, now positioned. From his overcoat pocket he lifted the pistol, ivory handle, blued barrel. His aim was true.

"Oh, Lordy!" And then the blood revealed itself. He did not miss, running into the Tennessee woods. No one told him not to fight within the bounds of civilization, on the brick streets of Memphis where women shopped. If only it could have been his blade. "If I so desired". The man stared, stricken, blood trickling between his white fingers from the blackness of his waistcoat. Stared straight into my eyes. Too late to rebuke him for this impudence. It had come after the last stroke of the pen was already made. After the last act was performed, perfect in its simplicity.

There is no honor in surrender.

CHAPTER 40

"Hey, Williams, didn't I tell you I don't want any interviews?" His voice echoed through the basement hall. "Don't let any more of those reporters in here, you hear me?"

I hesitated to step closer to the cell. "Honey, are you all right?" The bars, the dank odor, the darkness made this man who was my husband seem even more like a stranger than he had been.

"Is that you, Sallie? Oh, Sallie. Sallie, please forgive me. Oh, Sallie, dear Sallie." He pressed his face against the bars and gazed at me with such drunken sincerity, his bloodshot eyes glistening with tears, the stench of alcohol surrounding him. I could not bear to talk to him in his inebriated condition, and I could no longer contain my own tears. Returning to the entry way, I questioned the jailer. "Mr. Williams, can you tell me anything about what happened?"

"No, ma'am. I wasn't there. I just know what I hear." He leaned back against the wall in a rickety wooden chair, unconcerned that the back legs might slip out from under him, and attempted to twirl a heavy ring of keys around his stubby finger.

"What did you hear?"

"He done shot Dave Poston right there on Main Street in front of God and everybody. They brought him in here while I was eating my dinner, so he just sat right here in my office 'til I was done." His office consisted of the entryway to the jail cells, furnished with two chairs and a broken desk. Remnants of a biscuit were left before him on a piece of wrinkled waxed paper. "I wasn't gonna have no criminal messin' up my dinner. Anyhow, I gave the officer a receipt and put the man behind bars, where he belongs. The others that are in here were plum happy to have him amongst 'em. Andrew Jackson, Pat League, and the others."

"You mean you put him in there with those murderers?"

"Birds of a feather, I always say. Then he wanted me to call you, which I done. And then he yelled for a bottle of whisky. He was already drunk and I wasn't fixin' to let him have no more. He didn't seem too angry about that, though. I reckon he'd already had plenty for one day. He wouldn't talk none about what happened, but he's been right friendly with the folks that's come in. That's all that happened before you got here."

"Who came in before me?"

"Reporters. A couple of pickpockets."

"What about the men outside, guarding the jail? Someone said something about a lynching."

"Aw, that ain't nothing. I heard it, too. They say Poston's brother Frank was after Mr. King but he's safe in here. Judge DuBose sent a posse to guard the jailhouse from the mob. You ain't got nothing to worry about, ma'am."

"Excuse me." A young man with doughy cheeks appeared in the doorway, notepad in hand. "I'm with the *Commercial*. I've come to speak to Colonel King."

"He don't want no visitors."

"Yes, but I have just a couple of questions." He didn't wait for permission and hurried past us to the cell area.

"Don't say I didn't warn you," the jailer called after him.

I could not bring myself to converse with the hollow-eyed Mr. Williams any longer. My agitation was matched only by his indifference to our tragedy. Unsure of what to do, I paced the room, my hands trembling. I had never before been in a jail. The odor of bodily functions permeated the air, mixed with the stale smell of cheap cigars. Dirty gray walls surrounded me. My heart throbbed wildly.

"Get out of here, you dirty son of a bitch; if I had a knife I'd kill you, goddamn you; get out quick!" Clay's voice resounded through the corridor, unnerving me. This man I had married, whom I thought was a gentleman, could sink no lower.

Those doughy cheeks were pink with embarrassment as the reporter made a hasty exit. The jailer shook his head and laughed. I could find no humor in this wretched situation and knew I'd find no comfort from an insensitive jailer or a drunken husband. I had no idea what else he might say to the press in his inebriated state, and I wanted to make sure that no further embarrassing utterances spewed forth. Mr. Williams assured me, his chipmunk jaw filled with tobacco, that he would allow no more reporters in until I returned the next morning. I lowered my head to conceal my tears and left that hellhole to face the angry crowd outside, my exit punctuated by the disgusting sound of the jailer's spit.

I could not believe that my situation could possibly worsen. He had humiliated me just by becoming involved with that woman. As if that weren't enough, the press relished every detail of every motion, statement, hearing, continuously repeating each sordid story and accusation. Now he had become a felon an addition to his infamy, and I was forced to suffer the company of these horrible, gutter-living creatures. I suppose that's where he belonged. If only I had left town, taken the girls, settled in St. Louis, and started over. I certainly had the means. But the only thing worse than standing by his side was leaving—after this nightmare whatever I had left would have disappeared. Slander, gossip, vicious lies were difficult enough to endure; divorce, separation from my Church and my friends, loss of position, these were unthinkable. Staying by his side would at least give the appearance that I was loyally married to this troubled man and that I was indeed wronged by him. After watching her for so long, I had learned from her skills as a thespian.

🍁   🍁   🍁

"Yes, ma'am, we had an eventful night last night." The gash on Clay's forehead was no longer bleeding, but the dried blood had not been washed from his skin and his spectacles were bent.

"What happened?"

"I heard one of the men yelling last evening," the jailer explained, "and when I went to see what all the fuss was about, there he was, lying in his own vomit, passed out and bleeding."

"He done fell out of bed," the man in the cell said in a raspy voice. He sat in the corner on his bed without rising. "His head hit—*smack*—on the floor," he clapped his hands together loudly, "and seemed like his specs cut him right there, in his temple."

"Pat here and Andy Jackson took care of him, stopped the bleeding. But I had to clean the floor. Pretty nasty stuff."

"Thank you for your help," I said weakly, unaccustomed to this society of vulgar men and murderers.

"Have you heard from Weatherford?" Clay asked weakly, trembling, finally having made his way over to the bars.

"No, no, I haven't," I replied, still eyeing the man on the bed. He winked at me. I cringed.

"They're supposed to be here today, aren't they? Will you make sure they come?"

"Hey, ma'am, whatcha got in that basket?" the murderer asked insolently.

Instinctively, I swung the basket around to my side as if to conceal it. "Just a few things for my husband." I replied. Pastries, candies, fruit, and a small bottle of bourbon to renew his strength.

"You know that reporter was lying in his article this morning." Clay pointed to the haphazard pile of newspapers on the cot.

"Was he?" I asked, searching in my basket for what I knew he wanted most.

His shaking hand reached for the flask. "They got that all wrong. I never said those things." I repositioned myself to shield his desperate drinking from the jailer.

"Then you'd best set the record straight," Pat League suggested.

"It doesn't matter what I tell them. They wouldn't retract more despicable statements when I wasn't behind bars. They aren't likely to make retractions regarding the behavior of a prisoner. Is there anything in there about Poston?"

The jailer was hidden behind the pages of a newspaper. The front page depicted the murder, a drawing of a man with a gun and another walking into it. "Just says he's in pretty bad shape."

Clay began to pace, wringing his hands, running his fingers through his dirty hair.

"Ma'am, you know them reporters are chompin' at the bit to come in here and talk to him." The jailer folded his newspaper as he stood and slapped it onto his chair.

"I know." I did not want to face them, those loathsome men wielding pencils more deadly than knives, who wrote what they wished without regard to the consequences.

"Darling, I'm ready to talk with them. I'm afraid I might have given them a bad impression of me last night when they caught me unawares."

"I don't think it's a good idea to say too much. It's not just a matter of public humiliation any more. Let's wait for the lawyers."

Mr. Weatherford and Judge Brown did finally arrive and visited only briefly, long enough to advise which tact to take with the press. They did not object to his speaking with reporters, and having finished his bourbon and his lunch,

Clay seemed reinvigorated as he spoke freely with the dreaded vermin. Wisely, he did not speak about the reasons for his behavior.

"You know, you've got this all wrong," he said to them, rattling the papers in front of them. "As much respect as I have for the newspaper profession, I must inform you that the information from this reporter is simply incorrect." Clay seemed neither bitter nor angry. "I know what you are after. You want me to tell the cause of my action. I do not care to discuss the affair much, but my wife and I have arranged a brief statement. You can say this: What I have done was in defense of the honor of myself and my wife, who had been traduced by Dave Poston. He has charged that my wife was intimate with a Negro and not only that, but that I myself made the charge against my wife. It is a falsehood made out of whole cloth, and I naturally resented it. That is all I care to say about the affair. My wife and I have decided that it is better to say no more."

Those words cut deeper every time I heard them. Soon there would be no sensation left in me at all. Speaking this way, again, in front of these reporters was no better than what Poston had done. I had the feeling that if Poston had not uttered these words, Clay might have done it for him. I can't say he did it maliciously, or even stupidly, for he remained of reasonably sound mind throughout the entire ordeal. It was as if some demon had taken possession of him, some ghoulish being, speaking indifferently about how he had shamed me.

"Can you tell us what happened right before the shooting?" a reporter prodded.

"No, I don't care to say anything. I will say this though. The accounts given in the paper are materially incorrect. There were witnesses who know the facts. The papers have grievously misrepresented me. For instance you have noticed that a *Commercial* reporter says I cursed him out of the cell and threatened to kill him. That is not true. He came in here contrary to my expressed wishes, and I told him as politely as the circumstances would permit that I did not want to make a statement but he tried to bluff me. He wrote out a list of questions for me to answer and told me to write down the replies, his tone of voice implying a threat. Naturally I was indignant and may have ordered him away, but I did not use such language as he attributes to me."

"Don't you want to correct the mistakes reported by the papers?"

"No, I wouldn't say anything about it," I interrupted.

"I would," said Pat League. "I would give the whole facts and show the business in." The whole gaggle stopped scribbling and looked at the prisoner, who smiled impudently.

"No, I won't," Clay responded. "You see, my wife tells me not to. I will wait till my trial and then everything will come out. You will see then there is more at the back of this than the public dreamed of."

"Such as?"

He looked at me as if asking for permission to elaborate, but I cast him a warning glance. These men were not to be trusted.

"Colonel King, it has been reported that you made this statement yesterday: 'Poston made the objectionable statement in regard to me and Mrs. King many times and Mrs. King has the papers that contained it. I had repeatedly asked Poston to retract the charge but he declined to do so. I met him on the street Tuesday and asked him if he intended to retract the statement. He said he did not and so I shot him.'"

"Yes. And?"

"Well, sir, we read that statement to Frank Poston last night, and he denied that that was true. Said his brother described the whole incident differently there in the infirmary."

"What does Frank Poston know about the matter? And Dave Poston wouldn't know the truth if it bit him in the ass. The crux of the matter is this: I have the utmost confidence in my wife's honor. She asked me to ask for a retraction of the charge, and I did. A man has a right to protect his honor, doesn't he?"

"Mister King, sir." The unexpected voice of a child pierced the dense air of the jail. A boy no older than ten or eleven had slipped through the guards and made his way through the crowd of reporters for a face to face audience with the prisoner.

"What is it, son?"

"Mister King," the boy panted. "I figgered you'd want to know. They're saying that lawyer died."

CHAPTER 41

❀

June 1891

"Bailiff, what case am I hearing today?" the judge asked, knowing full well which one it was. His greasy white hair and preacher's robe made him look like Moses in a courtroom, if Moses ever used pomade.

"Case No. 91-213—The State of Tennessee vs. Henry Clay King."

"And what are the charges against Mr. King?"

"Murder in the first degree."

"Your Honor," Mr. Weatherford said, "the defendant was a colonel of the Confederacy and would prefer to be addressed as such."

"Oh, he would, would he? That's a mighty presumptuous request for a defendant in a murder case to be making, standing on ceremony and such. I don't believe I like that kind of request from a murder defendant. Sounds right insolent, if you ask me. Bailiff, why don't you take *Mister* King on down to the sweat box."

"But Your Honor…" Mr. Weatherford protested.

"Major Weatherford, one more word out of you, and I'll hold you in contempt. I imagine there's room enough for *two* more down there."

That lawyer didn't say nothing else. The bailiff disappeared with the Colonel, who was bound up in chains on his hands and his feet.

Judge J. J. DuBose was the main judge of Shelby County and was an enemy of the boss of all the politics in Memphis, David P. Hadden, according to the rumor at the courthouse. And come to find out, Boss Hadden was Mr. Poston's cousin. And I heard tell that Judge DuBose wanted to have Boss Hadden and the rest of Mr. Poston's family as his friends instead of his enemies. So Judge DuBose was planning to do everything he could during this murder trial to treat Mr. Poston's murderer as mean as possible to get on good terms with Boss Hadden. It looked to me like he was getting off to a good start.

After the bailiff and the Colonel were gone a few minutes, the judge banged his hammer and announced, "Court will now recess for 15 minutes. Bailiff, lead all the folks in the courtroom down to the basement. We're going to take a little 'educational' field trip." One of the bailiffs walked to the door next to where the judge was and signaled for everybody to follow him.

The Gantt Sweat Box was famous at the courthouse, because that's where they put all the colored men they thought were thieves. It was a little room down in the basement with no windows and a door made of iron bars. I heard they crowded just as many men into it as they could, and it made no difference to the judge how uncomfortable or how hot it became. Judge DuBose made his way up to the front of the line and stood right next to the cell door of the sweat box and started commenting, as everybody from the courtroom, even folks who might be on the jury, lined up and walked past, straining their necks to see who was in there, holding their noses, looking mighty smug, shaking their heads in sadness.

"Now, you see what comes of a life of crime," the judge remarked. "This is the punishment that comes to murderers, thieves, petty criminals, and men who do not respect the law of the land and the judges who administer the law. Now, watch your step, ma'am. No, no one gets away with crime in my city, and no one gets away with disrespect in my courtroom."

About twenty men were crowded into that one little room that day, and there sat the Colonel, the only white man among them all. He crouched on a bench squeezed between two other men, hunched over with his elbows on his knees and his hands grasping either side of his head, staring at the floor. His face was redder than usual, from the heat or the humiliation or both. The buzzing of green flies and the breathing of sweaty men were the only noises I could hear besides the judge's comments. When it came our turn to walk by the opening to the cell, Miss Marie paused and glared at him, but I just hung my head. I couldn't look at him. He had always been so kind to me and seemed to be such a good man. I sure didn't want to look him in the eye if he looked up, because I felt like, well, maybe I had something to do with his being there. It was so sad.

Every day that week while they were picking a jury, the judge took a break from court for fifteen minutes, and he ordered everybody to go downstairs and walk by the sweat box. And every day, there sat the Colonel among all those colored men, looking worse and worse. He got skinnier and sweatier. And smelly. It was hot down in the basement of the courthouse, it being summer and all, and none of those men all crowded in there had had a chance to wash. Poor Colonel King.

I know that judge did that out of spite, so he could get in good with the Postons and Boss Hadden. The Colonel might have killed a man, but that wasn't any reason for him to be treated like a common thief.

❧   ❧   ❧

While the Colonel was sitting in the sweat box all those days, the lawyers were picking a jury. "Mr. Campbell. Now, Mr. Campbell, did you ever know Mr. David Poston?"

"No, sir, but I done heard of him."

"And how have you heard of him?"

"He was that lawyer that done got shot downtown a couple of months back."

"And have you ever heard of Colonel King?"

"Why, shore I have. He's the one what shot him."

The judge couldn't find anybody to sit on the jury who hadn't heard of the case. Makes you wonder what kind of person hadn't heard of such a famous case, since the newspapers had written so much about it—first the assault trial, then the property lawsuit, and then the murder. So the lawyers didn't seem to have much choice but to let men who'd already heard about everything be on the jury. But sometimes that judge let the other side go a little too far.

"Mr. Short. Are you familiar with the victim in this case, Mr. David Poston?"

"I heard a him and the Colonel. Anybody what can read has."

"And will you be able to be objective about determining the verdict in this case?"

"Yeah, providin' that Colonel gits hung."

"Your Honor, the defense objects to this juror."

The judge looked annoyed that his newspaper reading had been interrupted. "Huh? Oh, an objection. Well, let me see." He inspected the man being questioned as he was flapping the paper, trying to turn the page. "No, no, I think this juror will do just fine."

"But Your Honor, this man has already passed judgment."

"Major Weatherford, you know as well as I do that everybody in this courtroom has an opinion about this case and about *Mister* King. We'd have to resort to letting illiterate women and Negroes on the jury if we looked for someone who didn't know enough to have an opinion. This juror stands."

Stunned, Mr. Weatherford shook his head in disbelief and sat down.

This went on for about a week. The lawyers were arguing about who could be fair, the judge wasn't even trying to be fair, and the Colonel was still sweating in the basement. Finally, on an especially hot morning, with the ladies in the courtroom flapping their paper church fans and even the judge wiping the sweat off his forehead, Mr. Weatherford and Judge Brown pitched a fit.

"Your Honor, I respectfully request that you release the defendant" (he'd stopped calling him "Colonel") "from his imprisonment in the basement so that he can witness the selection of the jury which will decide his fate. Please, sir. Consider the temperature outside at 9:15 in the morning. This approaches cruel and unusual…"

"All right, all right. I know a thing or two about mercy. Bailiff, go retrieve the defendant from the sweat box. Maybe now you two will learn a little about respect in my courtroom," he warned them, raising an eyebrow and sounding cranky.

The Colonel returned to the courtroom, red faced, filthy, and sweating. I sure hoped they would let him wash later on. That was a terrible thing to do to a man. Then I got to wondering about those other men, the colored ones. I wondered if they had lawyers pitching a fit for them. I reckon that's one advantage of being rich, so you can hire a lawyer, and being white, too.

Finally, after the judge let the Colonel out of the sweat box and after they picked the jury, they were ready to start the trial. Attorney General Peters made the first speech. Now, I don't rightly know why they called him a general, since he didn't wear a uniform or anything, but that was what they called him.

"Your Honor, gentlemen of the jury, I stand before you to prosecute the most straightforward of cases. We have here one man who shot another man. There were many witnesses to this murder, as it occurred in broad daylight in downtown Memphis. But the most heinous part of this premeditated crime is that the defendant is in fact a most dishonorable man who has murdered an honorable and devoted family man. When he was a soldier of the Confederate army, the defendant Mr. King deserted the noble Southern cause, and went on to lie about it. When he was married, he left his worn out wife and took up with a beautiful mistress, the widow of a Confederate General." Now I know Miss Marie liked that comment—she was always so proud of the way she looked, and she dressed up every day for the trial, wearing her widow's gray as much as possible. But Miss Sallie was sitting right there in the courtroom. She wasn't pretty like Miss Marie, that's true, and this whole lawsuit thing seemed to take all the spunk out of her, but that wasn't a reason to be calling her "worn out". That was just plain mean. Miss Sallie didn't even bring her girls with her to help her look pitiful.

"When he couldn't keep the promises he made to his mistress, he destroyed the deed to the property that he gave her and forced her to take her case to court." The Colonel stiffened up. Miss Sallie looked down at her lap sadly. I reckon Miss Marie didn't really mind being slandered like I thought she would. It was almost like she was proud of having people say such terrible things about her. Maybe she thought it would make people feel sorry for her even more.

"When the opposing attorney appealed the case, he shot him. This man has no more loyalty or decency in him than…than…" (he was looking around for something, he was so carried away with what he was saying) "than this chair. No more decency than an inanimate object. There could be no more disreputable man prosecuted for no more heinous crime. This is the nature of this very straightforward case which I bring before you."

The people in the courtroom began clapping and cheering. Judge DuBose banged his hammer. "Order. I will have order in my courtroom."

I didn't want to believe the things that he'd said about the Colonel. I knew the Colonel was an honorable man. I just knew it. The way he was so good to me and so polite to everybody. The way he tried to take care of us all. I thought at one time that Miss Marie really loved him, and I could understand why. But not any more. She stared at him with such hatred. But I reckon nobody ever knows nothing for sure, except the people involved. It just all seemed such a shame.

Mr. Weatherford walked slowly to the front of the courtroom and spoke in his usual dignified way. "Your Honor, gentlemen of the jury, Colonel Henry Clay King was indeed a member of the noble Confederate cause. A native of Kentucky, Colonel King brought together his own regiment of men to fight the advancing Union army, and eventually joined forces under the command of General Gideon Pillow. But there is not a shred of evidence that this brave man, this noble gentleman, was ever a deserter. None at all. In fact, he was a courageous soldier and was later captured and held as a prisoner of war. That accusation of his being a deserter is pure hogwash, made to further defame a good man. After the War, he enjoyed great success in the practice of law here in Memphis, and his reputation in the community was spotless. His lovely wife, to whom he is deeply devoted, sits here in the courtroom" (I think he was trying to shame the Attorney General by letting the jury know how he had insulted her) "ever loyal to her husband, as he has always been to her. And when misfortune struck the wife of his former commander, why, Colonel King once again did the honorable thing, the Biblical command, to care for the poor, the downtrodden, widows and their children."

Miss Marie crossed her arms and sighed. She never did like being called "poor and downtrodden."

"But this particular widow, no matter how noble her husband might have been, this particular widow, Mrs. Mary Eliza Pillow, is a grasping, conniving, stealing woman who took forcible possession of Colonel King's property, at one time holding his people at gunpoint, when he was out of town. This same woman defamed him publicly by her cross-bills to his suit to drive her from his property. Mr. David Poston, who represented Mrs. Pillow in this litigation, went so far as to publish false and degrading information about Colonel King's lovely wife, lies which are so specious, so outrageous, that I cannot repeat them here in polite company.

"Colonel King had been driven beyond the limits of human endurance by the lies and defamation spewed by Mrs. Pillow and her lawyer, Mr. Poston, and having recently heard that Mr. Poston was armed and angry, he decided that for his own protection he must arm himself as well. As much as he had desired to defend the honor of his wronged wife by killing Mr. Poston, he desisted and showed great restraint, considering his provocation. When approached on the street by an angry, shouting Poston, he feared for his life and defended himself. This was not premeditated murder, but self-defense, pure and simple. Add to that the frenzy into which Mr. Poston had driven Colonel King through his horrific allegations against Mrs. King, and it becomes clear that Colonel King could not have been in his right mind on the day of the tragedy. When Colonel King finally saw Mr. Poston on the street, why, his wrath and indignation and fear arose from within and overcame him, causing him to shoot this vile traducer of his wife's honor. It is only in seeing the full context of Colonel King's life and trials, provoked by this woman and by David Poston, that one can fully appreciate the extenuating circumstances which drove him to this most justifiable of deeds."

I thought Mr. Weatherford did a good job of explaining the Colonel's side of things, best as you can explain away a shooting.

❦   ❦   ❦

"Mr. Poston, what is your relationship to the deceased?"

"He was my older brother." Mr. Frank Poston had the same wolf like eyes and frightful sneer as his brother, but he didn't wave his arms as much.

"And how often did you ordinarily see your brother?"

"I worked with him every day. We practiced law together." He looked like he was fixing to cry.

"And how would you describe your brother's character?"

"Oh, my brother David was the kindest soul God ever placed on this earth. He wouldn't hurt a fly. He could be tough, that's for sure, but if he was tough, it was always on behalf of his client. He would never do or say anything that would be intentionally cruel." He wiped his eyes.

I never heard such nice talk about such a mean man. But it was his brother, so maybe he knew him back when he might have been nice. I think old man Poston was born with the devil in him. That happens in some folks, you know. They never even start to be nice. Even when they're little children, they act just like demons. I would have hated to be Mr. Poston's mama, what with a demon like that as a young'un.

"Now, Mr. Poston, tell me about your brother's family."

"His wife, Emma, is a good Christian woman. He has two sons, David and James, and two little girls, named Violet and Alice…" At that he started to bawl. He must have had a soft spot in his heart for poor little daddy-less Alice. It hadn't ever occurred to me that old man Poston might be married or have any children or anything. But I reckon even the meanest among us has got a human streak.

Judge DuBose broke in, in the middle of all the blubbering, and in the most tender way suggested that Mr. Poston take a break and get himself together. Mr. Poston pulled out a handkerchief and blew his nose with a loud honk before he plodded back through the courtroom and out the door.

"Since we have a small break in the proceedings," the judge said, "I think it would be appropriate for the jury to hear something of the facts that preceded this murder. I believe, Mr. Jackson, that you have some older copies of the *Appeal-Avalanche* that might be of interest to the jury."

"Yes, Your Honor. Here they are." And with that Mr. Jackson, the bailiff, handed the judge a stack of old newspapers. The judge started rummaging through them, until he found just what he wanted—Miss Marie's cross-bill, that whole front page in the newspaper. He began to read it out loud.

"Let's see, yes, here it is. Mrs. Pillow *'found herself…in a fraud so diabolical and malevolent in its deliberate and systematic plan and execution as to be almost too startling for belief, so skillfully creating a network of facts and circumstances so plausible as to answer his purpose even better than facts…'"*

He scanned the courtroom slowly. "'Diabolical' and 'malevolent'. Those are pretty harsh words, don't you think, Mr. Jackson?"

"Yessir. Real harsh," the burly man agreed.

The judge coughed and continued. "*She, a woman born to wealth and luxury, which he never knew, reared in all the elegance of an old-time Southern home, in order to support her little ones and preserve her self-respect and independence, tramped on foot, from daylight till dark, through mud and water, rain and sleet and snow, and through the heat of summer, over this plantation, imposing upon herself during these years the labors of a man, because she was not able to pay a superintendent…'"*

Miss Marie, tromping through the mud. That'll be the day.

That other teary eyed Mr. Poston wasn't quite ready to go back on the witness stand again, so the judge took to reading all the nastiness that the Memphis papers wrote back during the property hearing. "*Following the example of the Prince of Wales in the Mordaunt case, Colonel King has betrayed the confidence of a lady and has thereby sunk so low in the estimation of honorable men that he can sink no lower. It defies common decency that any man would defame any woman, let alone a widow'*…let's see now, yes, this is the part I was looking for…'*This foul-tongued traducer is not worthy to brush the dust from the shoes of her deceased husband…'"*

The room was silent except for the judge's gruff voice and the whirring of the ceiling fans. The people in the courtroom listened as if none of them had ever heard any of this before. But I didn't want to listen. I'd read it all, lived it all, and what I hadn't lived and knew was a lie gave me a knot in my stomach. So I just watched the ceiling fans, spinning round and round.

Finally, that other Mr. Poston composed himself enough to testify. He finished telling us all about old man Poston's family and his law practice and how he took care of the widows and children in his neighborhood and how he was an upstanding member of the Catholic Church. Then he explained what happened in March. He said he talked to old man Poston that night after the shooting, while he was dying in the infirmary. He said his brother said the Colonel had never done anything to show he was mad at him. That he'd seen him plenty of times on the street since the first trial and that nothing bad passed between them. That he wasn't expecting any trouble and that the only weapon he was carrying was a pocket knife. I wondered how a dying man could get around to saying so much. And, of course, the most interesting thing of all, he said that those doctors had to take out *three whole feet* of old man Poston's innards to try to save him. I reckon that didn't work.

Then it was the Widow Poston's turn. She was all dressed in black and kept her head down. Her eyes were watery before she even got started.

"Now, Mrs. Poston, I know this will be difficult for you, but we need to ask you a few questions. How long were you and Mr. Poston married?"

"It'd be seventeen years this August."

"And how long had he been practicing law?"

"I guess that would be almost twenty years." She brushed a strand of gray hair from her face and started to whimper. Oh, lawdy, I knew what was coming next.

"And did he ever discuss the content of his law work with you?"

Sniff. "Never. He knew he wasn't supposed to." She dabbed her handkerchief at her eye.

"But did you ever hear of the King-Pillow litigation?"

"Yes. But only that he was trying to help defend the honor of a poor...widow...woman." And with that she let out a wail you could have heard clear down to the banks of the Mississippi River. She moaned and sobbed so loud, my ears were hurting. I knew it must have hurt the jury members' ears, too, because she was sitting even closer to them. And the judge didn't make her stop. Why, she must have sat there for five minutes just a boo-hooing without nobody saying nothing. Finally, the judge said she wasn't any good as a witness with her being so upset and all and her not knowing anything about his law cases or the murder anyway, so he let her leave. I was just as glad, too.

I might have been driven to distraction, too, if I had a husband who was shot. But with a husband like old man Poston, I might have been driven to distraction anyway. I felt sorry for her, but not because he was dead. She just seemed so sad is all.

❧   ❧   ❧

"Your Honor, we would like to enter as evidence the record of the property dispute hearing between Colonel King and Mrs. Pillow," Mr. Peters announced.

"Objection, Your Honor," Judge Brown grumbled. "This is prejudicial."

"What is the purpose of this information, Mr. Peters?"

"We want to show Mr. King's motivation for the murder of Mr. Poston."

"Your Honor," Judge Brown explained in his gravelly voice, "the personal information contained in that record might not just reflect badly upon Colonel King. There is another party who might be calumnied by this information—Mrs. Pillow. Certainly the prosecution does not wish to defame a poor widow woman?" He raised his eyebrows, taunting Mr. Peters.

Mr. Peters responded angrily, "We do not wish to defame anyone, only to demonstrate that Mr. King had a reason to want to murder Mr. Poston."

"The record shouldn't be included because that case is under appeal, Your Honor," Mr. Weatherford reminded him. "Mr. Poston filed the appeals shortly before his demise."

"His murder, you mean. No, I don't think it would be inappropriate for the jury to have the record of the property dispute hearing in front of them."

"But Your Honor, it is irrelevant to the murder charge," Judge Brown tried again.

The judge leaned back in his chair, tapping his thumbs together. "It seems to me that the record of the property dispute could be a double-edged sword. The prosecution says it would show his motivation, but the defense could just as well use it to show how Colonel King was driven out of his mind, as you claim." He leaned forward and grinned. "I'll allow it."

What the court said in that property hearing didn't tell the whole story, so if I'd been one of the Colonel's lawyers, I would have called witnesses to tell all about the whole Sterling Hill mess. That way the Colonel might get a fairer shot. Mr. Weatherford could have told the judge how those Arkansas and Tennessee judges thought all of Miss Marie's witnesses were lying, just to make sure everybody knew that, or even Judge Brown could have said something. But I learned that you can't be a lawyer and a witness at the same time, which was a shame. The lawyers knew more about the whole situation than just about anybody.

Except for Miss Marie and me. I sure wouldn't have wanted be a witness again, but they could have asked Miss Marie. I'm not sure what she would have said, though, or how she would have acted. She probably would have just sat there, staring at the Colonel, like she did the whole time. I reckon she would have had to say something, seeing as how when you're a witness, you've got to talk. But what she did say might have been lies.

After several days of Attorney General Peters bringing in witness after witness telling what a good and decent man Mr. Poston was, he said his side was done, and it was time for the Colonel's side to start. The judge said we'd stop for the day and made his announcement.

"Gentlemen of the jury, I have the honor of inviting you to a picnic this Sunday at 2 o'clock out in East End Park. You can take the trolley to get there. All the refreshments will be provided by the court. Bailiff, find out if any of the jurors need directions to the picnic site. Court is now in recess until 9:00 a.m. Monday morning."

Now, I hadn't ever heard of a "jury picnic," but something about it didn't sound right. Mr. Weatherford rubbed his eyes with his fingers like he was trying to erase what just happened. Judge Brown whispered something to the Colonel, who shook his head sadly. I was just wondering about that jury picnic. I heard there was a merry-go-round out in East End Park. I wondered whether Miss Marie and I would be invited to that picnic. I reckon not.

CHAPTER 42

"Your Honor, it has come to our attention that certain improprieties have occurred regarding this jury," Attorney General Peters remarked nervously.

"Is that so?" Judge DuBose sat with his arms crossed, frowning.

"Yes, your Honor. There seems to have been some inappropriate contact between a juror and a witness, and we would like you to consider dismissing this juror."

"Who was it?" The judge scanned the jury threateningly. Mr. Peters called Mr. Smith to come to the witness stand. A lanky farmer ambled over to the chair, plopped down, and slumped down into the seat comfortably.

"Mr. Smith, are you familiar with any of the witnesses on this list?" the judge asked.

Mr. Smith pulled out his spectacles and squinted at the witness list. "I believe I ran into Mr. William Rollins here, just the other day."

"Are you a friend of Mr. Rollins?"

"No, but I was introduced to him down at the feed store."

"Did he say anything to you besides the usual pleasantries?"

"Well, yes. We got to talking about the weather. He told me the rain over in Arkansas had been pretty scarce."

"Bailiff, go round up Mr. Rollins and bring him on in to me," the judge barked.

So after a short recess, the bailiff came back in with Mr. Rollins, a farmer I'd seen at Sterling Hill a couple of times. I reckon Mr. Rollins was supposed to take the Colonel's side in the case and say something nice about him. But the judge had found a way out of that. After Mr. Smith said he'd talked to Mr. Rollins last week, the judge made that farmer Rollins pay a $10 fine and sent him to the work house for three weeks. Just like that. But he didn't do *nothing* to Mr. Smith. He went right back up to the jury box and sat down.

Now that ain't right. And the judge must have known it wasn't right. But the judge didn't say a word to that juror. Not one word. I reckon he wanted to get that juror on his side, the side against Colonel King, by being easy on him when he could have been rough. And he probably wanted to get rid of a witness that would have said something helpful about the Colonel. And that just wasn't fair.

Judge Brown stood and addressed Judge DuBose. "Your Honor, we respectfully request that you recuse yourself from this case."

"Recuse myself? What for?"

"Your Honor, it has become apparent to the defense that you have certain biases."

"Recuse myself? Not on your life!" the judge raged. You'd have thought that those lawyers would have learned about that judge, after that sweat box business, but they seemed to have forgotten all that.

"Then, Your Honor, we have to choice but to move for a mistrial."

"A mistrial? On what grounds?" Judge DuBose's face turned purple.

Judge Brown hesitated. "Several."

"Like what?"

"The jury picnic. It is outside of the bounds of all canons of legal ethics for a jurist to host, at the court's expense, a social gathering for a jury."

"Now looky here, Mr. Brown," the judge exploded. "There will be no mistrial in my courtroom—never! You can take your canons and you can just..."

Well, I won't repeat what the judge said. I wouldn't dare. I just never thought, well, never mind.

I heard tell that Judge DuBose had already let the whole jury leave after the trial every day to go out on the town and that he paid for all their whisky. I heard he sent them all out to supper once at Gaston's and paid the whole bill himself. Why, I heard they even went for a ferry boat ride over to Arkansas for an afternoon, and the judge went with them. So that jury picnic didn't seem any different. It wasn't supposed to be going on, but sure enough it was.

None of that seemed to bother Miss Marie, though. She sat perched on her wooden bench like a queen on her throne, waiting to spit on the traitor in chains before she sent him to the gallows. And she would have done just that, too, if she'd had the chance. Just because the Colonel tried to get his land back. I felt sorry for him, but I didn't say that to her. I wasn't fixing to get slapped again.

❧   ❧   ❧

"Now, Judge Morgan, would you describe for the court the petition for divorce you received from Colonel King in April of 1888?" Mr. Weatherford asked his first witness.

"Well," Judge Morgan began, leaning back in the chair and rubbing his whiskered cheek. "For one thing, it was almost illegible. I had to study it carefully to make out what it was. The handwriting looked like, well, like chicken scratch." His mutton chops seemed much too big for such a small man.

"Did it appear to be the handwriting of a sane person?"

"I don't know how one would describe the handwriting of a 'sane person,' Major Weatherford. But it could well be that Colonel King was inebriated either by whisky or by narcotics at the time that that petition was written."

"Do you have any reason to suspect, based on the content of that petition, that the author was not in his right mind?" Mr. Weatherford asked.

"Well, yes. There were some fairly unconventional aspects. For one thing, the reason given for the divorce was, shall we say, most unsavory." He eyed Judge DuBose and then Mr. Weatherford, as if he had said all he wanted to say on that subject.

"Did that reason have anything to do with Mrs. Sallie King?"

Judge Morgan repositioned himself and hesitated. I didn't think he could screw up his face into any more of a frown than he already had, but he did. "Yes."

"Please state for the record the reason for the divorce given in the petition."

"The best I could make out of that ungainly scrawl," Judge Morgan responded quietly, "was that Clay King was accusing his wife of having relations with a Negro."

The people in the courtroom gasped in unison. I thought everybody already knew all about that accusation and wouldn't be so surprised. But then I realized what he'd said. It wasn't just something Miss Marie made up—the business about Miss Sallie and Malcolm was something the Colonel really did say himself. A man is liable to say all kinds of things when he's drunk, I imagine.

Mr. Weatherford's head hung low, regretfully, even though he was the one who asked the question. "Sir, in your professional opinion, as a man who has seen a great deal in the legal world and in society at large, would this charge be made by a gentleman who is in his right mind?"

I reckon he wanted Judge Morgan to say no. "Clay King was desperately in love with Mrs. Pillow and was inclined to drink excessively." His tensed hands formed a small cage of fingers in front of him. "He even said as much when he came to me, asking me to return that divorce petition. He was afraid it would somehow be used against him in all these subsequent legal proceedings, although I suppose he didn't know it would be used in a murder trial."

"Thank you, Judge Morgan."

"No, the Clay King who came to my office, hat in hand, requesting that that petition be returned, he was not insane. Embarrassed? Yes. Desperate? Certainly. But he understood the consequences of that petition too clearly to be deemed insane."

❧   ❧   ❧

Rumor had it that all five of Mr. Poston's brothers were going to show up in the courtroom and shoot the Colonel right then and there, if he was found innocent. So the Colonel's friends were too scared to come to the courthouse any more. I even heard that somebody had threatened to kill one of the witnesses, and he plum run out a town. Seemed like anybody in Memphis who could have been a witness for the Colonel decided to stay as far away from that courthouse as they could.

It would be hard to admit you were a friend of a man that murdered another man. But considering how good a man the Colonel was to begin with, and how bad Mr. Poston was, and considering how the Colonel didn't start the whole mess anyhow, except that he was so generous with Miss Marie, well, you'd have thought somebody on his side would be there for him. But nobody was, except for Miss Sallie. And me, of course.

So the only ones they could get to testify for the Colonel were folks from Arkansas. And the strangest thing was that every one of those men from Lee County, every one of them, described the Colonel like he was crazy.

Mr. Derrick was the Recorder of the Deeds in Lee County, and he said Colonel King was as crazy as a betsy bug. He told a tale about running out to Sterling Hill to deliver a document one time. Said when he knocked on the back door and looked inside, he saw the Colonel sitting there in the kitchen, with Miss Marie cutting up his food for him and spoon-feeding him, just like he was a baby. And then Mr. Foster from LaGrange said one time he saw the Colonel driving into town in his carriage without his pants on. That story made the whole courtroom bust out laughing. Mr. Mills was from LaGrange, too, and he said he used to see the Colonel every evening wading in the river all the way up to his waist and singing hymns at the top of his lungs. He showed the judge how it happened: "'Shall we ga-ther at the ri-ver...'" Judge DuBose didn't much care for his singing.

But Attorney General Peters knew something about all of them. Mr. Derrick admitted he was the Colonel's cousin and was real sorry for letting Miss Marie record that deed like she did. Mr. Foster owed the Colonel $100 and might be inclined to say whatever it was the Colonel wanted him to because of it. And of course, Attorney General Peters made Mr. Mills tell everybody where LaGrange is—nowhere close to the river, so there's no way that a man who lived in LaGrange would be able to see the Colonel wading in it and singing every evening.

"Your Honor, the Defense calls Mr. Alfred Davis."

From the back of the courtroom shuffled a familiar dark man, with hair so white it looked like snow on the rich Delta soil. Someone had brought old Mr. Alfred all the way from Sterling Hill to testify for the Colonel. As he made his way up the aisle, he spotted me and gave me a little wave. I waved back, curious as to what he might say.

"Now, Mr. Davis, you told me you'd seen Colonel King act in some rather strange ways. Can you describe those to me?"

"Well, yassuh." He adjusted himself in the chair. "There was this one time over to the gate."

"What gate?"

"The gate that's at the front."

"Would that be the gate at the front of Sterling Hill?"

"Yassuh. That's where I mean."

"And what happened there at the gate?"

"Well, you see, there's this cabin there, over to the gate, and there was this one time that I was workin' around there, pullin' weeds. I couldn't help myself, but I looked in the window, and there they was."

"Who was there?"

"Colonel King and Miz Pillow."

"And what were they doing?"

"Well, the Colonel, he was down on his knees, with his head bowed, like he was prayin' or somethin'. And she, Miz Pillow, she was standin' over him, just a-cussin' and a-fussin'."

"How could you tell she was 'cussin'"?"

"One of the windows was broke. You could hear her blastin' him clear acrost to the river side of the place."

"Do you recall what she was saying?"

"She was cussin' him out right good. Using the Good Lord's name in vain. I ain't never heard nothin' like that comin' from no woman."

"And did you hear Colonel King say anything?"

"All I heard was him cryin', and he was callin' out to her like he was groanin' or somethin', cryin' 'Please. Please. I'll do whatever you want.' That's what he was sayin'. He just sounded so pitiful, I was right ashamed to say somethin' about it. Actin' like a child when he was a grown man." Mr. Alfred shook his head.

"So Colonel King was on his knees and she was cursing him?"

"Yassuh." Mr. Alfred nodded earnestly. "Them Yankees, they heard it, too, and they didn't know what to think. All gathering 'round with their guns and a cannon, too, just a-listenin' to her goin' at it. Strangest thing I ever did see, all them soldiers standin' there."

Nobody said anything for a minute, trying to figure out the story that Mr. Alfred was telling. He looked up at Mr. Weatherford, ready to take another question. But Mr. Weatherford just said, "Thank you, Mr. Davis," with eyes full of pity.

Attorney General Peters didn't ask him any questions about what he had said—he just left well enough alone. But I knew something that Mr. Peters didn't. I knew Mr. Alfred was Malcolm's daddy. And I knew how sorrowful he must have felt about what all Mr. Poston and Mr. Chambers and Miss Marie said and then what happened to his son. Mr. Alfred was just trying to help the Colonel. And even though he was liable to get confused sometimes—there wasn't a cabin by the front gate any more—I don't blame him one bit for saying what he did.

CHAPTER 43

"I have decided that representatives of the press should not be present during Colonel King's testimony." The rabble that filled the sweltering courtroom murmured louder than usual until the sound of the gavel silenced them.

Thank God. The press in this town had done enough damage to me and my family. It seemed there wasn't anything left of our lives to destroy. Our personal lives, our social lives, Clay's professional life had come crashing down around us because of the lies these men had printed. Some of the reporters sputtered indignantly at the judge's words. There they sat, with notepads and pencils on their laps, ready to write down everything that happened to take back to the newspapers and twist into some new convoluted tale, just like they'd done against us for years. Clay's testimony would undoubtedly be the most compelling, possibly the most damaging so far, and certainly the most easily misconstrued.

"Gentlemen?" the judge urged them, impatiently.

Probably fifteen men stood up, gathered their belongings, and slowly made their way out of the courtroom, some of them turning back around to look at the judge, as if expecting him to change his mind.

The bitch who had caused it all had blessedly stopped coming down to the courthouse every day, just as I wished I might. As angry as I had felt towards her, as many times as I wished I could rip her hair out and stomp her face, as many times as I wanted to shame her even more than she shamed me, I no longer had the energy—the venom had run dry. Numbness was all I felt toward her, toward the prosecutor, toward the world. Although I despised her, she did not force Clay to pick up that gun. The prosecutor did not create this crisis out of thin air. Clay was responsible for all his actions. This horrid man to whom I had attached myself, from whom I could not release myself, this horrid man was still my husband. And in the eyes of the world and of God, I had to be by his side. The world had already ostracized me. All that remained was the Almighty and Clay.

The trial was interminable—close to a month, by that time. The summer heat could not have added any more tension to that courtroom, brimming with curiosity seekers, the scandal mongers of the press, but none of our friends. None of them. We were completely bereft of the support and testimony of people we had known all our adult lives. The ties that bind are brittle, easily broken, in a society based on money and the illusions of status. Only Kizzie was there. I suppose Mrs. Pillow sent her as her personal emissary to give a more truthful account of the events in the courtroom than the newspapers were likely to give. I pitied the poor girl but welcomed her kind expressions each day, the only ones I knew.

"The Defense calls Colonel Henry Clay King." Hobbling to the witness stand, hunched, frightened, Clay seemed much less than even his name. He was no longer the valiant warrior or even the desperate lover he had been. He was just old.

"Now, Colonel King," Mr. Weatherford asked, "Please tell us the events of March 10th as you recall them."

He adjusted himself in the chair, cleared his throat, and peeked around Mr. Weatherford to see who was in the courtroom before he started quietly. "I went downtown," he cleared his throat again and spoke a little louder, "I went downtown that morning to try to find you. Bill Weatherford. First I went to your office, and then I looked in the courthouse."

"So you were not searching for David Poston that morning?"

"No, no, I wasn't. But if I'd found him…"

"That'll be just fine," Mr. Weatherford interrupted. "And at approximately 11:00 a.m. that morning, where were you?"

"I believe I was on Main Street about that time. Yes, that's it," he said, staring into his lap where one of his hands was squeezing the other one white.

"Now, we've had people come in here to say that you crossed Main Street in order to lie in wait for David Poston. Is that true?"

"No," he said calmly. "I crossed the street from the Memphis and Charleston ticket offices to get my shoes blackened. After that, I went into Lee's Cigar store, because they carry the particular brand of cigar that I prefer."

"Did you lie in wait for David Poston?"

"No, no, I had no idea he'd be walking down the street at that time."

"And exactly what happened that morning between you and Mr. Poston?"

He regarded Mr. Weatherford carefully. "Poston came running down Main Street toward me, yelling and waving his arms angrily. He looked me straight in the eye, and I knew what he was about to do. He looked me straight in the eye." By this time he was agitated. "I could see what he was thinking." He turned around to face the judge and said it again. "*He looked me straight in the eye.*"

"On the morning of March 10th, why did you bring a pistol with you in your overcoat pocket?"

"I believe that Mary Eliza and John, John Shields, I believe they were determined to kill me. They'd already attempted to steal my farm. And ruin my good name. They had already done that." Indeed, they had already done that and more.

"Did you have any reason to believe that David Poston was a threat to you?"

"Yes, yes, he was. He'd been carrying a double barrel shotgun around town, so I felt it necessary to arm myself and be prepared for anything. That's why I was carrying my gun."

"And when you saw him coming down Main Street that morning, you felt threatened by him?"

"Yes, I felt threatened. He was shouting and acting aggressive. *He looked me straight in the eye.* I decided I had to take care of the matter. I pulled out my gun, and I shot him in the gut." The quiet of the courtroom at that moment was unnerving. No one gasped in amazement. There were no sounds of paper rattling. This was a truth confirmed by too many, a reality too terribly accurate to be unexpected.

"Did you plan to kill David Poston that morning?"

"No, I did not, but I wanted to be prepared, just in case."

"Just in case…"

"Just in case I saw him, just in case I needed to protect myself."

"Colonel King, did you in any way provoke Mr. Poston on the day of the incident?"

"I did not see Mr. Poston on that day until he came running at me on Main Street. But he, he provoked me. He provoked me beyond what any man should have to bear." Then he stood up and bellowed, "That man was no gentleman, for saying the things that he did, that my wife had criminal intercourse…"

"That's fine, Colonel," Mr. Weatherford interrupted, uneasily. "Please sit down." I had heard those bitter words so many times, even from his own mouth, but I had never yet become inured to them. Hearing them made the truth sound so harsh, so ugly, not at all the gentle warmth I had known in his arms. These secrets, the private moments between a man and a woman could not adequately be described in even whispers, and certainly not in the hideous black words in newsprint for all the world to read and misconstrue and judge, words which tainted the brief passionate moments that I had known with Malcolm.

Mr. Weatherford turned around to the table where Judge Brown was sitting, and Judge Brown shrugged his shoulders helplessly.

"No further questions," Mr. Weatherford said.

"Now, Colonel King," Attorney General Peters began as he approached him, "did you communicate in any way with Mr. Poston on the morning of the murder?"

"I told Tom Stratton what I was prepared to do and that he should give him fair warning."

"What, precisely, was it that you were prepared to do?"

"I was prepared to kill him. I didn't want anybody else to get hurt, just that son of a bitch Poston. I wanted to give him fair warning that I was ready to kill him."

Mr. Peters let the sound of those words linger in the air as long as possible. "Colonel King, have you ever killed a man before?"

Clay glanced warily to each side. "Only in the War."

"Isn't it true that when you were living in Kentucky, that you drew a knife and threatened another lawyer?"

Clay was dumbstruck, as if Mr. Peters had drawn a knife on him.

"Please answer the question."

"He was threatening me. I had to defend myself. There's much more to it…" I had never heard this tale, but by this point, I had no doubt it was true.

"I'll take that as a 'yes'. And Colonel King, isn't it true that you were tried for 'assault with attempt to kill and murder' Mrs. Mary Eliza Pillow?"

"No. That is not true."

Mr. Peters flipped through his papers, with an annoyed look on his face. He walked back over to his table. One of the other lawyers there crooked his finger to him, and when the Mr. Peters leaned over, the other lawyer whispered something in his ear.

"All right, Colonel King. Isn't it true that you were tried on a charge of 'assault with a deadly weapon' in reference to an attack on Mrs. Pillow?"

"Yes. And I was found not guilty."

"Isn't it true, Colonel King, that the jury in that case found you not guilty on a statute of limitations issue, not on the facts of the case?"

His eyes were wild. "I was acquitted."

"And are you aware of the differences between the two charges, 'assault with intent to kill and murder' and 'assault with a deadly weapon'?"

"Of course, I am. I am a lawyer."

"And you are familiar with the distinctions in the Arkansas law regarding the statute of limitations for each charge?"

Clay glanced around the room nervously. "Of course I know those distinctions. They were the basis of my acquittal."

Mr. Peters smiled and turned toward the audience. "Now, Colonel King, is it true that you have been the editor of a scholarly legal periodical?"

"I am the founder and chief editor of *King's Tennessee Digest*."

"And how long have you been engaged in that endeavor?"

"Over twenty years."

"And are you still editing *King's Tennessee Digest*?"

"Yes. Well, I was until I was incarcerated."

"And have you ever had any difficulty understanding any of the legal matters that you read and edit?"

"Certainly not."

"So you have remained of sound mind, sound enough to study and comment upon difficult legal matters, for the past twenty years, up until this date?"

His eyes shifted from side to side. Cornered and desperate, he said nothing else.

"No further questions," Mr. Peters smirked.

Mr. Weatherford leaned on the table with his face in his hands. Judge Brown's eyes were closed tight, facing the ceiling. I steeled myself for yet another onslaught of interrogation by the press as I prepared to leave through the courtroom doors, those gates of Hell handcrafted for me by my husband, opening to my never ending torture.

CHAPTER 44

Mr. Weatherford carried a couple of books up to the front of the courtroom, set them down on a little table there, coughed to clear his voice, and began to say the last good thing anybody was going say about the Colonel in that court-room.

I'd had a hard time sleeping those last few nights of the trial, thinking about all the destruction, all the pain. The nighttime heat seemed to weigh upon me, like a heavy cat sleeping on my chest, almost smothering me. I felt that same heaviness in the heat of the courtroom that morning, and I wondered if it was my fault, if there was something I could have done. And even worse, I won-dered if I would have had the guts to do something if I could have. I didn't like none of the answers, neither.

Laura, all dressed in black, sat in the courtroom with me on that last day of speechmaking. She listened carefully, soaking up every word. With every phrase her eyes showed her feelings, sometimes anger, sometimes bitterness, but mostly the satisfaction of finally getting revenge. "He has disgraced my mother. That man has no character. None. He deserves every bad thing that happened to him." I'd heard those words over and over each day after the trial. I didn't try to tell her any different.

Mr. Weatherford held one fist over his heart, the other hand by his side, as he paced and argued. "Through the lawsuits and the accompanying calumny created by Mrs. Gideon Pillow and her attorney David Poston, Colonel King was driven right out of his mind. He firmly believed that the lawsuits filed against him were merely intended to goad him, to annoy him, and they hung over his head like a Sword of Damocles. He was thought by many to be a raving maniac. He was often seen wandering around the streets of downtown Memphis with a crazed look in his eye. He was ever approaching me and asking the same question: 'Is it over yet? Is it over yet?' These words echoed through the streets of Memphis, the desperate plea of a deranged man.'"

The Colonel had changed so much since I first met him. He seemed to be such a good man, such a kind man, even though he was prone to drinking and other weaknesses, I reckon. What those weaknesses were, deep down inside of him, I could only guess, but they seemed to tug at him, pulling him down into a whirlpool of confusion inside his head until they finally got the best of him. Until they finally made him kill a man. Temptation had done him in, and the old Colonel, the honorable gentleman who had been so kind to me, was gone forever.

"His honor and reputation were horribly impugned by these lawsuits and the publicity surrounding them, and because of that fact, his business suffered. His clients no longer entrusted him with their affairs. His wife's reputation was inalterably tarnished, and his daughters' chances for a life of respectability were diminished, just by the words of Mr. Poston and their publication. Colonel King sought solace in whisky, an act not a few of us are familiar with, and was unfortunately driven to intoxication by the pressures put upon him by lawsuit after lawsuit, disgrace after disgrace."

The Colonel and Miss Marie had done all they could do to shame each other. And every time they tried to shame the other one, they heaped more shame on themselves. You can't stay clean when you're fighting in the mud. And other folks got dirty along the way, too. Miss Sallie didn't do anything wrong, and yet she was pulled down into the slime, stuck in a swamp of disgrace for the rest of her life. It's awful how people's bad decisions can disgrace the folks around them. I felt so sorry for Miss Sallie and her girls.

"Is it any wonder that Colonel King, in whatever state of mind he might have been in, is it any wonder then that he kept himself armed? And when approached by the man who was the source of his demise—socially, economically, even mentally—and that man was approaching him in a loud and aggressive manner, is it any wonder that Colonel King, thinking Mr. Poston was himself armed and was accosting him on the street, that Colonel King would draw his weapon in self-defense?"

Shooting a man to keep him from shooting you. I reckon that made sense, and saying so was as good a way of getting out of such a fix as any. The Colonel was fighting against dying. Like Malcolm walking out that door. If he'd admitted what Miss Marie wanted him to, that he'd had relations with a white woman, even if it was a lie, he'd be dead anyway. They'd have got him either way. Wandering in the woods alone gave him at least a chance of escaping. But like a man fighting against drowning, there wasn't ever much chance he was going to come out of there alive.

By now Mr. Weatherford was holding one of the books open in his hand, pointing to something on the page. "The Bible entreats us to 'Do unto others as you would have done unto you.' If you, gentlemen of the jury, had found yourself entangled in the web of this beautiful woman, this dangerous, beautiful woman, would it not be likely that you too would be subject to her womanly wiles? The poet writes, 'A thing of beauty is a joy forever.' That's how it should be, but that's not how it is. Because you see, this great beauty, Mrs. Mary Eliza Pillow, has brought no joy to this man's life, only misery and suffering and disgrace. Have none of us made mistakes, in our devotion to Beauty? Is Colonel King the only man in this room who has fallen prey to a beautiful woman?"

What every woman envies and what every man desires. Miss Marie was surely beautiful on the outside, there was no doubt about that. But what was on the inside was surely ugly. Like the smooth glassy surface of a river that deceives you, hiding a churning undertow of destruction down below, only you can't see it till it's too late. She knew she could tempt the Colonel; she knew she could find his weakness; she knew she could deceive him, and in deceiving him, destroy him, just so she could get what she wanted. If she knew what it was she wanted.

"In Texas, they have created a most progressive law, that a person found guilty by reason of insanity should be hospitalized until he is recovered, or otherwise for the remainder of his life. In Tennessee, the law reads that a person found guilty by reason of insanity must be freed. Clearly, this formerly upstanding gentleman of the community, this legal scholar, this devoted family man and honored Confederate soldier poses no threat to anyone. He defended himself, his good name, and his wife's honor in this act of self-defense. His nemesis is now departed, and most tragically, so are his own mental faculties. It is your job, members of the jury, to see that justice is done and free this man to whom so many vile injustices have been done."

Mr. Weatherford did a right good job, considering what it was he had to do. It wouldn't be easy to help out a man who'd got himself into such a fix as this. I was real impressed with him and how he did everything he could to help the Colonel, even if he knew they didn't have a chance.

When we came back into the courtroom after the break, it was time for Attorney General Peters to say his piece. He walked right up to the front of the courtroom, while everybody was silent and waiting, loudly and dramatically, he hawked up and spit—*ping*—with perfect aim, into a tarnished brass spittoon. I reckon that was what he thought about Mr. Weatherford's speech.

❀　　　❀　　　❀

"Gentlemen of the jury," the judge announced right before he sent them out to decide the Colonel's fate. "There are several administrative matters which must be handled before you may begin your deliberations. You must elect a foreman, there are certain instructions that I must issue, et cetera. So I think it would be easier for us to adjourn for now, and then y'all come on over to my home for dinner this evening. That way we can tend to matters there without inconveniencing the lawyers and the other people in the courtroom. We can probably also concentrate better in the cool of the evening rather than in this hot courtroom. Bailiff, make sure all these good folks get my address. Oh, and if any of you need a ride, I'm sure Deputy Sheriff Harrell will be happy to oblige."

❀　　　❀　　　❀

The heat and humidity seemed a warning from the heavens that rain was coming, even though the dark clouds had only just begun to gather. Just as I had on most days of the trial, I spread my cloth and sat on the bluff overlooking the river to eat my lunch. The little boy Jeremiah had taken to me, and he made a point of finding me every day at lunchtime. I think the fact that I shared my meal with him might have had something to do with it.

Although Miss Marie hadn't been to the courthouse in more than a week, she was sure to come that morning when the verdict was expected. She had become a local celebrity: not just a name in the papers any more but a recognized face as well. On the trolley coming into town men whispered and women stared at her. From time to time someone would stop and speak to her, expressing their shared hope that Colonel King would come to much deserved justice.

The tension of waiting for the verdict was everywhere. Spectators and reporters wandered in front of the courthouse building, waiting for some word. Miss Marie and Laura didn't want to sit on the grass and eat lunch with me, preferring to stay inside the building just in case.

"How come you stay with Miz Pillow even when she treats you so bad?" Jeremiah had a mouthful of cake and dropped crumbs as he spoke.

"Oh, she doesn't treat me that bad. She's given me a pretty good life."

"Don't seem like it to me," he observed, taking another bite. The crumbs on his chin looked like the stubble of a blond beard. "If I had to stay with a lady like that, I think I'd run away. I don't like being beholden to nobody. Especially nobody who's mean."

I laughed at his spunk. He knew a lot more about getting along in the world all alone than I did, but I knew we were different folks with different ways.

"Kizzie. Are you happy?"

The rumble of thunder in the distance startled me. "I don't know. I'm happy helping other people, I reckon."

"But who helps you?"

"I don't need help," I replied as I began to gather my things.

"I reckon everybody needs help some time." He lay back on the grass, watching the darkening sky. The freckles on his elbows reminded me of my own and made me smile. His little dog Manny lay asleep in the grass beside him. "If you could do anything in the whole wide world, anything at all, what would it be?"

"I don't know. Never really thought about it. Never figured there'd be a time I could do anything in the whole wide world."

"I'd work at a newspaper," he said with certainty. "Those folks make lots of money and get to work with the machines. And smoke cigars, too. Some day I'm going to be an important newspaper man, and get the money that all the newsboys make."

"And I bet you can do that, too. Maybe you can even write articles and such."

"Nah. Working the machines would be enough for me. You're the one who could do the writing, as many good stories as you know." Jeremiah sat up suddenly, listening. The thunder was getting closer. A bright strike of lightening appeared in the distance over the river. He turned toward the courthouse up the hill.

"What's the matter?" A few people were stirring around the courthouse steps, with several hurrying into the building.

He stood up and began running. "It's in," he hollered back at me. "The verdict is in."

CHAPTER 45

The Newspapers

As Colonel King sat in conversation with his counsel and the audience spoke in whispers of the verdict, a loud scream broke the stillness.

It was so sudden, so unexpected and withal apparently so mournful that nobody could imagine whence it came.

Mr. Brooks rose and walked hastily into the hall and Criminal Court Clerk's office with the apparent expectation of finding his wife or some other of the relatives of Colonel King. None of them were to be seen.

Meanwhile hysterical cries, as of someone moaning could be heard all over the court house. Various rumors got abroad, many people saying they came from the basement, others that they proceeded from the third floor.

This proved correct. Mrs. Gideon J. Pillow, her daughter, Mrs. Shields, and a friend had posted themselves there to hear the verdict. Mrs. Pillow stood in the hall near the library door, while Mrs. Shields had posted herself on the rest in the stair leading to the second floor.

Observers standing below saw a man run up a few steps of the stair and call out the verdict.

Mrs. Pillow heard it. Her eyes beamed with joy. Clapping her hands she screamed hysterically and shouted: "Praise God, justice has been done and I am vindicated. Thank God, my prayers are answered and an honest jury has been found in Shelby County."

Mrs. Pillow was almost wild with joy. She danced around, laughed and moaned hysterically. To those who heard the sound without seeing the intoxication of pleasure it seemed a wail of despair rather than an expression of pleasure.

Librarian Tom Flanagan was about to go down stairs, perhaps in anticipation of the scene, when he thought it best to conduct Mrs. Pillow into the library office, for a crowd was gathering. There he succeeded in quieting her.

Mrs. Shields remained on the stair, whither Mrs. Pillow seemed bound when Mr. Flanagan stopped her. Rumor said they meant to stand where they could see Clay King descend from the Criminal Court, that they might wound him with their looks.

It has not been generally known that Mrs. Pillow and her daughter were in the city. Such was the rumor a few days ago, but nobody seemed to have seen them.

When General Peters began to speak Thursday morning, a young woman in black was recognized by a few in the audience as Mrs. Shields.

She sat enthralled by his eloquent excoriation of the defendant, her piercing black eyes gleaming with the thoughts that burned within her.

When the charge was delivered by Judge DuBose Thursday afternoon and the case given to the jury, Mrs. Shields could be seen pacing restlessly in the hall of the third floor.

Mrs. Pillow was at that time in the law library. Finding that a verdict would not be reached that afternoon they left, telling Mr. Flanagan they would return the next morning.

It is said that Judge DuBose's countenance assumed a dark hue when he heard it said that Mrs. Pillow was exulting over the verdict, and that he let fall such meaning words and "sweat-box" and "contempt of my court."

Mrs. Pillow visited the office of Attorney Walter Malone during the forenoon and talked with him in the same strain concerning her "vindication".

Among the many things she said was: "All Agnes wants now is to get a ticket in the front row to see her David Copperfield hanged."

Rumor said yesterday that Mrs. Pillow's visit to Memphis at this time, and the ominous presence of herself and Mrs. Shields were not unconnected with the kind of verdict returned by the jury. Indeed it was whispered that Colonel King's life is safer, for a year at least—and further, perhaps in view of the uncertainty of the law—than it would have been had he been acquitted.

Memphis Commercial July 4, 1891

❧   ❧   ❧

Mrs. Mary E. Pillow and her daughter, Mrs. Shields, are at the residence of Mr. William Gay on Union Street. An *Appeal-Avalanche* reporter called there last *night and interviewed the remarkable woman whose connection with H. Clay King was the remote cause of David H. Poston's death. The handsome presence and fascinating manner of Mrs. Pillow are well known, and it is hardly necessary to state that she is a fluent and entertaining talker. She was nervous last night and her handsome countenance bore the marks of anxiety. To the Appeal-Avalanche reporter she reviewed the history of her lawsuits with Colonel King and insisted that she had been vilified and plotted against by King, who never loved her but merely wished to rob her of her property.*

"I have been praying all the week," she said, "for the verdict this jury returned today. I could not have been satisfied with any other verdict nor do I think the peo-ple of Memphis would have permitted a less severe verdict to stand. They would have risen up in arms and declared that justice had been outraged. No one knows what I have had to endure at the hands of this man. He has not only attempted to ruin my character for the purpose of robbery, but on several occasions threatened my life. He threatened to shoot me at two different times while on the plantation in Arkansas.

He called me into his room one night, drew his pistol and told me he would kill me if I did not sign certain papers he had drawn up. I told him to shoot me but finally fled from the room and ran under the house to get away from him."

Mrs. Pillow seemed greatly amused at the idea of Colonel King calling her his "Agnes," and at the story told by the old darky of Colonel King falling on his knees to her, and at his conduct when demented. She stated that there was not a cabin near the front gate and that the old darky's story could not be true. She thinks Colonel King played crazy, in fact says he admitted as much to her, and that his reason for doing so was because he had threatened to shoot her, and was afraid she had gone to Helena and would have him arrested.

"I asked him afterward," continued Mrs. Pillow, "if he really meant to shoot me that night when I refused to sign those papers, and he said he did and intended to prove that I had committed suicide. He said he would have stated that he had told me he had intimated to certain parties that I was his mistress and that when confronted with the statement I could not bear up under the alleged disgrace and ended my own life. See what a deep laid scheme he had planned? His only purpose was to rob me, and he thought by making these charges against me that he had closed my mouth and that I would be compelled to submit…

"As for that matrimonial 'ad.,' which Colonel King read in his evidence. It did refer to me, but he wrote it and inserted it in the paper. His object was to publish me to the world as an adventuress, and thus injure me before the courts and in the eyes of the world. When he found out that I was investigating the matter, he went

to Mr. Scott, the representative of the paper, and told him if he ever divulged the author he would kill him. The whole scheme, from first to last, was a deep-laid plan to rob me of my money and property. This matrimonial 'ad.' was only one of the many schemes played to ruin and rob me."

Mrs. Pillow spoke feelingly of David H. Poston as a martyr to duty, a martyr who would wear a martyr's crown. She said that it is her intention to write a resume of the whole case for the press.

Memphis Appeal-Avalanche, July 4, 1891

❖   ❖   ❖

COLONEL KING TO HANG

Judge DuBose Read a Long Opinion
Adverse to the Defendant

The Aged Prisoner Stood Up
Without Flinching

Sentence of death was passed on H. Clay King yesterday morning.

The aged prisoner listened to the reading of a lengthy decision by Judge J. J. DuBose overruling his motion for a new trial without betraying unusual interest in the matter.

When the time came for the reciting of the death sentence he stood up without flinching while the judge in solemn and impressive tones announced that on November 6 he should be hanged by the neck until dead, dead, dead.

Memphis Appeal-Avalanche September 18, 1891

CHAPTER 46

Colonel King's old boots were tied tight around her calves as she made her way through the deep mud down to the first cotton field. Weeds that had grown as high as my shoulder crowded the small plants with a few white puffs that would be our crop. The harvest had been delayed by the October rain, and some half filled cotton sacks had been left in the deepening puddles of the turnrows.

"Gideon, try to gather these sacks onto the wagon. Maybe if we leave them in the barn for a while, they'll dry out." The boy followed his mother's instructions as best he could, but the waterlogged cotton was heavier than it looked. One of the few colored men left helped him lift it onto the wagon, then whipped the mule to move along down to the next abandoned bag. No one had the courage to tell her that soaked cotton was more likely to rot than to dry.

"You'd think these people would have the decency to fulfill their responsibilities," she complained as she surveyed the field. Back in March when word got around down in the quarters that the Colonel had shot a man and was in prison in Memphis, whole families of workers left before the crop could even be planted, to work more fertile fields and other harvests.

Mr. Worley had moved on, too. He had been willing to do his job, so long as the Colonel was running things, but once the Colonel went to prison, Mr. Worley didn't want to stay, even to farm the land for Miss Sallie and the girls. He said that as far as he was concerned, if Miss Marie was taking the reins, he wasn't going to be one of her mules. He left as soon as word came that the Colonel would be hanged, before the cotton harvest even started. He said she could do it. He moved on up to Memphis to work in a hardware store.

I didn't know what to do. I didn't want to stay with Miss Marie at Sterling Hill, but I couldn't rightly follow a man I wasn't married to, so I was stuck. And she didn't want to go to Memphis as much any more, now that all the fighting with the Colonel was pretty much over. She just wanted to stay on "her land." That's what she called it, whether or not the judges agreed.

With most of the field hands already gone, the children ended up doing more and more of the chores. They were practically grown people, Giddy and Annie were, and were probably getting ready to set out on their own when the time was right. Everybody seemed to be leaving or getting ready to leave. Even Mr. Alfred was gone. He died shortly after we heard the Colonel was set to hang. They said it was his heart. I believe that's probably right.

The drizzle became a downpour, beating down on us steadily, soaking our dresses. The black soil beneath us tried to hold our boots as we walked but could keep only our footprints, quickly filling with rainwater as we plodded through the field of unpicked cotton.

❧   ❧   ❧

"Mornin', Kizzie," the postmaster greeted me. "Looks like you've got some mail this mornin." The biting cold of February made the trip to town harder than it had to be, so I was glad to stand next to the stove in the warm post office.

"We do?"

"Yes, Mrs. Pillow has a letter, but so do you." I always did like getting letters from Laura, but I hadn't written any to her lately, so I wasn't expecting anything. "It's from Memphis," he said.

I took both our letters and a catalog and sat down on a bench next to the stove. Hers was an official looking one from the courthouse right there in Marianna. The handwriting on my letter was scrawled and crooked.

Dear Kizzie,

I got myself a good job at Griffin's Hardware Store, right on Shelby Street, lookin down at the river. I found a good room to live in not too far away. Now that I'm all settled down I want you to come to Memphis and git married. I miss you.

Kindest regards,

Tom Worley

❧   ❧   ❧

The Supreme Court decided that Sterling Hill belonged to the Colonel, even though he was up in the Tennessee State Penitentiary. When she heard their decision, she didn't throw a fit like she did when she got that first letter telling her about the lawsuit. She didn't slap me. She'd got even with the Colonel, she'd enjoyed six or seven good years at Sterling Hill, and it was time for her to move on, whether or not she wanted to.

A deputy sheriff with a brushy mustache appeared at our door. He was so short he looked more like a child playing dress up than like a real lawman. Except for his pistol. Mr. Chambers stood beside him. "Is Mrs. Pillow on the premises?"

"I'm afraid Mrs. Pillow isn't receiving visitors. You'll have to come again another time." I began to push the door closed.

The deputy pushed back and took one step into the hall. "I'm here on behalf of the court to enforce the order of eviction. I must speak with Mrs. Pillow."

"Yes, sir, I know why you're here," I told him, "but I'm afraid it will just be impossible for you to see Mrs. Pillow at the moment."

"I don't have no choice about this, ma'am. I got to talk to Mrs. Pillow herself, and deliver this here eviction notice, or I'm going to have to bring in some of the deputies to force her out. She didn't respond to the notice we mailed her, so this is how it's got to be. Now we can either do it the easy way…"

"Kizzie, it's important," Mr. Chambers explained. "Go get her, please."

"All right. I'll go get her, Mr. Chambers. Y'all come on in." I whispered to Annie to bring some refreshments for the gentlemen as they made their way solemnly into the parlor.

Miss Marie stood outside her bedroom door with her arms crossed tight in front of her.

"Miss Marie, Mr. Chambers and a…"

"I know they're here. You handle it, Kizzie. I don't want to talk to them."

"Yes, ma'am, but I'm afraid they need to talk to you. Maybe you ought to get dressed and ready so you can talk to them."

She hid her face with her hands for just a moment and took a deep breath. "Oh, if I must." I helped her on with her pretty gray suit and touched up her hair some. She stepped down the stairway slowly, reluctantly, but carrying herself with pride.

"Hello, Mr. Chambers. Officer. Kizzie, have Annie make us some coffee and some sweets." About that time Annie came in with a tray and set it on the table in the parlor.

"Please, sit down, gentlemen. What business do I have with you today?"

The deputy stood in the middle of the parlor—he wouldn't sit.

White puffs of smoke wafted from Mr. Chambers' pipe, spreading its sickly sweet stench throughout the room. "I'm afraid I have some bad news, Mrs. Pillow. As you know the Supreme Court has rejected our claim of your ownership of Sterling Hill. They completely upheld the lower court's decision."

"Yes, I understand that, and that will be appealed further, correct?"

"No, both the Arkansas Court and the Tennessee Court have ruled on this. Their decisions stand."

"Now, Miss Marie, how about some coffee? Would you like me to pour you some, Mr. Chambers? Officer?" I'd watched her long enough to know how I was supposed to act around gentlemen, even when she seemed to forget.

"I'm afraid those justices didn't think the facts were on our side," Mr. Chambers remarked sadly, exhaling a smoky breath.

"Oh, judges, what do they know? Who cares about facts, anyway? This will always be my land, whether or not anybody else thinks so."

"Mrs. Pillow, Mr. Pettis is here to enforce the decision." The deputy pulled a document from his shirt pocket.

"Let me see that." She extended her hand to the deputy. "Kizzie, get my spectacles." Quietly, she read the notice he brought. She paused, closing her eyes. "This notice is binding?"

"Yes, ma'am. I'm afraid we've reached the end of the road as far as appeals."

Miss Marie sat back in her chair silently, glancing around the room. Her eyes lit on the window. Rising slowly, she crossed the room and touched the glass. From that spot she could see the entire farm down the hill, the guest house, the barn, the quarters, now still and empty without life or movement, only the gray of neglect. The fields overtaken with unwanted growth could hardly be distinguished from the untilled land, but the colorless river was in clear view through the bare winter trees.

"I will require some time to pack my things."

"Yes'm. You can have 'til the end of the day, then you've got to get out." The deputy turned to leave, and I followed him to the door, with as stern a look on my face as I could muster, closing the door firmly behind him.

"I want to thank you for your assistance with these matters." She remained at the window, her arms folded in front of her. "David Poston told me you were a good man."

"I'm sorry this didn't work out as you wished." Mr. Chambers sat thoughtfully, holding the bowl of his pipe in his hand. "Mrs. Pillow, there is the matter of compensation."

"Ah, compensation." She continued to gaze out the window. The hall clock chimed the half hour.

"I understand that your crop this year was not as productive as you had hoped. But perhaps we can work something out."

"Yes, of course. It shouldn't be too long before I have the means to pay you." Shielding her eyes from the morning sun, she looked far into the distance. "When I am paid for my cotton claims, I shall send you your money post-haste."

❦   ❦   ❦

"Where are you going to go?" I asked her, folding her clothes and packing them in her trunk.

"Birmingham, I suppose. At least for a while. I may eventually move to Washington. I think I'd like to make a new start. Besides, it will probably be easier to pursue my cotton claims from there than from here. Have you seen my gloves?" Her eyes were still red even though the crying had stopped.

"Yes'm. Here they are. I reckon the congressmen up there will be able to help you," I offered.

"Yes, I suppose you're right. Congressman Dunn said he was still willing to help me. I'll be contacting him soon, I'm sure." She stared out the window at the wide delta sky. It was gray all afternoon that day. It looked like it might snow.

"I think I'd like to go to Memphis."

"Memphis?" She turned toward me. "Well, of course, we have to go to Memphis in order to take the train to Birmingham."

"No, ma'am. I mean I want to stay in Memphis."

"That's ridiculous. How could you stay in Memphis? You don't have any means. You don't know anyone."

I watched her while she gathered up her things. Seemed like she hadn't gotten one day older since we first moved there. I believed she was always going to stay the same—beautiful, selfish, cruel. Most of the time I don't believe she even knew I was in the room, except when she needed something. She just needed to have a servant. Somebody she could use. Somebody she could be more important than. She'd raised me, but not the way I saw Miss Sallie raise her girls, not the way she treated her own children. I watched her for a long time, understanding what she thought of me.

General Pillow sat at the head of the supper table like a defeated warrior, making sad pronouncements to his troops. Nobody said nothing when he told us we were losing our home there on "Millionaires' Row." After supper General Pillow retired early, but I needed to ask questions: where are we going to go? what are we going to do? Miss Marie didn't answer me. But I kept at it, being only 13 and not knowing any better. I started to cry and then to weep because I was worried it was all disappearing, that comfortable life, the only life I remembered well, there in Memphis. And in all my crying, through all those tears, I told her what I was scared of. That it wasn't real. That it was all just a fantasy, like her cotton claims. "I'll turn you out onto the streets alone to die and never give you a second thought if you ever, ever say anything like that again," she shouted at me after that first time she slapped me. If I behaved better, if I did like she told me, I knew I'd be safe.

The few leftover leaves were just barely dangling in the trees that February day, like they weren't fixing to fall no matter how hard the winter wind blew. I wondered what happened to them in the springtime when the new green-yellow leaves started to sprout. I looked out the window of her room to where the catbird used to sit in that old robin's nest. It was empty now. Even the catbird had moved on.

It didn't take too long to pick and choose among all the things in the house that were hers, to decide what she should take and what she shouldn't. She didn't take any of the ancestors, seeing as how they belonged to Miss Sallie. In fact, I don't think she took anything at all that belonged to Miss Sallie. She was careful about that.

What was left of the daylight peeked out between the clouds over the stubbled fields. Giddy and Annie lugged the trunks and boxes and packed them in her wagon, her old wagon, the one we brought with us from the old Pillow place. There weren't many menfolks around to help any more. As we were getting things all arranged, she remembered.

"Have you removed the bell as I asked?"

"Yes'm. It's already in the wagon." I knew enough about her to know that she wasn't fixing to leave behind something that she thought was rightfully hers if she didn't have to. I'd gotten a hammer and screwdriver and did the best I could to get that bell off the post. When it finally got loose, it fell to the ground with a thunderous clang. For the second time in my life, I picked up that old bell and heaved it up onto that same wagon. I didn't know I had it in me. Now she didn't have nothing at all left at Sterling Hill. That was about when the sheriff's deputy rode up on his horse. I helped Miss Marie into her rickety wagon, and I started the mule down the rutted up lane. And with the deputy following behind, we left Sterling Hill for the last time.

CHAPTER 47

❀

A long line had formed at the ticket counter in the Memphis train station that evening, so Miss Marie held our place and told me to go search for the leather glove she had dropped. I retraced my steps, studying more shoes than faces, hoping that this small task would focus my attention on more important problems than my own confusion. My heart pounded. The chill of the station made my anxiousness even more intense, until I heard a familiar sing-song call.

"Get your evening *Appeal-Avalanche* right here. Tutt's Pills for Torpid Liver. Prickly Ash Bitters. Wooldridge's Wonderful Cure. Get your evening edition right here."

"Jeremiah, is that you?"

The boy turned toward me frowning. Taller than I remember, his yellow hair in ragged cuts, he was thinner and had a bloody scrape on his cheek.

"Kizzie?"

I hadn't had a hug that big in years. "You're almost as tall as I am," I observed, mussing up his shaggy hair.

"Yeah, I reckon I am."

"Since when are you selling Tutt's Pills? I thought you wanted to be a newspaper man."

"I ain't selling them. There ain't nothing in the paper worth reading, exceptin' the ads. Best business I ever had was your murder trial last summer."

"Yeah. I know. I'm glad somebody got some good out of it."

"What are you doing here? I thought you was living in Arkansas."

"I was. I'm not any more." A train whistled and began to chug away from the station.

"You haven't broke loose from her yet, have you?"

"What?"

"Broke loose. From old lady Pillow."

I hadn't ever heard anybody call her that, and I couldn't help but smile. "No, not yet."

"What's keeping you?"

"Jeremiah, it's a hard thing to explain. She's like family to me."

"You ain't skeered, are you?"

"Of course not. I've lived with Miss Marie for so long, I'm not scared of nothing, except maybe for her."

He looked at me with such serious eyes, judging me for my actions or lack of them. The quiet between us was uncomfortable.

"Where's Manny?" I remembered to ask.

"Oh, he's hopping around outside somewheres. I imagine he's found hisself a girlfriend, at least until I go out and whistle for him."

"Don't you worry about him outside alone, what with all the trolley tracks and carriages and all?"

"No, I don't worry. He can take care of hisself. Even though it is nice to have him around."

"There it is." When the heavy woman stepped to the side, I saw the glove where her boot had been, wrinkled and smeared with dirt. "This is what I was looking for," I explained, shaking the dirty glove in front of him. "I've got to run give this to Miss Marie. I've got to go, Jeremiah." I walked away from him, but he followed me.

"Jeremiah," I stopped and turned. "You get back to your newspapers. I've got to go with her."

"You ain't got to do nothing." He stared at me with the intense expression of an older man. I continued toward her.

She was almost at the front of the line at the ticket window. "Where have you been?"

"Oh, nowhere. I just found an old friend is all."

"Who? Not this filthy street urchin."

The hairs on the back of my neck stood on end. "No, ma'am. This is Jeremiah."

"Hmmph. Jeremiah. Really, Kizzie, why do you waste your time?" The man in front of her had finished his business, and she stepped up to the window. "Two tickets to Birmingham."

"One ticket."

She turned her head and scowled at me. "Don't be silly. Of course, we need two tickets."

"No, ma'am. I ain't going with you."

"'Aren't' going with me, and of course, you are."

"No, ma'am," I said more firmly. "I'm going to stay here in Memphis."

"That's ridiculous. Of course, you're coming with me." She looked down at her money, and she laughed. She laughed at me. She had insulted Jeremiah, and she laughed at me.

A grizzled old man missing a front tooth approached her, close enough that I could smell his rotten breath. "Good evenin', madam. Could you be so kind as to lend me a nickel?"

"Shoo," she commanded. "Go away." She made a little brushing gesture with her hand, but he didn't leave. "I said 'shoo'. I want nothing to do with you." By then she noticed. "Kizzie. Where are you going?"

But I didn't answer her. I just grabbed my grip and left her standing there with nobody to help her. She called after me a couple of times, but I kept going, walking faster the farther I got from her. Jeremiah insisted on carrying my grip, and with a stack of newspapers under his other arm, we walked together out into the cold moonlight. I never felt so free, or so scared.

CHAPTER 48

SAVED FROM THE GALLOWS

GOVERNOR BUCHANAN COMMUTES THE SENTENCE OF COLONEL H. CLAY KING

*Irresistible Influences Brought to Bear on the
Governor to Procure the Commutation*

MEMPHIS, August 9*th*.—Gov. Buchanan, in Nashville this evening, commuted the sentence of Colonel H. Clay King, who was to have been hung on next
Friday, for the murder of David H. Poston, on March 15 last, on a public street in
this city. Unusual pressure was brought to bear upon the Governor for the past few
days…The prisoner heard the news with but little interest. He has been indulging
in stimulants of late and seemed indifferent to what was transpiring.

Arkansas Gazette, August 10, 1892

      ✤   ✤   ✤

Among the notable letters written in his behalf appears the following to Mrs. E.
K. White, a niece of King:

"Mrs. E. K. White:

Dear Madam–I sympathize deeply with you, and sincerely, in the conviction of
your uncle. I know but little of the facts in his case, but confess that my slight
information on the subject led me to suppose that enough of mitigation would
be shown upon his trial to reduce the grade of offense below that of the highest
known to our law. I have been so moved by your appeal that I have seriously
considered whether there was not something I might do to help you. I am
forced to the conclusion, however, that I ought not to interfere by applying to

the governor for the mitigation of the sentence pronounced upon your uncle. Such an application on my part would be based only upon the sympathy which I feel for you and my experience teaches me that such a consideration ought not to control executive action in cases of this kind. Notwithstanding this, I feel that there are circumstances in your uncle's case which ought to appeal strongly to the pardoning power, and I earnestly hope that such representations may be made to your governor as will avert the execution of the death sentence which has been pronounced.

Very truly yours,

Grover Cleveland
Gray Gables
Buzzard's Bay, Massachusetts, July 27, 1892"

A notable petition for clemency in the case was the following:

"To Hon. John P. Buchanan, Governor of Tennessee:

Whereas Col. H. Clay King has been convicted of the murder of David H. Poston and sentenced to be hanged on the 29th day of August, and

Whereas it is believed that the validity of his conviction has been thrown in doubt because the jury, while considering his case, left the State of Tennessee and went into the State of Arkansas and by the fact that competent evidence show that several of the jurors had, prior to the trial, expressed hostile sentiments against the defendant, which was not discovered in time for the courts to consider under their rules of practice; and

Whereas grave doubt of the sanity of the defendant, and

Whereas the decision affirming the judgment of the lower court was rendered by a divided court, therefore we, the undersigned representatives, upon information received from the record and from persons in whom we have confidence, respectfully submit that his case is a proper one for executive clemency, and we earnestly ask that you use your executive prerogative by commuting his sentence.

Signed: John G. Carlisle, Kentucky; Daniel W. Voorhees, Indiana; Isham G. Harris, Tennessee; Jo. C. S. Blackburn, Kentucky; Richard Coke, Texas; G. G. Vest, Missouri; Wilkinson Call, Florida, United States Senators.

B. A. Enloe, James D. Richardson, Rice A. Pearce, Tennessee; W. C. P. Breckinridge, J. H. Goodnight, Kentucky; John R. Fellows, New York; C. B. Kilgore, J. W. Bailey, John B. Long, Lewis Steward, J. D. Sayers, Charles Stewart, W. H.

Crain, Texas; Paul C. Edmonds, Virginia; W. S. Forman, Ben T. Cable, Scott Wike, S. T. Busey and Edward Lane, Illinois, Congressmen.

There were also letters from Gov. Hogg of Texas, Gov. John Young Brown of Kentucky; ex-Gov. Simon Bolivar Buckner or Kentucky, and Logan H. Roots of Colorado."

On August 9, Gov. John P. Buchanan commuted the death sentence to life imprisonment in the penitentiary.

The following night King had to be spirited away from Memphis to escape mob violence, while Buchanan's effigy was hanged to a telegraph pole at the corner or Main and Madison streets, the most central point in Memphis, and burned.

❉   ❉   ❉

DEATH LIBERATES H. CLAY KING FROM HIS PRISON CELL
Noted Memphis Lawyer and Convict Passes
Quietly Away at 10 O'Clock
Yesterday Morning
In State Penitentiary for Eleven Years

NASHVILLE, Tenn. Dec. 10 (Special) Colonel H. Clay King, who has been the central figure within the walls of the State prison for eleven years, is dead.

He passed quietly away at 10 o'clock this morning. His end was as peaceful as his life had been stormy.

For the past three months Colonel King has been sick. Then days ago his condition became critical and his death has been expected daily since.

Last night Drs. R. E. Fort and J. D. Witherspoon were called in by Dr. Black who had been attending him. So far advanced was the cancer in the stomach that they decided an operation would be futile. So he was allowed to die without the pain that would have been caused.

Up to his death King was conscious. To the last he retained his clearness of mind. He said last night to his family grouped around him: "I die in peace. I am perfectly resigned and have no fear for the future."

He has been a staunch member of the Catholic Church for thirty years.

Around Colonel King when he died were his three unmarried daughters, Misses Ida, Mary and Fannie King. His wife had been with him for a month. His son, Haughton King, was here a few days ago, but was forced to leave Saturday.

His son-in-law G. W. Brooks of St. Louis was also here a few days ago in an effort to secure his pardon.

The officials of the prison have treated King with consideration all the while he has been imprisoned. For two years he has done no work, but spent his time reading, considerably in French.

He kept abreast of the times and retained to the last his brilliancy of conversation and culture of bearing that had always marked him.

He was 73 years old.

Memphis Appeal-Avalanche, December 11, 1903.

CHAPTER 49

May 1913

"'And to this day when the cold February moon is full and shining bright over the hills along the river, the good people of Feliciana Parish remember the legend of the pirate John Murrell, who gave up his life and his treasure in his greedy search for even more, and they never, ever forget the powerful undertow that swallowed him down. The End.'"

"That was a scary one. You should write another one just like that." Thomas had twirled his blond cowlick during most of the reading, so I already knew he approved.

Mae sat cross-legged on the floor, her smock pulled up above her knees, examining her dirty toes. "No, she shouldn't. She should write another one about the fancy ladies in their lavender silk ballgowns meeting the president. I like those a lot better." She had lost her fourth front tooth that morning, and said "fanthy ladieth" and "thilk ballgownth", but I didn't dare laugh.

"What do you know? You're just a girl."

She squeezed her eyes shut and squealed. "Grandma!" Thomas smiled but covered his ears.

"Now, Thomas, don't be aggravating your sister," I warned, standing and stretching my legs from sitting for too long. I read my stories to them with a little too much energy. By the time I was finished, I was usually exhausted. "Mae, you know what they say. If you stick your lip out too far, a little bird might swoop down and perch there."

"Kizzie, you got a couple of little rapscallions here?" The dark silhouette of the man filled the doorway.

"Daddy!"

"Evenin', Jeremiah. How was the newspaper business today?"

He approached me and kissed me on the cheek, as his children reached for hugs. "Remarkable. Just remarkable." He rubbed the back of their heads, and Mae held tight to his leg. "I think they're going to print my editorial."

"Well, it's about time. After all the reporting you've done for them, they ought to be listening to what you have to say." I stepped toward the corner of the room that was my kitchen and began pulling out the bread and cheese for supper. "You checked your writing, didn't you? Made sure you didn't have any misspelled words?"

"If I misspelled anything, I can always blame it on the typesetters."

"Thomas, check to see if there's any ice left in the box for your father. I'm real happy for you, son. They liked to never get you out of that old greasy press room, and it's about time you moved up another notch. You always did have good sense about the news."

He moved over beside me in front of the cabinet and stole a bit of cheese to nibble. "They told me they might be interested in running some short stories in their Sunday editions."

I stopped slicing the bread and stared at him. "No. No, I don't think so."

Thomas plopped a melting chunk of ice in a glass for his father and poured in the water. "Come on, Grandma, you can write as good as anybody."

"'As well as anybody.' No, that's not for me. I'd much rather read them to y'all than have them printed for the whole world to see. Besides, you know what fancy ladies do with their newspapers, don't you? They use them to line the bottom of their bird cages."

Mae's mouth dropped open. "Somebody keeps a bird in a cage?" she almost shouted with her little hands open before her.

"Inside of their house," Thomas informed her smugly.

"I appreciate your vote of confidence in my profession, Kizzie," Jeremiah laughed, finishing the glass of water with an audible breath of relief.

"There's good and bad in everything," I instructed them with my long knife. "I just happened to have seen too much of the bad in newspapers in my life-time."

"Then I'll make sure you see more of the good to even it all out. Now, you kids, come on. Time for supper. Your mama is waiting. Tell Kizzie thank you."

"Thank you, Grandma Kizzie." Thomas waved as he turned to leave.

The little girl scampered after her brother and father out into the heat and hollered, "Thank you!" without looking back.

Jeremiah had lived with us for seven years before he married and had a family of his own. After all the kindness that had been shown to me for all those years, I was glad I could return the favor, show some kindness of my own, and take in an orphan. I never could stand the thought of him living out there on the streets by himself, even if he did think he could take care of himself. Every one of us can use some help now and then. And the funny thing was, I believe bringing him into our home did as much for Tom and me as it did for him. Like they say, charity is its own reward.

I remember Jeremiah asking me one time what I would do if I could do anything in the whole wide world. And I remember thinking what a childish question that was. Now I'm glad I stopped to consider it. If I could do anything in the whole wide world, I decided, I'd have a family of my own. Somebody to love and to love me back. I came to understand that that's a stronger force than any I've ever known, stronger than greed, stronger than revenge, stronger even than despair.

"Hey, Honeybunch." The back door creaked open, and I heard Tom's heavy feet stomping their dust on the mat.

"Don't you be tracking any dirt into my kitchen, mister. I just mopped the floor this morning."

"Yes, ma'am," he teased me. "I brung you something."

"'Brought.' What did you bring me?"

"A letter." Indifferently, he laid the envelope on the table and trudged over to my rocker. With slow exertion, he pulled the boots from his feet, leaned back in the rocker, and closing his eyes, heaved the happy sigh that comes with the end of a long day.

I picked up the letter and examined it. The same familiar blue script, the same smoky postmark. I took a dinner knife and ripped it open.

Dearest Kizzie,

I hope you and Tom are well. I wanted to let you know that my youngest, Mary Elizabeth, is getting married shortly, and she's very excited about having a "society" wedding. Wouldn't mother be proud!

I heard from Laura and Mr. John pretty regularly, but I never did hear from Miss Marie again. Of course, I didn't tell her where I was going when I left that train station, and I reckon she wasn't ever interested in knowing. Laura told me she'd moved to Washington, D.C., after all and was having a hard time. She didn't have much money, Laura said, even though her widow's pension finally did come through. She never did get her cotton claims paid for, but lawdy mercy, she kept on trying.

> *But our great joy with her wedding is dampened by great sadness. Our dear Mother was killed in a terrible, tragic accident. She was crossing Constitution Avenue, near the Capitol building, when she was hit by a passing street car. I don't know the details, except that she has passed on, and I hope that her eternal reward is at least as great as that which she sought here on earth.*
>
> *When John and I went to Washington to handle the arrangements, we found that she had mistakenly been buried in a small cemetery in town. I knew what she'd always wanted for her burial, so we had her reinterred in a manner more befitting the widow of a general, at Arlington Cemetery on the crest of a hill overlooking the Potomac River, all alone. I know she would have been pleased. May she always rest in peace.*
>
> *Yours affectionately,*
>
> *Laura*

My hand found the chair behind me so I could sit and ponder and read her words again. I studied her initials at the top of the page, graceful, intertwined ladylike letters that were just ordinary printer's ink, the kind you wipe off your hands, the kind that's a nuisance unless it's forming pretty letters or telling sordid stories in the newspapers or whispering desires mixed with teardrops on lonely evenings. The kind that's hard to wash away completely. I blinked away tears. Ashamed of my feelings, I sat quietly and wiped my eyes, listening for Tom's rhythmic breathing, constant, comforting, certain. Miss Marie was gone. And she got a pretty fancy piece of property after all. Rest in peace, Miss Marie. Rest in peace. The Good Lord knows you sure didn't live that way.

Driving up the shadowed lane to the top of the hill, we barely spotted the mansion house through the jungle of small trees and undergrowth. The steamy afternoon seemed the unreal setting of a dream, the haze and foliage hiding the beautiful home I once knew, changing the familiar perspective of it, until we were close enough to see something altogether unfamiliar. Underneath the green branches stood the remains of a house that looked more neglected than the old house over at the Pillow place had ever been. The white paint had mostly peeled away, and pieces of wood had been torn away and broken from someone trying to steal the boards. Through the windows edged with shards of glass, I could see leaves and branches from the stray bushes that had laid their claim on the inside. A sizeable hole in the roof exposed the rafters, and the far end of that pretty front porch that faced the river had collapsed, almost like a giant came along and squashed his thumb on top of it.

Where Miss Sallie's garden used to be, weeds had grown up taller than the front windows. Already tiny triangles of beggar lice clung to my skirt, and picking them off, I plodded through the weeds to that old post where the bell had sat, but it was rotten and wouldn't hold anything nearly as heavy as that bell any more. Then I noticed. Down at the bottom of the hill where the quarters and the smokehouse used to be, where we'd strolled along as a family and worked the acres and acres of farmland, there was only river water. The closest cotton field had been replaced by a sandbar. There wasn't a guest house any more. There wasn't a barn. Just gray-brown water, an occasional mossy post standing its ground, or the skeletal remains of a once vibrant home still fighting, still holding firm against the invisible current. The river had washed away most of Sterling Hill, and some of my best memories. And if it wasn't for that hill, what was left of the mansion house might have been washed away, too. This property was long past being worth fighting over.

"This is unbelievable," I called over to Tom, pointing out the new landscape at the bottom of the hill.

Grinning, he walked over towards me, breaking small branches and crushing grass with each careful step. "Looks like that old Queen of Floods earned her name." He slipped his arm around my waist, and we studied the changes down the hill. "This sort of thing happens regularly, you know. She twists and turns and changes her course every year. Sometimes she's making the land richer, sometimes she's washing it away." Still he smiled, as if it was a joke to see that place come to ruin, as if that's just exactly what such a place deserved. But all I saw was sadness.

The river was so much closer than it used to be, lapping up gently on its new banks. It looked so calm, so smooth, almost like it wasn't moving at all. I was tempted to scramble down the hill, take off my shoes, and wade in that cool water, it being such a hot afternoon. But I didn't dare. I know better now.

Notes

The newspaper passages I have included and cited in the text are the actual contemporaneous articles published about the litigation and the murder. Other passages that are described as newspaper quotations are also actual quotations, attributions listed below, with the two exceptions I have noted. As often as possible I have used the words attributed to Mrs. Pillow and Colonel King as I was able to find them in letters and in the newspapers.

Chapter 8

I have no reason to believe that the historical Colonel H. Clay King ever attempted the assassination of a commanding officer. He wrote a letter from Corinth, Mississippi, dated May 1, 1862, explaining a misunderstanding about a change of command and suggested in it that his men might have become mutinous because of this change. I have incorporated many of his words from this letter into this chapter. But the secret shared between Colonel King and General Pillow is a fabrication.

General Pillow's words at Fort Donelson are taken from *The Life & Wars of Gideon J. Pillow* by Nathaniel Cheairs Hughes, Jr., and Roy P. Stonesifer, Jr. (Chapel Hill: UNC Press, 1993).

Chapter 9

Quotations from Charlotte Bronte's *Jane Eyre* are from the Bantam Classic Edition, New York, 1981.

Chapter 32

Mrs. Pillow's cross-bill was published on the front page of the *Memphis Appeal-Avalanche*, July 28, 1889.

Chapter 34

The letter from the jurors was originally printed in the *Memphis Evening Democrat* and reprinted in the *Arkansas Gazette* on June 8, 1890.

Chapter 40

The words of Colonel and Mrs. King as they spoke to the press in his jail cell are quoted from the *Memphis Appeal-Avalanche* on March 11 and 12, 1891, although the Colonel did not make the crude statement about the Postons' knowledge of the truth and a different individual made the statement I have attributed to Pat League.

Chapter 41

Judge DuBose's quotations from the paper are taken from Mrs. Pillow's cross-bill in the *Memphis Appeal-Avalanche* on Sunday, July 28, 1889 ("Mrs. Pillow...facts," and "She...superintendent."). The "Prince of Mordaunt" quotation is based on Colonel King's paraphrase of an editorial (Letter, September 10, 1893) and the following "brush the dust" comment is a paraphrase of Mrs. Pillow's words (Letter, *Arkansas Gazette*, March 29, 1891).

Chapter 44

Mr. Weatherford's closing statement is based on the closing statements published in the *Memphis Appeal-Avalanche*, July 2, 1891, which were presented by both W. G. Weatherford and Judge T. W. Brown.

0-595-32209-3

Printed in the United States
21116LVS00003B/157-249